Honoré de Balzac, John Rudd, Ellen Marriage

A Prince of Bohemia And Other Stories

Honoré de Balzac, John Rudd, Ellen Marriage

A Prince of Bohemia And Other Stories

ISBN/EAN: 9783337168704

Printed in Europe, USA, Canada, Australia, Japan

Cover: Foto ©Andreas Hilbeck / pixelio.de

More available books at **www.hansebooks.com**

H. DE BALZAC

A

PRINCE OF BOHEMIA

AND OTHER STORIES

TRANSLATED BY

JNO. RUDD, B.A., and ELLEN MARRIAGE

WITH A PREFACE BY

GEORGE SAINTSBURY

PHILADELPHIA

THE GEBBIE PUBLISHING CO., Ltd.

1899

CONTENTS

LIST OF ILLUSTRATIONS

PREFACE.

"A PRINCE OF BOHEMIA," the first of the short stories which Balzac originally chose as make-weights to associate with the long drama of " Splendeurs et Misères des Courtisanes," is one of the few things that, both in whole and in part, one would very much rather he had not written. Its dedication to Heine only brings out its shortcomings. For Heine, though he could certainly be as spiteful and unjust as Balzac here shows himself, never failed to carry the laugh on his side. You may wish him, in his lampoons, better morals and better taste, but you can seldom wish him better literature. Had he made this attack on Sainte-Beuve, we should certainly not have yawned over it ; and it is rather amusing to think of the sardonic smile with which the dedicatee must have read Balzac's comfortable assurance that he, Heinrich Heine, would understand the *plaisanterie* and the *critique* which " Un Prince de la Bohème " contains. Heine " understood " most things ; but if understanding, as is probable, here includes sympathetic enjoyment, we may doubt.

It was written at the same time, or very nearly so, as the more serious attack on Sainte-Beuve in August 1840, and, like that, appeared in Balzac's own " Revue Parisienne," though it was somewhat later. The thread, such as there is, of interest is twofold—the description of the Bohemian *grand seigneur* Rusticoli or La Palférine, and the would-be satire on Sainte-Beuve. It is difficult to say which is least well done. Both required an exceedingly light hand, and Balzac's hand was at no time light. Moreover, in the sketch of La Palférine he commits the error—nearly as great in a book as on the stage, where I am told it is absolutely fatal—of delineating his hero with a sort of sneaking kindness which is neither dramatic impartiality nor satiric raillery.

La Palférine as portrayed is a "raff," with a touch of no aristocratic quality except insolence. He might have been depicted with cynically concealed savagery, as Swift would have done it; with humorous ridicule, as Gautier or Charles de Bernard would have done it; but there was hardly a third way. As it is, the sneaking kindness above referred to is one of the weapons in the hands of those who—unjustly if it be done without a great deal of limitation—contend that Balzac's ideal of a gentleman was low, and that he had a touch of snobbish admiration for mere insolence.

Here, however, it is possible for a good-natured critic to put in the apology that the artist has tried something unto which he was not born, and failing therein, has apparently committed faults greater than his real ones. This kindness is impossible in the case of the parodies, which are no parodies, of Sainte-Beuve. From the strictly literary point of view, it is disastrous to give as a parody of a man's work, with an intention of casting ridicule thereon, something which is not in the least like that work, and which in consequence only casts ridicule on its author. To the criticism which takes in life as well as literature, it is a disaster to get in childish rages with people because they do not think your work so good as you think it yourself. And it is not known that Balzac had to complain of Sainte-Beuve in any other way than this, though he no doubt read into what Sainte-Beuve wrote a great deal more than Sainte-Beuve did say.

There is a story (I think unpublished) that a certain very great English poet of our times once met an excellent critic who was his old friend (they are both dead now). "What do you mean by calling—— vulgar?" growled the poet. "I didn't call it vulgar," said the critic. "No; but you meant it," rejoined the bard. On this system of interpretation it is of course possible to accumulate crimes with great rapidity on

a censor's head.   But it cannot be said to be itself a critical
or rational proceeding.   And it must be said that if an author
does reply, against the advice of Bacon and all wise people,
he should reply by something better than the spluttering abuse
of the "Revue Parisienne" article or the inept and irrelevant
parody of this story.

"Un Prince de la Bohème," in its "Revue Parisienne"
appearance, bore the title of "Les Fantaisies de Claudine,"
but when, four years later, it followed "Honorine" in book
form, it took the present label.   The Comédie received it
two years later.

G. S.

A PRINCE OF BOHEMIA.

TRANSLATED BY ELLEN MARRIAGE.

To Henri Heine.

I inscribe this to you, my dear Heine, to you that represent in Paris the ideas and poetry of Germany, in Germany the lively and witty criticism of France; for you better than any other will know whatsoever this study may contain of criticism and of jest, of love and truth.

DE BALZAC.

"My dear friend," said Mme. de la Baudraye, drawing a pile of manuscript from beneath her sofa cushion, "will you pardon me in our present straits for making a short story of something which you told me a few weeks ago?"

"Anything is fair in these times. Have you not seen writers serving up their own hearts to the public, or very often their mistresses' hearts when invention fails? We are coming to this, dear; we shall go in quest of adventures, not so much for the pleasure of them as for the sake of having the story to tell afterward."

"After all, you and the Marquise de Rochefide have paid the rent, and I do not think, from the way things are going here, that I ever pay yours."

"Who knows. Perhaps the same good luck that befell Mme. de Rochefide may come to you."

"Do you call it good luck to go back to one's husband?"

"No; only great luck. Come, I am listening."

And Mme. de Baudraye read as follows:

Scene—a splendid salon in the Rue de Chartres-du-Roule.

(1)

One of the most famous writers of the day discovered sitting on a settee beside a very illustrious marquise, with whom he is on such terms of intimacy as a man has a right to claim when a woman singles him out and keeps him at her side as a complacent *souffredouleur* (drudge) rather than a makeshift.

"Well," says she, "have you found those letters of which you spoke yesterday? You said that you could not tell me all about *him* without them?"

"Yes, I have them."

"It is your turn to speak; I am listening like a child when his mother begins the tale of *Le Grand Serpentin Vert*" (The Big Green Toadstool).

"I count the young man in question in that group of our acquaintances which we are wont to style our friends. He comes of a good family; he is a man of infinite parts and ill-luck, full of excellent dispositions and most charming conversation; young as he is, he has seen much, and, while awaiting better things, he dwells in Bohemia. Bohemianism, which by rights should be called the doctrine of the Boulevard des Italiens, finds its recruits among young men between twenty and thirty, all of them men of genius in their way, little known, it is true, as yet, but sure of recognition one day, and when that day comes, of great distinction. They are distinguished as it is at carnival time, when their exuberant wit, repressed for the rest of the year, finds a vent in more or less ingenious buffoonery.

"What times we live in! What an irrational central power which allows such tremendous energies to run to waste. There are diplomatists in Bohemia quite capable of overturning Russia's designs, if they but felt the power of France at their backs. There are writers, administrators, soldiers, and artists in Bohemia; every faculty, every kind of brain is represented there. Bohemia is a microcosm. If the Czar would buy Bohemia for a score of millions and set its population down in

Odessa—always supposing that they consented to leave the as-phalt of the boulevards—Odessa would be Paris within the year. In Bohemia, you find the flower doomed to wither and come to nothing; the flower of the wonderful young manhood of France, so sought after by Napoleon and Louis XIV., so neglected for the last thirty years by the modern Gerontocracy that is blighting everything else—that splendid young man-hood of whom a witness so little prejudiced as Professor Tissot wrote: 'On all sides the Emperor employed a younger gener-ation in every way worthy of him; in his councils, in the general administration, in negotiations bristling with diffi-culties or full of danger, in the government of conquered countries; and in all places Youth responded to his demands upon it. Young men were for Napoleon the *missi dominici* of Charlemagne.'

"The word Bohemia tells you everything. Bohemia has nothing and lives upon what it has. Hope is its religion; faith (in one's self) its creed; and charity is supposed to be its budget. All these young men are greater than their mis-fortune; they are under the feet of Fortune, yet more than equal to Fate. Always ready to mount and ride an *if*, witty as a *feuilleton* (skit), blithe as only those can be that are deep in debt and drink deep to match, and finally—for here I come to my point—hot lovers, and what lovers! Picture to your-self Lovelace, and Henri Quatre, and the Regent, and Wer-ther, and Saint-Preux, and René, and the Marshal Richelieu—think of all these in a single man, and you will have some idea of their way of love. What lovers! Eclectic of all things in love, they will serve up a passion to a woman's order; their hearts are like a bill of fare in a restaurant. Per-haps they have never read Stendhal's 'De l'Amour' (Of Love), but unconsciously they put it in practice. They have by heart their chapters—Love-Taste, Love-Passion, Love-Caprice, Love-Crystallized, and, more than all, Love-Tran-sient. All is good in their eyes. They invented the burlesque axiom, ' In the sight of man all women are equal.' The actual text is more vigorously worded, but as in my opinion the spirit is false, I do not stand nice upon the letter.

" My friend, madame, is named Gabriel Jean Anne Victor Benjamin George Ferdinand Charles Edward Rusticoli, Comte de la Palférine. The Rusticoli came to France with Catherine de' Medici, having been ousted about that time from their infinitesimal Tuscan sovereignty. They are distantly related to the house of Este, and connected by marriage with the Guises. On the Day of Saint-Bartholomew they slew a goodly number of Protestants, and Charles IX. bestowed the hand of the heiress of the Comte de la Palférine upon the Rusticoli of that time. The county, however, being a part of the confiscated lands of the Duke of Savoy, was repurchased by Henri IV., when that great king so far blundered as to restore the fief; and in exchange the Rusticoli—who had borne arms long before the Medici bore them, to wit, *argent* a cross flory *azure* (the cross flower-de-luced by letters-patent granted by Charles IX.), and a count's coronet, with two peasants for supporters, with the motto IN HOC SIGNO VINCIMUS —the Rusticoli, I repeat, retained their title, and received a couple of offices under the crown with the government of a province.

" From the time of the Valois till the reign of Richelieu, as it may be called, the Rusticoli played a most illustrious part ; under Louis XIV. their glory waned somewhat, under Louis XV. it went out altogether. My friend's grandfather wasted all that was left to the once brilliant house with Mlle. Laguerre, whom he first discovered, and brought into fashion before Bouret's time. Charles Edward's own father was an officer without any fortune in 1789. The Revolution came to his assistance ; he had the sense to drop his title, and became plain Rusticoli. Among other deeds, M. Rusticoli married a wife during the war in Italy, a Capponi, a goddaughter of the Countess of Albany (hence La Palférine's final names). Rusticoli was one of the best colonels in the army. The Emperor made him a commander of the Legion of Honor and a count. His spine was slightly curved, and his son was wont to say of him, laughingly, that he was *un comte refait* (*contrefait*). *

"General Count Rusticoli, for he became a brigadier-general at Ratisbon and a general of the division on the field of Wagram, died at Vienna almost immediately after his promotion, or his name and ability would sooner or later have brought him the marshal's bâton. Under the Restoration he would certainly have repaired the fortunes of a great and noble family so brilliant even as far back as 1100, centuries before they took the French title—for the Rusticoli had given a pope to the church and twice revolutionized the kingdom of Naples—so illustrious again under the Valois; so dexterous in the days of the Fronde, that obstinate Frondeurs though they were, they still existed through the reign of Louis XIV. Mazarin favored them; there was the Tuscan strain in them still, and he recognized it.

"To-day, when Charles Edward de la Palférine's name is mentioned, not three persons in a hundred know the history of his house. But the Bourbons have actually left a Foix-Grailly to live by his easel.

"Ah! if you but knew how brilliantly Charles Edward accepts his obscure position! how he scoffs at the bourgeois of 1830! What Attic salt in his wit! He would be the king of Bohemia, if Bohemia would endure a king. His *verve* is inexhaustible. To him we owe a map of the country and the names of the seven castles which Nodier could not discover."

"The one thing wanting in one of the cleverest skits of our time," said the marquise.

---

* *Refait:* re-formed; *contrefait:* de-formed, thus reading: A count re-de-formed. An excellent pun, as the *m* and *n* have the same pronunciation.

" You can form your own opinion of La Palférine from a few characteristic touches," continued Nathan. " He once came upon a friend of his, a fellow Bohemian, involved in a dispute on the boulevard with a bourgeois who chose to consider himself affronted. To the modern powers that be, Bohemia is insolent in the extreme. There was talk of calling one another out.

" ' One moment,' interposed La Palférine, as much Lauzun for the occasion as Lauzun himself could have been. ' One moment. Monsieur was born, I suppose?'

" ' What, sir?'

" ' Yes, are you born? What is your name?'

" ' Godin.'

" ' Godin, eh!' exclaimed La Palférine's friend.

" ' One moment, my dear fellow,' interrupted La Palférine. ' There are the Trigaudins. Are you one of them?'

" Astonishment.

" ' No? Then you are one of the new dukes of Gaëta, I suppose, of imperial creation? No? Oh, well, how can you expect my friend to cross swords with you when he will be secretary of an embassy and ambassador *some day*, and you will owe him respect? *Godin !* the thing is non-existent! You are a nonentity, Godin. My friend cannot be expected to beat the air! When one is somebody, one cannot fight with a nobody! Come, my dear fellow—good-day.'

" ' My respects to madame,' added the friend.

" Another day La Palférine was walking with a friend who flung his cigar end in the face of a passer-by. The recipient had the bad taste to resent this.

" ' You have stood your antagonist's fire,' said the young count, ' the witnesses declare that honor is satisfied.'

" La Palférine owed his tailor a thousand francs, and the man instead of going himself sent his assistant to ask for the money. The assistant found the unfortunate debtor up six pairs of stairs at the back of a yard at the farther end of the

Faubourg du Roule. The room was unfurnished save for a bed (such a bed!), a table, and such a table! La Palférine heard the preposterous demand. 'A demand which I should qualify as illegal,' he said when he told us the story, 'made, as it was, at seven o'clock in the morning.'

" 'Go,' he answered, with the gesture and attitude of a Mirabeau, 'tell your master in what condition you find me.'

" The assistant apologized and withdrew. La Palférine, seeing the young man on the landing, rose in the attire celebrated in verse in 'Britannicus' to add, 'Remark the stairs! Pay particular attention to the stairs; do not forget to tell him about the stairs!'

" In every position into which chance has thrown La Palférine, he has never failed to rise to the occasion. All that he does is witty and never in bad taste; always and in everything he displays the genius of Rivarol, the polished subtlety of the old French noble. It was he who told that delicious anecdote of a friend of Laffitte the banker. A national fund had been started to give back to Laffitte the mansion in which the Revolution of 1830 was brewed; and this friend appeared at the offices of the fund with, ' Here are five francs, give me a hundred sous change!' (as 100 cents=$1). A caricature was made of it. It was once La Palférine's misfortune, in judicial style, to make a young girl a mother. The girl, not a very simple innocent, confessed all to her mother, a respectable matron, who hurried forthwith to La Palférine and asked what he meant to do.

" 'Why, madame,' said he, 'I am neither a surgeon nor a midwife.'

" She collapsed, but three or four years later she returned to the charge, still persisting in her inquiry: 'What did La Palférine mean to do?'

" 'Well, madame,' returned he, 'when the child is seven years old, an age at which a boy ought to pass out of women's hands'—an indication of entire agreement on the mother's

part—' if the child is really mine '—another gesture of assent
—' if there is a striking likeness, if he bids fair to be a gentleman, if I can recognize in him my turn of mind, and more
particularly the Rusticoli air ; then, oh—ah ! '—a new movement from the matron—' on my word and honor, I will make
him a cornet * of—sugar-plums ! '

"All this, if you will permit me to make use of the phraseology employed by M. Sainte-Beuve for his biographies of
obscurities—all this, I repeat, is the playful and sprightly yet
already somewhat decadent side of a strong race. It smacks
rather of the Parc-aux-Cerfs than of the Hôtel de Rambouillet.
It is a race of the strong rather than of the sweet ; I incline
to lay a little debauchery to its charge, and more than I
should wish in brilliant and generous natures ; it is gallantry
after the fashion of the Maréchal de Richelieu, high spirits
and frolic carried rather too far ; perhaps we may see in it
the *outrances* of another age, the Eighteenth Century pushed
to extremes ; it harks back to the Musketeers ; it is an exploit
stolen from Champcenetz ; nay, such light-hearted incon-
stancy takes us back to the festooned and ornate period of
the old court of the Valois. In an age as moral as the present, we are bound to regard audacity of this kind sternly ;
still, at the same time that ' cornet of sugar-plums ' may serve
to warn young girls of the perils of lingering where fancies,
more charming than chastened, come thickly from the first ;
on the rosy flowery unguarded slopes, where trespasses ripen
into errors full of equivocal effervescence, into too palpitating
issues. The anecdote puts La Palférine's genius before you
in all its vivacity and completeness. He realizes Pascal's
entre-deux (middle-space), he comprehends the whole scale
between tenderness and pitilessness, and, like Epaminondas,
he is equally great in extremes. And not merely so, his epigram stamps the epoch ; the *accoucheur* is a modern innova-

* Cornet is a military title, a musical instrument, and a paper packet.

tion. All the refinements of modern civilization are summed
up in the phrase. It is monumental."

" Look here, my dear Nathan, what farrago of nonsense is
this?" asked the marquise in bewilderment.

" Madame la Marquise," returned Nathan, "you do not
know the value of these 'precious' phrases; I am talking
Sainte-Beuve, the new kind of French. I resume. Walking
one day arm-in-arm with a friend along the boulevard, he was
accosted by a ferocious creditor, who inquired—

" ' Are you thinking of me, sir?'

" ' Not the least in the world,' answered the count.

" Remark the difficulty of the position. Talleyrand, in
similar circumstances, had already replied, ' You are very inquisitive, my dear fellow!' To imitate the inimitable great
man was out of the question. La Palférine, generous as Buck-
ingham, could not bear to be caught empty-handed. One
day when he had nothing to give a little Savoyard chimney-
sweeper, he dipped a hand into a barrel of grapes in a grocer's
doorway and filled the child's cap from it. The little one ate
away at his grapes; the grocer began by laughing, and ended
by holding out his hand.

" ' Oh, fie! monsieur,' said La Palférine, ' your left hand
ought not to know what my right hand doth.'

" With his adventurous courage, he never refuses any odds,
but there is wit in his bravado. In the Passage de l'Opera he
chanced to meet a man who had spoken slightingly of him,
elbowed him as he passed, and then turned and jostled him a
second time.

" ' You are very clumsy!'

" ' On the contrary; I did it on purpose.'

" The young man pulled out his card. La Palférine
dropped it. ' It has been carried too long in the pocket.
Be good enough to give me another.'

" On the ground he received a thrust; blood was drawn;
his antagonist wished to stop.

" ' You are wounded, monsieur ! '

" ' I disallow the *botte*' (thrust), said La Palférine, as coolly as if he had been in the fencing saloon; then as he riposted (sending the point home this time), he added, ' There is the right thrust, monsieur ! '

" His antagonist kept his bed for six months.

" This, still following on Monsieur Sainte-Beuve's tracks, recalls the *raffinés* (lit.: keen), the fine-edged raillery of the best days of the monarchy. In this speech you discern an untrammeled but drifting life; a gayety of imagination that deserts us when our first youth is past. The prime of the blossom is over, but there remains the dry compact seed with the germs of life in it, ready against the coming winter. Do you not see that these things are symptoms of something unsatisfied, of an unrest impossible to analyze, still less to describe, yet not incomprehensible; a something ready to break out if occasion calls into flying, upleaping flame? It is the *accidia* of the cloister; a trace of sourness, of ferment engendered by the enforced stagnation of youthful energies, a vague, obscure melancholy."

" That will do," said the marquise; " you are giving me a mental shower-bath."

" It is the early afternoon languor. If a man has nothing to do, he will sooner get into mischief than do nothing at all; this invariably happens in France. Youth at the present day has two sides to it; the studious or unappreciated, and the ardent or impassioned."

" That will do!" repeated Mme. de Rochefide, with an authoritative gesture. " You are setting my nerves on edge."

" 'To finish my portrait of La Palférine, I hasten to make the plunge into the gallant regions of his character, or you will not understand the peculiar genius of an admirable representative of a certain section of mischievous youth—youth strong enough, be it said, to laugh at the position in which it is put by those in power; shrewd enough to do no work, since work profiteth nothing, yet so full of life that it fastens upon pleasure—the one thing that cannot be taken away. And meanwhile a bourgeois, mercantile, and bigoted policy continues to cut off all the sluices through which so much aptitude and ability would find an outlet. Poets and men of science are not wanted.

"To give you an idea of the stupidity of the new Court, I will tell you of something which happened to La Palférine. There is a sort of relieving officer on the civil list. This functionary one day discovered that La Palférine was in dire distress, drew up a report no doubt, and brought the descendant of the Rusticoli fifty francs by way of alms. La Palférine received the visitor with perfect courtesy, and talked of various persons at Court.

"'Is it true,' he asked, 'that Mademoiselle d'Orléans contributes such and such a sum to this benevolent scheme started by her nephew? If so, it is very gracious of her.'

"Now La Palférine had a servant, a little Savoyard aged ten, who waited on him without wages. La Palférine called him Father Anchise, and used to say: 'I have never seen such a mixture of besotted foolishness with great intelligence; he would go through fire and water for me; he understands everything—and yet he cannot grasp the fact that I can do nothing for him.'

"Anchise was dispatched to a livery stable with instructions to hire a handsome brougham with a man in livery behind it. By the time the carriage arrived below, La Palférine had skillfully piloted the conversation to the subject of the functions of his visitor, whom he has since called 'the unmitigated misery man,' and learned the nature of his duties and his stipend.

"'Do they allow you a carriage to go about the town in this way?'

"'Oh! no.'

"At that La Palférine and a friend who happened to be

with him went down stairs with the poor soul and insisted on putting him into the carriage. It was raining in torrents. La Palférine had thought of everything. He offered to drive the official to the next house on his list; and when the almoner came down again, he found the carriage waiting for him at the door. The man in livery handed him a note written in pencil:

" 'The carriage has been engaged for three days. Count Rusticoli de la Palférine is too happy to associate himself with Court charities by lending wings to Royal beneficence.'

" La Palférine now calls the civil list the uncivil list.

" He was once passionately loved by a lady of somewhat light conduct. Antonia lived in the Rue du Helder; she had seen and been seen to some extent, but at the time of her acquaintance with La Palférine she had not yet 'an establishment.' Antonia was not wanting in the insolence of the old days, now degenerating into rudeness among women of her class. After a fortnight of unmixed bliss, she was compelled, in the interest of her civil list, to return to a less exclusive system; and La Palférine, discovering a certain lack of sincerity in her dealings with him, sent Madame Antonia a note which made her famous.

" 'MADAME:—Your conduct causes me much surprise and no less distress. Not content with rending my heart with your disdain, you have been so little thoughtful as to retain a toothbrush, which my means will not permit me to replace, my estates being mortgaged beyond their value.

" 'Adieu, too fair and too ungrateful friend! May we meet again in a better world.

" 'CHARLES EDWARD.'

" Assuredly (to avail ourselves yet further of Sainte-Beuve's

Babylonish dialect), this far outpasses the raillery of Sterne's
'Sentimental Journey;' it might be Scarron without his
grossness. Nay, I do not know but that Molière in his lighter
mood would not have said of it, as of Cyrano de Bergerac's
best—'This is mine.' Richelieu himself was not more complete when he wrote to the princess waiting for him in the
Palais Royal—'Stay there, my queen, to charm the scullion
lads.' At the same time, Charles Edward's humor is less
biting. I am not sure that this kind of wit was known among
the Greeks and Romans. Plato, possibly, upon a closer inspection, approaches it, but from the austere and musical
side——''

"No more of that jargon," the marquise broke in, "in
print it may be endurable; but to have it grating upon my
ears is a punishment which I do not in the least deserve."

"He first met Claudine on this wise," continued Nathan.
"It was one of the unfilled days, when Youth is a burden to
itself; days when Youth, reduced by the overweening presumption of Age to a condition of potential energy and dejection, emerges therefrom (like Blondet under the Restoration), either to get into mischief or to set about some colossal
piece of buffoonery, half excused by the very audacity of its
conception. La Palférine was sauntering, cane in hand, up
and down the pavement between the Rue de Grammont and
the Rue de Richelieu, when in the distance he descried a
woman too elegantly dressed, covered, as he phrased it, with
a great deal of portable property, too expensive and too care-
lessly worn for its owner to be other than a princess of the
Court or of the stage, it was not easy at first to say which.
But after July, 1830, in his opinion, there is no mistaking the
indications—the princess can only be a princess of the stage.

"The count came up and walked by her side as if she had
given him an assignation. He followed her with a courteous
persistence, a persistence in good taste, giving the lady from
time to time, and always at the right moment, an authoritative

glance, which compelled her to submit to his escort. Anybody but La Palférine would have been frozen by his reception, and disconcerted by the lady's first efforts to rid herself of her cavalier, by her chilly air, her curt speeches; but no gravity, with all the will in the world, could hold out long against La Palférine's jesting replies. The fair stranger went into her milliner's store. Charles Edward followed, took a seat, and gave his opinions and advice like a man that meant to pay. This coolness disturbed the lady, she went out.

"On the stairs she spoke to her persecutor.

"'Monsieur, I am about to call upon one of my husband's relatives, an elderly lady, Mme. de Bonfalot——'

"''Ah! Madame de Bonfalot, charmed, I am sure. I am going there.'

"The pair accordingly went. Charles Edward came in with the lady, every one believed that she had brought him with her. He took part in the conversation, was lavish of his polished and brilliant wit. The visit lengthened out. This was not what he wanted.

"'Madame,' he said addressing the fair stranger, 'do not forget that your husband is waiting for us, and only allowed us a quarter of an hour.'

"Taken aback by such boldness (which, as you know, is never displeasing to you women), led captive by the conqueror's glance, by the astute yet candid air which Charles Edward can assume when he chooses, the lady rose, took the arm of her self-constituted escort, and went downstairs, but on the threshold she stopped to speak to him.

"'Monsieur, I like a joke——'

"''And so do I.'

"She laughed.

"'But this may turn to earnest,' he added; 'it only rests with you. I am the Comte de la Palférine, and I am delighted that it is in my power to lay my heart and my fortune at your feet.'

"La Palférine was at that time twenty-two years old. (This happened in 1834.) Luckily for him, he was fashionably dressed. I can paint his portrait for you in a few words. He was the living image of Louis XIII., with the same white forehead and gracious outline of the temples, the same olive skin (that Italian olive tint which turns white where the light falls on it), the brown hair worn rather long, the black 'royale' (Anglice: imperial), the grave and melancholy expression, for La Palférine's character and exterior were amazingly at variance.

"At the sound of the name, and the sight of its owner, something like a quiver thrilled through Claudine. La Palférine saw the vibration, and shot a glance at her out of the dark depths of almond-shaped eyes with purpled lids, and those faint lines about them which tell of pleasures as costly as painful fatigue. With those eyes upon her, she said—
'Your address?'

"'What want of address!'

"'Oh, pshaw!' she said, smiling. 'A bird on the bough?'

"'Good-by, madame, you are such a woman as I seek, but my fortune is far from equaling my desire——'

"He bowed, and there and then left her. Two days later, by one of the strange chances that can only happen in Paris, he had betaken himself to a money-lending wardrobe dealer to sell such of his clothing as he could spare. He was just receiving the price with an uneasy air, after long chaffering, when the stranger lady passed and recognized him.

"'Once for all,' cried he to the bewildered wardrobe dealer, 'I tell you, I am not going to take your trumpet!'

"He pointed to a huge, much-dinted musical instrument, hanging up outside against a background of uniforms, civil and military. Then, proudly and impetuously, he followed the lady.

"From that great day of the trumpet these two understood one another to admiration. Charles Edward's ideas on the subject of love are as sound as possible. According to him, a man cannot love twice; there is but one love in his lifetime, but that love is a deep and shoreless sea. It may break in upon him at any time, as the grace of God found St. Paul; and a man may live sixty years and never know love. Perhaps, to quote Heine's superb phrase, it is ' the secret malady of the heart '—a sense of the Infinite that there is within us, together with the revelation of the ideal Beauty in its visible form. This Love, in short, comprehends both the creature and creation. But so long as there is no question of this great poetical conception, the loves that cannot last can only be taken lightly, as if they were in a manner snatches of song compared with Love the epic.

"To Charles Edward the adventure brought neither the thunderbolt signal of love's coming, nor yet that gradual revelation of an inward fairness which draws two natures by degrees more and more strongly each to each. For there are but two ways of love—love at first sight, doubtless akin to the Highland ' second-sight,' and that slow fusion of two natures which realizes Plato's ' man-woman.' But if Charles Edward did not love, he was loved to distraction. Claudine found love made complete, body and soul; in her, in short, La Palférine awakened the one passion of her life; while for him Claudine was only a most charming mistress. The devil himself, a most potent magician certainly, with all hell at his back, could never have changed the natures of these two unequal fires. I dare affirm that Claudine not infrequently bored Charles Edward.

" ' Stale fish and the woman you do not love are only fit to fling out of the window after three days,' he used to say.

" In Bohemia there is little secrecy observed over these affairs. La Palférine used to talk a good deal of Claudine; but, at the same time, none of us saw her, nor so much as knew her name. For us Claudine was almost a mythical personage. All of us acted in the same way, reconciling the requirements of our common life with the rules of good taste. Claudine, Hortense, the Baroness, the Bourgeoise, the Empress, the Spaniard, the Lioness—these were cryptic titles which permitted us to pour out our joys, our cares, vexations, and hopes, and to communicate our discoveries. Further, none of us went. It has been known, in Bohemia, that chance discovered the identity of the fair unknown; and at once, as by tacit convention, not one of us spoke of her again. This fact may show how far youth possesses a sense of true delicacy. How admirably certain natures of a finer clay know the limit line where jest must end, and all that host of things French covered by the slang word *blague*, a word which will shortly be cast out of the language (let us hope), and yet it is the only one which conveys an idea of the spirit of Bohemia.

"So we often used to joke about Claudine and the count. 'What are you making of Claudine?' 'How is Claudine?' 'Toujours Claudine?' sung to the air of 'Toujours Gessler.'

"'I wish you all such a mistress, for all the harm I wish you,' La Palférine began one day. 'No greyhound, no basset-dog, no poodle can match her in gentleness, submissiveness, and complete tenderness. There are times when I reproach myself, when I take myself to task for my hard heart. Claudine obeys with saintly sweetness. She comes to me, I tell her to go, she goes, she does not even cry till she is out in the courtyard. I refuse to see her for a whole week at a time. I tell her to come at such an hour on Tuesday; and be it midnight or six o'clock in the morning, ten o'clock, five o'clock, breakfast-time, dinner-time, bed-time, any particular inconvenient hour in the day—she will come, punctual to the minute, beautiful, beautifully dressed, and enchanting. And she is a married woman, with all the complications and duties of a household. The fibs that she must invent, the reasons she must find for conforming to my whims would tax the ingenuity of some of us! Claudine never wearies; you can always count upon her. It is not love, I tell her, it is in-

2   Q

fatuation. She writes to me every day; I do not read her letters; she found that out, but still she writes. See here; there are two hundred letters in this casket. She begs me to wipe my razors on one of her letters every day, and I punctually do so. She thinks, and rightly, that the sight of her handwriting will put me in mind of her.'

" La Palférine was dressing as he told us this. I took up the letter which he was about to put to this use, read it, and kept it, as he did not ask to have it back. Here it is. I looked for it, and I found it as I promised.

" ' Monday (*Midnight*).

" ' Well, my dear, are you satisfied with me? I did not even ask for your hand, yet you might easily have given it to me, and I longed so much to hold it to my heart, to my lips. No, I did not ask, I am so afraid of displeasing you. Do you know one thing? Though I am cruelly sure that anything I do is a matter of perfect indifference to you, I am none the less extremely timid in my conduct: the woman that belongs to you, whatever her title to call herself yours, must not incur so much as the shadow of blame. In so far as love comes from the angels in heaven, from whom there are no secrets hid, my love is as pure as the purest; wherever I am I feel that I am in your presence, and I try to do you honor.

" ' All that you said about my manner of dress impressed me very much; I began to understand how far above others are those that come of a noble race. There was still something of the opera girl in my gowns, in my way of dressing my hair. In a moment I saw the distance between me and good taste. Next time you shall receive a duchess, you shall not know me again! Ah! how good you have been to your Claudine! How many and many a time I have thanked you for telling me these things! What interest lay in those few words! You had taken thought for that thing belonging to you called Claudine? *This* imbecile would never have opened my eyes; he thinks that everything I do is right; and beside, he is much too humdrum, too matter-of-fact to have any feeling for the beautiful.

" 'Tuesday is very slow of coming for my impatient mind! On Tuesday I shall be with you for several hours. Ah! when it comes I will try to think that the hours are months, that it will be so always. I am living in hope of that morning now, as I shall live upon the memory of it afterward. Hope is memory that craves; and recollection, memory sated. What a beautiful life within life thought makes for us in this way!

" 'Sometimes I dream of inventing new ways of tenderness all my own, a secret which no other woman shall guess. A cold sweat breaks out over me at the thought that something may happen to prevent this meeting. Oh, I would break with *him* for good, if need was, but nothing here could possibly interfere; it would be from your side. Perhaps you may decide to go out, perhaps to go to see some other woman. Oh! spare me this Tuesday for pity's sake. If you take it from me, Charles, you do not know what *he* will suffer; I should drive him wild. But even if you do not want me, if you are going out, let me come, all the same, to be with you while you dress; only to see you, I ask no more than that; only to show you that I love you without a thought of self.

" 'Since you gave me leave to love you, for you gave me leave, since I am yours; since that day I loved and love you with the whole strength of my soul; and I shall love you forever, for once having loved *you*, no one could, no one ought to love another. And, you see, when those eyes that ask nothing but to see you are upon you, you will feel that in your Claudine there is a something divine, called into existence by you.

" 'Alas! with you I can never play the coquette. I am like a mother with her child; I endure anything from you; I, that was once so imperious and proud. I have made dukes and princes fetch and carry for me; aides-de-camp, worth

more than all the court of Charles X. put together, have done
my errands, yet I am treating you as my spoilt child. But
where is the use of coquetry? It would be pure waste. And
yet, monsieur, for want of coquetry I shall never inspire love
in you. I know it; I feel it; yet I do as before, feeling a
power that I cannot withstand, thinking that this utter self-
surrender will win me the sentiment innate in all men (so *he*
tells me) for the thing that belongs to them.

"'Wednesday.

" 'Ah! how darkly sadness entered my heart yesterday
when I found that I must give up the joy of seeing you. One
single thought held me back from the arms of Death! It
was thy will! To stay away was to do thy will, to obey an
order from thee. Oh! Charles, I was so pretty; I looked a
lovelier woman for you than that beautiful German princess
whom you gave me for an example, whom I have studied at
the opera. And yet—you might have thought that I had
overstepped the limits of my nature. You have left me no
confidence in myself; perhaps I am plain after all. Oh! I
loathe myself, I dream of my radiant Charles Edward, and
my brain turns. I shall go mad, I know I shall. Do not
laugh, do not talk to me of the fickleness of women. If we
are inconstant *you* are strangely capricious. You take away
the hours of love that made a poor creature's happiness for
ten whole days; the hours on which she drew to be charming
and kind to all that came to see her! After all, you were the
source of my kindness to *him;* you do not know what pain
you give him. I wonder what I must do to keep you, or
simply to keep the right to be yours sometimes. When I
think that you never would come here to me! With what
delicious emotion I would wait upon you! There are other
women more favored than I. There are women to whom you
say, "I love you." To me you have never said more than
"You are a good girl." Certain speeches of yours, though

you do not know it, gnaw at my heart. Clever men sometimes ask me what I am thinking. I am thinking of my self-
abasement—the prostration of the poorest outcast in the
presence of the Saviour.'

" There are still three more pages, you see. La Palférine
allowed me to take the letter, with the traces of tears that still
seemed hot upon it! Here was proof of the truth of his
story. Marcas, a shy man enough with women, was in
ecstasies over a second which he read in his corner before
lighting his pipe with it.

" ' Why, any woman in love will write that sort of thing ! '
cried La Palférine. ' Love gives all women intelligence and
style, which proves that here in France style proceeds from
the matter and not from the words. See now how well this is
thought out, how clear-headed sentiment is '—and with that
he read us another letter, far superior to the artificial and
labored productions which we novelists write.

" One day poor Claudine heard that La Palférine was in a
critical position; it was a question of meeting a bill of
exchange. An unlucky idea occurred to her; she put a tolerably large sum in gold into an exquisitely embroidered purse
and went to him.

" ' Who has taught you to be so bold as to meddle with my
household affairs ? ' La Palférine cried angrily. ' Mend my
socks and work slippers for me, if it amuses you. So !——
you will play the duchess, and you turn the story of Danaë
against the aristocracy.'

" He emptied the purse into his hand as he spoke, and made
as though he would fling the money in her face. Claudine,
in her terror, did not guess that he was joking; she shrank
back, stumbled over a chair, and fell with her head against the
corner of the marble mantel-piece. She thought she should
have died. When she could speak, poor woman, as she lay
on the bed, all that she said was, ' I deserved it, Charles ! '

"For a moment La Palférine was in despair; his anguish revived Claudine. She rejoiced in the mishap; she took advantage of her suffering to compel La Palférine to take the money and release him from an awkward position. Then followed a variation on la Fontaine's fable, in which a man blesses the thieves that brought him a sudden impulse of tenderness from his wife. And while we are upon this subject, another saying will paint the man for you.

"Claudine went home again, made up some kind of tale as best she could to account for her bruised forehead, and fell dangerously ill. An abscess formed in the head. The doctor—Bianchon, I believe—yes, it was Bianchon—wanted to cut off her hair. The Duchesse de Berri's hair is not more beautiful than Claudine's; she would not hear of it, she told Bianchon in confidence that she could not allow it to be cut without leave from the Comte de la Palférine. Bianchon went to Charles Edward. Charles Edward heard him with much seriousness. The doctor had explained the case at length, and showed that it was absolutely necessary to sacrifice the hair to insure the success of the operation.

"'Cut off Claudine's hair!' cried he in peremptory tones. 'No. I would sooner lose her.'

"Even now, after a lapse of four years, Bianchon still quotes that speech; we have laughed over it for half an hour together. Claudine, informed of the verdict, saw in it a proof of affection; she felt sure that she was loved. In the face of her weeping family, with her husband on his knees, she was inexorable. She kept her hair. The strength that came with the belief that she was loved came to her aid, the operation succeeded perfectly.

There are stirrings of the inner life which throw all the calculations of surgery into disorder and baffle all the laws of medical science.

"Claudine wrote a delicious letter to La Palférine, a letter in which the orthography was doubtful and the punctuation

all to seek, to tell him of the happy result of the operation,
and to add that Love was wiser than all the sciences.

"'Now,' said La Palférine one day, 'what am I to do to
get rid of Claudine?'

"'Why, she is not at all troublesome; she leaves you master
of your actions,' objected we.

"'That is true,' returned La Palférine, 'but I do not
choose that anything shall slip into my life without my consent.'

"From that day he set himself to torment Claudine. It
seemed that he held the bourgeoise, the nobody, in utter
horror; nothing would satisfy him but a woman with a title.
Claudine, it was true, had made progress; she had learned to
dress as well as the best-dressed women of the Saint-Germain
suburb; she had freed her bearing of unhallowed traces; she
walked with a chastened, inimitable grace; but this was not
enough. This praise of her enabled Claudine to swallow
down the rest.

"But one day La Palférine said, 'If you wish to be the
mistress of one La Palférine, poor, penniless, and without
prospects as he is, you ought at least to represent him worthily.
You should have a carriage and liveried servants and a title.
Give me all the gratifications of vanity that will never be
mine in my own person. The woman whom I honor with
my regard ought never to go on foot; if she is bespattered
with mud, I suffer. That is how I am made. If she is mine,
she must be admired of all Paris. All Paris shall envy me
my good fortune. If some little whipper-snapper seeing a
brilliant countess pass in her brilliant carriage shall say to
himself: "Who can call such a divinity his?" and grow
thoughtful—why, it will double my pleasure.'

"La Palférine owned to us that he flung this programme
at Claudine's head simply to rid himself of her. As a result
he was stupefied with astonishment for the first and probably
the only time in his life.

"' Dear,' she said, and there was a ring in her voice that betrayed the great agitation which shook her whole being, 'it is well. All this shall be done, or I will die.'

"She let fall a few happy tears on his hand as she kissed it.

"' You have told me what I must do to be your mistress still,' she added ; 'I am glad.'

"' And then ' (La Palférine told us) 'she went out with a little coquettish gesture like a woman that has had her way. As she stood in my garret doorway, tall and proud, she seemed to reach the stature of an antique sibyl.'

"All this should sufficiently explain the manners and customs of the Bohemia in which this young *condottiere** is one of the most brilliant figures," Nathan continued after a pause. "Now it so happened that I discovered Claudine's identity, and could understand the appalling truth of one line which you perhaps overlooked in that letter of hers. It was on this wise."

The marquise, too thoughtful now for laughter, bade Nathan "Go on," in a tone that told him plainly how deeply she had been impressed by these strange things, and even more plainly how much she was interested in La Palférine, of the many Christian names.

"In 1829, one of the most influential, steady, and clever of dramatic writers was du Bruel. His real name is unknown to the public ; on the play-bills he is de Cursy. Under the Restoration he had a place in the Civil Service ; and being really attached to the elder branch, he sent in his resignation bravely in 1830, and ever since has written twice as many plays to fill the deficit in his budget made by his noble conduct. At that time du Bruel was forty years old ; you know the story of his life. Like many of his brethren, he bore a stage dancer an affection hard to explain, but well known in the whole world of letters. The woman, as you know, was Tullia, one of the 'first ladies' of the Académie Royale de

---

* Mercenary soldiers.

Musique.   Tullia is merely a pseudonym like du Bruel's name
of de Cursy.

"For the ten years between 1817 and 1827 Tullia was in
her glory on the heights of the stage of the opera.   With
more beauty than education, a mediocre dancer with rather
more sense than most of her class, she took no part in the
virtuous reforms which ruined the corps de ballet; she continued the Guimard dynasty.   She owed her ascendency,
moreover, to various well-known protectors, to the Duc de
Rhétoré (the Duc de Chaulieu's eldest son), to the influence
of a famous superintendent of Fine Arts, and sundry diplomatists and rich foreigners.   During her apogee she had a neat
little house in the Rue Chauchat, and lived as opera nymphs
used to live in the old days.   Du Bruel was smitten with her
about the time when the duke's fancy came to an end in 1823.
Being a mere subordinate in the Civil Service, du Bruel tolerated the superintendent of Fine Arts, believing that he himself was really preferred.   After six years this connection was
almost a marriage.   Tullia has always been very careful to
say nothing of her family; we have a vague idea that she
comes from Nanterre.   One of her uncles, formerly a simple
bricklayer or carpenter, is now, it is said, a very rich contractor, thanks to her influence and generous loans.   This
fact leaked out through du Bruel.   He happened to say that
Tullia would inherit a fine fortune sooner or later.   The contractor was a bachelor; he had a weakness for the niece to
whom he is indebted.

"'He is not clever enough to be ungrateful,' said she.

"In 1829 Tullia retired from the stage of her own accord.
At the age of thirty she saw that she was growing somewhat
stouter, and she had tried pantomime without success.   Her
whole art consisted in the trick of raising her skirts, after
Noblet's manner, in a pirouette which inflated them balloon-
fashion and exhibited the smallest possible quantity of clothing
to the pit.   The aged Vestris had told her at the very begin-

ning that this *temps*, well executed by a fine woman, is worth all the art imaginable. It is the chest-note C of dancing. For which reason, he said, the very greatest dancers—Camargo, Guimard, and Taglioni, all of them thin, brown, and plain—could only redeem their physical defects by their genuis. Tullia, still in the height of her glory, retired before younger and cleverer dancers; she did wisely. She was an aristocrat; she had scarcely stooped below the noblesse in her *liaisons;* she declined to dip her ankles in the troubled waters of July. Insolent and beautiful as she was, Claudine possessed handsome souvenirs, but very little ready money; still, her jewels were magnificent, and she had as fine furniture as any one in Paris.

"On quitting the stage when she, forgotten to-day, was yet in the height of her fame, one thought possessed her—she meant du Bruel to marry her; and at the time of this story, you must understand that the marriage had taken place, but was kept a secret. How do women of her class contrive to make a man marry them after seven or eight years of intimacy? What springs do they touch? What machinery do they set in motion? But, however comical such domestic dramas may be, we are not now concerned with them. Du Bruel was secretly married; the thing was done.

"Cursy before his marriage was supposed to be a jolly companion; now and again he stayed out all night, and to some extent led the life of a Bohemian; he would unbend at a supper-party. He went out to all appearance to a rehearsal at the Opera-Comique, and found himself in some unaccountable way at Dieppe, or Baden, or Saint-Germain; he gave dinners, led the Titantic thriftless life of artists, journalists, and writers; levied his tribute on all the greenrooms of Paris; and, in short, was one of us. Finot, Lousteau, du Tillet, Desroches, Bixiou, Blondet, Couture, and des Lupeaulx tolerated him in spite of his pedantic manner and ponderous official attitude. But once married, Tullia made a slave of du Bruel. There was no help for it. He was in love with Tullia, poor devil.

"'Tullia' (so he said) 'had left the stage to be his alone, to be a good and charming wife.' And somehow Tullia managed to induce the most puritanical members of du Bruel's family to accept her. From the very first, before any one suspected her motives, she assiduously visited old Madame de Bonfalot, who bored her horridly; she made handsome presents to mean old Madame de Chissé, du Bruel's great-aunt; she spent a summer with the latter lady, and never missed a single mass. She even went to confession, received absolution, and took the sacrament; but this, you must remember, was in the country and under the aunt's eyes.

"'I shall have real aunts now, do you understand?' she said to us when she came back in the winter.

"She was so delighted with her respectability, so glad to renounce her independence, that she found means to compass her end. She flattered the old people. She went on foot every day to sit for a couple of hours with Mme. du Bruel the elder while that lady was ill—a Maintenon's stratagem which amazed du Bruel. And he admired his wife without criticism; he was so fast in the toils already that he did not feel his bonds.

"Claudine succeeded in making him understand that only under the elastic system of a bourgeois government, only at the bourgeois court of the Citizen-King, could a Tullia, now metamorphosed into a Mme. du Bruel, be accepted in the society which her good sense prevented her from attempting to enter. Mme. de Bonfalot, Mme. de Chissé, and Mme. du Bruel received her: she was satisfied. She took up the position of a well-conducted, simple, and virtuous woman, and never acted out of character. In three years' time she was introduced to the friends of these ladies.

"'And still I cannot persuade myself that young Madame du Bruel used to display her ankles, and the rest, to all Paris,

with the light of a hundred gas-jets pouring upon her,' Mme.
Anselme Popinot remarked naïvely.

"From this point of view, July, 1830, inaugurated an era
not unlike the time of the Empire, when a waiting-woman
was received at Court in the person of Mme. Garat, a chief-
justice's 'lady.' Tullia had completely broken, as you may
guess, with all her old associates; of her former acquaintances,
she only recognized those who could not compromise her.
At the time of her marriage she had taken a very charming
little hôtel between a court and a garden, lavishing money on
it with wild extravagance and putting the best part of her
furniture and du Bruel's into it. Everything that she thought
common or ordinary was sold. To find anything comparable
to her sparkling splendor, you could only look back to the
days when a Sophie Arnould, a Guimard, or a Duthé, in all
her glory, squandered the fortunes of princes.

"How far did this sumptuous existence affect du Bruel?
It is a delicate question to ask, and a still more delicate one
to answer. A single incident will suffice to give you an idea
of Tullia's crotchets. Her bed-spread of Brussels lace was
worth ten thousand francs. A famous actress had another
like it. As soon as Claudine heard this, she allowed her cat,
a splendid Angora, to sleep on the bed. That trait gives you
the woman. Du Bruel dared not say a word; he was ordered
to spread abroad that challenge in luxury, so that it might
reach the other. Tullia was very fond of this gift from the
Duc de Rhétoré; but one day, five years after her marriage,
she played with her cat to such purpose that the coverlet—
furbelows, flounces, and all—was torn to shreds, and replaced
by a sensible quilt, a quilt that was a quilt, and not a symptom
of the peculiar form of insanity which drives these women to
make up by an insensate luxury for the childish days when
they lived on raw apples, to quote the expression of a journal-
ist. The day when the bed-spread was torn to tatters marked
a new epoch in her married life.

"Cursy was remarkable for his ferocious industry. Nobody suspects the source to which Paris owes the patch-and-powder eighteenth century vaudevilles that flooded the stage. Those thousand-and-one vaudevilles, which raised such an outcry among the *feuilletonistes*, were written at Mme. du Bruel's express desire. She insisted that her husband should purchase the hôtel on which she had spent so much, where she had housed five hundred thousand francs' worth of furniture. Wherefore? Tullia never enters into explanations; she understands the sovereign woman's reason to admiration.

"'People made a good deal of fun of Cursy,' said she; 'but, as a matter of fact, he found this house in the eighteenth-century rouge-box, powder, puffs, and spangles. He would never have thought of it but for me,' she added, burying herself in her cushions in her fireside corner.

"She delivered herself thus on her return from a first night. Du Bruel's piece had succeeded, and she foresaw an avalanche of criticisms. Tullia had her At Homes. Every Monday she gave a tea-party; her society was as select as might be, and she neglected nothing that could make her house pleasant. There was bouillotte in one room, conversation in another, and sometimes a concert (always short) in the large drawing-room. None but the most eminent artists performed in her house. Tullia had so much good sense that she attained to the most exquisite tact, and herein, in all probability, lay the secret of her ascendency over du Bruel; at any rate, he loved her with the love which use and wont at length makes indispensable to life. Every day adds another thread to the strong, irresistible, intangible web, which enmeshes the most delicate fancies, takes captive every most transient mood, and, binding them together, holds a man tightly bound hand and foot, heart and head.

"Tullia knew Cursy well; she knew every weak point in his armor, knew also how to heal his wounds.

"A passion of this kind is inscrutable for any observer,

even for a man who prides himself, as I do, on a certain expertness. It is everywhere unfathomable; the dark depths in it are darker than in any other mystery; the colors confused even in the highest lights.

"Cursy was an old playwright, jaded by the life of the theatrical world. He liked comfort; he liked a luxurious, affluent, easy existence; he enjoyed being a king in his own house; he liked to be host to a party of men of letters in a hôtel resplendent with royal luxury, with carefully chosen works of art shining in the setting. Tullia allowed du Bruel to enthrone himself amid the tribe; there were plenty of journalists whom it was easy enough to catch and ensnare; and, thanks to her evening parties and a well-timed loan here and there, Cursy was not attacked too seriously—his plays succeeded. For these reasons he would not have separated from Tullia for an empire. If she had been unfaithful, he would probably have passed it over, on condition that none of his accustomed joys should be retrenched; yet, strange to say, Tullia caused him no twinges on this account. No fancy was laid to her charge; if there had been any, she certainly had been very careful of appearances.

"'My dear fellow,' du Bruel would say, laying down the law to us on the boulevard, 'there is nothing like one of these women who have sown their wild oats and got over their passions. Such women as Claudine have lived their bachelor life; they have been over head and ears in pleasure, and make the most adorable wives that could be wished; they have nothing to learn, they are formed, they are not in the least prudish; they are well broken in, and indulgent. So I strongly recommend everybody to take the "remains of a racer." I am the most fortunate man on earth.'

"Du Bruel said this to me himself with Bixiou there to hear it.

"'My dear fellow,' said the caricaturist, 'perhaps he is right to be in the wrong.'

"About a week afterward, du Bruel asked us to dine with him one Tuesday. That morning I went to see him on a piece of theatrical business, a case submitted to us for arbitration by the commission of dramatic authors. We were obliged to go out again ; but before we started he went to Claudine's room, knocked, as he always does, and asked for leave to enter.

"'We live in the grand style,' said he, smiling ; 'we are free. Each is independent.'

"We were admitted. Du Bruel spoke to Claudine. 'I have asked a few people to dinner to-day——'

"'Just like you !' cried she. 'You ask people without speaking to me ; I count for nothing here. Now' (taking me as arbitrator by a glance) 'I ask you yourself. When a man has been so foolish as to live with a woman of my sort ; for, after all, I was an opera-dancer—yes, I ought always to remember that, if other people are to forget it—well, under those circumstances, a clever man seeking to raise his wife in public opinion would do his best to impose her upon the world as a remarkable woman, to justify the step he had taken by acknowledging that in some ways she was something more than ordinary women. The best way of compelling respect from others is to pay respect to her at home, and to leave her absolute mistress of the house. Well, and yet it is enough to waken one's vanity to see how frightened he is of seeming to listen to me. I must be in the right ten times over if he concedes a single point.'

"(Emphatic negative gestures from du Bruel at every other word.)

"'Oh, yes, yes,' she continued quickly, in answer to this mute dissent. 'I know all about it, du Bruel, my dear, I that have been like a queen in my house all my life till I married you. My wishes were guessed, fulfilled, and more than fulfilled. After all, I am thirty-five, and at five-and-thirty a woman cannot expect to be loved. Ah, if I were a girl of

sixteen, if I had not lost something that is dearly bought at
the opera, what attention you would pay me, Monsieur du
Bruel! I feel the most supreme contempt for men who boast
that they can love and grow careless and neglectful in little
things as time grows on. You are short and insignificant,
you see, du Bruel; you love to torment a woman; it is your
only way of showing your strength. A Napoleon is ready to
be swayed by the woman he loves; he loses nothing by it;
but as for such as you, you believe that you are nothing apparently, you do not wish to be ruled. Five-and-thirty, my
dear boy,' she continued, turning to me, 'that is the clue to
the riddle. "No," does he say again? You know quite
well that I am thirty-seven. I am very sorry, but just ask
your friends to dine at the Rocher de Cancale. I *could* have
them here, but I will not; they shall not come. And then
perhaps my poor little monologue may engrave that salutary
maxim: "Each is master at home," upon your memory.
That is our charter,' she added, laughing, with a return of the
opera-girl's giddiness and caprice.

" 'Well, well, my dear little puss; there, there, never mind.
We can manage to get on together,' said du Bruel, and he
kissed her hands, and we came away. But he was very, very
wroth.

"The whole way from the Rue de la Victoire to the boulevard a perfect torrent of venomous words poured from his
mouth like a waterfall in flood; but as the shocking language
which he used on the occasion was quite unfit to print, the
report is necessarily inadequate.

" 'My dear fellow, I will leave that vile, shameless opera-
dancer, a worn-out jade that has been set spinning like a top
to every operatic air; a foul hussy, an organ-grinder's monkey!
Oh, my dear boy, you have taken up with an actress; may the
notion of marrying your mistress never get a hold on you. It
is a torment omitted from the hell of Dante, you see. Look
here! I will beat her; I will give her a thrashing; I will give

it to her! Poison of my life, she sent me off like a running footman.'

"By this time we had reached the boulevard, and he had worked himself up to such a pitch of fury that the words stuck in his throat.

"'I will kick the stuffing out of her!'

"'And why?'

"'My dear fellow, you will never know the thousand-and-one fancies that slut takes into her head. When I want to stay at home, she, forsooth, must go out; when I want to go out, she wants me to stop at home; and she spouts out arguments and accusations and reasoning, and talks and talks till she drives you crazy. Right means any whim that they happen to take into their heads, and wrong means our notion. Overwhelm them with something that cuts their arguments to pieces—they hold their tongues and look at you as if you were a dead dog. My happiness indeed! I lead the life of a yard dog; I am a perfect slave. The little happiness that I have with her costs me dear. Confound it all. I will leave her everything and take myself off to a garret. Yes, a garret and liberty. I have not dared to have my own way once in these five years.'

"But, instead of going to his guests, Cursy strode up and down the boulevard between the Rue de Richelieu and the Rue du Mont Blanc, indulging in the most fearful imprecations; his unbounded language was most comical to hear. His paroxysm of fury in the street contrasted oddly with his peaceable demeanor in the house. Exercise assisted him to work off his nervous agitation and inward tempest. About two o'clock, on a sudden frantic impulse, he exclaimed—

"'These damned females never know what they want. I will wager my head now that if I go home and tell her that I have sent to ask my friends to dine with me at the Rocher de Cancale, she will not be satisfied though she made the arrangement herself. But she will have gone off somewhere or other.

3

I wonder whether there is something at the bottom of all this, an assignation with some goat? No. In the bottom of her heart she loves me!'"

The marquise could not help smiling.

"Ah, madame," said Nathan, looking keenly at her, "only women and prophets know how to turn faith to account. Du Bruel would have me go home with him," he continued, "and we went slowly back. It was three o'clock. Before he appeared, he heard a stir in the kitchen, saw preparations going forward, and glanced at me as he asked the cook the reason of this.

" 'Madame ordered dinner,' said the woman. 'Madame dressed and ordered a cab, and then she changed her mind and ordered it again for the theatre this evening.'

" 'Good,' exclaimed du Bruel, 'what did I tell you?'

"We entered the house stealthily. No one was there. We went from room to room until we reached a little boudoir and came upon Tullia in tears. She dried her eyes without affectation, and spoke to du Bruel.

" 'Send a note to the Rocher de Cancale,' she said, 'and ask your guests to dine here.'

"She was dressed as only women of the theatre can dress, in a simply made gown of some dainty material, neither too costly nor too common, graceful, and harmonious in outline and coloring; there was nothing conspicuous about her, nothing exaggerated—a word now dropping out of use, to be replaced by the word 'artistic,' used by fools as current coin. In short, Tullia looked like a gentlewoman. At thirty-seven she had reached the prime of a Frenchwoman's beauty. At this moment the celebrated oval of her face was divinely pale; she had laid her hat aside; I could see a faint down like the bloom of fruit softening the silken contours of a cheek itself so delicate. There was a pathetic charm about her face with its double cluster of fair hair; her brilliant gray eyes were veiled by a mist of tears; her nose, delicately carved as a Roman cameo, with its quivering nostrils; her little mouth, like a child's even now; her long, queenly throat, with the veins standing out upon it; her chin flushed for the moment by some secret despair; the pink tips of her ears, the hands that trembled under her gloves, everything about her told of violent feeling. The feverish twitching of her eyebrows betrayed her pain. She looked sublime.

"Her first words had crushed du Bruel. She looked at us both, with that penetrating, impenetrable cat-like glance which only actresses and great ladies can use. Then she held out her hand to her husband.

"'Poor dear, you had scarcely gone before I blamed myself a thousand times over. It seemed to me that I had been horribly ungrateful; I told myself that I had been unkind. Was I very unkind?' she asked, turning to me. 'Why not receive your friends? Is it not your house? Do you want to know the reason of it all? Well, I was afraid that I was not loved; and indeed I was half-way between repentance and the shame of going back. I read the newspapers, and saw that there was a first night at the Variétés, and I thought you had meant to give the dinner to a collaborator. Left to myself, I gave way, I dressed to hurry out after you—poor pet.'

"Du Bruel looked at me triumphantly, not a vestige of a recollection of his orations *contra Tullia* in his mind.

"'Well, dearest, I have not spoken to any one of them,' he said.

"'How well we understand each other!' quoth she.

"Even as she uttered those bewildering sweet words, I caught sight of something in her belt, the corner of a little note thrust sidewise into it; but I did not need that indication to tell me that Tullia's fantastic conduct was referable to occult causes. Woman, in my opinion, is the most logical of created beings, the child alone excepted. In both we behold a sublime phenomenon, the unvarying triumph of one dominant, all-excluding thought. The child's thought changes every moment; but while it possesses him, he acts upon it with such ardor that others give way before him, fascinated by the ingenuity, the persistence of a strong desire. Woman is less changeable, but to call her capricious is a stupid insult. Whenever she acts, she is always swayed by one dominant passion; and wonderful it is to see how she makes that passion the very centre of her world.

"Tullia was irresistible; she twisted du Bruel round her fingers, the sky grew blue again, the evening was glorious. And ingenious writer of plays as he is, he never so much as saw that his wife had buried a trouble out of sight.

"'Such is life, my dear fellow,' he said to me, 'ups and downs and contrasts.'

"'Especially life off the stage,' I put in.

"'That is just what I mean,' he continued. 'Why, but for these violent emotions, one would be bored to death! Ah! that woman has the gift of rousing me.'

"We went to the Variétés after dinner; but before we left the house I slipped into du Bruel's room, and on a shelf among a pile of waste papers found the copy of the 'Petites-Affiches,' in which, agreeably to the reformed law, notice of the purchase of the house was inserted. The words stared me in the face—'At the request of Jean François du Bruel and Claudine Chaffaroux, his wife——' *Here* was the explanation of the whole matter. I offered my arm to Claudine, and allowed the guests to descend the stairs in front of us. When we were alone—'If I were La Palférine,' I said, 'I would not break an appointment.'

"Gravely she laid her finger on her lips. She leant on my arm as we went downstairs, and looked at me with almost something like happiness in her eyes because I knew La Palférine. Can you see the first idea that occurred to her? She thought of making a spy of me, but I turned her off with the light jesting talk of Bohemia.

"A month later, after a first performance of one of du

Bruel's plays, we met in the vestibule of the theatre. It was raining; I went to call a hack. We had been delayed for a few minutes, so that there were no hacks in sight. Claudine scolded du Bruel soundly; and as we rolled through the streets (for she set me down at Florine's), she continued the quarrel with a series of most mortifying remarks.

" ' What is this about ? ' I inquired.

" ' Oh, my dear fellow, she blames me for allowing you to run out for a hack, and thereupon proceeds to wish for a carriage.'

" ' As a dancer,' said she, ' I have never been accustomed to use my feet except on the boards. If you have any spirit, you will turn out four more plays or so in a year; you will make up your mind that succeed they must, when you think of the end in view, and that your wife will not walk in the mud. It is a shame that I should have to ask for it. You ought to have guessed my continual discomfort during the five years since I married you.'

" 'I am quite willing,' returned du Bruel. ' But we shall ruin ourselves.'

" ' If you run into debt,' she said, ' my uncle's money will clear it off some day.'

" ' You are quite capable of leaving me the debts and taking the property.'

" ' Oh ! is that the way you take it ? ' retorted she. ' I have nothing more to say to you ; such a speech stops my mouth.'

" Whereupon du Bruel poured out his soul in excuses and protestations of love. Not a word did she say. He took her hands, she allowed him to take them ; they were like ice, like a dead woman's hands. Tullia, you can understand, was playing to admiration the part of corpse that women can play to show you that they refuse their consent to anything and everything ; that for you they are suppressing soul, spirit, and life, and regard themselves as beasts of burden. Nothing so provokes a man with a heart as this stratagem. Women can only use it with those who worship them.

"She turned to me. 'Do you suppose,' she said scornfully, 'that a count would have uttered such an insult even if the thought had entered his mind? For my misfortune I have lived with dukes, ambassadors, and great lords, and I know their ways. How intolerable it makes bourgeois life! After all, a playwright is not a Rastignac nor a Rhétoré——'

"Du Bruel looked ghastly at this. Two days afterward we met in the greenroom at the opera, and took a few turns together. The conversation fell on Tullia.

"'Do not take my ravings on the boulevard too seriously,' said he; 'I have a violent temper.'

"For two winters I was a tolerably frequent visitor at du Bruel's house, and I followed Claudine's tactics closely. She had a splendid carriage. Du Bruel entered public life; she made him abjure his Royalist opinions. He rallied himself; he took his place again in the administration; the National Guard was discreetly canvassed, du Bruel was elected major, and behaved so valorously in a street riot that he was decorated with the rosette of an officer of the Legion of Honor. He was appointed master of requests and head of a department. Uncle Chaffaroux died and left his niece forty thousand francs per annum, three-fourths of his fortune. Du Bruel became a deputy; but beforehand, to save the necessity of reëlection, he secured his nomination to the Council of State. He reprinted diverse archæological treatises, a couple of political pamphlets, and a statistical work, by way of pretext for his appointment to one of the obliging academies of the Institute. At this moment he is a commander of the Legion, and (after fishing in the troubled waters of political intrigue) has quite recently been made a peer of France and a count. As yet our friend does not venture to bear his honors; his wife merely puts 'La Comtesse du Bruel' on her cards. The sometime playwright has the order of Leopold, the order of Isabella, the cross of Saint-Vladimir, second-class, the order of Civil Merit of Bavaria, the papal order of the Golden Spur—all the lessers orders, in short, beside the Grand Cross.

"Three months ago Claudine drove to La Palférine's door in her splendid carriage with its armorial bearings. Du Bruel's grandfather was a farmer of taxes ennobled toward the end of Louis Quatorze's reign. Chérin composed his coat-of-arms for him, so the count's coronet looked not amiss above an escutcheon innocent of Imperial absurdities. In this way, in the short space of three years, Claudine had carried out the programme laid down for her by the charming, light-hearted La Palférine.

"One day, just a month ago, she climbed the miserable staircase to her lover's lodging; climbed in her glory, dressed like a real countess of the faubourg Saint-Germain, to our friend's garret. La Palférine, seeing her, said, 'You have made a peeress of yourself I know. But it is too late, Claudine; every one is talking just now about the Southern Cross, I should like to see it!'

"'I will get it for you.'

"La Palférine burst into a peal of Homeric laughter.

"'Most distinctly,' he returned, 'I do *not* wish to have a woman as ignorant as a carp for my mistress, a woman that springs like a flying-fish from the greenroom of the opera to Court, for I should like to see you at the Court of the Citizen-King.'

"She turned to me.

"'What is the Southern Cross?' she asked, in a sad, downcast voice.

"I was struck with admiration for this indomitable love, outdoing the most ingenious marvels of fairy tales in real life —a love that would spring over a precipice to find a roc's egg, or to gather the singing flower. I explained that the Southern Cross was a nebulous constellation even brighter

than the Milky Way, arranged in the form of a cross, and
that it could only be seen in southern latitudes.

" ' Very well, Charles, let us go,' said she.

"La Palférine, ferocious though he was, had tears in his
eyes; but what a look there was in Claudine's face, what a
note in her voice! I have seen nothing like the thing that
followed, not even in the supreme touch of a great actor's
art; nothing to compare with her movement when she saw
the hard eyes softened in tears; Claudine sank upon her knees
and kissed La Palférine's pitiless hand. He raised her with
his grand manner, his ' Rusticoli air,' as he calls it—' There,
child!' he said, ' I will do something for you; I will put you
—in my will.'

" 'Well,'' concluded Nathan, " I ask myself sometimes
whether du Bruel is really deceived. Truly, there is nothing
more comic, nothing stranger than the sight of a careless young
fellow ruling a married couple, his slightest whims received as
law, the weightiest decisions revoked at a word from him. That
dinner incident, as you can see, is repeated times without
number; it interferes with important matters. Still, but for
Claudine's caprices, du Bruel would be de Cursy still, one
vaudevilist among five hundred; whereas he is in the House
of Peers.''

"You will change the names, I hope!'' said Nathan, addressing Mme. de la Baudraye.

" I should think so! I have only set names to the masks
for you. My dear Nathan,'' she added in the poet's ear, " I
know another case in which the wife takes du Bruel's place.''

"And the catastrophe?'' queried Lousteau, returning just
at the end of Mme. de la Baudraye's story.

" I do not believe in catastrophes. One has to invent such
good ones to show that art is quite a match for chance; and
nobody reads a book twice, my friend, except for the details.''

" But there is a catastrophe,'' persisted Nathan.

"What is it?"

"The Marquise de Rochefide is infatuated with Charles Edward. My story excited her curiosity."

"Oh, unhappy woman!" cried Mme. de la Baudraye.

"Not so unhappy," said Nathan, "for Maxime de Trailles and La Palférine have brought about a rupture between the marquis and Madame Schontz,* and they mean to make it up between Arthur and Béatrix."

1839–1845.

* See "Beatrix."

A HISTORICAL MYSTERY.

TRANSLATED BY JNO. RUDD, B.A.

To Monsieur de Margone.

His host at the Château de Saché: in the grateful memory of

DE BALZAC.

PART I.

THE CHAGRIN OF THE POLICE.

THE autumn of the year 1803 was one of the most lovely in the first part of this century which we now call the "Empire." In October numerous rains had refreshed the earth and this had caused the trees to be still leafy and green in the month of November. The people were beginning to believe in a secret understanding between the skies and Bonaparte, who was at this time declared Consul for life ; it was this belief that was the cause of much of his prestige ; and, strangely enough, on the day the sun failed him, in 1812, his good-luck waned also.

About four o'clock in the evening of November 15th, the sun cast what seemed like red dust upon the tops of four rows of venerable elms, which graced a long baronial avenue ; it sparkled on the sand and grassy tufts of an immense *rond-point*, such as is frequently noticed in the country where land is valued cheaply enough to be sacrificed to ornament. The air was so pure, the atmosphere so mild, that a family was sitting out in the fresh air like it had been a mid-summer day.

A man habited in a hunting-jacket of green duck with green buttons, and breeches of the same stuff, and wearing shoes with thin soles and leggings to the knees, was cleaning a carbine with the minute care a skillful hunter gives to that work during his hours of leisure. This man had neither game nor game-bag; neither had he any accoutrements that showed his intending departure or a recent return from the chase; two women, seated near-by, were gazing at him as though overcome with a terror they would fain conceal but could not wholly disguise. Any one looking upon the scene, hidden in this shady glade, would without doubt have shuddered as the old mother-in-law and wife of the man now shuddered. It was plain to all that no huntsman takes such minute precaution with his weapons when he only intends the killing of small game, neither does he, in the department of l'Aube, use such a heavy rifled carbine.

"Shall you slay a roebuck, Michu?" said his beautiful young wife, endeavoring to assume a smiling air.

Before replying, Michu looked at his dog, who lay in the sun, its paws stretched out, its nose on its paws in the charming attitude of a trained hunting-dog; it had just raised its head and was snuffing the air, first along the avenue which lay stretched before them for a mile in length, and then up the cross-road where it entered the left side of the *rond-point*.

"No," replied Michu, "but a monster which I don't wish to miss—a lynx."

The dog, a magnificent spaniel, in a natural robe of white with brown spots, growled.

"Good!" said Michu, speaking to himself; "spies! The country is alive with them."

Madame Michu looked up to heaven appealingly. A beautiful blonde woman with blue eyes, formed like an antique statue, composed and pensive in manner, she seemed devoured by some secret and bitter grief. The appearance of her husband may explain to some extent the terror of the two women. Physiognomy's laws are definite, not only in their application to the character, but also to the fatalities of life. There is such a thing as a prophetic physiognomy. If it were possible, and such vital statistics would be of much value to society, to obtain an exact likeness of those who perish on the scaffold, the science of Lavater and that of Gall would indubitably prove that the heads of all these persons, even those who may be innocent, show strange signs.

Yes, fate sets its stamp on the faces of those who are doomed to a violent death of any kind ! Now, this seal, visible to the observing eye, was imprinted on the expressive face of the man with the carbine. Short and stout, quick and agile in his motions as a monkey, though of a calm temperament, Michu had a white face injected with blood, with features set close together like those of a Tartar, to which his red hair lent a sinister expression. His eyes bright and yellow, like those of a tiger, showed depths behind them in which the look of those examining them might lose itself without finding either motion or warmth. Fixed, luminous, and rigid, those eyes terrified whoever looked into them. The contrast between the immobility of his eyes and the activity of his body increased the chilly sensation experienced at the first sight of Michu.

This man's ever-prompt action was but the echo of a single thought ; the same as the life of animals is the outcome of instinct without reflection. Since 1793 he had trimmed his beard into the shape of a fan. Even had he not been, which he had during the Terror, president of a Jacobin club, this peculiarity in the shape of his face would alone have made him terrible to behold.

His Socratic face with its blunt nose was surmounted by a very fine forehead, but it projected so much that it overhung the features. The ears, well detached, possessed a kind of mobility like those in savage beasts, which are always on the *gui-vive*. The mouth, half-open, as is so often the custom in the country, displayed the teeth that were strong and white as almonds, but irregular. Gleaming red whiskers enshrined this face, which was white, but mottled in places. The hair cropped short in front and long at the sides and back of the head, brought into relief, by its savage redness, all the singular and fateful physiognomy. The thick, short neck seemed to tempt the axe. At this moment the sun, falling in long rays over the group, lighted up the three heads, at which the dog would glance from time to time.

This scene took place on a magnificent stage. The *rond-point* is at the extreme end of the Gondreville park, one of the wealthiest estates in France, and without contradiction the finest in the department of l'Aube: it has splendid avenues of elms, a castle built on Mansard's designs, a park of fifteen hundred acres inclosed in a stone wall, nine great farms, a forest, mills, and meadows. This almost royal property belonged prior to the Revolution to the Simeuse family. Ximeuse is a feudal estate situated in Lorraine. The name is pronounced Simeuse, and in time it came to be written as pronounced.

The great fortune of the Simeuses, gentlemen adherents of the House of Burgundy, goes back to the time when the Guises were embroiled with the Valois. Richelieu at first, then Louis XIV., remembered the devotion of the Simeuses to the factious house of Lorraine and rebuffed them. The then Marquis de Simeuse, an old Burgundian, old Guiser, old Leaguer, old frondeur* (he inherited the four great rancors of the noblesse against royalty), came to live at Cinq-Cygne.

This courtier, rejected at the Louvre, married the widow of the Comte de Cinq-Cygne, the younger branch of the celebrated family of Chargebœuf, one of the most illustrious names in Champagne, but now become as opulent and famous as the elder.

The marquis, one of the richest men of the day, instead of ruining himself at Court, built Gondreville and enlarged his domains by the purchase of other estates and joined them all

---

* One who declaims against the government of a country.

in one for the sole purpose of a beautiful hunting-ground. He also constructed the Hôtel Simeuse at Troyes, a short distance from the Hôtel Cinq-Cygne. These two old houses were for a long time the only stone-houses in Troyes. The marquis sold Simeuse to the Duke of Lorraine. His son sóon dissipated the savings of his father and also some part of his great fortune under the reign of Louis XV.; but he afterward entered the navy, became a vice-admiral, and redeemed his youthful follies by brilliant services. The Marquis de Simeuse, son of this mariner, perished with his wife on the scaffold at Troyes, leaving twin children, who emigrated, and were, at this time, still abroad following the fortunes of the House of Condé.

This *rond-point* was formerly the site of the meet of the Grand Marquis—the name given in the family to the Simeuse who erected Gondreville. Since 1789 Michu had inhabited the hunting-lodge at the park entrance, built in the time of Louis XIV., and called the pavilion of Cinq-Cygne.

The village of Cinq-Cygne is at the end of the forest of Nodesne (a corruption of Notre-Dame), which was reached through the avenue of four rows of elms where Courant suspected spies. After the death of the Grand Marquis this pavilion had been entirely neglected. The vice-admiral preferred the Court and the sea to Champagne, and his son gave this pavilion to Michu as a dilapidated dwelling.

This noble building is of brick, ornamented with vermiculated stone-work at the angles and on the door and window casings. On each side is a gateway of exquisite wrought iron, eaten by rust, connected by a railing. Beyond the grille extends a wide and deep moat now filled with vigorous trees, while on the parapets bristle iron arabesques, the innumerable sharp points of which are a warning to evil-doers.

The park-walls begin on each side of the circumference made by the *rond-point.* On one hand the noble semicircle is defined by slopes planted with elms; on the other, inside the park, a like half-circle is formed by groups of exotic trees. The pavilion thus occupies the centre of this round open space, which extends before it and behind in the shape of two horseshoes.

Michu had made the rooms of this ancient hall, on the lower floor,.into a stable, a kitchen, and a wood-shed. Of its old splendor but one trace remained, this was an antechamber paved with black and white slabs of marble ; this was entered on the park side through a door with small leaded panes, like those which might yet be seen at Versailles before Louis-Philippe turned that castle into a hospital for the glories of France.

The interior of the pavilion is divided by an old staircase of worm-eaten wood, full of character, the same as the first story, into five rooms at the base of the stairway ; above is an immense garret. This venerable edifice is covered by one of those vast roofs with four gables, a ridge-pole decorated with ornaments of lead, and a projecting window, circular in shape, on either side ; such as Mansard took just and keen delight in ; for, in France, the Italian attics and flat roofs constitute a folly against which our climate makes protest. In this garret Michu stored his fodder. All the park which surrounds the pavilion is English in style.

A hundred feet away a one-time lake, now merely a pond, well stocked with fish, makes its vicinity known by a thin mist which arises above the tree-tops, as well as by the croaking of a thousand frogs, toads, and other amphibious gossips who make discourse at sunset. The time-worn appearance of everything, the deep silence of the woods, the perspective of the avenue, the forest in the distance, a thousand details, the rusty iron work, the masses of stone velveted in moss, all formed the poetry of this building which still exists.

At the time of the commencement of this history, Michu was leaning against a mossy parapet on which he had laid his powder-horn, cap, handkerchief, a screw-driver, some rags ; in fact, all the necessary implements for his suspicious operations. His wife's chair was against the wall, beside the outer door of the pavilion; above it there still remained the richly sculptured arms of the Simeuse family, with their noble motto: CY MEURS.   The mother, dressed as a peasant, had moved her chair in front of Madame Michu, so that she might place her feet upon the rungs and keep them from the dampness.

"The little one, where is he?" asked Michu of his wife.

"He is roaming about the pond; he is crazy after frogs and insects," said the mother.

Michu whistled in a manner that made them tremble.   The speed with which his son ran to him was proof plain enough of the despotism wielded by the steward of Gondreville. Michu since 1789, but more especially since 1793, had been all but the master of the estates.   The terror he inspired in his wife, his mother-in-law, a little servant-boy named Gaucher, and a domestic named Marianne, was shared through a circumference of ten leagues.   Perhaps it may be as well without further delay to give the reason for this dread; further, it will fill out the moral portrait of Michu.

The old Marquis de Simeuse had transferred the greater portion of his property in 1790, but had been unable, owing to circumstances, to place the estates of Gondreville into safe hands.   Accused of corresponding with the Duke of Brunswick and the Prince of Cobourg, the Marquis de Simeuse and his wife were cast into prison and condemned to death by the Revolutionary tribunal of Troyes, the president of which was Marthe's father.   This noble domain of Gondreville was sold as national property.   It was remarked with horror that the head-keeper of the Gondreville estates was present at the execution of the marquis and marquise, in his capacity as president of the Jacobin club at Arcis, whither he went from Troyes to assist.   The orphan son of a simple peasant, Michu, who had been the recipient of countless benefactions of the marquise's, who had him brought up in her own household and made game-keeper, was, by exalted demagogues, hailed as a Brutus, but all the rest of the world ceased to recognize him after this act of base ingratitude.

The purchaser was a man from Arcis named Marion, a grandson of a former bailiff of the Simeuse family. This man, a lawyer before and after the Revolution, was in fear of his game-keeper; he made him steward at a salary of three thousand francs and an interest in the sales. Michu, who passed for having some ten thousand francs laid by, married the daughter of a tanner at Troyes, prompted by his patriotism, an apostle of the Revolution in that town, where he was the president of the Revolutionary tribunal.

This tanner, a man of conviction, who in character resembled Saint-Just, was later on mixed up in the Babeuf conspiracy and killed himself to escape condemnation. Marthe was the most beautiful girl in Troyes. In spite of her shrinking modesty she had been compelled by her formidable father to represent the Goddess of Liberty in some republican ceremony.

The purchaser only came three times to Gondreville in the course of seven years. His grandfather had been steward of the Simeuse family, so all Arcis took it for granted that the Citizen Marion was the secret representative of the Messeiurs de Simeuse.

As long as the Terror lasted the steward of Gondreville, a devoted patriot, son-in-law of the president of the Revolutionary tribunal of Troyes, flattered by Malin, who represented the department (de l'Aube), was the object of a certain kind of respect. But when the Mountain was overthrown and after his father-in-law had committed suicide, Michu became a scapegoat; everybody hastened to accuse him, as well as his father-in-law, of acts to which, so far as he was personally concerned, he was totally a stranger.

The steward resented the injustice of the populace; he repaid it with a hostile mien. He talked brave. In the meantime, after the 18th Brumaire, he maintained an unbroken silence, which is the philosophy of the strong. He no longer combated public opinion, he contented himself with his own affairs; this wise conduct caused him to be regarded as sly, for he possessed, it was said, in lands alone a fortune of about a hundred thousand francs.

In the first place, he spent nothing; next, this fortune was legitimately come by from inheriting his father-in-law's estate and the savings of six thousand francs a year, his salary, with its profits and perquisites. He had been steward for a dozen years, and every one estimated his savings, so that, when the Consulate was proclaimed, he bought a farm for fifty thousand francs the suspicions attaching to his former doings were diminished, and the people of Arcis gave credit to him in consideration of his great fortune. But unfortunately at the very time that public opinion was condoning his past a silly affair, envenomed by the country-side gossip, revived the general belief in the ferocity of his nature.

One evening, coming away from Troyes, in company with some peasants, among whom was the farmer at Cinq-Cygne, he dropped a paper on the highway; the farmer, who was walking behind him, stooped down and picked it up. Michu turned around, saw the paper in the hand of that man, he drew a pistol from his belt and threatened the farmer—who knew how to read—to blow out his brains if he opened the paper.

Michu's action was so sudden and violent, the tone of his voice so frightful, his eyes blazed so savagely, that all about him turned cold with fear. The farmer of Cinq-Cygne was already an enemy of Michu's.

Mademoiselle de Cinq-Cygne, a cousin of the Simeuses, had only this one farm left for her fortune and resided at her castle of Cinq-Cygne. She lived for her cousins, the twins, with whom she had played in childhood at Troyes and at Gondreville. Her only brother, Jules de Cinq-Cygne, who emigrated previous to the Simeuses, died before Mayence; but by a somewhat rare privilege, and will be told of later, the name of Cinq-Cygne was not to perish for lack of heirs male. This affair between Michu and the farmer made a great stir in the arrondissement, and further darkened the already mysterious veil which seemed to enfold Michu; but this was not the only circumstance that made him feared.

Some months after this scene, the Citizen Marion, with the Citizen Malin, came to Gondreville. Rumor had it that Marion was about to sell the estate to this man, who had profited by politics, having just been appointed by the First Consul on the council of State, as a recompense for his services on the 18th Brumaire. The politicians of the little town of Arcis now divined that Marion had been the agent of Citizen Malin instead of that of the Messrs. de Simeuse.

The all-powerful councilor of State was the most important personage in Arcis. He had obtained for one of his political friends the prefecture of Troyes, and he had been able to get an exemption from the conscription for the son of a farmer at Gondreville, named Beauvisage; in fact, he had rendered services to all. This business then aroused no opposition in the country where Malin reigned, and where he still reigns absolute.

It was the dawn of the Empire.

Those who in these days read the history of the French Revolution can form no idea of the immense intervals which were traveled by public thought between the various events which now appear so close together. The general desire for peace and tranquillity that each one felt after the violent commotions brought about a complete forgetfulness of important facts thereto anterior. History matured quickly under the march of new and ardent interests. No person, except Michu, searched into the past of this affair, which was accounted a simple matter.

Marion, who had, at the time it was offered for sale, bought

Gondreville for six hundred thousand in assignats, had sold
it for a million crowns; but the only amount disbursed by
Malin were the fees for registration.   Grévin, a clerical companion of Malin's, assisted in the transaction, and the councilor rewarded his help by naming him notary at Arcis.
When this new sale was known at the pavilion, brought
thither by a farmer, whose farm was situated between the
forest and the park on the left side of the grand avenue, by
name Gronage, Michu turned pale and went out; he lay in
wait for Marion, and at last met him alone in one of the walks
of the park.

"Monsieur, has he sold Gondreville?"

"Yes, Michu, yes.   You will have a powerful man for your
master.   The councilor of State is the friend of the First Consul; he is very intimate with all the ministers; he will protect
you."

"You, then, were saving the estate for him?"

"I don't say that," answered Marion.   "I knew not at
that time where to place my money, and, for the best security,
I invested it in national property; but it is not pleasant for
me to hold an estate that belonged to a family in which my
father——"

"Was a servant, a steward!" said Michu, violently.   "But
you shall not sell it; I want it, and I can pay you for it,
me——"

"You?"

"Yes, me; seriously, and in good gold, eight hundred
thousand francs——"

"Eight hundred thousand francs; where did you find
them?" said Marion.

"Don't you bother about that," replied Michu.

Then, softening his voice, he added, in a low tone:

"My father-in-law saved the lives of many people."

"You are too late, Michu; the affair is settled."

"You must defer it, monsieur!" cried the steward, seizing

his master's hand, which he squeezed as tight as a vise. " I am hated; I would be rich and powerful; I must have Gon-dreville ! Listen, I don't cling to life; you sell me that place or I'll blow your brains out !——"

" But give me time in which to be off with Malin; he's a hard man to accommodate."

" I will give you twenty-four hours. If you drop one word about this matter, I'll chop off your head as I would chop a turnip."

Marion and Malin left the castle during the night. Marion was frightened; he told the councilor of State of the meeting, and asked him to keep an eye on the steward. It was impossible for Marion to get off delivering the estate to the man who had been the genuine purchaser, and Michu was not the man to comprehend any such puerile reason. Moreover, the service rendered by Marion to Malin was to be, and ended, in fact, by being, the origin of the former's political fortune, as well as that of his brother.

In 1806 Malin had the advocate Marion appointed first president of an imperial court, and when tax-collectors were created he nominated his brother receiver-general of l'Aube. The councilor of State told Marion to stay in Paris; he gave warning to the minister of police, who issued orders that the steward should be closely watched. Nevertheless, he did not wish to push the man to extremities, so Malin kept him on as steward, under the rule of the notary of Arcis.

From that instant Michu became more absorbed and taciturn than ever, and gained the reputation of a man that would not stick at committing a crime. Malin, councilor of State, a function which the First Consul raised to that of a ministry, and one of the framers of the Code, played a great rôle in Paris, where he purchased one of the most splendid mansions in the faubourg Saint-Germain, after having married the only daughter of Sibulle, a wealthy contractor, who was sufficiently discredited, with whom he was associated in obtaining the

post of receiver-general at l'Aube for Marion. He never returned to Gondreville, but he left all matters concerning the
estate to the management of Grévin, who looked after his
interests. Finally, what had he to fear? he, the former representative of l'Aube, and a one-time president of a Jacobin
club at Arcis?

And still the same unfavorable opinion of Michu held by
the lower classes was shared equally by the bourgeoisie, and
Marion, Grévin, Malin, without any explanation or reason or
compromising themselves on the subject, showed that they
looked upon him as an excessively dangerous person. The
instructions which obliged his surveillance, given by the minister of police to watch the steward, did not in any wise
lessen this belief. To end all, the whole country wondered
that he kept his place, but thought that it was on account of
the terror he inspired. Who now but can comprehend the
deep melancholy impressed on Michu's wife?

In the first place, Marthe had been piously raised by her
mother. Both, good catholics, had suffered a great deal from
the opinions and conduct of the tanner. Marthe never
thought without blushing of that time when she had paraded
through the town of Troyes, garbed as a goddess. Her father
had constrained her to marry Michu, whose ill reputation was
then on the increase, and she experienced too much fear of him
to properly estimate him. Nevertheless she knew that he loved
her, and at the bottom of her heart lay a genuine affection for
this awe-inspiring man; she had never known him to do an
unjust act, never had he spoken brutally, to her at least; he
endeavored, in fact, to anticipate her desires.

This poor pariah, who imagined himself as being disagree-
able to his wife, for the most part passed his days outdoors.
Marthe and Michu, in distrust of each other, lived in what
to-day we call an "armed peace." Marthe, who never saw
any one, suffered keenly from the ostracism that for the past
seven years had surrounded her as the daughter of a head-

cutter-off (*coupe-tête*) and whose husband was a so-called traitor. More than once she had heard the farmer's people, on the neighboring farm, occupied by a man named Beauvisage, greatly attached to the Simeuse house, say as they passed by the pavilion :

" That's Judas' house."

The singular resemblance between the head of the steward and that of the thirteenth apostle, which his character seemed to complete, had earned him that so odious a nickname through all the country-side. It was this unhappiness of mind, added to vague but continual dread of the future, which had given Marthe her pensive and subdued air. Nothing causes such deep sadness as an unmerited degradation from which no way of escape seems open. A painter could have made a great picture of this family of pariahs in the bosom of the prettiest site in Champagne, where the scenery is generally cheerless.

" François ! " cried the steward to hurry up his son.

François Michu, a child of ten, played in the park of the forest and collected his little perquisites like its master ; he ate the fruits he hunted ; he at any rate had neither cares nor troubles ; he was the only being in the family that was really happy at being isolated in such a situation between the park and the forest and in the still greater solitude of general repulsion.

" Gather up those things there and put them away," said the father to the son, pointing to the parapet. " Look at me ! you love your father and your mother ? "

The child sprang to his father, as if to embrace him ; but Michu made a movement with the carbine which pushed him back.

" Good ! you have sometimes prattled about things that are done here," said he, fixing his eyes, dangerous as a wild-cat's, on him. " Now, bear this in mind ; if you tell the Gaucher or Gronage or Bellache people the least thing that occurs here, or even to Marianne who loves us, you will kill your father,

Don't do this, and then I will forgive you yesterday's indiscretion.''

The child began to cry.

"Don't cry; but if any one asks you questions, reply the same as peasants do: ' I don't know.' There are people about the country that I can't trust. There!'' Then turning to the two women: "You have heard?'' said he, "you two, now keep a dead-close mouth.''

"My friend,'' to her husband, "what are you going to do?''

Michu, who was carefully measuring a charge of powder into the barrel of his carbine, leaned it against the parapet and said to Marthe:

"No person knows of my having that gun ; stand in front of it!''

Courant sprang up on his feet and barked furiously.

"Beautifully intelligent creature,'' cried Michu; "I am confident there are spies around.''

They both felt a spy. Courant and Michu, who seemed each to possess the same soul, lived together like the Arab and his horse live in the desert. The keeper knew every modulation of Courant's voice, the same as the dog knew the thoughts of his master in his eyes, or felt it exhaling in the air from his body.

"What say you to that?'' cried Michu in a low voice, as he pointed out to his wife two inauspicious people who appeared in a by-path leading to the *rond-point*.

"What do they want in the country? They are Parisians!'' said the widow.

"Ah! there you are!'' cried Michu. "Hide my carbine,'' said he in the ear of his wife; "they are coming here.''

The two Parisians who now crossed the open space of the *rond-point* were certainly types for the painter. The one who seemed to be the subaltern, wore top-boots, turned down rather low, showing well-shaped calves encased in colored silk stockings of doubtful cleanliness. The breeches of ribbed cloth, of apricot color and with metal buttons, were much too large; they were baggy around the body, and the creases seemed to indicate the style of a clerk in an office. A pique vest, overdone with salient embroidery, open, and buttoned with only one button just above the stomach, gave to this personage a dissipated look, while his black hair, in cork-screw curls, hid his forehead and hung down his cheeks. Two steel watch-chains were festooned on his breeches. The shirt was adorned with a white and blue cameo-pin. The coat, cinnamon-colored, would have tickled a caricaturist by its long tails, and, when viewed from behind, bore such a resemblance to a cod that that name was applied to them. This codfish-tail fashion lasted for ten years, nearly the whole period of Napoleon's empire. The cravat, tied in a number of large pleats, permitted this individual to bury his visage in it up to his nose. His pimply skin, his high cheek-bones, his big, long nose of the color of brick-dust, his mouth lacking half its teeth (but greedy for all that and menacing beside), his ears ornamented with huge gold earrings, all these details, which might have appeared grotesque in any other man, were rendered terrible by two little eyes set in their place like those of pigs, expressing insatiable covetousness and insolent half-jolly cruelty. These two ferreting and perspicacious blue eyes, icy and glassy, might have served as the model of the redoubtable emblem, the famous EYE, of the police, invented during the Revolution. His hands were encased in black silk gloves, and he carried a switch. He must have been some official personage, for his bearing, his manner of taking snuff and jamming it into his nose, the bureaucratic importance of a subordinate man, but one who answers for his superiors and acquires a temporary sovereignty by enforcing their given orders.

The other, whose dress was in the same style, but elegant and well put on, showing care in the minutest details, wore Suwaroff boots which came high up on the legs over a pair of tight pants, and creaked as he walked ; over his coat he wore a spencer, a garment of the aristocracy adopted by the Clichiens and the young dandies, and which survived the Clichiens and the young dandies, both. In those times fashions often lasted longer than parties; a symptom of anarchy which 1830 has again presented to us. This accomplished dude (*muscadin*) seemed to be about thirty years old. His manners showed familiarity with good society; he wore valuable jewels. The collar of his shirt came to the tops of his ears. His conceited, impertinent air betrayed a kind of secret superiority; his pallid face was bloodless; his thin, flat nose had that sardonic expression seen in a death's head, and his green eyes were impenetrable: their glance was discreet, as also was the screwed-up mouth.

The first one seemed on the whole a good fellow compared with this young man who was slashing the air with a cane, the golden top of which glistened in the sun. The first one might have cut off a head himself, but the second was capable of entangling innocence, virtue, and beauty in the nets of calumny and intrigue and then of poisoning or drowning them.

The rubicund-faced man would have consoled his victim with a jest, the other was incapable of even a smile. The first was forty-five years of age, and undoubtedly loved both women and good-cheer. This kind of men have passions which binds them as slaves to their business. But the young man had neither passions nor vices. If he was a spy, he was of the diplomatic service, and worked at it for the art's sake. He conceived, the other executed ; he was the idea, the other was the figure.

" We are at Gondreville, eh, my good woman ?" said the young man.

" Here we don't say 'my good woman,'" replied Michu. " We yet remain simple enough to say 'citizen' and 'citizeness' down here."

"Ah!" said the young man with a natural air and not, seemingly, at all annoyed.

Players of écarti in society will remember often having had a sense of inward disaster when some person has sat down at the same table with them in the middle of the game, a player whose voice, manner, look, mode of shuffling the cards, all, give a presentiment of defeat. At the appearance of this young man Michu felt an inward prophetic prostration. He was appalled by a fatal presentiment; he had a confused foreboding of the scaffold; a voice whispered him that this dude would be his fate, though there was nothing in common between them. It was for this reason that his words were so rude; he wished to be vulgar.

"Do you not belong to the Councilor of State Malin?" demanded the second Parisian.

"I am my own master," replied Michu.

"Again, ladies," said the young man, putting on a most polite manner, "are we not at Gondreville? Monsieur Malin is there expecting us."

"There is the park," said Michu, pointing to the open gate.

"And why hide you that carbine, my pretty?" said the jovial companion of the young man who, in passing through the gate, had caught sight of the barrel.

"Always at your work, even in the country!" cried the young man, smiling.

They both turned about with a feeling of distrust which was at once detected by the steward, although their faces remained impassive; Marthe allowed them to examine the carbine, what time Courant accompanied with his barks; for she was convinced that Michu meditated some evil deed and was glad of the strangers' curiosity. Michu cast a glance at his wife which made her tremble; then he took up the gun and began to load it with a bullet; he took all the chances of this fatal bad-luck and the discovery of his weapon; he seemed to have no further care about his life, and his wife quite grasped that thought.

"You have wolves here, then?" said the young man to Michu.

"Always where there are sheep wolves are also. You are in Champagne, and there is a forest; but we have also wild boars, large and small vermin, both; we have a little of everything," said Michu, banteringly.

"I'll wager, Corentin," said the elder of the two men, after exchanging a look with the other one, "that this is my Michu——"

"We never kept pigs together," said the steward.

"No, but we have been presidents of Jacobins, citizen," replied the old cynic, "you at Arcis, I elsewhere. You have retained the civility of the Carmagnole;* but it is now out of fashion, old boy."

"The park seems to me to be pretty large, we might easily get lost; if you are truly the steward show us the way to the castle," said Corentin in a peremptory tone.

Michu whistled to his son and went on driving home the bullet. Corentin gazed at Marthe with indifference, while his companion seemed charmed by her; but the young man noted the signs of her inward distress which had escaped the old libertine, who had noted the carbine with dread. These two natures were disclosed by this trifling but important circumstance.

"I have an engagement on the other side of the forest," said the steward. "I cannot take you, but my son will show you the way to the castle. How came you to Gondreville? By the way of Cinq-Cygne?"

"Like yourself we had business in the forest," said Corentin, without apparent irony.

"François," cried Michu, "conduct these gentlemen to the castle unseen by others; they don't follow the beaten paths.

* A vulgar but highly popular song of early Revolutionary times.

Come here ! '' said he, as the two strangers turned their backs, talking to each other in a low voice.

Michu caught up his child, and embraced him almost with solemnity and with an expression which confirmed the apprehensions of his wife ; she was chilled to the back and looked with haggard eyes at her mother, for she could not weep.

" Go," said Michu to his son.

He watched the boy till he was lost to view.

Courant was vigorously barking on the side of the road nearest to the Gronage farm.

" Oh ! that's Violette," said he. " That makes the third time he has passed here to-day. What's in the wind ? Quiet, Courant ! ''

Soon afterward he heard the trot of a pony approaching.

Violette, mounted on one of those little nags, used so universally by the farmers in the vicinity of Paris, appeared under a round, broad-trimmed hat, which shaded his wood-colored, wrinkled face. His gray eyes, twinkling and mischievous, somewhat concealed the treachery of his nature. His skinny legs, draped in white linen gaiters which came up to the knees, seemed to rather hang than rest in the stirrups, they seemed to maintain their position by the weight of his hob-nailed shoes. Over his vest of blue cloth he wore a cloak of coarse wool in black and white stripes. His gray hair fell in curls at the back of his head. This dress, this gray horse with its little short legs, the style in which Violette rode him, stomach projecting and shoulders thrown back, the dirty, chapped hands which grasped the shabby bridle, all depicted him as the avaricious, ambitious peasant, who has the earth hunger and who will buy land at any price.

His mouth, with its blue lips parted as if some surgeon had pried them open with a scalpel, the innumerable wrinkles on his face and brow hindered the play of his features. Those hard, fixed lines expressive of menace, which belied the humility which country folk assume to conceal their schemes and feelings, as Orientals and savages envelop theirs in an imperturbable gravity. From a simple peasant day-laborer he had become, by a long course of evil-doing, the farmer of Gronage; after he had accomplished this purpose, which far exceeded his former hopes, he still continued his persistent evil practices. He wished ill to all, and he wished it vehemently. He was delighted at any opportunity to injure another.

Violette was openly envious; but, with all his maliciousness, he kept within the limits of the law—neither more nor less than like the parliamentary Opposition. He believed his prosperity was dependent on others' ruin, and that whoever it might be that was above him was an enemy against whom every weapon was good. This is a very common character among the peasantry.

His business at this time was to get an extension of the lease of his farm from Malin; it had only about six months longer to run. Jealous of the steward's fortune, he was for ever narrowly watching him; the country people upbraided him for his intimacy with Michu; but he, wishing to obtain a twelve years' lease, was really spying out for a chance to be of use to either the government or Senator Malin, who mistrusted Michu.

Violette, with the assistance of the game-keeper at Gondreville, by the steward, and by some others on the estate, kept the commissary of police at Arcis fully informed of all Michu's actions. This functionary had unsuccessfully endeavored to win over Marianne, Michu's servant, in the interest of the government; but Violette and his satellites learned everything from Gaucher, the boy helper upon whose fidelity Michu absolutely relied, but who betrayed him for cast-off clothes, vests, buckles, cotton socks, and candy. This boy had no comprehension of the importance of his chatter. Violette blackened Michu's every action, he gave them a criminal aspect by the most absurd suggestions; all this was, of course, unknown to the steward, who knew, however, of the treachery of the farmer, and was delighted to mystify him.

"You must have a lot of business at Bellache that you are here again?" said Michu.

"Again! Is that a word of reproach, Monsieur Michu? You are not going to whistle for sparrows on that clarionet. I didn't know you had a carbine like that."

"It grew in a field of mine where carbines grow," replied Michu. "Look, this is how I sow them."

The steward took aim at a viper thirty paces away and cut it in two.

"Is that to protect your master, that bandit's gun? It was perhaps him who gave it to you——"

"He came from Paris for the express purpose of bringing it me," replied Michu.

"All the country is talking of this journey of his. Some say he is in disgrace, and has retired from office; others that he is here to see things for himself. But say, why does he come, like the First Consul, without notice? Did you know of his coming?"

"I don't know him well enough to be wholly in his confidence."

"You have not yet seen him then?"

"I did not know of his arrival until I returned from my rounds through the forest," said Michu, reloading his carbine.

"He has sent for Monsieur Grévin from Arcis; they are up to some game or other."

"If you are going by the way of Cinq-Cygne," said the steward to Violette, "give me a lift, I'm going there."

Violette was too regardful of his crupper to have a man of Michu's weight thereon, he spurred up. Judas slung his gun over his shoulder and walked rapidly along the avenue.

"With whom can Michu be angry?" said Marthe to her mother.

"Ever since he heard of the arrival of Monsieur Malin, he

has been gloomy,'' replied she. "But it is getting damp, let us go inside.''

When the two women had settled themselves in the chimney corner, they heard Courant barking.

"There's my husband!" cried Marthe.

Directly Michu came in he mounted the stairs; his wife, worried, followed him to their bedchamber.

"See if you can see anybody about," said he to Marthe in a voice of emotion.

"Nobody," she answered. "Marianne is in the field with the cow, and Gaucher——"

"Where is Gaucher?" he demanded.

"I don't know."

"I distrust that little joker. Go up to the granary, look all through the garret, and search every little corner of the pavilion."

Marthe went out to obey this order. When she returned she found Michu on his knees praying.

"What hast thou done?" said she, frightened.

The steward took his wife by her waist, drew her toward him, kissed her forehead, and replied, in a voice shaken with emotion:

"If we never see each other again, remember, my poor wife, that I loved you well. Follow, point by point, the instructions that I have written in a letter interred at the foot of the larch in that copse; it is in a tin canister. Don't touch it until I am dead. And bear in mind that, whatever may happen to me, despite man's injustice, that my arm has but been the instrument of God's justice."

Marthe, who had turned pale by degrees, became as white as her own linen; she gazed on her husband with an eye fixed by fear. She tried to speak, and found her throat was too parched. Michu disappeared like a shadow; he had tied Courant to the foot of his bed, where the dog, like all other dogs, howled in despair.

Michu's choler against M. Marion had serious reasons, but now it was concentrated on another man, much more criminal in his eyes; on Malin, whose secrets were known to the steward, he being better able to appreciate the conduct of the State councilor. Michu's father-in-law had had, politically speaking, the confidence of Malin, named as representative of l'Aube to the Convention by Grévin.

It might not be useless, perhaps, to here relate the circumstances which brought the Simeuse and Cinq-Cygne houses into connection with Malin, and which weighed heavily on the fate of the twins and Mademoiselle de Cinq-Cygne, but still more heavily on Marthe and Michu.

At Troyes the Cinq-Cygne hôtel stands opposite the Hôtel Simeuse. When the populace, incited by minds that were as shrewd as they were cautious, had pillaged the Hôtel Simeuse, and there discovered the marquis and marquise, accused of corresponding with their enemies, and had delivered them to the National Guards, who carried them off to prison, the mob shouted: "To the Cinq-Cygne!" To them the Cinq-Cygnes were no more innocent of crime than were the Simeuses. The dignified and brave Marquis de Simeuse in trying to save his two sons, aged eighteen, whose courage was like to compromise them, had confided these two, some time before the outbreak, to their aunt, the Comtesse de Cinq-Cygne. Two domestics attached to the house of Simeuse accompanied them to her house.

The old man, who did not desire that his name should perish, had requested that what had occurred should be hidden from his sons, even if the very worst should happen. Laurence, then aged twelve years, was loved equally by both brothers, and she also equally loved them. Like most other twins, the Simeuse brothers were so alike that for a long time their mother clothed them in different colors in order to know them apart. The first-comer, the eldest, was called Paul-Marie, the other Marie-Paul. Laurence de Cinq-Cygne, to

5

whom was confided the secret of the situation, right well played her rôle of woman. She petted her cousins and coaxed them, looked after them to the very moment that the populace surrounded the Hôtel Cinq-Cygne.

This was the first inkling the brothers had of danger, and the two glanced at each other. Their resolution was instantly taken ; they armed their own servants and those of the Comtesse de Cinq-Cygne, barricaded the door, and stood guard at the windows, after having closed the shutters, with the five men-servants and the Abbé d'Hauteserre, a relative of the Cinq-Cygnes. These eight courageous champions poured a deadly fire into the crowd. Every shot killed or wounded an assailant. Laurence, instead of despairing, loaded the guns with an extraordinary coolness, passing the bullets and powder to those who needed them. The Comtesse de Cinq-Cygne was on her knees.

" What do you, my mother ? " said Laurence.

" I pray," she replied, " for them and for you ! "

Sublime words ; said also by the mother of the Prince of the Peace, in Spain, under similar circumstances.

In an instant eleven people lay dead upon the ground among a heap of wounded. This style soon cools or further excites a populace ; it either becomes enraged at such work or discontinues rioting. The more advanced soon recoiled ; but the entire mob, when they saw their own dead, cried out :

" At the assassins ! At the murderers ! "

The more prudent folk went in search of the people's representative. The twins, who now understood the disastrous events of the day, supposed that the member of the Convention desired the ruin of their family, and their suspicion was soon a certainty. Animated by revenge these two posted themselves under the *porte-cochère*, armed with their guns, to kill Malin as soon as he showed himself.

The countess had lost her head ; she saw her house in ashes and her daughter assassinated ; she blamed her relatives for their heroic defense and compelled them to desist, although it made a nine days' talk throughout France. Laurence slightly opened the door, when summoned to do so by Malin; and seeing her the representative thought to overawe such a mere child and entered the house.

"Tell me, monsieur," replied she to the first word he had uttered when he demanded the reason for this resistance, "how you who wish to give liberty to France, do not protect us from such people as these! They would demolish our hôtel, assassinate us, and you say we have no right to repulse force with force?"

Malin stood rooted to the ground. He found himself confronted by the armed brothers.

"You the son of a mason, employed by the Grand Marquis to build his castle!" exclaimed Marie-Paul, "you have allowed them to drag our father to prison—you have listened to calumnies!"

"He shall be liberated at once," said Malin, who thought he was lost when he saw each young man convulsively grasp his gun.

"You owe your life to that promise," Marie-Paul said solemnly. "But if it is not done this evening, we shall find you again!"

"As to that howling horde," said Laurence, "if you do not pack them off, the first blood shed will be yours. In the meantime, Monsieur Malin, get out!"

The conventionalist did quit, and harangued the multitude, speaking on the sacred rights of the domestic hearth, the *habeas corpus*, and the English "home." He informed them that the law and the people were sovereign, that the law was the people, that the people could only act through the law, and that power was vested in the law. This law of necessity made him eloquent, it dispersed the crowd. But he never forgot the contemptuous expression of the two brothers, nor the "get out!" of Mademoiselle de Cinq-Cygne.

So it was that when the question arose of the selling the estates of the Comte de Cinq-Cygne, Laurence's brother, the proceedings were rigorously carried out. The district agents left Laurence nothing but the castle, the gardens, and the farm called Cinq-Cygne. After being instructed by Malin, the appraisers informed Laurence that she had no legitimate rights, the nation had a legal possession of lands of emigrants who had taken up arms against the Republic. The evening of this furious tempest Laurence so entreated her two cousins to leave the country, as she feared some treachery on the part of the representative, or a trap being set into which they might fall, that they took horse that night and gained the outposts of the Prussian army. At the moment that they had arrived at the forest of Gondreville, the Cinq-Cygne mansion was surrounded; the representative in person came to arrest the heirs of the house of Simeuse.

He dared not seize upon the Comtesse de Cinq-Cygne, then in bed of a horrible nervous fever, or on Laurence, a child only twelve years of age. The servants, afraid of the severity of the Republic, had all disappeared. The next morning the news of the two brothers' resistance and their flight to Prussia was known to the neighborhood; a crowd of three thousand met before the Cinq-Cygne mansion and demolished it with remarkable celerity. Mme. de Cinq-Cygne, who was carried to the Hôtel Simeuse, died there from an increase of her fever.

Michu did not appear on the political scene until after these events, for the marquis and marquise remained in prison for nearly five months. During this time the representative of l'Aube was away on a mission. But when M. Marion sold Gondreville to Malin, when all the country had forgotten the effects of the late popular ebullition, Michu understood the whole business; Michu just thought he did; for Michu was like Fouché, one of those people who are so profound in their several aspects that, when they play a part, they are simply

incomprehensible when they act it, and never become understood until after the drama is over.

In the majority of circumstances of his life, Malin had never
failed to consult his faithful friend Grévin, the notary of
Arcis, whose judgment of men and things was, at a distance,
sharp, clear, and precise. This faculty is the wisdom of force
of habit of second-rate men. Now, in November, 1803, circumstances were very grave with the councilor of State, so
much so that a letter might have compromised the two friends.
Malin, who hoped for the nomination as senator, was afraid
of giving explanations in Paris ; he left his hôtel and came to
Gondreville, and gave the First Consul as his only reason for
this course his desire to be on the spot ; this gave him an air
of zeal in Bonaparte's eyes ; but really his reason, instead of
being the interests of the State, was only to look after his own
concerns.

Now, while Michu was watching in the park and looking
for a propitious chance for his revenge, after the manner of
the savages, the shrewd Malin, accustomed to turn all things
to his own benefit, was leading his friend toward a lawn in
his English garden, a lone place, and very favorable to a
secret conference. Standing there alone in the middle, and
speaking in a low voice, the two friends were too far away to
be overheard by any one who might be lurking around ; they
could, beside, be confident of having time enough in which to
change the conversation if some indiscreet one approached.

" Why not have remained in some chamber of the castle ? "
said Grévin.

" Did you not notice those two men, the envoys of the
prefect of police ? "

Though Fouché made himself in the affair of the conspiracy
of Pichegru, Georges, Moreau, and Polignac, and was the
soul of the Consular cabinet, he did not then direct the
minister of police, but was simply a councilor of State like
Malin.

"Those two men are Fouché's two arms. One, that young dude whose face resembles a bottle of lemon-soda, that has vinegar on his lips and verjuice in his eyes, put an end to the insurrection in the West, in the year VII., in five days. The other one is a follower of Lenoir; he is the only one that still retains the great traditions of the police. I had asked for an agent of little repute, supported by an official personage, and they sent me these two masters in the craft (*compères là*). Ah! Grévin, Fouché would, without doubt, like to get on to my game. This, then, is why I have left those gentlemen dining in the castle; they won't find Louis XVIII., nor the least sign of him."

"Ah, just so! but," said Grévin, the notary, "what is your game?"

"Eh! my friend, a double game is always dangerous, but, by being friendly with Fouché, makes it a triple one, and it may be that he perhaps has caught on to the fact that I am in the secrets of the house of Bourbon."

"You?"

"Me," replied Malin.

"You have forgotten Favras, eh?"

These words impressed the councilor.

"Since when?"

"Since the Consulate for life."

"But are there no proofs?"

"Not that!" said Malin, clicking his thumb-nail against one of his teeth.

In a few words Malin made an outline of the critical position in which Bonaparte would have England, menaced with destruction by the camp at Boulogne; he explained to Grévin the outlook of that scheme, unknown by France and Europe, but of which Pitt had a suspicion. Also the desperate position in which England would place Bonaparte. An imposing coalition, Prussia, Austria, and Russia, bought by English gold, were to raise an army of seven hundred thousand men.

While at the same time a formidable conspiracy was hatching over entire France, having amongst its members Mountain-men, Chouans, Royalists, and their princes.

"It was held by Louis XVIII. that so long as there were three Consols anarchy must prevail, and that he would take some favorable opportunity for avenging the 13th Vendémiaire and Fructidor 18th," said Malin; "but the Consulate for life has unmasked Bonaparte's designs; he will soon be Emperor. This former sub-lieutenant meditates the creation of a dynasty! This time his life is really in jeopardy; and the plot far better planned than that of the Rue Saint-Nicaise. Pichegru, Georges, Moreau, the Duc d'Enghien, Polignac, and Rivière, the two friends of the Comte d'Artois, are in it."

"What an amalgamation!" exclaimed Grévin.

"France is being silently invaded; there will be a general uprising; the last trick in the bag will be utilized. A hundred picked men, commanded by Georges, will attack the Consular guard and the Consul hand-to-hand."

"Eh, well, denounce them!"

"For the past two months the Consul, his minister of police, the prefect, and Fouché have held a few clues of this great plot; but they don't know the whole of it, and, at this present moment, they are liberating the parties concerned that they may discover more about it."

"As for the right," said the notary, "the Bourbons have a much better right to conceive, plan, and execute a plot against Bonaparte than Bonaparte had on Brumaire 18th against the Republic of which he was the offspring; he assassinated his mother, and planted himself in their house. I understand easily enough that when they see the lists of the *émigrés* closed, mortgages annulled, the Catholic faith restored, anti-revolutionary arrest increasing, that all the multiple radiations should begin perceiving that their return becomes more difficult, if not impossible. Bonaparte being the only remaining obstacle, they wish to be rid of him; nothing can be plainer.

Vanquished, conspirators become brigands; if successful, heroes; and your perplexity seems quite natural to me."

"It is being agitated," said Malin, "to have Bonaparte throw the head of the Duc d'Enghien at the Bourbons, like the Convention threw the head of Louis XVI. at the kings, so as to commit him to this government; otherwise we must upset the real idol of the French people and their future emperor and seat the true throne on the ruins. I am at the mercy of chance; some lucky pistol-shot, or some infernal machine *à la* the Rue Saint-Nicaise. Even I don't know all. It has been proposed that I call together the council of State at the critical moment and direct its action to the legal restoration of the Bourbons."

"Wait," answered the notary.

"And why?"

"The two Simeuses are conspirators; they are in this part of the country; I must either watch them, let them compromise themselves, and so be quit of them, or else I must needs protect them privately. I asked for subalterns and they have sent me their choicest lynxes, who came hither through Troyes and secured the gendarmes on their side."

"Gondreville is what you are after and this conspiracy favors you," said Grévin. "Neither Fouché nor Talleyrand nor those two partners of theirs have anything to do with it: play fair with them. Pshaw! those who beheaded Louis XVI. are in the government; France is filled with the acquirers of National lands, and you would talk of restoring those who would re-demand Gondreville? If they are not imbeciles, the Bourbons would pass a sponge over all that has been done. Warn Bonaparte!"

"A man of my rank cannot denounce," said Malin, quickly.

"Of your rank?" cried Grévin, smiling.

"They have offered me the seals."

"I understand your bewilderment, and it is for me to get

a clear view through this political darkness and find a way out for you. Now it is quite impossible to forefend results if the Bourbons return, when a General Bonaparte has eighty line of battle-ships and four hundred thousand men. The most difficult thing in a policy of expectation is to know when a tottering power may fall; but, my old boy, that of Bonaparte is in the ascendant. May it not be that Fouché is sounding the bottom of your mind and thinks then to rid himself of you?"

"No; I am sure of my ambassador. Beside, Fouché, in such an event, would never send me two such as these; he would know that I should be suspicious."

"I am afraid of them," said Grévin. "If Fouché does not distrust you, and is not trying you, why should he send them? Fouché doesn't play such a game without some reason."

"What decides me," exclaimed Malin, "is that I should never know an easy mind with these two Simeuses around; perhaps Fouché, who recognizes my situation, wants to be assured that they cannot escape him and thinks, through them, to reach the Condés."

"Eh! my old boy, it is not under Napoleon that the possessor of Gondreville will be ousted."

As he raised his eyes Malin perceived in the foliage of a great clump of lindens the muzzle of a gun.

"I was not mistaken; I heard the click of a gun-trigger," said he to Grévin, after he had hidden behind a big tree-trunk where the notary, uneasy at this abrupt movement, soon joined his friend.

"That is Michu," said Grévin; "I can see his red beard."

"We won't appear to be afraid," replied Malin, who slowly walked away, repeatedly saying: "What has that man against the owner of this estate? It certainly wasn't you that he covered. If he overheard us, I would recommend his asking for prayers for himself! We had better get in an open field. Who the devil would think of distrusting the air?"

"There's always something to learn," said the notary; "but he was pretty far away and we spoke low and cautiously!"

"I will speak a few words to Corentin," replied Malin.

Some few moments after Michu had returned to his house, with a pale face and contracted features.

"What is the matter with you?" said his wife, afraid.

"Nothing," replied Michu, seeing Violette, whose presence was like an icy chill.

Michu took a chair and quietly seated himself before the fire, and threw a letter therein after he had removed it from a tin tube like those served out to soldiers for the carrying of their papers. This action caused Marthe to draw a long breath like one relieved of a great burden, and greatly puzzled Violette. The steward-keeper laid his carbine on the mantel with an admirable *sang-froid.* Marianne and the old mother were spinning by the light of a lamp.

"Come, François," said the father, "it is our bedtime. Go to bed!"

He lifted his son roughly by the middle of his body and carried him off.

"Go down into the cellar," he whispered when they had gained the stairs, "empty two bottles of the Mâcon wine of one-third its contents, and fill them up with Cognac brandy which is on the shelf; then take a bottle of white wine and mix it with one-half of brandy. Do this carefully and place the three bottles on the empty cask which stands near the cellar entrance. When you hear the window opened by me, come out of the cellar, saddle my horse, mount it and wait for me at Poteau-des-Gueux. That little rogue dislikes going to bed," said the steward on his return; "he likes to do as his elders do, to see all, hear all, and know all. You spoil my folk, Father Violette."

"Good God!" cried Violette, "what has loosened your tongue? You never spoke as much before!"

" Do you believe that I let myself be spied upon without knowing it ? You are not on the right side, my father Violette. If, instead of serving those who dislike me, you were for me, I could do better by you than only renewing your lease——"

" How ? " said the avaricious peasant, with wide eyes.

" I'll sell my property in a good market."

" No market is a good one where one has to pay anything at all," said the sententious Violette.

" I am about leaving the district and I'll give you my farm at Mousseau, the buildings, the granaries and cattle for fifty thousand francs."

" Truly ? "

" How's that ? "

" Bless me ! I must think——"

" We'll reason it out. But I shall want an advance."

" I have nothing."

" A note."

" The same."

" Tell me who sent you here."

" I am returning from the place that I went to recently, and I only stopped to pass good-evening."

" Returning without your horse ? For what kind of an idiot do you take me ? You are lying, you shall not have my farm."

" Eh, well, it was Monsieur Grévin, he said to me : ' Violette, we want Michu, you fetch him. If he is not home, await him.' I could understand that I should have to stay here the whole evening."

" Those sharks from Paris, are they still at the castle ? "

" Ah ! I can't say as to that ; but there was company in the salon."

" You shall have my farm, let us settle the arrangement now. My wife, go and find some wine to wet the contract. Take the best wine of Roussillon, the wine of the ex-marquis.

We are not children. You will find two bottles on the empty cask at the entrance of the cellar, and a bottle of white wine, too.''

"That's it," said Violette, who never got drunk, "let's have a drink."

"You have fifty thousand francs under the floor of your room, under the bed, give them to me a fortnight after the contract passes Grévin.''

Violette gazed fixedly at Michu and turned livid.

"Ah! you came spying out a Jacobin who has had the honor of the presidency of the Arcis club, and you thought you could get the better of him, eh? I have eyes, I saw where the tiles had been freshly relaid, and I naturally concluded that you did not lift them up to sow wheat there. Drink.''

Violette, troubled, took a large glass of wine without paying any attention to its quality. Terror had placed, as it were, a hot iron in his stomach, the brandy scorched less than his avarice; he would have given much for his part to be returned home, so that he might change the place of his treasure. The three women smiled.

"Do you like it?" said Michu to Violette, refilling his glass.

"Yes, sure.''

"You would like to be home, old knave!''

After a half-hour's pleasant discussion as to the time when he might enter into possession, and on the thousand punctilios used by peasants in concluding a bargain, in the middle of assertions, of filling and emptying glasses, of filling promises with words, of denials, and so on: "Not true?" "Good truth!" "My good word!" "Like I said!" "Why should I cut off your head?" "What if this glass of wine that he gives me is poisoned, if it be not genuine! (*varté*).''

Violette tumbled over, his head on the table, not tipsy, but dead drunk. Michu at once opened the window.

" Where is that rascal, Gaucher ? " he asked his wife.

" He is in bed."

" You, Marianne," said the steward-keeper to his faithful servant, " stand in front of the door and watch him. You, my mother, stay down here," said he, " and keep an eye on this spy; watch him and do not open the door until you hear François' voice. It is a matter of life or death ! " he added in a solemn voice. " Now everybody beneath this roof must remember that I have never left the house this night ; every one of you must say that—even if your head was on the block. Come," said he to his wife ; " come, mother, put on your shoes, take your hood, and off we go ! No questions, I accompany you ! "

For three-quarters of an hour this man held them by gestures and looks of despotic authority, irresistible, powerful, flowing from the unknown source and possessing extraordinary properties like that of great generals on the field of battle who inflame an army, and great orators inspiring immense crowds, and, also, we must say it, great criminals in their audacious schemes. They seem then to exhale from the head and they issue from the tongue ; even the gesture can inject into another man the will of the one.

The three women knew very well that they were in the midst of some horrible crisis ; without being warned of their danger, they felt it in the rapid actions of that man, whose shining countenance, whose forehead spoke, whose brilliant eyes glittered like stars ; they saw in the sweat that bathes his hair to the ends, while more than once his words broke with impatience and rage. Marthe passively obeyed. Armed to the teeth, his gun on his shoulder, Michu dashed down the avenue, followed by his wife ; and very shortly they arrived at the cross-roads where François was hidden in the thicket.

" The boy has quick intelligence," said Michu, when he saw him.

This was his first word. His wife had run after him and was unable to speak a word.

"Return to the pavilion, hide yourself in a thick tree, watch the country and the park," said he to his son. "We have all gone to bed, no one is stirring, your old grandmother will not open to you until she hears you speak. Remember every word I have spoken to you. On that depends the life of your father and that of your mother. Justice must not catch on to us being out all night."

After whispering the above to his son, who instantly disappeared in the forest, like an eel in the mire, through the wood, Michu said to his wife:

"To horse! and pray that God be with us. Hold fast! the beast may play out under us."

As he thus spoke he gave the horse two kicks with his feet and then pressed him with his powerful knees, making the horse start off with the celerity of a hunter; the animal seemed to understand his master; and he had crossed the forest in a quarter of an hour. Michu without deviating from the shortest cut soon found himself where the roofs of Cinq-Cygne could plainly be seen by the light of the moon. He fastened his horse to a tree and mounted a little knoll, which overlooked the valley of Cinq-Cygne.

The castle at which Marthe and Michu looked at for a few moments had a charming effect in the landscape. Although of minor importance both in architecture and extent, yet it has certain meritorious points to the archæologist. This old edifice of the fifteenth century, situated on an eminence, surrounded by a deep moat, large and still filled with water, is constructed of boulders and cement; but the walls are of a thickness of seven feet. In its simplicity it recalls the rough and warlike life of feudal times.

This truly simple castle consists of two great, reddish towers connected by a long main building pierced by crosses of real stone, forming windows, and the roughly carved mul-

lions of which somewhat resemble vine-tendrils. The stairway is outside on the middle in a kind of pentagonal tower
with a little arched door. The interior of the first floor,
which, together with that of the second floor, was modern-
ized under Louis XIV., is surmounted by an immense roof
pierced by windows with carved triangular pediments. Before
the castle is found a vast lawn from which the trees had been
but recently cut away. On either side of the entrance bridge
are two small dwellings in which the gardeners live, separated
by a paltry iron-railing, without any style, and evidently
modern. To right and left of the lawn, divided in two parts
by a paved path, are the stables, cow-sheds, barns, woodhouse,
bakery, chicken-coops, and the out-offices, placed doubtless
in the remains of two wings resembling the real castle.
Formerly this castle must have been hard to force, fortified
as it was at the four angles, defended by an enormous tower
with an arched door, at the bottom of which was, in place of
the present iron-railing, a drawbridge. The two great towers
with their pepper-box roofs, which had not been razed, and
the belfry-tower in the middle gave a handsome appearance to
the village. The church, also ancient, was seen near by, and
its pointed steeple harmonized with the mass of the castle.
The moon distinctly showed the various roofs and towers in
grand relief by playing and sparkling upon them.

Michu looked on this lordly dwelling in a manner that
quite upset the ideas of his wife, for his face, now calmer,
bore an expression both hopeful and proud. His eyes embraced the horizon with a certain defiance; he stood in a
listening attitude; it was now nine o'clock; the moon threw
its light on the border of the forest and lighted up the little
knoll on which they stood. He regarded this position as too
dangerous and descended, as he was afraid of being seen.
Meanwhile, no suspicious sound troubled the peace of the
beautiful valley, surrounded on one side by the forest of
Nodesme. Marthe, trembling and exhausted, awaited the

denouement of their hurried ride.   To what was she committed? to a good deed or a crime?   At this moment Michu
whispered in his wife's ear:

"Go you to the Comtesse de Cinq-Cygne and ask for
speech with her; when you see her, ask to speak to her in
private.   If you are not afraid of listeners being about, then
say to her:

"'Mademoiselle, the life of your two cousins is in danger,
and he who can explain the why and ·wherefore awaits to
attend on you.'   If she is afraid, if she distrusts you, add:
'They are conspiring against the First Consul, and the conspiracy is discovered!'   But no names, they distrust us too
much."

Marthe raised her face toward her husband and said:

"Is it that you would help them?"

"Eh, what if I did?" said he, frowning and knitting his
brow, believing it a reproach.

"You don't understand me!" exclaimed Marthe, as she
pressed Michu's big hand; and, falling on her knees, she
kissed it and bathed it in her tears.

"Hurry, now! you shall weep afterward," said he, em-
bracing her vehemently.

When his wife had gone, his eyes filled with tears.   He had
been distrustful of Marthe because of her father's opinions;
he had hidden the secrets of his life from her; but the beautifully simple character of his wife had suddenly become apparent to him, the same as his grandeur had dazzled her.
Marthe passed from deep humiliation, caused by the degradation of a man whose name she bore, to the rapture given by
his nobleness; the change was without transition; it made her
tremble.   A prey to a troubled life, she told him afterward
that she had marched through blood from the pavilion to
Cinq-Cygne, and had in a moment been lifted up amongst
the angels.   He who knew that he had not been appreciated,
who mistook the melancholy and grieved air of his wife to her

lack of affection, and had for that reason left her to herself, and had turned all her son's tenderness toward himself, had in a moment understood the significance of his wife's tears; she had cursed the part that her beauty and her father's will had forced her to play. Her happiness was now playing about her like lightning in the midst of a storm. And it was lightning! Each now thought of the ten years of misunderstanding and blamed themselves alone.

Michu stood motionless, his elbow resting on his carbine and his chin upon his elbow, lost in a profound reverie. Such a moment makes one recognize all the sorrows of a painful past.

Agitated by a thousand similar thoughts of her husband, Marthe now was troubled at heart by the danger threatening the Simeuses, for she now understood all, even the faces of the two Parisians; but still she could not solve the mystery of the carbine. She darted onward like a doe and soon reached the path to the castle; she was surprised by the steps of a man behind her; she uttered a cry, and the large hand of her husband covered her mouth.

"From the top of the knoll there I saw the silver-lace embroideries of their hats! Go in by the breach in the moat between mademoiselle's tower and the stables; the dogs won't bark at you. Pass through the garden and call the countess by the window, order them to saddle her horse, and tell her to come out through the breach; I'll join you there after I have studied the Parisians' schemes and how to escape them."

This danger, which seemed rolling round them like an avalanche, gave wings to Marthe.

The Frank name Duineff was common to both the Cinq-Cygne and Chargebœuf families. Cinq-Cygne became the name of the younger branch of the Chargebœuves after the defense of the castle by five daughters of that house, made during the absence of their father, all remarkably fair, and of

6 S

whom no person had thoughts of such bravery.   One of the first Comtes de Champagne wished, by this pretty name, to perpetuate the memory of their deed as long as the family should exist.

After this singular feat of arms, the daughters of this race were proud, but they were not, perhaps, always nice.   The last of the family, Laurence, had, contrary to the Salic law, inherited the name, the coat-of-arms, and the manor.   The King of France had approved of the charter to the Comte de Champagne, in commemoration of this bravery, to that family and its successors in tail for ever.   Laurence was, therefore, Comtesse de Cinq-Cygne; her husband would have to take both her name and her blazon, which bore the device made glorious by the answer given by the elder of the five sisters, when summoned to surrender the castle: MOURIR EN CHANTANT! or, we die singing.

Worthy of those beautiful heroines, Laurence possessed a fair and lily-white complexion.   The lines of her blue veins could be traced through the delicate, close texture of her skin. Her most beautiful golden hair harmonized prettily with her deep, blue eyes.   All pertaining to her expressed the Darling. Within her fragile, though active, body, and, as it were, in defiance of its pearly whiteness, lived a soul like that of a man of noble character; but the person who was not a close observer would have guessed at it from the gentle countenance and rounded features, which, when seen in profile, bore some vague resemblance to that of a lamb.   This exceeding gentleness, although noble, had something in it of the stupidity of a lamb.

"I look like a dreamy sheep," she would remark, with a smile.

Laurence, who talked but little, seemed to be more dormant than dreamy.   Suddenly, at any serious moment, the Judith hidden in her was revealed, sublime; and, unfortunately, circumstances had afforded opportunity too often.

At thirteen, Laurence, after the events of which you know, was an orphan, living in a house opposite the place where of old had stood, in Troyes, a mansion which had been one of the most curious specimens in France of the architecture of the sixteenth century—the Hôtel Cinq-Cygne.

Monsieur d'Hauteserre, one of her relatives, now her guardian, carried the heiress off to the country to live at her castle of Cinq-Cygne. This brave provincial gentleman, alarmed at the death of his brother, the Abbé d'Hauteserre, who was shot down in the square at the moment when he attempted his escape, disguised as a peasant, was not in any position to defend his ward's interests: he had two sons in the army of the princes, and every day, at the least noise, he believed that the municipals of Arcis had come to arrest him.

Laurence, proud of having withstood a siege and possessed of the historic whiteness of her ancestors, despised the prudent cowardice of the old man who bent his neck to the tempest; she dreamed of distinguishing herself. So she audaciously hung in her poor salon at Cinq-Cygne the portrait of Charlotte Corday, crowning it with little sprigs of oak leaves. She corresponded by faithful agents with the twins in defiance of the law, which punished that crime with death. The agent also risked his life in returning the answers. Laurence lived, after the catastrophes at Troyes, only for the triumph of the royal cause. After she had soberly judged M. and Mme. d'Hauteserre and learned their honest nature, but without energy, she placed them outside her sphere. Laurence, however, had too much judgment and too sound a mind to be otherwise than indulgent to their natures; always good, amiable, and affectionate toward them, she nevertheless imparted none of her secrets to them. Nothing so shapes the soul as a constant dissimulation in one's family. At her majority, Laurence still retained the goodman d'Hauteserre, the same as in the past.

So that her favorite mare was well groomed, that her maid

Catherine was dressed in a manner to please her, and her little page, Gothard, was suitably habited, she cared for little beside. Her thoughts were elevated high above the occupations and interests which in different times might, without doubt, have pleased her. Her toilet was but a small matter to her; moreover, her cousins were not there to see her.

When she went riding, Laurence wore a bottle-green habit, with a dress of some common woolen goods, and a cape trimmed with Brandebourg braid when she went walking; in the house she was always seen in a wrapper of silk. Gothard, her little groom, a bright, courageous boy of fifteen, was her escort wherever she might go; she was nearly always out of doors, riding or hunting over the Gondreville farms, neither Michu nor the farmers raising the slightest objection. She was a splendid mount, managing her horse most admirably, and her good hunting was deemed a miracle; even during the Revolution the country-side never addressed her by any other name than " Mademoiselle."

Whoever may have read the grand romance " Rob Roy " will recollect that rare woman, for whose conception the imagination of Walter Scott went out of its usual frigidness, Diana Vernon. This recollection may serve to give a proper understanding of Laurence, if you add the exalted qualities of the Scottish huntress to those of Charlotte Corday, but suppressing the charming vivacity that made Diana so attractive.

The young countess had seen her mother die, the shooting down of the Abbé de Hauteserre, and the Marquis and Marquise de Simeuse executed. Her only brother had died of his wounds; her two cousins, now serving in Condé's army, liable to death at any moment; finally, the fortune of the Simeuse and Cinq-Cygne families had been wasted by the Republic without any profit to the State. Her gravity, degenerating into an appearance of stupor, can readily be conceived.

M. d'Hauteserre had made an upright, careful guardian. Cinq-Cygne became under his administration in some sort like a farm. The goodman, who resembled more a clever business man than a chevalier proprietor, had turned the park and garden to profit, and their two hundred acres of meadow and woodland he used for pasturage for horses and fuel to burn. Thanks to his most rigorous economy the countess, on attaining her majority, had recovered by his State investments a competent fortune. In 1798 the heiress possessed twenty thousand francs a year in the Funds and twelve thousand francs per annum from the Cinq-Cygne rentals; for a fact, she had some dividends still due on the government stock and had re-let the farms at a much increased rate.

M. and Mme. d'Hauteserre had retired into the country with three thousand livres of annuity invested in the Lafarge tontines. This remains of their fortune did not permit of their living elsewhere than at Cinq-Cygne; there Laurence's first action was to give them the use for life of the wing of the castle which was occupied by them. The d'Hauteserres, as avaricious for their ward as for themselves, and who every year laid by the whole of their thousand crowns in trust for their two sons, kept the heiress on wretched board. The total expenses of Cinq-Cygne did not exceed five thousand francs per annum. But Laurence would not condescend to such paltry details and found everything all right.

The guardian and his wife, insensibly dominated by the imperceptible influence of her strong character, felt even on the trivial side of things, finished by admiring her whom they had known as a child; a very rare sentiment. But Laurence had in her manner, her guttural voice, her imperious look, her I know not what style, that inexplicable power which impresses all, even when it is not apparent, for among the simple it seems to resemble the profound. Now to the vulgar the profound is incomprehensible. Perhaps it is for this reason that the admiration of the mob is so prone to be excited by what it cannot understand.   M. and Mme. d'Hauteserre, impressed by her habitual silence and the vagaries of the young countess, were constantly in the expectation of some great marvel from her.

In doing good with intelligence and never allowing herself to be deceived, Laurence was held in the greatest respect by the peasantry, although she was an aristocrat.   Her sex, her name, her misfortunes, the originality of her life, all contributed to give her a certain sense of authority over the inhabitants of the Cinq-Cygne valley.

She sometimes would be away for one or two days, accompanied by Gothard; but never on her return had M. or Mme. d'Hauteserre asked the reason for her absence.   Please remark, though, that there was nothing of the fantastical about her.   This virago was hidden or masked under a most feminine figure, and a more feeble appearance.   Her heart was excessively tender, but she carried her head with the resolute, virile air of the firm stoic.   Her clairvoyant eyes knew not the way to weep.   To see that white, delicate wrist would be to disbelieve in its strength, defying that of the most determined cavalier.   Her hand, so refined, so flexible, handled the pistol and gun with all the skill and energy of an experienced sportsman.   Out of doors she never wore any other head covering than a jockey cap like those worn by women horseback riders, peaked and with a green veil.   Her delicate countenance and fair throat were enveloped in and protected by a black cravat, and never suffered injury by her long rides in the fresh air.

Under the Directory and up to the beginning of the Consulate, Laurence had been able to elude the observation of the country folk; but, when the government became more settled and was regularly installed, the new authorities, the prefect of l'Aube, the friend of Malin, and Malin himself, essayed to destroy her influence.   Laurence thought only of the overthrow of Bonaparte, whose ambition and triumph had excited her rage, but a rage that was cool and calculating. The obscure and unknown enemy of this man encased in glory, she visited him, in the depths of this valley in the forest, with a terrible fixity; there were times when she thought of killing him somewhere in the vicinity of St. Cloud or the Malemaison.

The ideas for executing this design may be the explanation of some of her past actions; but initiated, during the rupture of the peace of Amiens, into the conspiracy of the men who intended to make the 18th Brumaire return on the First Consul, she had thenceforward subordinated her individual efforts and hatred to the very vast and most excellently devised plans laid to strike at Bonaparte from the exterior, by the tremendous coalition of Russia, Austria, and Prussia (whom the Emperor vanquished at Austerlitz); and from the interior by a coalition of men who were politically opposed to each other, but united by one common hatred, and whose chief design, like Laurence's, was the death of that man, and who did not shrink from the name—assassin.

This young girl, seemingly so frail, so strong to those who best knew her, was at this time the faithful guide and helper of the exiled gentlemen who had arrived from England to take a hand in this deadly game.

Fouché relied on the coöperation of the emigrants beyond the Rhine to lure the Duc d'Enghien into the plot. The presence of that prince in the territory of Baden, at a short distance from Strasbourg, gave some weight to this supposition. The great question as to whether that prince knew of the enterprise and was awaiting an opportune moment in which to cross the frontier into France is one of the many secrets about which, as about many others also, the house of Bourbon has ever maintained the deepest silence.

As that period of history becomes older the impartial historian finds that at least it was imprudent of the prince to place himself on the frontier at the very instant that a colossal conspiracy was about to break forth, the secret of which,

most undoubtedly, was known to every member of the royal
family.

The prudence displayed by Malin while talking with Grévin
in the open air, this young woman applied to her every act.
She received the emissaries, conferred with them at different
points in the forest of Nodesme, or beyond the valley of Cinq-
Cygne, between Sézanne and Brienne. She frequently rode
fifteen leagues on a stretch with Gothard, returning to Cinq-
Cygne without any trace of fatigue or preoccupation upon her
fresh young face.

She had some time before surprised in the eyes of a little
cow-boy, then nine years old, the naïve admiration which is
often shown by children for that which is out of the common
run ; she constituted him her page, taught him how to groom
a horse with all the care and attention of an Englishman.
She recognized a desire to do his best, a bright intelligence,
and a total absence of calculation; she tested his devotion,
but found only one mind, and that was of nobleness; he never
thought of recompense. She trained this so young soul, she
that was so young herself; she was good, but dignified with
him; she attached him to her by attaching herself to him;
and by herself polishing a nature that was half-wild, but saving its freshness and simplicity. When she had sufficiently
tested and proved his faithfulness—almost dog-like—which
she had nurtured, Gothard became her clever and ingenious
accomplice.

The little peasant, whom none could suspect, went from
Cinq-Cygne to Nancy, and frequently returned before many
were aware that he had even left the country. He knew how
to practice all the dodges of a spy. The excessive distrust
which had been imparted to him by his mistress had not
changed his natural self. Gothard, who had all the tricks of
a woman, the candor of a child, and the constant observation
of a conspirator, concealed all these admirable traits under the
dense ignorance and the torpidity of a country-johnny.

This little fellow had a weak, silly, and clumsy appearance; but once at his work he became supple as a fish, he escaped like an eel; he understood, like dogs do, the slightest glance; he nosed a thought. His good, fat face, red and round, his sleepy brown eyes, his hair cut like the peasants, his livery, and his slow growth gave him the appearance of a ten-year-old boy.

Under the protection of their cousin, who, from Strasbourg to Bar-sur-Aube, had journeyed under her eyes, Messrs. d'Hauteserres and the Simeuses, accompanied by a number of other *émigrés*, had just passed through Alsace and Lorraine, and were now in Champagne, at the same time that other no less bold conspirators were entering France by the cliffs of Normandy.

Dressed like workmen the d'Hauteserres and the Simeuses had marched from forest to forest, guided one after another by persons chosen three months back in each department, by Laurence, from amongst the least suspected of the Bourbon adherents living in each place. The emigrants slept by day and traveled by night. Each was accompanied by two devoted soldiers; one going in advance to ward off danger, the other in the rear to protect a retreat in case of accident. Thanks to these military precautions, this valuable detachment had reached without bad luck the forest of Nodesme, chosen as the rendezvous. Twenty-seven other gentlemen had entered France from Switzerland and crossed Burgundy, guided toward Paris with the like caution.

Monsieur de Rivière planned on getting together five hundred men, of which one hundred were to be young noblemen; the officers of this sacred battalion, Messrs. de Polignac and de Rivière, whose conduct as the chiefs was most remarkable, afterward maintained an absolute secrecy as to the names of their accomplices, who remained undiscovered. It might perhaps be said, now that the Restoration has somewhat cleared matters up, that Bonaparte never knew the extent of the

danger he than ran, any more than England understood the
peril she had escaped from the camp at Boulonge; and,
nevertheless, the police of France was never more intellec-
tually or ably managed.

At the time of the commencement of this history, a coward,
for cowards are always to be found among conspirators who
are not all equally strong men in a little number; a sworn
confederate, brought face to face with death, gave certain information, happily insufficient to cover the whole plot, but
precise enough to disclose the scheme. As Malin had informed Grévin, the police had loosed the prisoners, hoping
that by watching them they might discover the ramifications
of the plot. In the meantime the government had its hand
forced, as it were, by one Georges Cadoudal, a man of action
who took council only of himself, and who had hidden himself in Paris with twenty-five Chouans to attack the first
Consul.

Both hatred and love were combined in the thoughts of
Laurence. Destroy Bonaparte and reinstate the Bourbons,
then would not Gondreville be recovered and would it not
make the cousins' fortunes? These two sentiments, one the
exact opposite of the other, sufficed, especially at twenty-
three years of age, to excite all the faculties of her soul and
every force in her life. So for two months past she had appeared to the inhabitants of Cinq-Cynge more beautiful with
each new moment. Her cheeks had become rosy; hope encased her brow with pride; but when hearing the "Gazette"
read of an evening and the conservative doings of the First
Consul were given, she lowered her eyes to conceal her passionate longing for the coming fall of that enemy of the
Bourbons.

Those in the castle had not the slightest idea that on the
last night the young countess had met her cousins. The two
sons of M. and Mme. d'Hauteserre had passed that night in
Laurence's own room; under the same roof with their father

and mother ; as for Laurence, after knowing they were safely
in bed, and without exciting suspicion in them, between one
and two o'clock in the morning she had kept her tryst with
her two cousins in the forest, where she had hidden them in
the deserted hut of a wood-broker's man.

Sure of meeting them again on the following day she yet made
no manifestations of joy, she betrayed not the least emotion ;
she effaced all signs of pleasure at having again met them ;
she was, in fact, impassible. Her pretty Catherine, the
daughter of her nurse, and Gothard, both in the secret,
modeled their style and behavior after her own.

Catherine was nineteen. At that age a girl is a fanatic and
rather than speak a word would have her throat cut. As to
Gothard, only to inhale the perfume used by the countess on
her tresses and among her garments he would have withstood
the rack without speaking.

At the moment that Marthe, in an endeavor to avert the
imminent peril, was gliding like a shadow to the breach
indicated by Michu, a peaceful sight was presented in the
salon of the château de Cinq-Cygne. Its occupants had no
suspicion of the storm about to burst upon them ; their quiet
attitudes would have excited the compassion of the first person who should learn their situation.

The large fireplace, the mantel of which was finely decorated with a mirror and shepherdesses in panniers, was brilliant
with a great fire such as can only be seen in castles situated on
the borders of forests. At the corner of this fireplace, on a
great, square wooden lounge in gilt, draped in magnificent
green china silk, sat the young countess, or in some sort lay
stretched out in utter weariness. Returning alone at six
o'clock from the confines of Brie, after having played scout
to the troupe which she had safely guided to their last hiding-
place before the four gentlemen entered Paris, she had surprised M. and Mme. d'Hauteserre just finishing their dinner,

Pressed by hunger, she had seated herself at table without changing her muddy hunting-habit or boots. After dinner, instead of at once doing this, she had suddenly succumbed to fatigue, and her beautiful fair head, with its golden ringlets, had drooped back on the cushion of the lounge, her feet resting on a stool. The warmth of the fire had dried the mud upon her "amazon" and boots. Her gloves of doeskin, her little jockey-cap with its green veil, and her riding-whip lay on the table as she had thrown them down on entering. She looked at times on the old Boule clock which decked the mantel of the fireplace between the two candelabra, to see if, after a certain hour, her four conspirators were yet asleep; sometimes she looked at the boston game set out in front of the fireplace, and at which Monsieur and Madame d'Hauteserre, the curé of Cinq-Cygne and his sister were playing.

Even though these persons were not included in this scene, their portraits deserve the merit of a representation, for they were one of the aspects of aristocracy after their defeat in 1793. From this point of view, a painting of the salon at Cinq-Cygne savors of the raciness of history in dishabille.

The gentleman, then fifty-two years old, tall, spare, sanguine, and healthily robust, would have seemed the embodiment of vigor but for his great eyes of porcelain blue, the appearance of which denoted extreme simplicity. It existed in his face, which terminated in a long, pointed chin; between his nose and his mouth there seemed, judging by the rules of design, an unnatural distance, which gave him an air of submission quite in keeping with the other traits of his physiognomy.

His forehead, much wrinkled by life in the open air and by ever-recurring anxieties, was flat and without expression. His gray hair, flattened by his cap, which he wore the whole day through, looked much like a skull-cap on his head, and further defined its pear-shaped form. His face was somewhat redeemed by an aquiline nose; but the only indication of strength was to be found in his bushy eyebrows, which still

retained their blackness, and in the bright color of his skin;
but these signs were not altogether misleading, for this gentleman, although very gentle and simple, was Catholic and
monarchical in faith, and no consideration whatever could
ever make him change sides. This goodman would have
allowed himself to be arrested without any attempt at defense;
he would not fly from the municipality; he would, if need
were, ascend the scaffold with equanimity. His three thousand livres of income, his sole resource, had hindered his
emigrating. Therefore he obeyed the government *de facto*
without ceasing in his love for the royal family, and he prayed
for their reëstablishment; but he had refused to compromise
himself by partaking in any effort in favor of the Bourbons.
He belonged to that class of royalists who knew when they
were beaten and never forgot that fact nor their despoiling;
he therefore remained dumb, economical, rancorous; without
spirit, but equally incapable of any sacrifice; he waited patiently to greet triumphant royalty; the friend of religion and
the priests, but firmly resolved to silently bear every shock
of fate. Such an attitude does not support any opinion; it is
only sheer obstinacy.

Action is the essence of party.

Without pluck, but loyal; avaricious as a peasant, but yet
noble in manner; bold in his wishes, but discreet of word and
action; turning everything to profit; willing to be even made
mayor of Cinq-Cygne, Monsieur d'Hauteserre made an admirable representative of those honorable gentlemen on whose
brow God has written the word *mites:* those who burrowed in
their country houses and allowed the storms of the Revolution
to pass over their heads, who under the Restoration again rose
to the surface, wealthy with their hidden niggard savings,
proud of their discreet attachment, and who, after 1830, recovered their estates. His costume, expressive envelope of
his character, painted both the man and the times.

M. d'Hauteserre wore one of those nut-brown riding-coats

with small collars which the last Duke of Orleans had made
the fashion after his return from England, and which were,
during the Revolution, like a compromise between the hideous
popular garment and the elegant redingotes of the aristocracy.
His velvet vest in raised flowered stripes, after the fashion
which brings to mind Robespierre and St. Just, was sufficiently
open to allow a view of the upper part of a shirt-frill in fine
pleats. He still preserved his small-clothes, but they were of
coarse, blue cloth, with burnished steel buckles. His stockings
of black stuff showed his stag-legs, the feet of which were
shod in thick shoes, supported by gaiters of black cloth. He
kept up the old style of a lawn cravat in folds innumerable,
fastened at the throat by a gold brooch. The goodman had
not intended a point of political electicism in adopting this
costume, in the combined fashion of a peasant, a revolutionist,
and an aristocrat; he had very innocently bowed himself to
circumstances.

Madame d'Hauteserre, aged forty, and wasted by emotions,
had a faded face, which always seemed to be posing for a
portrait; and her lace cap, trimmed with bows of white satin,
singularly aided in giving her a solemn air. She still wore
powder, in spite of a white fichu, and a dress of puce silk with
tight sleeves and a full skirt, the last, sad costume of Queen
Marie-Antoinette. She had a pinched nose, a pointed chin,
her face triangular, her eyes worn with weeping; but she wore
a *trace* of rouge, which gave a brightness to their gray. She
took snuff, every time she did this using all the pretty precautions of the fashionable women of her early days; all the
details of this constituted a ceremony which was explainable
by one word—she had pretty hands.

For the two years past the former tutor of the two Simeuses,
a friend of the Abbé d'Hauteserre, named Goujet, abbé of
Minimes, had taken as a retreat the parish of Cinq-Cygne out
of friendship for the d'Hauteserres and the young countess.
His sister, Mademoiselle Goujet, rich by seven hundred francs

of income, added that amount to the meagre salary of her brother for their housekeeping.

Neither the church nor parsonage had been sold during the Revolution, on account of their small value. The Abbé Goujet lived quite near the castle, for the wall of the parsonage garden and that of the park were one and the same at places. Then twice a week the Abbé Goujet* and his sister dined at Cinq-Cygne, where, every evening they played a game with the d'Hauteserres. Laurence did not know one card from another.

The Abbé Goujet, an old man with white hair and a face as white as that of an old woman, dowered with a kindly smile and a gentle persuasive voice, relieved the insipidity of his plump face by a forehead bristling with intelligence, and a pair of very keen, fine eyes. Of medium height and well-made, he still wore the old French style of black coat, wearing silver buckles on his breeches and shoes, black silk stockings, a black vest on which lay his ecclesiastical bands, which gave him a distinguished air and detracted not at all from his dignity.

This abbé, who became bishop of Troyes after the Restoration, had, during the whole course of a long life, made the studies of young people his especial care; he fully understood the character of the young countess; he realized her true worth; he had shown her from the very first a respectful deference which had contributed much toward her independence at Cinq-Cygne, for it caused the austere old lady and the good gentleman to yield to her who should have yielded to them.

During six months the Abbé Goujet had watched Laurence with that particular intuition of priests, the most sagacious of men; and although he was not aware that this young girl of twenty-three meditated overturning Bonaparte at the moment that she was with feeble hands picking at the brandebourg

* The Philéas Goujet of "The Deputy for Arcis."

trimming of her riding habit, he well knew that she was certainly in the throes of some great project.

Mademoiselle Goujet was one of those old maids whose portrait is struck in two words, which will enable the least imaginative person to picture her—she was ungainly. She recognized her own ugliness and was the first to laugh at her hideousness, showing her long teeth, yellow as her complexion, and her bony hands. She was gay and hearty. She wore the famous corsage of a past age, a very ample skirt with pockets full of keys, a cap decked with ribbons, and a false front. She had become forty at an early age, but had, so she said, caught up with herself by keeping at that age for twenty years. She venerated the nobility, knowing how to guard her own dignity by giving to persons of birth the respect and homage that is their due.

This company was a godsend for Mme. d'Hauteserre, who, unlike her husband, had no rural occupations, nor had she, like Laurence, the tonic of hatred to help her bear the dullness of solitude. Beside this, there had been several ameliorations during the past six years. The Catholic religion had been permitted reëtablishment,* and this allowed the faithful to perform their religious duties, which play more of a part in country life than elsewhere.

M. and Mme. d'Hauteserre, reassured by the conservative acts of the First Consul, had corresponded with their sons, a great novelty, and now being no longer in dread of what might happen to them they looked for the erasure of their names and a speedy, happy return to France. The Treasury had liquidated the arrears of past-due dividends and was now prompt in paying its interest. The d'Hauteserres therefore now received a sum of eight thousand francs a year. The old man applauded himself upon his sagacity in premising this result when he had placed the whole of his savings, about twenty thousand francs, together with those of his ward,

---

* In 1802.

before the 18th Brumaire, in the Funds, which went up, as we all know, from twelve to eighteen francs.

For a long time Cinq-Cygne had been empty and denuded even of its furniture. From calculations the prudent guardian did not think proper to make any alterations for the better during the commotions of the Revolution, but, at the peace of Amiens, he made a trip to Troyes, where he gathered some relics of two pillaged mansions, which he bought from second-hand dealers. The salon was furnished for the first time. White brocade curtains with green flowers, stolen from the Hôtel de Simeuse, draped the six windows of the salon in which we just found the party assembled. The walls of this vast hall were entirely wooden and encased in beaded mouldings with gargoyles at the angles; painted in two tints of gray. The spaces over the four doors were filled in the style of Louis XV., with pictures in black and white. The goodman had found in Troyes certain console tables, a green damask couch, a crystal candelabra, a card table in marquetry, and these and much other stuff served to the restoration of the old traditions of Cinq-Cygne.

In 1792 all the furniture of the castle had been taken or destroyed, for the pillage of the mansions had been imitated in this valley. Each time the old man went to Troyes he returned with some relic of its ancient splendor. Sometimes a beautiful carpet intended for the floor of the salon, at another time it would be portions of a dinner service or maybe some old porcelains of either Dresden or Sèvres. During the past six months he had ventured to dig up the family plate of Cinq-Cygne, which the cook had buried in the "little house," an outhouse of the dwelling, belonging to him at the end of one of Troyes' long faubourgs.

That faithful servant, by name Durieu, with his wife, had followed the fortune of their young mistress. Durieu was the factotum of the household, his wife being the housekeeper. Durieu was assisted in his cooking by Catherine's sister, to whom he was teaching his art and who would become an excellent cook.   An old gardener, his wife, their son, paid by the day, and their daughter, who served as dairymaid, made up the household of the castle.

Madame Durieu, during the past six months, had been making in secret a livery in the Cinq-Cygne colors for Gothard and the gardener's son.   Although blamed for this imprudence by the gentleman, she had the pleasure of seeing dinner served on Sainte-Laurence's day, the young countess' fête day, in the same style as of old.   This slow and painful restoration of departed things caused much delight to M. and Mme. d'Hauteserre and the Durieus.   Laurence smiled at what she termed "such nonsense."   But the goodman d'Hauteserre looked equally well after the more solid matters: he repaired the buildings, renewed the walls, planted trees wherever there was chance for such to grow, and left not one inch of unproductive land.   In the whole of the Cinq-Cygne valley he was regarded as an oracle on agriculture.

He had contrived to recover one hundred acres of contested land, remaining unsold, as it was in some way confounded with that of the commune; this land he had turned into artificial meadows which pastured the beasts belonging to the castle, and he had surrounded it with poplar trees which were now, at the end of six years, making a vigorous growth.   He had the intention of purchasing some of the old estate, utilizing the buildings around the castle to form a second farm which he would manage himself.

Life at the castle during these two years had thus been a nearly happy one.   Monsieur d'Hauteserre rose with the sun and overlooked his laborers, for he kept them all the time employed whatever the weather; then home to breakfast, mounted his farm galloway as soon as his meal was finished and took the rounds of the place; at dinner he returned again and finished his day with a game at boston.

Every occupant of the château had his appointed task;

life was regulated as in a convent. Laurence alone disturbed the routine by her sudden journeys, her uncertain absences, and by what Madame d'Hauteserre termed her whims. In the meantime there existed two policies at Cinq-Cygne, and this caused dissension.

In the first place, Durieu and his wife were jealous of Gothard and Catherine, who shared the intimacy of their young mistress, the idol of the household, more than themselves.

Then the two d'Hauteserres, encouraged by Mademoiselle Goujet and the curé, wished their two sons, as well as the Simeuse twins, to take the oath and return to this quiet life instead of leading a wretched life among strangers. Laurence flouted at this odious compromise and represented royalty pure, militant, and implacable.

The four old folk, who had no wish to compromise their happy existence, anxious that their haven of refuge should not be risked after being saved from the furious torrent of the Revolution, endeavored to convert Laurence to their wise doctrines, presaging that in such case her influence would result in their sons' and the two Simeuses' speedy return to France. The superb disdain of their ward frightened these poor people, who were not mistaken when they apprehended that she contemplated what they termed *un coup de tête*, or some foolish scheme.

This jarring discord became apparent after the explosion of the infernal machine in the Rue Saint Nicaise, the first Royalist attempt against the conqueror of Marengo, after he had refused to treat with the house of Bourbon. The d'Hauteserres regarded it as lucky that Bonaparte had escaped that danger and believed that the Republicans were its instigators. Laurence wept with rage when she learned that the First Consul was saved. Her despair overcame her usual reticence, she accused God of having betrayed the sons of Saint-Louis.

"For me," she exclaimed, "I would have succeeded!

Have we not a right," said she to the Abbé Goujet, as she noticed the deep stupefication produced by her words on all the faces about her, "the right to attack usurpation by any and every possible means?"

"My child," answered the Abbé Goujet, "the church has been attacked and blamed by philosophers for having declared in former times that the same weapons might be turned against usurpers that usurpers had themselves employed so success-fully; but, nowadays, the church owes too much to Monsieur the First Consul not to be his protector against that maxim which, by-the-by, is of the jesuits."

"So, then, the church abandons us!" she gloomily replied.

From that day, what time the four old people talked of submission to the decrees of Providence, the young countess left the salon. For some time now the curé, shrewder than her late guardian, instead of discussing principles, drew atten-tion to the material advantages of the consular government, less to convert the countess than to try and detect in her eyes some expression which might lend him a clue to her projects.

Gothard's absences, the numerous long rides of Laurence, her evident preoccupation, which in these last days were apparent in her countenance, with many other little signs not possible to be hidden in the silence and tranquillity of the life at Cinq-Cygne, had aroused the unquiet feelings of the d'Hauteserres, the Abbé Goujet, and the Duricus; all their eyes showed the feeling of fear in these submissive royalists. But as all went on as peacefully as before, no event occurring, in the usual calm manner of the political atmosphere, all was peace; after a few days the life at this little castle resumed its usual course. Each had attributed the long rides of the countess to her passion for the chase.

One can easily imagine the deep silence which reigned in the park, in the courtyards, and outside, at nine o'clock, in the castle of Cinq-Cygne, where at this moment the persons we have described were harmoniously grouped, where reigned a deep peace, where abundance prevailed, where the good and wise gentleman still hoped to convert his ward to his system of obedience to the ruling powers by helping the continuity of these happy results.

These royalists continued to play their *boston*, which had spread ideas of independence through the whole of France under a frivolous form; for it was invented in honor of the insurgents in America, all its terms applying to that struggle which Louis XVI. encouraged. While making their "independences" or their "poverties," they kept their eyes on the countess, who, overcome by fatigue, had fallen asleep, with a singular smile of irony on her lips; her last thought had been what a picture of terror would be seen at that table by her speaking but two words, which should apprise the d'Hauteserres that their sons had slept only last night beneath their own roof.

What young girl of twenty-three would not have been, like Laurence was, proud to play the part of destiny? and who would not have felt, as she did, a feeling of compassion for those so far inferior to herself?

"She sleeps," said the abbé. "I have never seen her so fatigued."

"Durieu tells me that her mare is nearly foundered," remarked Mme. d'Hauteserre. "Her gun has not been fired, the breech is clean, therefore she has most certainly not been hunting."

"Ah! by the paper-sack!" replied the curé, "that's neither here nor there."

"Bah!" exclaimed Mlle. Goujet, "when I was twenty-three, and perceived that I was condemned to always be an old maid, I rushed around and fatigued myself in a dozen ways. I understand that the countess scours the country for hours without ever thinking of killing the game. Soon it will be a dozen years since she saw her cousins, whom she loves: eh, well, in her place, if I were as young and pretty, I'd make a bee-line for Germany ! Poor darling, perhaps she is studying up the frontier."

" You are joking, Mademoiselle Goujet," said the curé, smiling.

" But," she replied, " I see you all uneasy about the way-wardness of a young girl of three-and-twenty, and I explain it to you."

" Her cousins returned, and she, finding herself rich, will end by calming down," said goodman d'Hauteserre.

"God so will it," exclaimed the old lady, taking out a gold snuff-box, which during the life of the Consulate had again received the light of day.

" There is something new in the country," said goodman d'Hauteserre to the curé. " Malin has been at· Gondreville since yesterevening."

" Malin ? " cried Laurence, awakened by the name, al-though in a deep sleep.

" Yes," responded the curé, " but he departs again to-night ; everybody is conjecturing the motive of his speedy journey."

" That man," said Laurence, " is the evil genie of our two houses."

The young countess had been dreaming of her cousins and the d'Hauteserres ; she had seen them in danger. Her beau-tiful eyes grew fixed and glassy as her mind thus warned thought of the perils about to be incurred in Paris ; she rose suddenly and went to her chamber without a word. Her room was the state bedchamber, it came next to a dressing-room, and beyond it was an oratory, situated in a tower overlook-ing the forest. Soon after she had retired from the salon, the dogs barked, the bell at the wicket-gate rang, and Durieu, the picture of fear, rushed into the salon :

" Here is the mayor ! there is something the matter ! "

This mayor, a former huntsman of the house of Simeuse, came at times to the castle, where, out of policy, the d'Hau-

teserres showed him a deference to which he attached much
value. This man, named Goulard, had married a wealthy
market-woman of Troyes whose property was in the commune
of Cinq-Cygne; he had further augmented it by the purchase
of a fine abbey and its lands, which acquisition had absorbed
all his savings. The vast abbey of Val-des-Preux, situated
about a quarter of a league from the castle, he had turned
into a dwelling almost as splendid as Gondreville itself, and
where now he and his wife figured like rats in a cathedral.

"Goulard, thou hast been greedy!" said mademoiselle,
laughingly, to him, the first time she saw him at Cinq-Cygne.

Though much attached to the Revolution and coldly received by the countess, the mayor always felt himself bound
to respect the Simeuse and Cinq-Cygne families. Therefore
he shut his eyes to what went on at the castle. He called it
shutting his eyes by not seeing the portraits of Louis XVI.,
Marie Antoinette, and the royal family; of MONSIEUR, of
Comte d'Artois, of Cazalès, of Charlotte Corday, which ornamented the panels in the salon. Neither did he resent the
wishes freely expressed in his presence for the ruin of the
Republic, or the ridicule heaped upon the five directors and
all other governmental combinations then extant. The position of this man, who, like most parvenus, having now made
his fortune, reverted to his early faith in the ancient families
and would willingly have attached himself to them, was now
being used to their profit by the two persons whose profession
had been so quickly guessed by Michu, and who had recon-
noitred the neighborhood before going to Gondreville.

In Corentin, the phœnix of spies, the finer traditions of
the ancient police were revived; he had a secret mission.
Malin had caught on to the right idea of a double purpose
being intended by these star-artists of the tragio-farce. Perhaps, though, before seeing them in their rôles it might be as
well to show the head of which they were the arms.

Bonaparte, on becoming First Consul, found Fouché chief

of police.　The Revolution had with frankness and good
reason appointed a special minister of police.　But after his
return from Marengo, Bonaparte created the prefecture of
police ; there he placed Dubois in charge and called Fouché
to the council of State, naming as his successor in the ministry
the conventional Cochon, since known as Comte de Lap-
parent.

Fouché, who considered the ministry of police as one of
the most important in the government of great views and
fixed policy, saw disgrace or, the same thing, distrust in the
change.　After he came to know, by the affair of the infernal
machine and of the conspiracy in which we are concerned, the
great superiority of this brilliant statesman, Napoleon returned
him to the ministry of police.　Later again he became alarmed
at the talent displayed by Fouché during his, Napoleon's, absence in the Walcheren episode, the Emperor then gave this
ministry to the Duc de Rovigo and sent the Duke of Otranto
—Fouché—to be governor of the Illyrian provinces, a veritable
exile.

This singular genius, who struck Napoleon with a kind of
terror, did not reveal itself at first or all at once.　This obscure
member of the Convention, one of the most remarkable men
of those times, and the most ill-judged, was moulded, as it
were, by the storm.　Under the Directory he raised himself
to that height whence men of genius can view the future and
estimate the past ; and then, like certain mediocre actors who
have suddenly become divine through the light of some bright
perception, he gave proofs of his dexterity during the hasty
revolution of the 18th Brumaire.

This pale-faced man, trained to monastic dissimulations,
possessing the secrets of the *montagnards* to whom he belonged, and those of the royalists to whom he afterward ended
by belonging, had silently and slowly studied the men, the
events, the sides of the interests on the political stage ; he
penetrated Bonaparte's secrets ; he gave him useful counsel and

precious intelligence. He had been well satisfied to remain at the head of affairs and Fouché would have properly safeguarded the whole policy, but Napoleon's uncertainties and restless uneasiness caused him to be liberated from his post.

The ingratitude, or otherwise the distrust of the Emperor after the Walcheren affair, explains this man, who, unfortunately for himself, was not a *grand seigneur* and whose conduct of affairs was modeled on that of Prince Talleyrand. At that time neither his former colleagues nor his more recent ones had suspected the extent of his genius, purely ministerial, essentially administrative, just in its forecasts and of unbelievable sagacity. To-day certainly all impartial historians perceive that Napoleon's excessive self-love was one of the thousand causes of his fall, a punishment which cruelly expiated his wrong-doing.

That distrustful sovereign nourished a constant jealousy in his own rising power which influenced his least and every act and caused his secret hatred for men of talent, the Revolution's precious legacy, with whom he could have constructed himself a cabinet, which might have become the depository of his ideas. Talleyrand and Fouché were not the only ones who gave him umbrage.

Now, it is the misfortune of usurpers to have for enemies those from whom they have received the crown as well as those from whom it was wrenched. Napoleon's sovereignty was never entirely and convincingly felt by those who had been his superiors or his equals, nor yet by those who recognized the doctrine of Divine right ; none of these persons believed that their oath to him was in any way binding on them.

Malin, an inferior man, incapable of appreciating Fouché's mysterious genius or of distrusting his own shrewd perceptions, burned himself like a moth in a candle, by asking him in confidence to send certain of his agents to Gondreville, where, he said, he hoped to obtain some light on the conspiracy.

Fouché, without alarming his friend by asking any questions, asked himself why Malin went to Gondreville, and why he did not give, while in Paris and immediately, the information already possessed by him. The ex-oratorian, fed from infancy on trickery, and well aware of the double-dealing of a number of the members of the Convention, said to himself:

"By what means should Malin know more than ourselves, who know little or nothing?"

Fouché, therefore, concluded that either there was some latent complicity or one in embryo, and carefully kept his own counsel, not informing the First Consul. He liked the better to make an instrument of Malin than to ruin him. Fouché made a habit of reserving to himself a great portion of the secrets he detected; he thus obtained a power over those people superior to that wielded by Bonaparte. One of Napoleon's charges against his minister was this very duplicity. Fouché was well acquainted with the swindling scheme by which Malin had acquired the Gondreville estate, and which obliged him to keep the Messrs. Simeuse under constant surveillance.

The Simeuses were now serving in the army of the Condé; Mlle. de Cinq-Cygne was their cousin; it was possible that they were to be found in her neighborhood, and were sharers in the plot; this would imply that the house of Condé was concerned in the plot, as they were its ardent supporters. Messrs. de Talleyrand and Fouché intended casting light into this very dark corner of the conspiracy of 1803.

These considerations were grasped by Fouché at a glance, rapidly and with clearness. But there existed between Talleyrand, Malin, and himself strong ties that compelled him to use great circumspection, and made him anxious to fully understand the exact state of affairs inside Gondreville castle.

Corentin was unreservedly attached to Fouché, as Monsieur de la Besnardière was to Talleyrand, Gentz to M. de Melternich, Dundas to Pitt, Durac to Napoleon, Chavigny to Cardinal Richelieu. Corentin was not in the counsel of this minister, but his friend-tool, the secret Tristan to this Louis XI. of low degree; beside Fouché had naturally left him in the ministry of the police (when he had to quit it), thus preserving an eye to see and to be able to keep a finger in the pie.

This fellow, it was said, belonged to Fouché by some unavowed tie of relationship, for he furnished him profuse recompense after every successful service. Corentin had in Peyrade a tried friend, who was raised under the last lieutenant of police; nevertheless he kept a number of his secrets from him. Corentin had Fouché's order to explore the Château de Gondreville, to impress on his memory the plan, and to learn every secret hiding-place therein.

"Perhaps we may be compelled to return there," said the ex-minister, precisely as Napoleon told his lieutenant to thoroughly examine the field of Austerlitz on which he intended falling back.

Also Corentin was to study Malin's conduct, find out what influence he possessed in the country, and to observe the men that he employed. Fouché was convinced of the presence of the Simeuses in that vicinage. By carefully spying on those two officers who were friends of the Prince of Condé, Peyrade and Corentin could acquire some precious light on the ramifications of the conspiracy beyond the Rhine. In any case Corentin had the means, the orders, and the requisite agents to surround Cinq-Cygne and watch the country from the forest of Nodesme into Paris.

Fouché advised the utmost circumspection, and only would he allow a domiciliary visit to Cinq-Cygne in case of some positive information given by Malin. Finally, by way of instructions, he gave Corentin an account of the inexplicable personage, Michu, who for three years past had been under the surveillance of the police. Corentin's thoughts were those of his chief:

"Malin knows all about the conspiracy! But," he added to himself, "it may be that Fouché knows also, eh?"

Corentin started for Troyes before Malin; he had made arrangements with the commander of the gendarmes, who had picked out the most intelligent men and placed over them a capable captain as chief. Corentin chose the castle of Gondreville as the rendezvous, and directed the captain to deploy some of his men at night to take up positions in four different points in the valley of Cinq-Cygne and at a great enough distance from each other as not to give the alarm, each picket consisting of a dozen men.

These four pickets were to form a square and gradually close in around the castle of Cinq-Cygne. By the master of the castle being away during his consultation with Grévin, Malin had given Corentin the chance to accomplish a part of his mission in exploring the château. On his return from the park the councilor of State when he came in told Corentin most positively that the Simeuses and d'Hauteserres were in the country, so the two agents dispatched the captain and his men, who, luckily for the gentlemen, were crossing the forest by the avenue during the time that Michu was making drunk the spy, Violette.

The councilor of State had begun explaining to Peyrade and Corentin of his narrow escape. The two Parisians then told of the incident of the carbine they had seen the steward load, and Grévin had sent Violette to get information of what was going on in the pavilion. Corentin advised the notary, to make assurance doubly sure, to take Malin to his own house in the little town of Arcis, there to sleep in safety.

At the moment when Michu had rushed through the forest in the direction of Cinq-Cygne, Corentin and Peyrade were starting from Gondreville in a ramshackle wicker cabriolet drawn by a post-horse, driven by the corporal of Arcis, one of the shrewdest men in the legion, and whom the commandant at Troyes had recommended to them.

"The surest plan to seize them all is to warn them," said Peyrade to Corentin. "At the moment when they are thoroughly frightened and are trying to save their papers or to escape, we tumble upon them like thunder. The cordon of gendarmes have by now surrounded the château and they are caught as in a net. We shall capture every one of them."

"You should send the mayor to warn them," said the corporal. "He is on good terms with them and would not like to see them harmed; they won't distrust him."

Just as Goulard was getting ready for bed, Corentin, who had stopped and left the cabriolet in a little thicket, began speaking confidentially to him at his house. He told him that in a few moments an agent of the government would require him to enter the castle of Cinq-Cygne and arrest the Messieurs d'Hauteserre and Simeuse; in case they had already gone, he would have to learn if they had slept there the previous night, search for Mademoiselle de Cinq-Cygne's papers, and, most likely, arrest the people and master and mistress of the castle.

"Mademoiselle de Cinq-Cygne," said Corentin, "is without doubt protected by some great persons, for I have received private instructions to give her notice of this visit. I am to do all I can for her without compromising myself. Once on the spot I shall not be able to do so—I shall not be alone; run you to the castle and warn them."

This midnight visit of the mayor was the more bewildering to the players when they saw Goulard's agitation.

"Where can I find the countess?" he asked.

"She is in bed," said Mme. d'Hauteserre.

The mayor, incredulous, could hear sounds on the second floor.

"What's up with you, now, Goulard," said Mme. d'Hauteserre.

Goulard was dumb in his so great astonishment as he noticed the tranquil ease of their faces and their evident freedom from fear which may obtain in all ages. At the aspect of this calm and innocent party playing at boston and which he had interrupted, he could not conceive that there was anything in the suspicions of the police of Paris.

At this moment Laurence, kneeling in her oratory, was fervently praying for the success of the conspiracy. She prayed the God of the priest to help and succor the murderers of Bonaparte ! She implored the God of love to crush that fatal man ! The fanaticism of Harmodius, Judith, Jacques Clément, Ankarstroëm, of Charlotte Cordray, and Limcëlan animated this lovely spirit, virgin and pure.

Catherine was preparing the bed, Gothard was closing the blinds, when Marthe Michu arrived under the windows of Laurence, at which she flung a pebble, at once seen.

"Mademoiselle, there's some one there," said Gothard, seeing an unknown woman.

"Silence !" said Marthe in a low voice, "come down and speak to me."

Gothard was in the garden in less time than a bird would have taken to fly from a tree to the ground.

"In a moment the castle will be surrounded by gendarmes. You saddle," said she to Gothard, "mademoiselle's horse without making any noise, then take it down through the breach in the moat between the stables and this tower."

Marthe trembled at seeing Laurence two paces away, having followed Gothard.

"What is it ?" said Laurence simply and without being at all affected.

"The conspiracy against the First Consul is discovered," replied Marthe, in the ear of the young countess. "My husband, who seeks to save your two cousins, sends me to ask you to come and speak with him."

Laurence recoiled a pace or two and looked with suspicion at Marthe.

"Who are you ?" said she.

"Marthe Michu."

"I cannot understand what you wish with me," replied Mademoiselle de Cinq-Cygne, coldly.

"Be careful, you will kill them! Come, in the name of the Simeuses!" said Marthe, falling on her knees and stretching out her hands toward Laurence. "Have you not papers here; nothing that will compromise you? From the knoll in the forest my husband just saw the silver-laced hats and bright guns of the gendarmes."

Gothard had already climbed to the granary and perceived the silver-lace of the soldiers; in the deep silence of the country he heard the noise of their horses; he slipped down and into the stable, saddled his mistress' horse, whose feet, Catherine, at a word from Gothard, muffled in linen.

"Where shall I go?" said Laurence to Marthe, whose look and words bore an inimitable accent of sincerity.

"Through the breach," said she, and pulled Laurence along. "My noble husband is there. You shall learn the worth of a Judas!"

Catherine went into the salon, quickly picked up the hat, whip, gloves, and her mistress' veil and went. This sudden apparition and Catherine's actions were so striking a commentary on the mayor's words, that Mme. d'Hauteserre and the Abbé Goujet exchanged a look which contained this dreadful thought:

"Farewell to our happiness! Laurence conspires, she has destroyed her cousins and the two d'Hauteserres."

"What was it you said?" asked M. d'Hauteserre of Goulard.

"The castle is surrounded; you are about to have a domiciliary visit. If your sons are here, bid them and the de Simeuses to save themselves."

"My sons!" exclaimed Mme. d'Hauteserre, stupefied.

"We have seen no one," said M. d'Hauteserre.

"All right," said Goulard. "But I care too much for the family of Cinq-Cygne and that of the Simeuse to see them

come to harm.   Listen well to me; if you have any compromising papers——"

"Papers?" echoed the gentleman.

"Yes; if you have any, burn them," replied the mayor.
"I'll go and amuse the officers."

Goulard who wished to run with the royalist hounds and
hark with the republican hare left the chamber, and the dogs
commenced barking violently.

"You have not time; they are here," said the curé.   "But
who will warn the countess?   Where is she?"

"Catherine did not come for her whip, gloves, and hat to
convert them into relics," said Mlle. Goujet.

Goulard endeavored to detain the two officers for a few
minutes, as he announced the perfect ignorance of the occupants of Cinq-Cygne.

"You don't understand this sort of people," said Peyrade,
laughing, finger on nose, at Goulard.

The two men, so smoothly sinister, at once entered, followed by the corporal from Arcis and a gendarme.   Their
appearance froze the four peaceful boston players, who kept
their seats, alarmed by such a display of force.   The noise
made by a dozen gendarmes whose horses were champering
on the terrace outside reached them across the lawn.

"I miss Mademoiselle de Cinq-Cygne here," said Corentin,
insinuatingly.

"But she is doubtless asleep in her chamber," replied M.
d'Hauteserre.

"Come with me, ladies," said Corentin, turning into the
antechamber and the stairway, and whither Madame d'Hauteserre and Mademoiselle Goujet followed him.   "Trust in
me!" whispered Corentin to the old lady.   "I am yours.
It was I who sent the mayor to warn you.   Distrust you,
though, my colleague, confide only in me, I can save you
all!"

"But what means all this?" asked Mlle. Goujet.

"A matter of life or death. Can you understand that?" answered Corentin.

Mme. d'Hauteserre fainted. To the great astonishment of Mlle. Goujet and Corentin's greater disappointment, Laurence's room was found to be vacant. Sure that no one could possibly have escaped either from the park or the castle in the valley, for every egress was guarded, Corentin stationed a gendarme in each room, ordering the others to search the outbuildings and stables, and then descended to the salon, where, beside Durieu and his wife, the rest of the household had rushed in the wildest excitement.

Peyrade studied their features with his little blue eyes; he remained cold and calm in the midst of this uproar. When Corentin reappeared alone—for Mlle. Goujet stayed behind to care for Mme. d'Hauteserre—he heard the tramp of horses, and soon after the weeping of a child. The horses entered by the small wicket-gate. In the midst of the general hubbub a soldier was seen pushing forward Gothard, whose hands were tied, and Catherine, both of whom he turned over to the police agents.

"Here are some prisoners," said he. "That little scallawag tried to escape on horseback."

"Imbecile!" said Corentin in his ear, "why didn't you leave him alone? We should have learned something by following him."

Gothard chose to melt into tears and put on an idiotic appearance. Catherine took on an attitude of blissful innocence, which caused the old agent to become reflective. Lenoir's pupil, after comparing these two children each with the other, and after examining the simple air of the old gentleman, whom he thought awfully sly, the intelligent curé, who still fingered the cards, the stupefication of the people and Durieu, neared Corentin and whispered:

"They are not by any means flats (*gnioles*) with whom we have to deal!"

Corentin responded with a glance at the card-table; then he added:

"They were playing at boston! They were making the bed for the mistress of the house; she has escaped; it's a deuce of a surprise; we shall catch them, though."

There is always a reason and a purpose for a breach. Here, then, is the why and wherefore of the one found between the tower called the "Mademoiselle tower" and the stables, and why made.

After his installation at Cinq-Cygne, the goodman d'Hauteserre converted a long ravine, through which the waters of the forest fell into the moat, into a path between two large sections of the grounds belonging to the castle, by the unique plan of planting out about a hundred walnut-trees which he found in the nursery. In eleven years these walnut-trees had grown and branched out so as to nearly cover the road, already encased by embankments six feet in height, and which ran into a little wood of thirty acres extent, recently purchased.

When the castle had its full complement of occupants, each one preferred taking this way to the main road of the commune, which skirted the walls of the park and led to the farm, rather than to go around by the gate. By thus passing along this way, without their intending it, the breach had become gradually enlarged on both sides, with the less scruple that in this nineteenth century moats are absolutely useless and d'Hauteserre had often talked of turning it to a better use.

This constant treading down of the earth, gravel, and stones had ended by filling up the bottom of the moat. The water, not being able to pass this way, only covered the walk after very heavy rains. In the meantime, notwithstanding this fact, all the folk, and particularly the countess, used this path; but the banks were still so steep and abrupt that it was a work of difficulty to make a horse descend them, and still harder to get them to ascend by that means to the communal road.

But horses sometimes seem to enter into the knowledge of the dangers in their masters' thoughts.

While the young countess was hesitating about following Marthe, and had demanded further explanations, Michu, from the top of his hillock, had followed the lines described by the gendarmes and understood their scheme; he became desperate as the time went by at not seeing the countess. A picket of gendarmes followed the park wall, stationing themselves as sentinels, each man being near enough to communicate with those on either side of him by voice and looks, listening and watching at the least noise or the least movement. Michu, lying flat on his stomach, ear to earth, like an Indian, gauged the length of time remaining to him by the sound.

"I was too late!" said he to himself. "Violette shall pay for this! What a long time it took to make him drunk. What can be done?"

He heard the detachment passing through the gate after debouching from the forest, where, by a similar manœuvre, it would presently meet the picket coming by the communal road; he took another look around:

"Still five or six minutes!" said he.

At this moment he caught sight of the countess. Michu seized her with a firm hand and pushed her into the covered path.

"Keep on right before you! Lead her," said he to his wife, "to where my horse is; and bear in mind that gendarmes have ears."

Seeing Catherine, who carried the whip, gloves, and hat; above all, seeing the good sense of Gothard, this man, keen-witted in peril, resolved to play a game on the gendarmes, a trick which should be as successful as the one he had played on Violette. Gothard, like magic, had forced the mare to climb the moat bank.

"You have muffled the horse's feet—good! I kiss you!" said the steward-keeper, taking Gothard by his arm.

Michu let the mare follow her mistress after taking the gloves, hat, and whip. Speaking to Gothard:

"You are plucky and sensible, you will understand me," said he. "Force your horse on to the path up here, mount him, then start off and let the gendarmes chase after you across the farm-meadows; get the whole gang after you," pointing out the way he should follow. "As for you, my pretty," said he to Catherine, "there are other gendarmes on the road between Cinq-Cygne and Gondreville; you glide off in the opposite direction to that taken by Gothard, and draw them toward the forest and the castle. Do this in such manner that we be not interfered with in the covered path in the fosse."

Catherine and the grand little fellow who had in this affair given proof of such remarkable intelligence executed the manœuvre so as to make both lines of gendarmes think they had them safe. The moon's dim light did not permit of their pursuers distinguishing the form, clothing, sex, or the number of those they followed. The course was made on the virtue of the false maxim: "It is best to arrest all those who flee!" the folly of this high policy was energetically demonstrated by Corentin to the corporal. Michu, who had reckoned on this instinct of the gendarmes, was able to reach the forest soon after the countess, whom Marthe had guided to the indicated tryst.

"Ride to the pavilion now," said he to Marthe. "The forest is watched by the Parisians; it is dangerous to stay here. We all doubtless wish our liberty."

Michu unfastened his horse and begged the countess to follow him.

"I shall not take another step," said Laurence, "without you give me some earnest of the interest you take in me, for, after all's said—you are Michu——"

"Mademoiselle," replied he, in a gentle voice, "the part I am playing can be explained in a few words. I am, unknown to the Messrs. Simeuse, the guardian of their fortune. In this matter I received the last instructions of their deceased father, and their dear mother, my protectress. I have played the rôle of a virulent Jacobin to render the better service to my young masters; unfortunately I began my game too late and was unable to save my old master and mistress."

Here Michu's voice faltered.

"Since the flight of the young men I have regularly sent them sufficient sums for their station in life."

"Through the house of Breintmayer, of Strasbourg?" said she.

"Yes, mademoiselle, the correspondents of Monsieur Girel, of Troyes, a royalist who, like myself, for good reasons made himself a Jacobin. The paper which your farmer picked up one evening, as we were returning from Troyes, related to this business and would have proved compromising to us : my life is no longer mine, but theirs ; do you understand?

"I could not make myself the master of Gondreville. In my position I should have lost my head when they demanded whence I obtained my gold. I preferred to wait and buy it in later; but that scoundrel of a Marion was the creature of another scoundrel—Malin. Gondreville, all the same, shall yet be restored to its rightful owners.

"That's my lookout. It is but four hours ago since I had Malin covered by my gun ; ah! he nearly went to pot, that time! Lady, he once dead, the property put up for sale, and then you could have purchased it.

"In case of my death my wife would have brought you a letter which would have given you the means. But this brigand told his fellow-villain Grévin—another *canaille* like unto himself—that the Simeuses were conspiring against the First Consul, that they were in this part of the country, and that he intended giving them up and thus enjoy Gondreville in tranquillity. Now, I myself, saw the two police spies, I laid aside my carbine, and lost no time in coming here, thinking that

you would best know how to give warning to the young people.   That's all."

"You are worthy the dignity of nobility," said Laurence,
offering her hand to Michu, who wished to kneel and kiss
that hand.

Laurence saw his movement and prevented it, saying:

"Stand up, Michu!" with a tone of voice and look which
rendered in that one moment of bliss full repayment for all
his unhappiness during the past dozen years.

"You reward me as though I had done all that remains for
me to do," said he.   "But listen now, don't you hear the
huzzars of the guillotine?   Let us go elsewhere and talk."

Michu took the mare's bridle, and, walking beside the
countess, led her a little distance away; then he said:

"Only keep a firm seat and lookout that you don't get
struck by the branches of the trees on your head or whipped
about the face by them."

Then he guided her for half an hour at full gallop; they
turned and twisted, striking into wood-paths and crossing the
clearings, all the time bewildering their tracks, of which all
trace was lost, until they reached a point at which he stopped.

"I don't know where I am, I who know the forest as well
as you know it," said the countess, looking about her.

"We are right in the middle of it," he replied.   "We have
two gendarmes after us, but we are safe."

The picturesque spot to which the keeper had guided Laurence was destined to be so fatal to the principal personages
of this drama, and to Michu particularly, that it becomes the
duty of the historian to describe it.   The more as this place
became, as we shall afterward learn, one of the most famous
in the judicial annals of the Empire.

The forest of Nodesme belonged to the monastery of Notre-
Dame.   That monastery, seized, sacked, demolished, had entirely disappeared—monks and possessions.   The forest was
an object for cupidity, and was finally taken into the domain

of the Comtes de Champagne, who afterward mortgaged it
and allowed it to be sold.

In the course of six centuries nature had covered the ruins with
her rich and vigorous mantle of green, and had so thoroughly
effaced them that the existence of one of the most noble con-
vents was no longer indicated but by a slight eminence, shaded
by beautiful trees, and encircled by a dense, impenetrable
shrubbery with which, since 1794, Michu had taken much pains
by planting the thorny acacia in every breach between the
bushes. At the foot of this eminence a pond was found,
which showed the existence of an unknown stream and which
had, without doubt, determined the site of the monastery.

The owner of the title of the forest of Nodesme was the only
one to recognize the etymology of the word or name, dating
back for eight centuries, and to discover that in former times
a monastery had existed in the centre of the forest. When he
heard the first thunder-claps of the Revolution, the Marquis
de Simeuse had been compelled to test his title by a law-suit,
and had thus, by chance, as it were, learned the facts; he began with a secret thought, not difficult to imagine, to search
out the site of the late monastery. The keeper, who knew the
forest thoroughly, had naturally assisted his master in his
labors; it was his knowledge as a forester that led to the site
of the monastery. By observing the trend of the five principal roads in the forest, some of which had become effaced, he
saw that they all abutted on to the knoll or the pond, whether
coming from Troyes, from the Valley of Arcis, or from that
of Cinq-Cygne and Bar-sur-Aube.

The marquis desired to probe the mound, but he thought it
best that this should be done by strangers to the country.
Pressed by circumstances he abandoned his researches, leaving
a strong impression on Michu's mind that the eminence hid
either treasures or the foundations of the abbey. Michu continued this archæological enterprise; he probed the ground,
he sounded the holes, he plumbed the pond, and on its level,

between two trees at the foot of the mound, he found the ground rang hollow.

One fine night he came armed with a pickaxe and labored until he discovered a range of cellars which were descended by a flight of stone steps. The pond, only three feet in depth at most, was in the shape of a shovel, the handle of which seemed to issue from the mound; a spring evidently rose in the artificial rockery and became lost by filtration in the vast forest. This marshy spot, surrounded by aquatic trees, ashes, willows, and alders, was the terminus of all the old roads and leafy by-paths long since abandoned.

The water appeared to be stagnant, although it was constantly running, for it was covered with large-leafed plants, duck-weed, and cresses, giving it a beautifully green surface hardly to be distinguished from its margin of thick, delicate grasses. This lonely place was too far from any habitation for any except wild animals to come there to feed. Well convinced that nothing could exist near the marsh, and the mound being difficult of access, keepers and hunters never visited it; the timber in this corner of the forest had not been felled for many years; Michu was reserving it until its growth was fully matured.

At the end of the cellar he found a clean, dry, vaulted cell, built of hewn stone, something like a convent-dungeon, such as in old times was called an *in pace*. The salubrity of the cavern and the state of preservation of the stairs and vaults were explained by the presence of the fountain, which at some time had been inclosed by a wall of great thickness, built of brick and cement, like those of the Romans, to safely hold the water.

Michu covered the entrance to this retreat with huge stones; then, to render the secret still more his own, he never entered it except from the wooded eminence by clambering down the crags instead of going thither by the pond-side.

At the moment of the arrival of the two fugitives the moon

cast her beautiful silvery light on the century-old tree-tops on
the mound; it flickered on the magnificent leafy glades of
the several paths, there ending—sometimes showing clusters
of trees, at other times a single one.

On all sides the eyes were irresistibly drawn to their vanish-
ing perspectives, following the curves of some path, by some
black leaves of shadow, or the solemn stretch of the dark
forest avenues. The light filtered through the branches above
the crossings, found the tranquil water out of sight between
the cresses and the water-lilies, and here and there lit up a
diamond spark. The croaking frogs broke the deep silence
of this pretty nook of the forest, while the wild scents incited
thoughts of liberty in the soul.

"Are we truly safe?" said the countess to Michu.

"Yes, mademoiselle. But we have each of us something
to do. Do you tie up our horses to the trees on the top of
the little bank, and then muzzle them," said he, offering his
cravat; "both are intelligent creatures; they will understand
to keep quiet. When that is done drop right down by the
water-side by that crag; take care that your habit does not
get caught anywhere; you will find me below."

While the countess hid the horses and fastened them up,
after gagging them, Michu removed the stones and uncovered
the entrance to the cavern. The countess, who thought she
thoroughly knew the forest, was amazed to the last degree when
she saw the vaulted chamber. Michu replaced the stones as
dexterously as any mason. Scarcely had he done this than the
noise of the tramping of horses and the voices of the gendarmes broke the silence of the night; but he quietly kindled a
pine torch and led the countess to the *in pace*, where they
found a candle-end left behind by him when on one of his exploring expeditions in the cellar. The ponderous iron door,
although nearly an inch in thickness, had in parts become
eaten through with rust; but it had been put in good order by
the keeper and was secured with bolts. The countess, nearly

dead with fatigue, sank down upon a stone-bench, above which still hung an iron-ring fastened to the wall.

"We have a salon in which to chat," said Michu. "The gendarmes may prowl around as much as they wish; at the worst, they can only take our horses."

"Take our horses!" said Laurence; "that would be the death of my cousins and the Messieurs d'Hauteserres! Tell me what you know."

Michu recounted what he had overheard of the conversation between Malin and Grévin.

"They are now on their way to Paris; they are to enter it this morning," said the countess, when he had done.

"They are lost then!" exclaimed Michu. "Understand this, that men are surely stationed at the barriers to examine every one going in or out. Malin has the best of reasons to allow my masters to compromise themselves so as to have them killed out of his way."

"And I, who know nothing of the general plan of this affair!" cried Laurence. "How can I send warning to Georges, Rivière, and Moreau? Where are they? Let us only think of my cousins and the d'Hauteserres, we must overtake them, be the cost what it may."

"The telegraph* can beat the best horse," said Michu; "and of all the nobles implicated in this conspiracy your cousins are the most carefully tracked. If I can find them and hide them here; here we could keep them until the matter blows over; their poor father perhaps had a vision of this hiding-place: he had a presentiment that they would be here safe from danger!"

"My mare comes from the stables of the Comte d'Artois, she was sired by one of his finest English horses; but she has done about six and thirty leagues; she would drop dead on the road," said she.

"Mine is in good condition," said Michu; "and if you have

---

* The semaphore.

ridden thirty-six leagues, I should not have to ride more than eighteen."

"Twenty-three," said she. "They have been on the march since five o'clock! You would catch up with them beyond Lagny, at Coupvrai, whence they are to leave at day-break, disguised as sailors; it is their intention to enter Paris by boat. Here," she continued, giving him a half broken off her mother's wedding ring, "is the only token they will believe; I gave them the other half. The keeper of Coupvrai is the father of one of their soldiers; to-night he found them a hiding-place in a charcoal-burner's hut in the middle of the wood. They are eight in all, Messieurs d'Hauteserre and four other men are with my cousins."

"Mademoiselle, no one is looking after the soldiers; let us only think of the Messieurs de Simeuse, let the others look out for themselves. Is it not quite enough to warn the others by crying out: 'Lookout for your heads.'"

"Abandon the d'Hauteserres? never!" said she. "They must all perish or be saved together."

"They are only petty squires," objected Michu.

"They are only chevaliers," she replied, "that I know, but they are related to the Cinq-Cygnes and Simeuses. Bring back my cousins and the d'Hauteserres, and advise with them as to the best method of gaining this forest."

"The gendarmes are here! Do you hear them. They are in consultation."

"Well, this evening you have twice had good-luck. Go, bring them back, hide them in this cellar; they'll be safe against all search! I am good for nothing," cried she in a rage; "I should only be a beacon to give light to the enemy. The police would never imagine that my cousins were in the forest if they see me at my ease. The whole question resolves itself into this—how to find five good horses to bring them in six hours from Lagny into our forest, five horses to then be killed and concealed in some thicket."

"And the money?" replied Michu, who thought intently as he listened to the young countess.

"I gave a hundred louis to my cousins this evening."

"I'll answer for them;" cried Michu.   "Once hidden here you must not make any effort to see them; my wife or my little boy shall bring them food twice a week.   But, as I cannot tell what may happen to myself, remember, mademoiselle, in case of misfortune, that the main beam in the granary of my pavilion has had a hole bored in it with an auger.   In it you will find, after removing the little plug of wood, a chart of this part of the forest.   The trees marked with a red dot on the plan have a black mark on them near the ground.   Each of these trees is a sign-post.   Under the third old oak which stands to the left of each sign-post, two feet in front of the trunk and buried seven feet deep in the ground, you will find a tin canister, each of which contains one hundred thousand francs in gold.   These eleven trees—there are only eleven— are the whole fortune of the Simeuses, since Gondreville has been taken from them."

"It will take a hundred years for the nobility to recover from the blows dealt them!" said Mlle. de Cinq-Cygne, slowly.

"Is there a password?" asked Michu.

"'France' and 'Charles' for the soldiers; 'Laurence' and 'Louis' for Messieurs d'Hauteserre and Simeuse.   My God! to think that yesterday I saw them for the first time in eleven years, and now to know that to-day they are in danger of death—and such a death!   Michu," said she with an expression of melancholy, "be as prudent during the next fifteen hours as you have been grand and devoted during the past dozen years.   If disaster overtakes my cousins I shall die. No," she quickly added, "I would live until I had killed Bonaparte!"

"There will be two of us for that on the day that all is lost."

Laurence took the coarse hand of Michu's in her own and shook it in the warm English manner. Michu looked at his watch; it was midnight.

"We must get out at whatever cost," said he. "Death shall be the portion of the gendarme that stops my passage! And you, Mademoiselle the Countess, would it not be better for you to ride back to Cinq-Cygne at full gallop; there they are—fool them."

The hole once opened, Michu heard nothing; he flung himself flat upon the ground, his ear to the earth, and then suddenly arose.

"They are on the outskirts of the forest going toward Troyes," said he; "I'll fool them yet!"

He assisted the countess to climb out and then replaced the stones. When he had done this he heard her gentle voice calling him, she wished to see him mounted before herself. There were tears in the rough man's eyes as he exchanged a last look with his young mistress, but her eyes were tearless.

"Fool them! yes, he is right!" said she, when she no longer heard him. Then she started off at a full gallop for Cinq-Cygne.

Madame d'Hauteserre knowing that her sons were in danger of death and believing that the Revolution was not yet over, and still fearing the summary justice of the times, was aroused to a sense of her surroundings by the very violence of the anguish that had made her lose them. Led by a terrible curiosity she descended to the salon, which presented a picture worthy a painter of genré.

The abbé still occupied his seat at the card-table and was mechanically fingering the counters; the while he kept a corner of his eye fixed in a furtive manner on Corentin and Peyrade, who stood together by the fireside and spoke to each other in whispers. Several times Corentin's quick eye caught the not less keen glance of the curé; but, like two expert fencers who know themselves evenly matched, and who return to their guard after crossing weapons, each averted his eye at the instant they met.

The goodman d'Hauteserre, planted on his two legs like herons', stood beside the big, burly, overgrown, and avaricious Goulard, in an attitude of utter stupefication. Although dressed as a bourgeois the mayor had all the appearance of a servant. Both gazed with stupid eyes at the gendarmes between whom stood Gothard, who was still sobbing, and whose hands were so tightly bound that they were purple and swollen. Catherine did not change her air of artless simplicity, which was quite inscrutable.

The corporal, who, according to Corentin, had made such a silly blunder in arresting these little folk, did not seem able to make up his mind whether to stay or depart. He stood pensively in the middle of the salon, his hand resting on the hilt of his sabre and his eyes on the two Parisians. The bewildered Duricus and the rest of the domestics of the castle formed an admirable tableau of expressive anxiety. Only for the convulsive sobs of Gothard one could have heard a fly moving around.

When the mother, pale and terrified, opened the door and entered, almost carried by Mlle. Goujet, her eyes red with weeping, every glance was at once turned upon them. The two agents hoped, as the others feared, to see Laurence enter. The spontaneous movement of the whole household seemed caused by some mechanical arrangement which makes wooden figures wink their eyes and move themselves all alike.

Madame d'Hauteserre made three quick strides toward Corentin and in a broken but violent voice said :

"For pity's sake, monsieur, tell me of what my sons are accused ? And why do you think they are here?"

The curé seemed to say as he watched the old lady : "She'll make a mess of it ;" and lowered his eyes.

"My duty and the mission in which I am engaged forbid

my answering you," answered Corentin with an urbane mockery.

This refusal, which the detestable affability of the vulgar fop seemed to render more emphatic, petrified the old mother, who sank into an easy chair beside the Abbé Goujet ; she clasped her hands and breathed a prayer.

"Where did you arrest that cry-baby?" asked Corentin, addressing the corporal and pointing out Laurence's little page to him.

"On the road to the farm along the park walls; the rascal had nearly reached the Closeaux woods."

"And the girl?"

"She? Olivier pinched her."

"Where was she going?"

"Toward Gondreville."

"Going in different directions, eh?" said Corentin.

"Yes," replied the gendarme.

"Is he not the page and the girl the maid of the Citizeness Cinq-Cygne?" said Corentin to the mayor.

"Yes," replied Goulard.

After a few whispered words between Corentin and Peyrade, the latter left the room, accompanied by the corporal of the picket.

At this moment there entered the Arcis corporal, he went up to Corentin and, in a low voice, said :

"I know the premises well. I have searched everywhere, outbuildings and all ; there is nobody there, unless the young fellows are buried. We have sounded all the floors and walls with the butts of our guns."

Peyrade soon returned, he made a sign to Corentin to come outside ; he took him to the breach in the moat and pointed out the hidden way.

"We have discovered how the trick was done," said Peyrade.

"And I'll tell you how it was," said Corentin. ˻ The little

scallawag and the girl put those stupid gendarmes on the wrong scent, and thus the game had time to escape."

"We shall not learn the truth until daylight," answered Peyrade. "The road is damp; I have ordered two gendarmes to guard it at top and bottom. After daylight we can see who went thither by the footprints."

"There is the track of a horseshoe," said Corentin; "let us go to the stables."

"How many horses have you here?" asked Peyrade of MM. d'Hauteserre and Goulard, when they returned to the salon.

"Now, Monsieur the Mayor, you know, speak!" cried Corentin, noticing that that functionary hesitated to reply.

"Well, there's the countess' mare, Gothard's horse, and Monsieur d'Hauteserre's——"

"We only saw one in the stable," said Peyrade.

"Mademoiselle is out riding," said Durieu.

"Out riding, after nightfall, your ward?" asked the libidinous Peyrade of M. d'Hauteserre.

"Very frequently," replied the goodman, with exceeding simplicity. "Monsieur the Mayor can swear to that."

"All the world knows she has her fancies," put in Catherine. "She looked at the sky before she went to bed, and I think the glitter of the bayonets shining in the distance sort of puzzled her. She told me she wanted to find out if there was going to be another revolution."

"When did she go out?" asked Peyrade.

"When she saw the guns."

"And by which road?"

"I don't know."

"And the other horse?" said Corentin.

"The gen-en-en-darmes t-t-took it awa-a-ay from m-m-me!" said Gothard.

"And where, then, were you going?" said one of the gendarmes.

"I was fol-low-wing my mis-mis-mistress to the fa-a-arm."

The gendarme looked up toward Corentin, as if he expected an order; but this language was so natural and yet so artful, with such a depth of innocence yet so crafty, that the two Parisians eyed each other again as if repeating Peyrade's words: "These are not flats."

The gentleman appeared to be unable to understand a taunt. The mayor was stupid. The mother, imbecile by her maternal fears, questioned the agents of police with hopelessly silly interrogations. All the servants had been really surprised out of their sleep. With all these little facts before him and by judging the various characters, Corentin came to the only conclusion possible, that Mademoiselle de Cinq-Cygne was his only real adversary.

Although the police may be shrewd they have to labor under many disadvantages. Not only must they discover all that is known to a conspirator, but they must needs test each side of their suppositions before they strike the truth. Beside, the conspirator is always watching after his own safety, whereas the police are only on duty during certain hours. Without there were traitors, it would be the easiest thing for conspiracy to accomplish its desire. A conspirator possesses more ingenuity than the whole body of police with all its resources. Finding themselves stopped short morally, as they might be physically, by a door, which they expected to find open, being shut in their faces and the weight of several men at the back of it, Corentin and Peyrade knew that some one had "tumbled to their game," but whom this was they did not know.

"I assure you," whispered the Arcis corporal, "that if the two Messieurs de Simeuse and d'Hauteserre passed the night here, that they slept in the beds of either the father or the mother, or of Mademoiselle de Cinq-Cygne, the servants or the men; or they must have walked the park, for there is not the least trace of their presence."

"Who can have warned them?" said Corentin to Peyrade. "It could only have been the First Consul, Fouché, the min-

isters, the prefect of police, or Malin, for only these knew anything of it."

"We will leave some *moutons* (sheep—spies) in the vicinity," said Peyrade, in the ear of Corentin.

"And your sheep will be in Champagne,"* said the curé;
he could not forbear a smile as he heard the word "sheep"
and guessed what it meant.

"My God?" thought Corentin, who answered the smile of
the curé by one of his own. "There is one intelligent man
here; I'll see what I can get out of him. Here's for a trial."

"Gentlemen——" said the mayor, who wished to prove
his devotion to the First Consul by addressing his two agents.

"Say *citizens*, the Republic still exists," interrupted Corentin, regarding the curé with a look of raillery.

"Citizens," resumed the mayor, "just as I came into the
room, and before I had opened my mouth, Catherine rushed
in and seized the whip, gloves, and hat of her mistress."

A low murmur of horror issued from the depths of every
chest but that of Gothard. All eyes but those of the gendarmes and agents turned menacingly upon Goulard the in-
former—they seemed to flash fire at him.

"Good citizen mayor," said Peyrade, "all is now made
clear. Somebody warned the Citizeness Cinq-Cygne in time!"
and he looked with an eye of distrust at Corentin.

"Corporal, handcuff that youngster," said Corentin to the
gendarme, "and shut him up by himself. Also lock up the
girl," pointing to Catherine. "You will overlook the search
for any papers," he went on, addressing Peyrade; then
whispered him: "Turn out everything, spare nothing. Monsieur l'Abbé," said he to the curé, confidentially, "I have
an important communication to make to you."

He took him into the garden.

---

* An illusion to a French saying without an English equivalent, though
it might be rendered "will be shorn;" the herbage being scant in this
district.

"Listen, Monsieur l'Abbé: you have all the cleverness of a bishop, and (no one can overhear us) you know what I mean ; I no longer have any hope of saving these two families except by your assistance ; they are very foolishly letting themselves blunder to the brink of a precipice over which once fallen nothing can bring them back. Messrs. Simeuse and d'Hauteserre have been betrayed by one of the infamous spies introduced by governments into all conspiracies to worm out their objects, methods, and members. Do not confound me with the wretch who accompanies me; he belongs to the police; I am honorably attached to the honorable Consular Cabinet, with whom I have the last word.

"It is not desired that the Simeuses shall be ruined ; it is more than probable that Malin would like to see them shot, but the First Consul, if they are here and they have no evil intentions, wishes to draw them back from the edge of the precipice, for he likes good soldiers. The agent who is with me possesses all the power ; I, in appearance, am a nobody, but I know how things are. The agent is pledged to Malin, who has undoubtedly promised him his protection, an office, and, possibly, money, if he finds the two Simeuses and gives them up.

"The First Consul, who is a really great man, never favors selfish schemes. I don't care to know if the two young men are here," continued Corentin, in reply to a gesture of the curé's ; "but I wish to warn you that only one way of safety is open. You know the law of 6th Floreal, of the year X.; it grants amnesty to those *émigrés* who were still in a foreign country, on condition that they return before 1st Vendemiaire, of XI., that is to say, in the September of last year. But the Messieurs Simeuse having, the same as the Messieurs d'Hauteserre, held commands in the army of Condé, have brought themselves into the category of exceptions made by that law. Therefore their presence in France is criminal; under the circumstances, it will be taken as a proof that they are among the irreconcilable enemies of the government; they will appear as the accomplices of a horrible conspiracy.

"The First Consul saw the mistake in this exception, which has raised up enemies; he wishes the Messieurs Simeuse to know that no steps will be taken against them, if they address a petition to him saying that they have reëntered France with a full intention of submitting to the laws and promising to take the oath to the Constitution. You of course understand that the document ought to be in my hands before they are arrested, and bearing a date some days earlier; I then could be the bearer of it——

"I don't ask where these young men are," said he, noticing that the curé had made a new gesture of denial. "Unfortunately, we are sure to find them; the forest is patroled, the entrances to Paris are watched, as are also the frontiers.

"Listen carefully to what I am about to say! If these gentlemen are between the forest and Paris, they will be taken; if they are in Paris, they will be found; if they turn back, the unfortunates will be arrested. The First Consul is amiably disposed to the *ci-devants*, and cannot endure the Republicans; and this is but natural—if he wants a throne he must needs murder liberty. Let the secret be our own. Here is what I will do: I will wait until to-morrow; I will be blind; but beware of the agent; this hated Provençal is the devil's own lackey; he has Fouché's directions, the same as I have those of the First Consul."

"If the Messieurs Simeuse are here," said the curé, "I would give ten pints of my blood and an arm to save them; but if Mademoiselle de Cinq-Cygne is in their confidence not the least word has escaped her, this I swear on my eternal salvation; neither has she done me the honor of asking my advice. I am more than satisfied at her discretion, supposing that discretion be needed.

"To-night we played boston as usual in absolute silence until half-past ten o'clock; we neither saw nor heard anything. Not a child can pass through this solitary valley but that everybody sees and knows it, and for the last fifteen days or so not a single stranger has been seen. Now the d'Hauteserres and Simeuses would make a party of four. The goodman and his wife have submitted to the Government; they have made every effort imaginable to persuade their sons to return; they wrote them only yesterday. Thus I can only say, upon my soul and conscience, it is only your visit here that has shaken my belief of their being in Germany. Between ourselves, there is no one here, except the young countess, who does not do justice to the eminent abilities of Monsieur the First Consul."

"Foxy!" thought Corentin. "Well, if these young folk are shot," he said aloud, "it is well-deserved; I wash my hands of it."

He had walked with the Abbé Goujet to an open space where the moon shone brightly upon them, and, as he uttered these fatal words, he looked sharply at him. The priest was much distressed, but he seemed to be both surprised and ignorant.

"Understand this, Monsieur l'Abbé," continued Corentin, "that their rights in the Gondreville estates renders them doubly criminal in the eyes of the lower orders! I would rather they were in the hands of God than in his saints."

"There is a plot, then?" asked the curé, simply.

"Base, odious, cowardly, utterly contrary to the generous spirit of the nation," replied Corentin; "it will meet universal opprobrium."

"Oh, well, Mademoiselle de Cinq-Cygne is incapable of baseness!" exclaimed the abbé.

"Monsieur l'Abbé," answered Corentin, "look here; we have (that is, between you and me) proof positive of her complicity, but not enough as yet to prove the case in a law-court. She took flight when we came—— And understand. I sent the mayor to give warning."

"You did; but for one who desired to save them, you followed pretty closely on his heels," said the abbé.

At these words they looked at each other—there was no more to be said. Both one and the other were profound anatomists of thought to whom a mere inflection of the voice, a look, a word, reveals the soul just as a savage knows his enemies by indications, invisible to the eyes of an European.

"I thought to get something out of him, but he has tumbled to me!" thought Corentin.

"Oh, the scallawag!" said the curé to himself.

Midnight was tolled by the old church-clock at the moment that Corentin and the curé reëntered the salon. The opening and shutting of the doors and windows of the rooms and closets could be heard. The gendarmes pulled the beds apart. Peyrade, with the quick wit of a spy, ferreted and sounded everything. This pillaging excited the terror and indignation of the faithful servitors, who, as before, stood motionless. M. d'Hauteserre exchanged pitiful glances with his wife and Mlle. Goujet. A species of horrible curiosity kept every one on the alert. Peyrade just then came down with a box in his hand; a sandal wood-casket, carved, which had some time, most likely, been brought from China by the Admiral de Simeuse. This pretty box was flat, and about the size of a quarto volume.

Peyrade beckoned Corentin to the window-bay.

"I have it!" said he. "This Michu, who was prepared to pay Marion eight hundred thousand francs for Gondreville, and who yesterday meant to shoot Malin, is the man of the Simeuses; his motive in threatening Marion and stalking Malin shows the same game. He showed it when I saw a capacity of his having ideas; he has but one thought—he found out what was going on and came here to give the alarm."

"Malin most likely talked about the conspiracy to his friend the notary," said Corentin, following his colleague's inductions, "and Michu, being in hiding, overheard him speaking about the Simeuses. Maybe Michu only postponed the charge from his carbine to prevent the evils of a more pressing necessity—a loss even greater than that of Gondreville."

"He well knew what we were," said Peyrade. "My first glance at him showed that he was amazingly intelligent for a peasant."

"Oh! that proves that he was on his guard," replied Corentin. "But, after all, old fellow, don't let us make any mistake. Treachery makes a prodigious stink and primitive people smell it from afar."

"Well, all the better for us," said the Provençal.

"Call in the Arcis corporal," cried Corentin, to one of the gendarmes. "Let us send him to the pavilion," said he to Peyrade.

"Violette, our ear, is there," said the Pronvençal.

"We set out before getting any news from him," said Corentin. "We should have brought Sabatier with us. Two of us are not enough—Corporal," said he, seeing him enter, and edging him between Peyrade and himself, "don't let them fool you as they did just now the gendarme from Troyes. It appears to us that Michu is mixed up in this business; go to the pavilion, keep an eye on everything, and report all."

"One of my men heard horses in the forest at the time they arrested the young servants; and I have four spirited fellows on the track of whoever may be hiding there," replied the gendarme.

He went out; the sound of his galloping horse echoing on the paved path across the lawn rapidly died away.

"Come, now! they have either gone to Paris or are retracing their steps into Germany," said Corentin to himself.

He sat down, took a note-book out of the pocket of his spencer, wrote two orders in pencil, sealed them, and beckoned one of the gendarmes.

"Get off to Troyes on full gallop; wake up the prefect

and tell him to get the telegraph* at work as soon as there is light enough.''

The gendarme went off at a hand gallop. The intent of this move was so evident that the occupants of the castle felt their heart sink within them ; but this new anxiety was an addition to another that made martyrs of them all, for all eyes were fixed upon the precious casket. All the time the two agents were speaking together each one was taking furtive glimpses at their eager eyes. A kind of cold fury rendered the unfeeling hearts of these agents insensible ; they relished the general terror they inspired. The detective and sportsman have each the same emotions ; but where one employs his powers in slaying a hare, a partridge, or a roebuck, the other is thinking of saving the State or a prince and to gain a great reward.

Again, the hunt for men is superior to the other chase by all the distance existing between man and brute. Moreover, the spy is compelled to elevate his part to the importance of the interests in which he is engaged. Without going further into the matter, it must be easy for each one to see that the soul must be as ardent in the chase of a man as the other's is in pursuing game. As these two men gained a glimmering of the truth, the more eager they became ; but their expressions, their eyes remained cold and calm, the same as their ideas, suspicions, and schemes remained inscrutable. But for those who followed the effects of this moral scent on these two bloodhounds on the track of concealed facts, who could have watched and noted the quick movements of canine agility which led them to reach the truth in their rapid examination of probabilities, there was in all this something to make one shudder ! How and why had men of such genius fallen so low when their powers were so high?

What imperfection, what vice, what passion has debased him? Is a man a police-spy as another is a thinker, writer,

* Telegraphing was then done by semaphore signaling.—TRANSLATOR.

statesman, painter, general, because he knows nothing but how to play the spy, as the others know only how to speak, write, govern, paint, or fight? The castle household had but one heartfelt wish: "Why does not thunder fall upon these miscreants?" They thirsted for vengeance. But for the presence of the gendarmes there would have been an outbreak.

"Nobody, of course, has the key of this box?" asked the cynical Peyrade, questioning the company as much by the movement of his great, red nose as by his words.

The Provençal noticed, not without a qualm of terror, that the gendarmes had quit the room. Corentin and himself were alone. Corentin drew a small dagger from his pocket and began to force it under the lid of the box. At this moment they heard the galloping of a horse, first on the road, then on the little paved path across the lawn; it was the noise of a desperate gallop; but more horrible yet was the fall and awful sigh of the horse, who seemed to tumble in a heap at the foot of the central tower. A commotion like that produced by a thunder-clap shook the spectators when they saw Laurence, whose entrance was announced by the rustle of her riding-habit; the servants hastily formed two lines, through which she passed.

Despite the rapidity of her ride, she had yet experienced the anguish the discovery of the conspiracy must cause; all her hopes were overthrown! She had galloped through ruins as her thoughts turned upon the necessity of submission to the Consular government. Only for the danger that encompassed the four gentlemen, which served as a tonic to conquer her fatigue and despair, she would have fallen in a swoon. She had all but killed her mare to return and take her stand between death and her cousins.

Seeing this heroic girl, pale, with drawn features, her veil thrown back, riding-whip in hand, each one knew—as her burning glance grasped the whole scene and took in its meaning—from the almost imperceptible twitch of Corentin's sour face that the real adversaries had met face to face. An awful duel was about to begin.

Seeing the casket in Corentin's hands, the countess raised her riding-whip and sprang quickly to him; she struck his hands so violent a blow that the casket fell to the floor; she snatched it up, flung it into the middle of the fire and stood in a defiant attitude, with her back to the fireplace, before either of the agents recovered from their surprise. The scorn which flashed from the eyes of Laurence, her pale brow and disdainful lips, were even more insulting to these men than the haughty action by which she spurned Corentin as a venomous reptile.

Once more old d'Hauteserre felt himself a cavalier, his blood surged red to his face, he regretted that he had no sword. For a moment the servants trembled with joy. The vengeance invoked upon these creatures had fallen. But their happiness was driven deep into their souls by a hideous fear; they still heard the gendarmes going and coming in the garrets.

The spy—vigorous epithet, under which term are confounded all the shades distinguishing all the police, for the public will never seek to be more specific in speaking of the various grades of those who comprise this dispensary so necessary to every government—the spy whose make-up is at once magnificent and curious; he is never angry; he has the humanity of a Christian priest; he has stolid eyes, and he opposes, as it were, with them as a barrier against a world of ninnies which does not understand him; his brow is adamant at insult; he seeks his end like a reptile whose outer shell can only be fractured by a cannon-ball; but, again, like that creature, he is but the more furious when the blow falls, as he felt himself securely protected by his armor. The blow of the whip-stock upon his fingers was to Corentin, pain apart, the blow of the cannon-ball that broke his carapace; given by that noble and magnificent girl, with all the loathing of her glance, not only humiliated him in the eyes of the others, but still more in his own.

Peyrade, the Provençal, sprang to the hearth ; he received a kick from Laurence's foot, but he caught it and forced her, out of modesty, to throw herself on the couch where so short a time past she had lain asleep. This was burlesque in the midst of terror, a frequent contrast in human life. Peyrade scorched his hand in snatching the box from the fire, but he got it, threw it down upon the floor, and sat upon it. These little events passed quickly and without a word. Corentin, recovering from the smart with the blow of the riding-whip, caught and held Mademoiselle de Cinq-Cygne by both hands.

" Do not compel me to use force against you, *my beautiful citizeness*," said he with a mocking courtesy.

Peyrade's act had extinguished the fire, the result of stifling the flames.

" Here, gendarmes ! " he cried, still maintaining his absurd position.

" Will you promise to behave yourself ? " said Corentin, insolently to Laurence, and picking up his dagger, but without committing the fault of threatening her.

" The secrets of that casket are no concern of the government," she replied, with a trace of melancoly in her manner and accent. " When you have read the letters therein, you will, in spite of your infamy, feel ashamed of having done so —that is, if you have any sense of shame," she added after a pause.

The curé glanced at Laurence as who would say : " For God's sake ! Keep calm."

Peyrade rose. The bottom of the casket, being nearest the coals, was nearly burned through, and left a scorch-mark on the carpet. The lid was almost reduced to charcoal and the sides gave way. This grotesque Scævola, who had sacrificed to the god of Police and Fear the seat of his apricot-colored breeches, opened the two sides of the box like it had been a

book and slid three letters and two locks of hair upon the
baize of the card-table.   He was just about to smile significantly at Corentin when he perceived that the two locks of
hair were almost white, of different shades.   Corentin released
Mlle. de Cinq-Cygne and went toward the table and picked
up one of the letters from which the hair had fallen.

Laurence also rose and stood beside the two spies and
said :

"Oh ! read it up ; that shall be your punishment."

As they continued to read to themselves, she herself took
up the remaining letter and began :

DEAR LAURENCE :—My husband and myself have heard of your noble
conduct on the day of our arrest.   We know that you love our twin dears
as much, or nearly equal, as we love them ourselves ; so we charge you
with a gift which will be at the same time precious and sad to them.   M.
the Executioner has come to cut off our hair, for we are to die in a few
moments ; he has given us his promise to place in your hands the two only
souvenirs we can leave our dearly beloved orphans.   Keep these our last
remains, and give them to them in happier days.   We have put our last
kiss upon each with our blessing for them.   Our last thought will be of
our sons, then of you, and afterward of God !   Love them dearly.

                                    BERTHE DE CINQ-CYGNE.
                                    JEAN DE SIMEUSE.

In all eyes there were tears as the letter was being read.

Laurence, in a firm voice and with a stony look, said to the
two agents :

"You are less merciful than *Monsieur the Executioner.*"

Corentin composedly replaced the hair in the letter, laid the
letter aside on the table, and put a pile of counters on the
top of it.   His coolness in the midst of the general emotion
was something awful.   Peyrade unfolded the other two letters.

"Oh ! as for those," said Laurence, " they are much alike.
You have heard the will read, you can now learn how it was
carried into effect.   In future my heart will be without secrets ; this is all :

1794, AUDERNACH,
Before the battle.

MY DEAR LAURENCE:—I love you for life and I want you to be assured of this. But you ought to know, in case of my death, that my brother, Paul-Marie, loves you as much as I love you. My sole consolation in dying would be the thought that some day you would certainly take my dear brother for your husband; and I shall not then be consumed by jealousy, as I should be if I remained in this life and you should prefer him to me. After all that preference seems the most natural, for, perhaps, he is more worthy than me—— and so forth.

MARIE-PAUL.

"Here is the other letter," said she, with a charming color flushing her forehead.

My kind Laurence, I have sadness in my heart, but Marie-Paul is full of gayety; his nature will doubtless please you more than mine. Perhaps some day you may have to choose between us. Eh, well—though I love you passionately——

"You are in correspondence with *émigrés!*" said Peyrade, interrupting Laurence and holding the letters, as a matter of precaution, between himself and the light to see if anything written in sympathetic ink appeared between the lines.

"Yes," said Laurence, as she refolded the precious letters, the paper of which was yellow with age. "But in virtue of what right do you force an entrance into my house and violate my personal liberty and that of my household?"

"Ah, exactly so!" said Peyrade. "By what right? You shall be let know, my fair aristocrat," he replied, taking a warrant from his pocket issued by the minister of justice, and countersigned by the minister of the interior. "See, citizeness, the ministers have this bee in their bonnets——"

"We might also ask you," said Corentin, in a voice intended for her own ear, "by what right you harbor in your house the assassins of the First Consul? You struck me just now with your riding-whip on my fingers; that justifies me in giving a blow in my turn to dispatch messieurs, your cousins, whom I came here to save."

At the first movement of her lips and the look which Laurence cast upon Corentin, the curé guessed what that unknown great actor was saying, and he made her a sign of distrust. Only Goulard saw this gesture.

Peyrade knocked little blows on the lid of the box to see if it had a double bottom.

"Oh! my God!" said Laurence to Peyrade, snatching away the lid; "don't break it—wait."

She took a pin, pushed the head of one of the figures, a spring gave way, and the two halves opened and disclosed two miniatures of the Messieurs de Simeuse in the uniform of the army of Condé, two portraits painted on ivory in Germany. Corentin, who found himself face to face with an adversary worthy of his anger, withdrew with Peyrade into a corner of the room to hold a secret conference with him.

"You could throw that on the fire?" said the Abbé Goujet to Laurence, pointing to the letter of the marquise and the hair.

For all answer the young girl gave a significant shrug of her shoulders. The curé then understood that she had sacrificed all this to mislead the spies and gain time. He raised his eyes to heaven in mute admiration.

"Where did they catch Gothard? I can hear him crying," she asked, loud enough to be overheard.

"I don't know," replied the curé.

"Had he gone to the farm?"

"The farm?" said Peyrade to Corentin. "Let us send there."

"No," replied Corentin, "this girl would not intrust the safety of her cousins to a farmer. She amuses herself at our expense. Do as I tell you. After all we may do something here, although we made a great blunder in coming at all."

Corentin went and stood before the fire, lifting the long

pointed tails of his coat to warm himself, putting on the style, tone, and manner of a gentleman paying a visit.

"Mesdames, you may go to bed, and the servants also. Monsieur le Maire, your services are no longer required. The strict orders we received permitted no other course to be adopted by us; but as soon as the walls, which appear to me to be inordinately thick, have been examined, we shall take our leave."

The mayor saluted the company and went out; neither the curé nor Mlle. Goujet made a move. The servants were too anxious to leave without knowing the fate of their young mistress. Mme. d'Hauteserre, who, since the arrival of Laurence, had studied her with the curious instinct of a despairing mother, rose, took her by the arm into a corner of the room, and in a low voice said:

"Have you seen them?"

"How could I have allowed your sons to come beneath your roof without your knowledge?" replied Laurence. "Durieu," said she, "see if it is possible to save my poor Stella; she is still breathing."

"She must have come a long way?" said Corentin.

"Fifteen leagues in three hours," she answered, addressing herself to the curé, who regarded her with astonishment. "I started at half-past nine and returned a little after one."

She looked at the clock; it was half-past two.

"So," remarked Corentin, "you don't deny that you have ridden fifteen leagues?"

"No," said she. "I admit that my cousins and the Messieurs de Simeuse, in their perfect innocence, did not expect other than to be included in the amnesty, and were on their way to Cinq-Cygne. When I had cause to believe that Malin was trying to implicate them in some treasonable conspiracy, I sent to caution them to return to Germany, where they will be before the telegraph at Troyes can signal the frontier. If I have committed a crime, let me be punished."

This answer, the result of profound meditation by Laurence, and so probable in every way, quite shook Corentin's convictions; the young countess noted its effect out of the corner of her eye. At this decisive moment, when every soul was, as it were, in a state of suspense and turned upon their two countenances, first that of Laurence, then that of Corentin, then from Corentin's back to Laurence's, the sound of a galloping horse reached them coming from the forest, down the road, then through the gate and over the paved pathway across the lawn. A frightful anxiety was stamped on every face.

Peyrade entered, his eyes gleaming with joy; he went to his colleague with great impressment and said, loud enough for the countess to hear:

"We have caught Michu!"

Laurence, to whom the agony, fatigue, and the tension of her whole intellectual faculties had given a rosy color, turned white and fell almost fainting into an armchair. La Durieu, Mademoiselle Goujet, and Mme. d'Hauteserre sprang toward her, for she was suffering; she made a gesture for them to cut the braided frogging of her amazon.

"That caught her——, *they* are on their way to Paris!" said Corentin to Peyrade. "Change the orders."

They went out, leaving a gendarme at the door of the salon. The infernal smartness of these two men had gained a terrible advantage in this duel; they had ensnared Laurence by one of their stock tricks.

At six o'clock in the morning, as day was breaking, the two agents returned. They had explored the covered path and were satisfied that three horses had passed that way to the forest. They were now awaiting the report of the captain of gendarmes that had been watching the neighborhood. They left the château in charge of a corporal while they went to breakfast at a wine-shop at Cinq-Cygne, but not until after they had given orders that Gothard, who had answered their every question with a torrent of tears, and Catherine, who still remained perversely silent and stolid, should be liberated. Catherine and Gothard went into the salon and kissed Laurence's hands, she laying exhausted on the lounge. Durieu also went in to tell her that Stella would recover, but that she needed the best of care.

The mayor, uneasy and inquisitive, met Corentin and Peyrade in the village. He allowed that he could not suffer such officials of the government of so high a rank to breakfast in a measly cabaret; he therefore took them to his own house. The abbey was but three-quarters of a mile away. On the way Peyrade remarked that the corporal of Arcis had not sent any news of either Michu or Violette.

"We are dealing with very smart folk," said Corentin; "for they are more clever than ourselves. Undoubtedly the priest has a hand in it."

At the time that Mme. Goulard was ushering the two officials into the great, fireless dining-room, the lieutenant of gendarmes, anxiety depicted on his face, arrived.

"We came upon the corporal of Arcis' horse in the forest without his master," said he to Peyrade.

"Lieutenant," cried Corentin, "ride at once to Michu's lodge and find out what is going on! They must have killed the corporal."

This news spoiled the mayor's breakfast. The Parisians swallowed their food with the rapidity of sportsmen halting for a meal; they returned to the castle in their wicker cabriolet so as to be in readiness to start for any point whither the exigencies of the case rendered their presence necessary. When the two men reappeared in the salon into which they had brought such trouble, terror, sorrow, and anxiety, they found Laurence, in a loose wrapper, the gentleman and his wife, the Abbé Goujet and his sister grouped around the fire, to every appearance perfectly tranquil.

"If they had caught Michu," Laurence meditated, "they

10   U

would have brought him in. I am vexed to think that I lost my presence of mind and that I threw some light on the suspicions of those vile wretches; but the damage can be repaired—— For how long do we remain your prisoners?" she asked the two agents with a satirical, unconcerned air.

The two spies exchanged glances.

"How can she know anything about our uneasiness in regard to Michu? No outsider can possibly have gotten into the castle. She is guying us!" said the two spies to each other by a look.

"We shall not bother you much longer," replied Corentin; "in three hours from now we shall offer our regrets for having disturbed your solitude."

No one replied. This contemptuous silence redoubled Corentin's inward fury. He had been reckoned up by Laurence and the curé, the two intellects of this little group, to their mental understanding of him. Gothard and Catherine set the table by the fire for breakfast and the curé and his sister had joined the family at their meal. Neither masters nor servants paid the least attention to the two spies, who went out and promenaded the garden, the courtyard, the road, returning once in a while to the salon.

At half-past two the lieutenant reappeared.

"I have found the corporal," said he to Corentin; "he was lying on the road leading from Cinq-Cygne to Bellache's farm; he has no wound except a bad contusion on the head, which looks as though it had been caused by his fall. He told me that he had been knocked off his horse so quickly and thrown so violently to the ground that he was quite unable to say how it was done; his feet slipped out of the stirrups, luckily for him, or he might have been dragged to death by the horse as he ran across the fields. We left him in the care of Michu and Violette——"

"How! you found Michu in his pavilion?" said Corentin, looking at Laurence.

The countess smiled shrewdly, like a woman who tastes revenge.

"It seems they were bargaining about a purchase last night, which began early in the evening and was about completed when I arrived," the lieutenant went on. "They were both pretty drunk apparently; but it's not to be wondered at, for they had been the whole night drinking and trading and haven't yet come to terms."

"Did Violette say this?" cried Corentin.

"Yes," said the lieutenant.

"That's it—if you want a thing done you must do it yourself!" exclaimed Peyrade, looking at Corentin, who distrusted the lieutenant's report quite as much as the other did.

The young man nodded his assent to the old man's gesture.

"At what time did you arrive at Michu's lodge?" said Corentin, noticing that Mademoiselle de Cinq-Cygne had glanced at the clock on the mantel.

"Around two o'clock," replied the lieutenant.

Laurence took in M. and Mme. d'Hauteserre and the Abbé Goujet and his sister in one glance that seemed to enfold them in an azure mantle; the joy of triumph sparkled in her eyes, she blushed, tears gathered under the lashes; this girl who had shown such strength was unable to weep except from pleasure. At this moment, especially to the priest, she was sublime; he was at times distressed by her virile characteristics; but he now had a glimpse of the woman's infinite tenderness; but in her these feelings lay like a hidden treasure in some infinite depth beneath a block of granite.

A gendarme came and asked if he might bring in Michu's son, who wished to speak with the gentlemen from Paris. Corentin made an affirmative gesture. François Michu, a smart chip of the old block, was in the courtyard where Gothard, now at liberty, had no chance to speak to him ex-

cept before the eyes of the gendarme. The little Michu, un-
perceived by the gendarme, managed to slip something into
Gothard's hand. Gothard stole in behind François and
reached Mlle. de Cinq-Cygne and with an innocent air gave
her both halves of the ring; she kissed it with ardor, for she
now well knew that Michu had accomplished his mission:
that the four gentlemen were in safety.

"My dad *(m'n p'a)* wants to know what to do with the
copiril, what ain't doing well?" said François, imitating the
speech of the peasantry.

"What's the matter with him?" asked Peyrade.

"It's his yed; he kim a cropper, and don't you forget it.
For a gindarme what should know how to ride, that is funny;
but I guess the hoss tumbled! There's a hole, oh! bigger'n
your fist on back o' his yed. 'Pears like he'd cracked it on a
nasty cobble-stone. Poor man! he's a dandy gindarme, but
it hurts him all the same—even us is sorry for him."

Here the captain of gendarmes from Troyes entered the
courtyard; he dismounted, and made a sign to Corentin,
who, when he recognized him, hurried to the window and
pushed it open to save time.

"What is it?"

"We have returned like the Dutchmen! We have found
five horses dead with fatigue, their coats stiff with sweat, in
the very middle of the main avenue of the forest; I am keeping them to find out whence they came and whose they are.
The forest is surrounded; those that are inside cannot get
out."

"At what time do you suppose these horsemen came into
the forest?"

"At half-past twelve, noon."

"Don't let a hare leave that forest without being seen!"
whispered Corentin. "I'll detail Peyrade to help you; I,
myself, will go to see the poor corporal. Go to the mayor's,"
he whispered the Provençal; "I'll send a clever fellow to re-

lieve you. We must make use of the country-folk ; examine every one of the faces here."

He turned to the company and said, a threatening ring in his voice : "*Au revoir !*"

Nobody saluted the agents as they went.

"What would Fouché say of a domiciliary visit from which nothing resulted ?" cried Peyrade, as he helped Corentin into the wicker cabriolet.

"All is not over yet," answered Corentin in Peyrade's ear ; "our gentlemen are in the forest for sure."

He pointed out Laurence, who was standing at one of the great windows with little panes, in the salon ; he cast a sinister look at her.

"I once did for a woman quite her equal, and one who stirred my bile much less than this one has ! If this one crosses my path I'll pay her for that cut with the whip."

"The other was a strumpet," said Peyrade ; "this one is of high rank——"

"What difference is that to me ? All is fish in the sea !" said Corentin, making a sign to the gendarme who drove him to whip the post-horse.

Ten minutes later the castle was completely evacuated.

"How was the corporal got out of the way ?" said Laurence to François Michu, whom she seated at the table to have some breakfast.

"My father and my mother said to me that it was a matter of life and death, that nobody must get into the house. So I knew when I heard horses going about in the forest that I had to do with them dogs of gindarmes, but I meant to keep 'em out. So I got some big ropes out of the granary and just fastened one of 'em to a tree right at the corner of the road. Then I drawed the rope high up so as it would hit the breast of a man on hossback and tied it on another tree facing it, and listened for a gallopin' hoss. The road was barred. It turned out fine. The moon had set ; my copiril just kim a cropper—but it didn't kill him. But what would you! for they are tough, is them gindarmes! After all, I did all I could."

"You saved us!" said Laurence, kissing François Michu, as she took him to the gate.

There she looked cautiously around, and, seeing no one, whispered:

"Have they provisions?"

"I have just taken them a twelve-pound loaf and four bottles of wine. They'll be all snug for six days."

When she returned to the salon, the young girl was beset with mute interrogations by M. and Mme. d'Hauteserre, the Abbé Goujet and his sister, each of whom regarded her with as much admiration as anxiety.

"But have you really seen them again?" cried Mme. d'Hauteserre.

The countess put her finger on her lips and smiled; then she left the room and went to bed. The victory once won, weariness overcame her.

The shortest road from Cinq-Cygne to Michu's pavilion was that which led from the village to Bellache's farm to the *rond-point* where the spies had first appeared to Michu. The gendarme who was driving Corentin followed this route, which was the one that the corporal of Arcis had taken. As they went along the agent was on the lookout for signs which should show how the corporal had been unhorsed. He rated himself for having sent but one man on an errand so important, and he drew from this fault an axiom for a police code which he was compiling for his own use.

"If they put the gendarme out of the way, they must have done the same by Violette. The five dead horses have evidently brought the four conspirators and Michu from the environs of Paris. Has Michu a horse?" said he to the gendarme, who belonged to the contingen from Arcis.

"Ah! and a famous nag it is; a hunter from the stables of

the *ci-devant* Marquis de Simeuse. Although fifteen years old, there's not a better beast in the country. Michu can ride it a full twenty leagues and the animal's hide would be as dry as my hat. Oh, he is careful of him; he has refused lots of money for it."

"What does the horse look like?"

"Dark brown, with white stockings above the shoes, thin, all sinew, like an Arabian."

"Have you seen Arabian horses?"

"I returned from Egypt a year ago; I have ridden the Mameluk's horses. We have to serve eleven years in the cavalry. I was on the Rhine with General Steingel, then in Italy afterward, then followed the First Consul in Egypt. Soon I shall be a corporal."

"When I am inside Michu's lodge, go you to the stables; if you have lived eleven years among horses, you can easily tell if a horse is blown."

"See, that is where our corporal was thrown," said the gendarme, pointing out the place where the road joined the *rond-point*.

"Tell the captain to pick me up at Michu's, and we'll go back to Troyes together."

Corentin got down and stood for a few moments examining the ground. He scrutinized the two elm-trees which faced each other, one against the park wall, the other on the high bank of the *rond-point*, here intersected by the cross-road; then he saw, what as yet had not been noticed, the button off a gendarme's uniform lying in the dust. He picked it up, and soon entered the pavilion, where he perceived Violette and Michu sitting at the kitchen table and disputing eagerly. Violette rose, saluted Corentin, and offered him a drink.

"Thanks; I came to see the corporal," said the young man, who at half a glance saw that Violette had been drinking for a full dozen hours.

"My wife is nursing him upstairs," said Michu.

"Well, corporal, how are you?" said Corentin, who had run up the stairs and found the gendarme with a bandaged head lying on Mme. Michu's bed. The hat, sword, and shoulder-belt lay on a chair.

Marthe, faithful to her womanly instincts, and not aware of her son's prowess, was, with her mother, nursing the corporal.

"We expect Monsieur Varlet the Arcis doctor," said Mme. Michu. "Gaucher has gone after him."

"Leave us for a moment," said Corentin, much surprised at the scene, which made the innocence of the two women obvious. "Where were you struck?" asked Corentin, looking at the man's uniform.

"On the breast," replied the corporal.

"Show me your shoulder-belt," said Corentin.

Now the yellow band with a white edge had been recently given as a part of the uniform of the gendarmes now called "National Guard;" the law for which prescribed the uniform, stipulating the minutest details. On the belt was a metal plate, much like that worn by foresters, upon which was engraved these singular words: RESPECT TO PERSONS AND TO PROPERTIES. The rope had left a deep score across the belt. Corentin took up the coat and found the place of the missing button he had found upon the road.

"At what time did they find you?" asked Corentin.

"Just at daybreak."

"Who helped you up?"

"The women and Michu's boy."

"Good!" said Corentin to himself. "Evidently they did not go to bed. The corporal was not knocked off his horse by a gun-shot, nor by the blow of a bludgeon, for an antagonist must have been at his own height to strike such a blow; he must have been on horseback also; he must have been disarmed by some obstacle across his path. A piece of wood? Impossible. An iron chain? That would have left its mark. What did you feel?" he said aloud.

"I was knocked off so suddenly——"

"The skin is grazed under your chin."

"It seems to me," said the corporal, "that my face was sawed by a rope."

"I have it," said Corentin. "Somebody fastened a rope from one tree to another to bar your way."

"Most likely," said the corporal.

Corentin went down and into the kitchen.

"Come, old cock, let's make an end of it!" Michu was saying to Violette, as he saw the spy. "One hundred thousand francs in all and you become master of my lands. I shall then retire on my income."

"As sure as there is but one God, I haven't more than sixty thousand, I tell you."

"But I offer you your own time in which to pay the balance! Here you've kept me bargaining since yesterday. The land is the best around."

"The land is all right," replied Violette. "I know all about that, but——"

"Wife, bring more wine," cried Michu.

"What, haven't you had enough to drink?" cried Marthe's mother. "That is the fourteenth bottle since nine o'clock——"

"You, then, have been here since nine o'clock this morning?" said Corentin to Violette.

"No, begging your pardon. Since last evening I have not left the place, and after all I've done no good—the more he drinks the higher the price."

"In every market a raise of the elbow means a rise in the price," said Corentin.

A dozen empty bottles ranged along the table bore silent testimony to the truth of the old woman's words. Just then the gendarme outside made a sign to Corentin, and whispered to him as he stood on the threshold:

"There is no horse in the stable."

"You have sent your little son to the town on horseback, I guess?" said Corentin to Madame Michu when he went into the house again.

"No, monsieur," said Marthe, "he went afoot."

"What's become of your horse, then?"

"I have lent him," replied Michu, curtly.

"Come here, my good apostle," said Corentin, speaking to the keeper and beckoning him: "I have two words I wish to slip down your ear-tube."

Corentin and Michu went out.

"That carbine you were loading at four o'clock yesterday was meant to kill the councilor of State—Grévin, the notary, saw you; but we can't pinch you for that—plenty of malice intended, but few witnesses. You managed, how I know not, to stupefy Violette, and you, your wife, and boy passed the night out of doors to warn Mademoiselle de Cinq-Cygne of our arrival and save her cousins, whom you have in hiding here—though just now I don't know where. Your son or your wife threw the corporal pretty nicely. You have us beaten. You're a pretty smart chap. But all is not yet said: and you won't have the last word. Hadn't you better compromise? your masters will gain by it."

"Come this way, we cannot talk here without being overheard," said Michu, leading the spy through the park toward the pond.

When Corentin saw the sheet of water, he looked fixedly at Michu, who doubtless counted on his great physical strength to heave this man into the mud beneath seven feet of water. Michu answered with a look that was quite as steady. It was absolutely as though a cold and flabby boa-constrictor was glaring defiance at one of those tawny-red, fierce jaguars of Brazil.

"I am not thirsty," quoth Corentin, stopping short on the border of the meadow and thrusting his hand down into a side-pocket to feel for his little dagger.

"We shall never reach an understanding," said Michu, coldly.

"Mind what you're about, my dear boy; Justice has her eye on you."

"Well, if she can't see any clearer than you, everybody is in danger," retorted the keeper.

"You refuse, then?" asked Corentin, significantly.

"I'd sooner have my head cut off a hundred times over, if a man's head could be cut off a hundred times, than come to any agreement with such a villain as you."

Corentin hastily climbed into the chaise, after a comprehensive glance at Michu, the pavilion, and Courant, who barked after him. He gave some kind of orders as he passed through Troyes, and returned to Paris. All the brigades of gendarmes were the recipients of secret instructions and special orders.

During the months of December, January, and February the search was diligently kept up in even remote villages. Ears were in every tavern. Corentin learned three important facts—a horse like that of Michu's had been found dead near Lagny. The five horses buried in the forest of Nodesme had been sold for five hundred francs each by certain farmers and millers to a man who signally resembled Michu. When the decree was passed against the accomplices and those who harbored them, Corentin confined the search and surveillance of the police to the forest of Nodesme. Then, after the arrest of Moreau, the royalists, and Pichegru, no strangers were to be seen around the countryside.

Michu had now lost his place; the notary of Arcis had carried him a letter from the councilor of State, now become a senator, authorizing Grévin to receive the accounts of the steward-keeper, and giving him notice to quit. In three days Michu had asked and been given a formal discharge in due form and became a free man. To the great astonishment of the country he went to live at Cinq-Cygne, where Laurence made him the farmer of all the reserves of the castle. The day of his installation fatally coincided with the execution of the Duc d'Enghien. Nearly the whole of France heard at the same time of the capture, trial, condemnation, and death of the prince—terrible reprisals which preceded the trials of Polignac, Rivière, and Moreau.

PART II.

CORENTIN'S REVENGE.

It was intended to build a new farm-house for Michu, but while this was being constructed the so-called Judas was lodged in the rooms over the stables, by the side of the famous breach. Michu bought two horses, one for himself and one for his son, for they both joined Gothard in esquiring mademoiselle in all her rides, which had, as most people may imagine, for their object the feeding of the four gentlemen and to see that they wanted for nothing. François and Gothard, assisted by Courant and the countess' dogs, looked out that the vicinity of the hiding-place was clear. Laurence and Michu carried the provisions which Marthe, her mother, and Catherine prepared, unknown to the rest of the household, so as to keep the secret to themselves, for they knew without any doubt that the village contained spies. From motives of prudence these expeditions were never made oftener than twice a week, and always at a different hour, sometimes by day and sometimes at night. These precautions continued even during the trials of Rivière, Polignac, and Moreau.

When the Senate (*sénatus-consulte*) called the Bonaparte dynasty to the throne, and Napoleon's nomination as Emperor was submitted to the French people, M. d'Hauteserre gave his signature to the register brought to him by Goulard. When it was made known that the pope would anoint and crown Napoleon, Mlle. de Cinq-Cygne no longer opposed a petition being sent asking that the two young d'Hauteserres and her cousins might have their names struck off the list of *émigrés* and to be allowed to resume their rights as citizens of France.

(157)

The old man went off to Paris forthwith, and there had a consultation with the *ci-devant* Marquis de Chargebœuf, who was acquainted with Talleyrand. That minister, who was then in favor, undertook that the petition should be presented to Josephine, she in turn gave it to her husband, who was now addressed as Emperor, Majesty, Sire, although the result of the popular vote was as yet unknown.

M. d'Hauteserre, M. de Chargebœuf, and the Abbé Goujet, who also went to Paris, obtained an audience with Talleyrand, who gave them the promise of his support. Already Napoleon had pardoned some of the principals in the great royalist conspiracy against him ; but, although the four gentlemen were merely suspected of complicity, yet after the rising of the council of State the Emperor called Senator Malin, Fouché, Talleyrand, Cambacérès, Lebrun, and Dubois, the prefect of police, into his cabinet.

"Gentlemen," said the future Emperor, still wearing the dress of the First Consul, "we have received petitions from the Sieurs de Simeuse and d'Hauteserre, officers in the army of the Prince of Condé, praying permission to reënter France."

"They are here now," said Fouché.

"Like a thousand others that I come across in Paris," remarked Talleyrand.

"I think," returned Malin, "that you have not come across them, for they are in hiding in the forest of Nodesme, where they feel themselves quite at home."

He was very careful to avoid letting the First Consul and Fouché learn of his having spoken those few words which had saved his own life ; but he made advantageous use of Corentin's reports and convinced the council of the participation of the four gentlemen in the plot of Messieurs de Rivière and Polignac, and that they had Michu as an accomplice. The prefect of police confirmed these assertions of the senator.

"But how could this keeper know that the conspiracy had been discovered ?" asked the prefect of police. "The

Emperor, his council, and myself were the only persons who possessed the secret."

No one paid any attention to this remark of Dubois'.

"If they have been hidden in a forest and you have not been able to find them in seven months," said the Emperor to Fouché, "they have fully expiated their wrong-doings!"

"I am content," said Malin, alarmed at the perspicacity of the prefect of police, "to imitate your majesty's example, although they are my personal enemies; therefore I make myself their advocate and beg that their names be stricken off the lists."

"They will be less dangerous to you reinstated than as *émigrés,* for they must take the oath of allegiance to the constitution of the Empire and its law," said Fouché, looking steadily at Malin.

"In what way are they dangerous to Monsieur the Senator?" asked Napoleon.

Talleyrand on this spoke for some time to the Emperor in a low voice. The erasure from the lists and the reinstatement of Messrs. de Simeuse and d'Hauteserre seemed to be granted.

"Sire," said Fouché, "depend upon it that you will hear of these people again."

Talleyrand, by the earnest request of the Duc de Grandlieu, gave pledges in the name and on the honor of these gentlemen—a term which had much influence with Napoleon—that they would attempt naught against the Emperor and would give their submission without equivocation.

"The Messieurs d'Hauteserre and de Simeuse are most unwilling to bear arms against France after recent events. It is true they have not much sympathy with the Imperial government; they are people which your majesty would do well to conciliate; but they will be satisfied to live on French soil and obey the laws," said the minister.

Then he laid a letter he had received expressing these sentiments before the Emperor.

"This is so frank that it is most likely sincere," said the Emperor, looking at Lebrun and Cambacérès. "Have you any further objections?" he asked Fouché.

"In the interest of your majesty," replied the future minister of police, "I ask to be charged with the transmission to these gentlemen of their reinstatement, *when it is definitely granted,*" said he in a louder voice.

"So be it," said Napoleon, seeing a dissatisfied frown on Fouché's face.

This little council rose without the matter being positively decided ; but it had the result of implanting a vague distrust of the four gentlemen in Napoleon's memory. M. d'Hauteserre, who believed he had succeeded, had written a letter announcing the good news. The occupants of Cinq-Cygne were therefore not surprised when, a few days latter, Goulard came to inform the countess and Mme. d'Hauteserre that they were bidden to send the four gentlemen to Troyes, where the prefect would annul the decree for their arrest and reinstate them in their rights, after they had made their oath of allegiance to the Empire. Laurence made reply to the mayor that she would duly inform her cousins and the d'Hauteserres.

"Then they are not here?" said Goulard.

Madame d'Hauteserre looked with anxiety after the young girl, who left the mayor to consult with Michu. The latter saw no reason against the immediate release of the *émigrés.* Laurence, Michu, his son, and Gothard started therefore for the forest, taking with them an additional horse, for the countess intended accompanying the four gentlemen to Troyes and then to return with them. The whole household, apprised of the good news, gathered on the lawn to see the departure of the joyous cavalcade.

The four young gentlemen left their hiding-place, mounted their horses, and were soon on the road to Troyes, accompanied by Mlle. de Cinq-Cygne. Michu, assisted by his son and Gothard, reclosed the entrance to the cellar, and all three returned on foot. Michu recollected, while on the way, that he had left the forks, spoons, and a silver cup that his masters had been using in the cavern, and he returned for them alone. When he reached the borders of the pond he heard voices in the cellar, and went straight to the entrance of the cave through the brush.

"You have doubtless come to look for your silverware?" said Peyrade, grinning and showing his big red nose among the leaves.

Without knowing why—for at any rate his young masters were safe—Michu experienced a dull horror in his every joint, so keen was his sense of vague, indefinable forebodings of evil; meanwhile, he at once went forward and found Corentin on the stairs, a wax-taper in his hand.

"We are not spiteful," said he to Michu; "we might have pinched your *ci-devants* any time during the past week, only we knew they were off the list. You're a pretty tough citizen! You gave us too much trouble for us not to wish to satisfy our curiosity."

"I'd give something handsome," said Michu, "to know by whom and how we have been sold!"

"If that puzzles you, my boy," said Peyrade, grinning, "look at your horses' shoes, then you'll see that you betrayed yourselves."

"No rancor," said Corentin, whistling a signal for the captain of gendarmes and their horses.

"That miserable Parisian blacksmith who shod the horses so well in the English fashion, and who has just left Cinq-Cygne, was a rat of theirs!" cried Michu. "They had only to follow our tracks when the ground was damp, disguised as fagot-cutters or poachers, after those nails had been put in the shoes of the horses. We are quits."

Michu was soon consoled by thinking that the discovery of the hiding-place was of no moment, as the gentlemen were again Frenchmen, reinstated, and had recovered their free-

11

dom. Nevertheless, his first presentiment had reason. The police and jesuits possess the virtue of never abandoning their enemies or their friends.

The goodman d'Hauteserre returned from Paris, and was not a little surprised at not being the first to bring the news. Durieu prepared an excellent dinner, the servants donned their best liveries, and the whole household awaited with impatience the arrival of the exiles, who came about four o'clock; at the time of their arrival they were joyous but humiliated, for they were placed under police surveillance for a term of two years; obliged each month to present themselves at the prefecture, and during that time were compelled to remain in the commune of Cinq-Cygne.

"I will send you the register to sign," the prefect had said to them. "Then, in a few months, you can ask for a remission of these conditions, which have been imposed on all Pichegru's accomplices. I will support your request."

These restrictions, although merited, somewhat dampened the young men. Laurence, however, only laughed.

"The Emperor of the French," said she, "was badly raised; he has not as yet acquired the knack of giving favors with grace."

The gentlemen found all the occupants of the castle at the gates, and on the roads a goodly number of the villagers, for the adventures of these young men had made them famous throughout the department. Mme. d'Hauteserre, her face bathed in tears, held her sons in a long embrace; she was unable to utter a word; she was silent, but happy, for a great part of the evening.

The Simeuse twins had hardly dismounted than a general cry of surprise went up, caused by their astonishing likeness to each other—the same look, the same voice, the same little mannerisms. Each made the same movement in rising from the saddle, throwing their leg over the horse's crupper in dismounting, and alike threw their reins over the animals' necks; their dress, absolutely the same, made them the more like a pair of veritable Ménechmes. They wore Suwaroff boots, which fitted the instep; tight, white skin breeches; green hunting-jackets with metal buttons; black cravats and buckskin gloves. These two young men, then thirty-one years of age, were, in the language of the day, "charming cavaliers." Of medium height, but well made, they had brilliant eyes, with long lashes, liquid and floating like those of children; black hair, noble foreheads, and of olive skin. Their speech, gentle as a woman's, fell graciously from their well-shaped red lips. Their manner was more polished and courteous than that of the provincial gentry; it plainly showed that a knowledge of men and things had given them a secondary education more finished than their first and constituting each a polished gentleman.

Thanks to Michu, ample money had been supplied them to visit foreign Courts in befitting style and to travel during their emigration. The old gentleman and the abbé thought them rather haughty; but, in their present situation, it was perhaps the result of a lofty character. They showed all the little ear-marks of a careful education, to which was added a wonderful address in all physical exercises. The only lack of resemblance was in the region of thought. The youngest was charming in his gayety, the eldest in his melancholy; but this contrast, purely spiritual, was not apparent until after a long intimacy.

"Ah, my girl," whispered Michu to Marthe, "how can one help devoting himself to these two young lads?"

Marthe, who admired the twins as a wife and mother, nodded her head prettily and pressed her husband's hand. The servants had permission to embrace their new masters.

During the seven months' seclusion to which the four young men had condemned themselves, they had several times imprudently, though it was necessary imprudence, taken their walks abroad, being, however, carefully guarded by Michu, his son, and Gothard. During these promenades, usually taken on clear nights, Laurence reunited the past with the present time, but found it utterly impossible to choose between the two brothers. A pure and equal love for each of the twins possessed her heart. She thought indeed that she had two hearts. On their side the two Pauls dared not speak to themselves of their impending rivalry. Perhaps all three were trusting to accident to decide. This anomalous situation no doubt acted upon Laurence, for, after a visible momentary hesitation, she took an arm of each of the brothers as she entered the salon, whither she was followed by M. and Mme. d'Hauteserre, who clung to and plied their sons with questions. At this moment all the servants shouted:

"Long live the Cinq-Cygnes and the Simeuses."

Laurence, still between the two brothers, turned around and thanked them with a charming gesture.

When these nine persons came to observe each other closely, for in all reunions, even in the bosom of the family, there comes a time when one observes the other after a long absence, the first look that Adrien d'Hauteserre cast on Laurence, and which was caught by his mother and the Abbé Goujet, seemed to show pretty plainly that that young man was in love with the countess. Adrien, the youngest of the d'Hauteserres, had a gentle, kindly soul. His heart had remained adolescent despite the catastrophies that had hardened him into manhood. Like a great many soldiers who remain virgin in mind in the midst of great peril, he showed the diffidence and timidities of youth. In this he differed wholly from his brother, a rough-looking man, a great sportsman, an intrepid soldier, full of resolution, but lacking in delicacy, and of little mental alertness in affairs of the heart. One was all soul, the other all action ; but yet each possessed in the same degree that nice sense of honor which is the life of a gentleman.

Dark, short, slim and wiry, Adrien d'Hauteserre gave an

impression of strength; while his brother, tall, pale, and fair, seemed weakly. Adrien, nervous in temperament, had strength of soul; Robert, who was lymphatic, was fond of athletic exercises. Families frequently present these fantastical contrasts, the causes of which it might be interesting to examine, but it is only recorded here to show that Adrien need not fear a rival in his brother. Robert's affection for Laurence was that of a relative, and he showed all the respect of a noble for a young girl of his own caste.

In matters of sentiment the eldest of the d'Hauteserres belonged to that class of men who look upon woman as an appendage to man, limiting her physical sphere to the functions of maternity, who demand perfection in that respect, but considering woman as naught in all else. To such the idea of admitting her as an integral portion of society in the body politic, or in the family, meant a social upheaval. To-day we are so far removed from such a primitive theory that nearly every woman, even those who do not aim at the fatal emancipation offered by the new sects, will be shocked by only hearing such opinions; but Robert d'Hauteserre had the misfortune to think thus.

Robert was a man of the middle ages, the younger man was of to-day. These differences, instead of hindering their affections, had but knit them the closer together. On the first evening these shades of character were seen and appreciated by the curé, Mademoiselle Goujet, and Madame d'Hauteserre, who were secretly reading the future while playing their boston.

At twenty-three, having passed through a long solitude of deep reflection and the anguish of an enterprise defeated, Laurence had become a woman; feeling within herself a powerful longing for affection, she put forth all the graces of her mind and was charming. She revealed the charms and tenderness with all the innocence of a girl of fifteen. During the past thirteen years she had been a woman only in suffering; she hoped for amends; she now showed herself gentle and winning as before she had proven herself strong and great.

The four old people were the last to leave the salon; they shook their heads as if they felt uneasy at this new manifestation of that charming girl. What power of passion might there not be hidden in a young woman of her temper and nobility? The two brothers loved with an equal love the same woman, and with an equal tenderness; which of these two would Laurence choose? Would she, in choosing one, kill the other?

Countess in her own right, she would bring her husband a title and great privileges, together with an illustrious name; perhaps, in thinking of these advantages, the Marquis de Simeuse would sacrifice himself to espouse Laurence to his brother, who, by the old laws, was poor and without title; but the younger, would he deprive the elder of the happiness of having Laurence for a wife? While they were distant from her this strife of love had created but little inconvenience; moreover, the two brothers were so often in danger, the chances of war might put an end to the difficulty; but what would result from this reunion? When Marie-Paul's and Paul-Marie's passion had attained its greatest height could they share, as they now did, the looks, the feelings, the attentions, the words of their cousin? would they not break out into a jealousy the consequences of which might result most horribly? What would be the end of this pleasant life, where they were one in heart though divided in person?

To these suppositions, bandied between each other as they finished their last game of boston, Madame d'Hauteserre replied that she would marry neither of her cousins. The old lady had that evening experienced one of those inexplicable presentiments which are and remain secrets between mothers and God.

Laurence, in her inward consciousness, was no less afraid

MADAM. D'HAUTESERRE REPLIED THAT SHE WOULD MARRY
NEITHER OF HER COUSINS.

of this *tête-à-tête* with her cousins. To the exciting drama of
the conspiracy, to the dangers incurred by the two brothers,
to the miseries of their emigration, now succeeded another
drama of a kind she had never contemplated. This noble
girl could not resort to refusing both twins; she was too honest a woman to marry one and nurse an irresistible passion for
the other in her heart. To remain unmarried, to weary her
cousins by her refusal to come to a decision, and then to take
as husband the one who remained faithful in spite of her
caprices, was less thought of as a conclusion than vaguely admitted. As she fell asleep she told herself the wisest thing
to do was to leave all to chance. Chance is, in love,
woman's Providence.

The next morning Michu started for Paris, whence some
four days later he returned with four fine horses for his new
masters. In six days the hunting season opened, and the
young countess sagely reflected that the violent exercises
would be a buffer against the difficulties of the *tête-à-tête* at
the castle. The first result, though, was quite unexpected;
it at once surprised the onlookers of this strange love and
excited their admiration. Without any preceding agreement
the two brothers rivaled each other in their attentions to
Laurence; they experienced a sense of pleasure in acting thus,
which appeared to suffice them. Nothing more natural.
After such a long absence they felt the necessity of studying
her, of knowing her thoroughly, beside letting her know and
understanding them, leaving her free to make her own choice;
they were sustained in their mutual trial by their double life,
which was one life.

Love, the same as motherhood, was unable to distinguish
between the two brothers. Laurence was obliged, in order to
know them apart, to present them with different cravats—a
white one for the eldest-born and a black one for the younger.
Without this perfect resemblance, this identity of life, which
misled them all, a similar position would have seemed im-

possible. It can only be explained by the fact itself, one of those things which men can never be brought to believe in unless actually seen ; and, when it is seen, the mind becomes even more bewildered by having to explain them than to believe.

If Laurence spoke, her voice echoed in two hearts equally loving and faithful. Did she say anything ingenious, pleasant, or noble, her look encountered the pleasure expressed in two glances which followed her every movement, interpreted her lightest wish ; with eyes that beamed upon her with an ever-new expression of gayety in the one or tender melancholy in the other.

In anything concerning their mistress the two brothers showed an admirable spontaneity of heart, together with a concord of action which, to quote the Abbé Goujet, reached the sublime. Often, in the question of petty services, or if something had to be searched for, the little things that a man delights to render to the woman whom he loves, the elder would leave the pleasure of the doing it to the younger brother, casting a look at Laurence that was proud and tender in one. The younger put his honor in the due payment of every such debt. This noble rivalry in a sentiment in which man in his jealousy often falls below the ferocity of brutes simply amazed the ideas of the old folk who contemplated it.

Little things such as these often brought tears into the eyes of the countess. A single sensation, but perhaps all-powerful in certain privileged organizations, may give some slight idea of Laurence's feelings : it may be realized by a remembrance of the perfect concord of two fine voices like, say, those of Sontag and Malibran, in some harmonious duet, or the complete unison of two instruments touched by the hand of genius, when the blended sounds of their melody enter the soul like the passionate sighing of a single soul.

Sometimes to the curé, who was watching them, as he saw the Marquis de Simeuse buried in an arm-chair and glancing from time to time at his brother with melancholy eyes as he laughed and talked with Laurence, it seemed as though he was capable of making an immense sacrifice; but soon he caught in his eye an expression of unconquerable passion. Should either of the twins find himself alone with Laurence, he might well believe that he was loved exclusively.

"It seems to me that there is but one of them," said the countess to the Abbé Goujet, when he questioned her about the state of her heart.

The priest then recognized that coquetry was absolutely lacking in her. Laurence could not realize that two men loved her.

"But, my dear girl," said Mme. d'Hauteserre one evening, though her own son was silently dying of love for Laurence, "you must decide between them."

"Leave us in our happiness," she rejoined. "God will save us from ourselves!"

Adrien d'Hauteserre hid his consuming jealousy in the depths of his heart, and guarded his secret tortures, keeping his despair to himself. He endeavored to be content with the happiness of seeing this charming being who, during these few months of suspense, shone most radiantly. In effect Laurence had become a coquette; she took that dainty care of her person which women, who are loved, take such pleasure in. She followed the fashions, and, more than once, went to Paris, to reappear more beautiful than before, decked in some new *chiffon* or other finery. Finally, to give her cousins that full idea of home, even to its least enjoyment, from which they had so long been disassociated, that, despite her late guardian's remonstrances, she made hers the most completely comfortable place in all Champagne.

Robert d'Hauteserre did not understand one thing in this hidden drama. He had not even perceived the love his brother bore Laurence. He loved to rally his cousin on her coquetry, for he confounded that odious defect with a desire to please ; but he was always mistaken in questions of taste, feeling, and culture. So, whenever this man of the Middle Ages made his appearance on the scene, Laurence very soon caused him to take the clown's part, though quite unsuspected by him. She amused her cousins by discussing with Robert, leading him insidiously on step by step into the middle of some bog of ignorance and stupidity. She excelled in those ingenious mystifications which, to be perfect, must leave the victim well satisfied with himself. Nevertheless, although coarse by nature, Robert not once during those happy months, the only really delightful time in the lives of these three charming people, uttered one virile word which might have brought things to a crisis between the Simeuses and Laurence. The brothers' sincerity impressed him.

Robert without doubt guessed that a woman might well hesitate before according a sign of preference for one when the other must suffer chagrin by it, as must be should one brother be made happy at the expense of the other, who would suffer in the depths of his heart. This respect on Robert's part admirably explains the situation, which would certainly have obtained the privilege of being submitted to the higher powers in the days of faith, when the sovereign pontiff had the power of intervention and of cutting the Gordian knots in such rare phenomena and such impenetrable mysteries. The Revolution had strengthened these hearts in the Catholic faith, and religion had increased the gravity of this terrible crisis, for the grandeur of their characters augmented the sublimity of the situation. Again, neither M. nor Mme. d'Hauteserre, nor the curé, nor his sister looked for anything common or vulgar from the two brothers or from Laurence.

This drama, which remained a secret locked in the bosom of the family circle, where each in silence observed its slow yet rapid progress, carried with it unlooked-for joys, trifling contests, frustrated preferences, little despairs, anxious waitings, explanations deferred to the morrow, mute avowals, and all the rest, so that the occupants of Cinq-Cygne paid no attention to the coronation of the Emperor Napoleon. These passions found a truce and a distraction in the violent exercises of the chase; excessive physical fatigue removed from the soul every occasion of wandering in the dangerous steppes of dreamland. Neither Laurence nor her cousins gave a thought to public affairs, for each day brought its own palpitating interest.

"In truth," said Mlle. Goujet, one evening, "I don't know which of all these lovers loves the most."

Adrien, who chanced to be alone in the salon with the four boston players, raised his eyes and turned pale. For some days past his only hold on life had been the joy of seeing Laurence and hearing her speak.

"In my opinion," said the curé, "the countess, being a woman, loves with the most abandon."

Laurence, the two brothers, and Robert entered shortly afterward. The newspapers had just been delivered. Seeing the inefficacy of conspiracies within the land, England was now arming Europe against France. The disaster at Trafalgar had entirely overthrown one of the most tremendous schemes ever invented by human genius. The Emperor had intended, as a repayment for his election, to ruin the English power, but now the Boulogne camp was broken up. Napoleon, whose soldiers were always inferior in numbers, was about to carry war into new fields in Europe. The whole world breathlessly awaited the result of the campaign.

"Oh! this time he will surely be beaten," said Robert, laying down the journal.

"He has on his hands the whole forces of Austria and Russia," said Marie-Paul.

"He has never manœuvred in Germany," added Paul-Marie.

"Of whom are you speaking?" asked Laurence.

"Of the Emperor," replied the three gentlemen.

Laurence disdainfully glanced at her two lovers, which, while it humiliated them, gave joy to the heart of Adrien. The slighted suitor made a gesture of admiration and gave her a proud look, which spoke plainly as words that his whole thoughts were of Laurence.

" You see, love has not made her forget her hate," said the Abbé Goujet, in a low voice.

This was the first, last, and only reproach the two brothers incurred; but, at that instant, they were found inferior in love to their cousin—who had, two months after its occurrence, first learned of the grand triumph at Austerlitz by overhearing a discussion between d'Hauteserre senior and his two sons.

Faithful to his plan, the old man wished his boys to proffer their services to the Emperor; he thought that they would doubtless be reinstated in their rank with a chance of military greatness for their future.   But pure Royalism was the stronger at Cinq-Cygne.   The four gentlemen and Laurence laughed at the prudent old man, who seemed to scent coming evil. Prudence, perhaps, is less of a virtue than an exercise of intellectual *sense*, if it is allowable to couple these two words; but without doubt a day will come when physiologists and philosophers will admit that the senses are, in some sort, the sheath of a vivid and penetrating power proceeding from the mind.

After the conclusion of peace between France and Austria, toward the end of the month of Febraury, 1806, a relative, who had asked for the reinstatement of the Messrs. Simeuse, and who was later destined to give signal proofs of his attachment, the *ci-devant* Marquis de Chargebœuf, whose estates extended from Seine-et-Marne into l'Aube, arrived at Cinq-Cygne in a species of *calèche*, in that day derisively called a *berlingot*.*   When this shabby vehicle came along the narrow, paved road, the occupants of the castle, who were at break-

* A single-seated berlin.

fast, burst into a fit of laughter; but when they recognized
the bald head of the old man, which he had thrust out between
the two leather curtains of the *berlingot*. M. d'Hauteserre
named him, and every one rose to receive and do honor to the
head of the house of Chargebœuf.

"We have not done well in allowing him to come to us,"
said the Marquis de Simeuse to his brother and the d'Hauteserres; "we ought to have visited and thanked him."

A servant, in the dress of a peasant, who drove the vehicle,
planted his wagoner's whip in a cumbersome leather tube
and then went round to assist the marquis to alight; but
Adrien and the younger Simeuse prevented this: they un-
buttoned the leather apron, and, despite his protestations,
helped the old man to descend. The marquis maintained
that his yellow *berlingot* with its leather curtains was a most
excellent and commodious carriage. The servant and
Gothard, who assisted him, soon unharnessed the sturdy
horses with shiny flanks, more accustomed, without much doubt,
to dragging the plough than drawing a carriage.

"In spite of the cold? Why you are as doughty as a knight
of old!" said Laurence to her aged relative, taking his arm
and leading him into the salon.

"It is not for you to come and see an old fogy like me,"
said he, as a delicate reproach to his young relatives.

"What brings him?" asked old d'Hauteserre of himself.

M. de Chargebœuf, a handsome old man of sixty-seven,
in light-colored breeches, his frail, little legs encased in
ribbed stockings, wore powder, pigeon-wings, and a queue.
His green cloth hunting-coat, with gold buttons, was oramented
with brandebourgs, also golden. His white vest dazzled with
its enormous amount of golden embroideries. This apparel,
still the style among old people, well became his face, which
much resembled that of the great Frederick. He never put on
his three-cornered hat for fear of destroying the effect of the
crescent-moon of powder on his cranium. He supported his

right hand on a cane with a hooked handle, and held both his
cane and hat in a manner worthy of Louis XIV.

This dignified old man doffed his wadded silk pelisse and
planked down into an easy-chair, holding his three-cornered
hat and cane between his knees in an attitude which none
but the *roués* of the Court of Louis XV. have ever possessed the secret; a pose which left the hands at liberty to
make play with the snuff-box, alway a precious trinket. In
fact, the marquis drew from the pocket of his vest, which was
closed with a flap covered with gold-lace arabesques, a very
valuable snuff-box. As he fingered his own pinch and proffered
the box to those around him, accompanying the same with
charming gestures and looks of affection, he remarked the
pleasure which his visit had given. He appeared to realize
why the young *émigrés* had been remiss in their duty to him.
He had the air of saying: "When one makes love, one cannot make visits."

"We shall have you for some days, of course?" said
Laurence.

"It is quite out of the question," he replied. "If we
were not so divided by events, for you have made journeys of
greater distance than that between our houses, you would
realize, dear child, that I have daughters, daughters-in-law,
and grandchildren; all these would be uneasy if they did not
see me at my hôtel this evening; and I have over forty miles
to drive."

"Your horses—they are in good condition," said the
Marquis de Simeuse.

"Oh! I have come from Troyes, where yesterday I was on
business."

After the usual inquiries about his family, the Marquise de
Chargebœuf, and other really uninteresting matters, but in
which politeness assumes we are keenly concerned, it dawned
upon M. d'Hauteserre that M. de Chargebœuf's object was
to warn his young relatives against imprudence. The old

marquis remarked that times were much changed; no person was able to prophesy what the Emperor might become.

"Oh!" said Laurence; "he'll become God."

The good old man spoke of making concessions. When he stated with much emphasis and authority, in fact more than he put into his own doctrines, M. d'Hauteserre looked supplicatingly at his sons.

"Would you serve that man?" said the Marquis de Simeuse to the Marquis de Chargebœuf.

"Why, yes, if the interests of my family needed it."

At length the old man hinted vaguely at distant dangers. When Laurence asked an explanation, he urgently advised the four gentlemen to give up hunting and to live indoors as much as possible.

"You always look upon the Gondreville estates as being your own," said he to the Simeuses; "you thus keep alive a terrible hatred. I see by your start of surprise that you are in ignorance of the ill-will existing against you at Troyes, though your courage is not forgotten there. People speak of how you foiled the police of the Empire; some praise you, while others regard you as enemies of the Emperor. Some fanatical partisans have it that Napoleon's clemency is inexplicable. But this is nothing. You have turned the tables on people who believed themselves smarter than you, and men of such low degree never forgive. Sooner or later justice, which in your department emanates from your enemy, Senator Malin (for he has his creatures everywhere, even in the ministerial offices), his justice will be only too delighted to find you implicated in some bad scrape. A peasant quarrels with you for crossing his field; you will have your loaded guns; you are hot-headed, and evil quickly ensues. In your position people must be in the right a hundred times over if they are not to be considered in the wrong. It is not without good reason that I speak thus. The police have your arrondissement under strict surveillance; they even keep a commissary in that little hole of a place, Arcis, expressly to protect the senator of the Empire from your designs. He lives in fear of you and openly declares it."

"But this certainly slanders us!" exclaimed the younger Simeuse.

"It slanders you! I guess it does, but does the public think so? That's the question. Michu once lay for the senator, who has not by any means forgotten. Since your return the countess has taken Michu into her service. Most people, a great majority of the public, in fact, think that Malin is right. You evidently do not realize how delicate the position is when an *émigré* is brought into contact with those who possess his property. The prefect, an intelligent man, let fall a few words yesterday which caused me much uneasiness. In short, I would rather not see you remain here."

This reply was received in deep amazement. Marie-Paul rang the bell.

"Gothard," said he to the little fellow, when he entered, "go and seek Michu."

The former steward-keeper of Gondreville soon put in an appearance.

"Michu, my friend," said the Marquis de Simeuse, "is it true that you tried to kill Malin?"

"Yes, Monsieur le Marquis, and when he again comes here I shall stalk him——"

"Do you know that we are suspected of instigating this? That our cousin by taking you on as her farmer is accused of complicity in your designs?"

"Good heavens!" cried Michu, "I must be under a curse. Shall I never quietly get rid of Malin?"

"No, my boy, no," replied Paul-Marie. "But you must leave the country and our service; we will care for you and put you in the way of fortune. Sell all that you own here, realize everything; we will send you to Trieste, there we have a friend with immense business connections; you can be very useful to him until things mend here for us all."

Tears came into Michu's eyes; he was rooted to the spot on the polished floor.

"Were there any witnesses when you ambushed and aimed at Malin?" asked the Marquis de Chargebœuf.

"Grévin the notary was talking with him; that prevented my killing him, very fortunately; Mademoiselle la Comtesse knows why," said Michu, looking at his mistress.

"This Grévin is not the only one who knows?" said M. de Chargebœuf; he appeared annoyed at these questionings, although none but the family was present.

"That spy who came down at that time to trap my masters he knew also," replied Michu.

M. de Chargebœuf rose as if to look over the gardens, and said:

"Indeed, you have made the most of Cinq-Cygne, eh?" Then he went out, followed by the two brothers and Laurence, who divined the meaning of his inquiry.

"You are frank and generous, but imprudent as ever," said the old man. "I give you warning of a public rumor, *which you rightly say is a calumny*, nothing more natural; and now see what you have done! you go on to prove that it is well-founded before such weak people as Monsieur and Madame d'Hauteserre and their sons—— Oh! you young people! you young people! You ought rather to leave Michu here and go away yourselves! But, in case you desire to stay here, write a letter and send it to the senator about Michu, telling him that you have become aware of the rumor concerning him and that he is dismissed your employ."

"We!" exclaimed the two brothers; "write Malin, the assassin of our father and mother, the impudent plunderer of our property!"

"All very true: but he is one of the greatest personages of the imperial Court, and the king of l'Aube."

12   V

"He who cast his vote for the death of Louis XV., in case the army of Condé entered France, and otherwise for perpetual imprisonment ! " said the Countess de Cinq-Cygne.

"He who probably advised the death of the Duc d'Enghien ! " cried Paul-Marie.

"Eh, well ! if you wish to recapitulate his titles of nobility," exclaimed the marquis, "give him that, also, of having pulled Robespierre by the tails of his coat when he saw that his enemies were more powerful than he ; he, who would have shot Bonaparte if the 18th Brumaire had failed of its purpose ; he, who is always found on the strongest side, with the pistol or sword ever ready to rid himself of any adversary inspiring his fear ! But so much the more reason ! "

"We have fallen very low ! " said Laurence.

"Children," said the old Marquis de Chargebœuf, taking all three by the hand and leading them toward the lawn, then lightly covered with a sprinkling of snow; "you will fly off in anger when you hear the advice of a wise man, but I must do it ; here is what I should do :

"I would take as a mediator some old gentleman—like myself, say—I would commission him to ask Malin a million francs for a ratification of the sale of Gondreville. Oh ! he would readily consent if the thing were kept secret. You would then have, as Funds now stand, one hundred thousand livres of income ; you could thus purchase some other fine estate in another part of France ; Cinq-Cygne you could leave safely in the hands of Monsieur d'Hauteserre, and you can draw straws to decide which of the two shall become the husband of this beautiful heiress. But the talk of an old man is, in the ears of young folk, like the speech of the young to the ears of the old—sound without sense."

The old marquis signified by a gesture that he wished no reply ; he returned to the salon whither, during their conversation, the Abbé Goujet and his sister had arrived.

The proposition of drawing straws for the hand of their

cousin had aroused indignation in the Simeuses; while Laurence was, so to speak, revolted at the unpleasant remedy advised by her relative. The three became less gracious than before to the old man, but without ceasing to be duly courteous. Their affection was chilled. M. de Chargebœuf, who experienced this chill, cast frequent looks full of kindly compassion on these three charming people. The conversation became general; he dwelt on the necessity of submitting to events; further, he lauded M. de Hauteserre for his persistence in wishing his sons to enter the service.

"Bonaparte," said he, "makes dukes. He has created fiefs of the Empire; he will make counts. Malin wishes to become Comte de Gondreville. That is an idea which, perhaps," added he, looking at the Simeuses, "might be utilized to your benefit."

"Or made disastrous," said Laurence.

When the horses had been put in, the marquis went out, accompanied by the whole company. After he found himself in the vehicle, he made a sign to Laurence to come; she sprang upon the carriage-step with the lightness of a bird.

"You are not an ordinary woman; you ought to understand me," he whispered. "Malin's conscience is too uneasy for him to leave you in peace; he will set some snare to catch you. At least be careful of all your actions, even your slightest. In short, negotiate; that is my last word."

The two brothers stood passively by their cousin in the middle of the lawn, motionless and mute, watching the *berlingot* as it turned through the iron gates and took the road to Troyes; for Laurence had repeated the last word of the old gentleman to them. Experience always makes an error when it comes in a *berlingot*, wearing striped stockings, and with a queue on the nape of the neck. None of these young hearts had the least conception of the changes then taking place in France. Every nerve quivered with indignation, honor, like their noble blood, was boiling in their veins.

"And he is the head of the house of Chargebœuf!" said the Marquis de Simeuse; "a man who bears for a device: VIENNE UN PLUS FORT! (*Adsit fortior!*) one of the greatest of war-cries."

"There is only the *bœuf** left," said Laurence, with a bitter smile.

"We are no longer in the days of Saint-Louis!" said the younger Simeuse.

"MOURIR EN CHANTANT—we die singing," exclaimed the countess. "The cry of the five young girls who founded our house shall be mine!"

"And ours is: CY MEURS! Therefore no surrender," replied the elder Simeuse; "for on reflection we shall find that our relative the ox had ruminated sagely upon what he came to tell us. Gondreville to become the name of a Malin!"

"And his residence!" cried the younger.

"Mansard designed it for nobles, and the people would raise their broods therein!" said the eldest.

"If it should so happen, I would rather see Gondreville burned," exclaimed Mlle. de Cinq-Cygne.

A man from the village, who had come to look at a calf that old d'Hauteserre wished to sell, overheard these words as he came out of a cow-shed.

"Let us return to the salon," said Laurence, smiling. "We have nearly committed an imprudence and given reason for the prophecy of the Ox about a calf. My poor Michu," she went on, as they entered the salon, "I had forgotten your adventure, but we are not in the odor of sanctity in the countryside, so you must not compromise us. Have you any other peccadillos with which to reproach yourself?"

"I reproach myself for not having killed the assassin of my old masters before hurrying to the rescue of my present ones."

"Michu!" cried the curé.

* Ox.

"But I won't leave the country," said he, continuing, without heeding the curé's exclamation, "till I know that you are in safety. I see fellows prowling around here that I don't like the looks of. The last time we hunted in the forest that imitation keeper, who took my place at Gondreville, came up to me and asked if we thought ourselves at home there. 'Ah! my boy,' said I, 'it is no easy matter to break yourself of a habit in two months that has been practiced for two hundred years.'"

"That was wrong, Michu," said the Marquis de Simeuse, smiling with pleasure.

"What answer did he make?" asked M. d'Hauteserre.

"He just said," replied Michu, "that he would acquaint the senator with our pretensions."

"Comte de Gondreville!" cried the elder d'Hauteserre. "Ah! a fine farce! You know, though, they say *your majesty* to Bonaparte."

"And *your highness* to my lord the grand-duke of Berg," said the curé.

"Who may he be?" asked M. de Simeuse.

"Murat, Napoleon's brother-in-law," answered old d'Hauteserre.

"Good!" commented Mlle. de Cinq-Cygne. "And do they say *your majesty* to the widow of the Marquis Beauharnais?"

"Yes, mademoiselle," replied the curé.

"We ought to visit Paris and see all this!" cried Laurence.

"Alas! mademoiselle," said Michu, "I went there to put my son to school, and I swear to you that there's no nonsense about what they call the Imperial Guard. If all the army is modeled after that, it may outlast our time and longer."

"They speak of noble families that are entering the service," said M. d'Hauteserre.

"And as the law now stands your children will be compelled to serve," the curé replied. "The law recognizes neither rank nor name."

"This man is doing us greater harm with his Court than the Revolution did with its axe!" cried Laurence.

"The church prays for him," said the curé.

These remarks, made quickly one after the other, were so many commentaries on the wise counsel of the old Marquis de Chargebœuf; but these young folk had too much faith, were too honorable to accept a compromise. They told themselves, as every defeated party has done in every age, that there would come an end to the prosperity of their conquerors; that the Emperor had only the support of the army; that the power of might must sooner or later give way before right, and so on. So, despite the wise counsel, they fell into the pit that was digged before them, while more prudent and docile folk, like the goodman d'Hauteserre, might have avoided it. If people were only frank they might perhaps admit that misfortunes never come upon them without their giving an actual or occult warning. Many only perceive the deep significance of this mysterious signal until after the calamity is upon them.

"In any case, Mademoiselle la Comtesse knows that I cannot leave the country until I have put in my accounts," said Michu to Mademoiselle de Cinq-Cygne, in a low and meaning voice.

For all answer she gave a sign of intelligence to her farmer, who went out. Michu very soon sold his lands to Beauvisage, the farmer of Bellache, but he could not be paid under fifteen days. A month after the visit of the marquis, Laurence, who had told her two cousins of the existence of their fortune, proposed that in the Mid-Lent feast they should unearth the million buried in the forest. The heavy fall of snow had prevented this being done before, but Michu was none the less pleased that this operation of recovering the treasure should take place in his masters' presence. He had quite made up his mind to leave that part of the country, he was afraid of himself.

" Malin has arrived quite suddenly at Gondreville, but no one knows why," said he to his mistress; "and I cannot control myself at the thought of Gondreville being offered for sale in consequence of the decease of the owner. I seem to think myself a guilty man as I do not act on the inspiration."

" Whatever reason can he have for leaving Paris in the middle of winter?"

" All Arcis is talking about it," replied Michu; "he has left his family in Paris, being only accompanied by his valet. Monsieur Grévin, the Arcis notary, Madame Marion, the wife of the receiver-general and sister-in-law of the other Marion, who swears by the name of Malin, are keeping him company in the château."

Laurence believed Mid-Lent would be a good day, for it gave the opportunity of getting the servants out of the way.

The masqueraders would attract the peasants to the town; and nobody would be at work in the fields. But the choice of this day was just the cause of its bad-luck, as often occurs in criminal matters. Chance had calculated as ingeniously as had Mlle. de Cinq-Cygne and more to the purpose. The uneasiness of M. and Mme. d'Hauteserre, which would be increased if they knew that eleven hundred thousand francs was buried in the park situated on the outskirts of the forest, caused the young d'Hauteserres, after holding a council, to withhold this knowledge from them.

The secret of the expedition was restricted to Gothard, Michu, the four gentlemen, and Laurence. After careful calculations it seemed possible that each horse could carry forty-eight thousand in a long bag over the crupper. Three trips would be enough. For the sake of prudence they sent off all the people, whose inquisitiveness might prove dangerous, to Troyes to join in the Mid-Lent rejoicings. Catherine, Marthe, and Durieu, who might be relied upon, were left to guard the castle. The servants gladly embraced the holiday that had been given them and were off before daybreak. Gothard, assisted by Michu, rubbed down the horses and saddled them early in the morning. The caravan went by way of the gardens, and from thence masters and servants gained the forest. At the moment they were mounting their horses, for the park gate was so low that each one had gone through the park on foot leading the horses after them, old Beauvisage, the Bellache farmer, came by.

"Halloo!" cried Gothard, "here's somebody coming, what——"

"Oh! it is only me," said the honest tenant, coming out upon them. "I salute you, gentlemen. You are going hunting in spite of the prefect's instructions, eh? I am not one to blab, but lookout for yourselves. If you have friends, you have also a number of enemies."

"Oh!" answered the burly d'Hauteserre, with a smile, "God send success to our hunting, and you will soon find your masters back again."

This speech, on which events were to put a very different sense, caused Laurence to look severely at Robert. The elder de Simeuse imagined that Malin would make restitution of the Gondreville estates, if indemnified. These children were of the contrary opinion to that of the Marquis de Chargeboeuf. Robert, sharing these hopes, had them in his thoughts when he spoke these fatal words.

"In any case *mum* is the word, my old boy," said Michu, who was the last out, as he took the key out of the gate.

It was one of those fine days about the end of March, when the air is crisp and dry, the ground is hard, the temperature pleasant, the warmth seemingly at variance with the leafless trees, and the weather is cloudless. So mild was the weather that here and there they could see patches of green in the countryside.

"We go to search for treasure, and all the time you are the

real treasure of our house, cousin," laughed the eldest de Simeuse.

Laurence rode slowly in front, her two cousins being on either side of her horse. The two d'Hauteserres came next, followed in turn by Michu. Gothard went on in front to see that the road was clear.

"Since our fortune is recovered, in part at least, marry my brother," said the younger, in a low voice. "He adores you; you would be quite as wealthy as most of the nobles of to-day."

"No. Leave all the fortune to him, and I will marry you, since I am rich enough for two," she replied.

"So be it, then," said the Marquis de Simeuse. "As for myself, I will leave you to search for a wife worthy of being your sister."

"Then you love me less than I thought?" asked Laurence, looking at him with a jealous expression.

"No; I love both of you more than you love me," retorted the marquis.

"So you would sacrifice yourself for us?" asked Laurence of the eldest de Simeuse, with her eyes filled with a glance of momentary preference.

The marquis was silent.

"Well, as for me, I should always be thinking of you, and my husband would find that insupportable," replied Laurence, his silence drawing a gesture of impatience from her.

"How could I live without you?" cried the younger, looking at his brother.

"Nevertheless, you cannot marry both of us," said the marquis. "And," he added, with the brusque tone of a man whose heart is touched, "it is time you made your decision."

He pushed his horse forward so that the two d'Hauteserres might not hear. Laurence's and his brother's horse followed this movement. When they had placed a reasonable distance between themselves and the other three, Laurence made an effort to speak, but tears were her only response.

"I will enter a convent," she said at last.

"And be the last of the Cinq-Cygnes?" asked the younger Simeuse; "and so, instead of leaving one unhappy man who would be content in his lot, you would leave two. No; the one who can only be your brother will resign himself to his fate. When we learned that we were not so poor as we thought ourselves, we had an explanation," said he, looking at the marquis. "If I am preferred, all our fortune goes to my brother. If I am the unfortunate one, he will make the fortune over to me, in addition to the title, for he will become Comte de Cinq-Cygne. In any case the unlucky one will have a chance of an establishment. Finally, if he feels heartbroken, he will enter the army, there to be killed, so that he may cast no shadow on the other's household."

"We are true knights of the Middle Ages, we are worthy of our ancestors!" cried the elder. "Speak, Laurence."

"We cannot continue longer like this," said the younger de Simeuse.

"Think not, Laurence, that there is no luxury in this sacrifice," said the eldest.

"My dearly beloved," said she, "I am incapable of making a decision. I love you both, as if you were only one; the same as you loved your mother. God will help us. I cannot choose. We will leave it to chance to decide, I make but one condition."

"What?"

"That the one who is to be my brother for the future shall not go away until I give him permission. I wish to be the sole judge of the expediency of his going."

"Yes," said both brothers, without having any idea of what was in the mind of their cousin.

"The one of you to whom Madame d'Hauteserre addresses the first word this evening at table, after the blessing, shall be my husband. But each of you must abstain from trickery; neither must prompt her to question him."

"We shall play fairly," said the younger.

Both the brothers kissed Laurence's hand. The certainty of the ending being favorable to himself made the spirits of both eminently joyous.

"In any case, dearest Laurence, you will make a de Cinq-Cygne," said the eldest.

"And in our game the one who wins loses his name," said the younger.

"I think, by the look of things," said Michu, behind the two d'Hauteserres, "that mademoiselle will become madame before long. My masters are very jolly. If my mistress makes her choice I shall not go; I shall want to see that wedding."

Neither of the d'Hauteserres replied. A magpie suddenly alighted between the d'Hauteserres and Michu, who, superstitious like all primitive people, thought he could hear the bell tolling for his funeral. The day began gayly for the three lovers, who when going through the woods together seldom see magpies.

Michu, provided with his map, soon found the spot; each of the gentlemen carried a pickaxe; the money was gotten out. That part of the forest in which the hiding-place was, a lonely spot far from any house or path, was entirely deserted, so the cavalcade, laden with gold, met no one. This was unfortunate. Going from Cinq-Cygne to fetch the last two hundred thousand francs the caravan, emboldened by success, took a short cut instead of following their former trail. This path went over the highest point of the forest, whence they could see the park at Gondreville.

"A fire!" said Laurence, seeing a column of bluish smoke.

"It is some bonfire," replied Michu.

Laurence, who knew every forest track, left the cavalcade and cantered to the Cinq-Cygne pavilion, Michu's old residence.   The lodge was empty and closed, but the iron gate was open, and the tracks of a number of horses struck Laurence's eyes.   The column of smoke rose from a lawn in the English park, and she supposed they must be burning weeds.

"Ah! so you are in it, too, mademoiselle," exclaimed Violette, who had come at a gallop from the park on his pony, pulling up when he saw Laurence.   "But it is only a carnival farce, is it?   They won't kill him, will they?"

"Whom?"

"Your cousins; they don't wish to kill him?"

"Kill whom?"

"The senator."

"You are an idiot, Violette."

"Well, what are you doing here, then?" he asked.

At this suggested idea of danger menacing her cousins, the intrepid rider dashed off at full speed, and reached them just as the bags were filled.

"Quick!   Something is the matter.   What, I don't know; but let us hurry back to Cinq-Cygne."

While the gentlemen had been busy carrying off the fortune saved by the old marquis, a strange scene had occurred at the Château de Gondreville.

At two o'clock that afternoon, the senator and his friend Grévin were playing a game of chess before the fire in the great drawing-room on the first floor.   Mme. Grévin and Mme. Marion sat chatting in the chimney-corner, seated on a couch.   All the servants of the castle had gone to see a curious masquerade, long advertised, in the Arcis arrondissement.   The family of the keeper who had replaced Michu in the lodge at Cinq-Cygne had also gone.   The senator's valet and Violette were all that remained at the castle.   The gatekeeper, two gardeners and their wives were at their posts; but the lodge was at the entrance to the drive at the farther end of the Arcis avenue, and at the distance which existed between the *rond-point* and the castle it would have been impossible to hear the report of a gun.

Moreover, all the folk were at the door looking in the direction of Arcis, whence the mummers were expected to come, and which was over a mile away. Violette was sitting in the great entrance-hall, waiting for an interview with the senator and Grévin about a renewal of his lease. At this moment five men, masked and gloved, four of whom were of the height and general appearance of the d'Hauteserres and the de Simeuses, while the other resembled Michu, burst in upon Violette and the valet, gagged them with pocket-hand-kerchiefs, and tied them down to two chairs in the butler's pantry. Despite the celerity of the aggressors this was not done without the crying out of the two victims. These cries were heard in the salon. The two women said they knew it was a cry of terror.

" Listen ! " said Mme. Grévin, " there are thieves——"

" Pshaw ! it is a Mid-Lent yell," said Grévin; " the mummers are coming up to the castle."

This discussion gave the five strangers time to shut the gates of the great courtyard and to lock up the valet and Violette. Mme. Grévin, a woman with a will of her own, would go out to learn the cause of the noise. She ran across the five masks, and met the same fate as the valet and Violette. Then they burst into the salon where the two most powerful of them tackled the Comte de Gondreville, gagged and bound him, and hurried with him into the park; meanwhile the other three had served out the like treatment to Mme. Marion and the notary, each of these being securely fastened to their chairs. The whole affair did not take more than a half-hour.

The three unknown men were soon rejoined by those who had carried off the senator; the whole of them then began a thorough search through the castle from cellar to garret. They opened every closet door without picking a single lock; they sounded the walls; and, in short, the whole place was in

their hands until five in the evening. At that time the valet
had gnawed with his teeth through the cords that bound
Violette's hands. Violette then ungagged himself and shouted
for help. Hearing his cries the five masks made off across
the gardens, mounting horses like those ridden by the Cinq-
Cygnes, and escaped. After he had unbound the valet, who
in turn released the women and the notary, Violette bestrode
his pony and rode after the miscreants. He was astounded,
when he reached the pavilion, to see the gate thrown open
and Mlle. de Cinq-Cygne acting as sentinel.

When the young countess had disappeared, Violette was
joined by Grévin on horseback, accompanied by the policeman
of the commune of Gondreville, the gate-keeper having given
him a horse from the castle stables. The gate-keeper's wife
had gone to Arcis to alarm the gendarmes there. Violette at
once informed Grévin of his meeting with Laurence and the
flight of that daring young woman, whose depth, decision,
and fearlessness they well knew.

"She was the lookout," said Violette.

"Is it possible that the Cinq-Cygne nobles can have made
this attack?" exclaimed Grévin.

"What!" replied Violette. "Did you not recognize the
burly Michu? It was he that sprang upon me. I felt his fist
in good style. Moreover, the five horses belong to Cinq-
Cygne."

Looking at the tracks of the horses' shoes on the sand of the
road, the notary left the policeman at the gate to watch over
the precious imprints, sending Violette to bring the justice of
the peace from Arcis to verify them. Then he hurried back
to the castle and entered the drawing-room, where he found
that the lieutenant and sub-lieutenant of the imperial gendarmerie had arrived, together with four men and a corporal.

This lieutenant, as might be anticipated, was the corporal
who two years ago had had a hole made in his head by François, and to whom Corentin had made known the name of

his malicious adversary. This man, named Giguet,* whose brother was in the army and who became one of the leading colonels of artillery, rose by merit to the rank of an officer in the gendarmerie, subsequently commanding the Aube cavalry.

The sub-lieutenant, named Welff, had once driven Corentin from Cinq-Cygne to the pavilion, and from thence to Troyes. On the way the Parisian was edified by this Egyptian soldier on the "carryings on" and "dodges" of Laurence and Michu. These two officers naturally entered with great enthusiasm in anything against the residents of Cinq-Cygne.

Malin and Grévin had both worked together on the Code of Brumaire of the year IV., the judicial work of the so-called National Convention, and promulgated by the Directory. So Grévin, who knew to the bottom of this piece of legislation, was enabled to work this affair with terrible celerity, as the presumption, amounting almost to certainty, showed the criminality of Michu, the d'Hautescrres, and the de Simeuses. People of to-day, save perhaps some old magistrate. cannot realize the judicial organization overturned by Napoleon about this very time by the promulgation of his Code and by the institution of the magistracy now obtaining in France.

The Code of Brumaire of the year IV. reserved the conducting of the prosecution of the misdemeanor committed at Gondreville entirely to the director of the jury of the department. It may be remarked, by the way, that the Convention had stricken the word "crime" out of the judicial phraseology. It admitted nothing but misdemeanors—misdemeanors against the law, misdemeanors which were punishable by fine, imprisonment, or disgrace. Death was the last or "corporal" punishment. This latter was, however, destined after the Peace to be commuted to twenty-four years of hard labor. So the Convention estimated that twenty-four years of hard

* See "The Deputy for Arcis."

labor was equal to death, what then must be said of the penal Code which inflicts a punishment of hard labor in perpetuity?

The codification of the laws then being prepared by Napoleon's council of State suppressed the magistracy and the directory of juries, because of the enormous power it placed in their hands. In reference to the conduct of the prosecution and the drawing up of the indictment, a director of the jury was in some sort at this time an agent of the judicial police, the public prosecutor, the examining judge, and the court of appeal in one. Only his procedure and indictment were submitted to the commissary of the executive power and to the verdict of a jury of eight, to whom were submitted all the facts in the case; these heard the accused and the witnesses and finally brought in a preliminary verdict, called the "accusation."

The director was able to bring his influence to bear upon the jury, for they met in his private office, so that in a sense they were almost compelled to work in coöperation with and not against him. These, then, were the juries of accusation. The other juries which formed the "trial" juries were composed of entirely new names and passed on the evidence brought before the court.

The criminal tribunal, to which Napoleon gave the name of criminal court, was composed of a president, four judges, a public accuser, and a government commissary. Nevertheless, from 1709 to 1806 there still existed special courts, so-called, empowered to try without a jury, in certain departments and sundry cases, and which consisted of judges from the civil tribunal.

This conflict of special and criminal justice courts raised questions as to competence, which were passed upon by the tribunal of "cassation." If the department of the Aube had had a special court, a case touching an attempt on the life of a senator of the Empire would undoubtedly have been brought before it; but in that quiet department no provision was made for special cases. Grévin, therefore, sent off the sub-lieutenant to the director of juries at Troyes. The Egyptian soldier rode with a loose rein from Gondreville and returned with that all but sovereign functionary.

The director of the jury at Troyes had formerly been a lieutenant of the bailiwick, and had been appointed a salaried clerk to a committee of the Convention; he was a friend of Malin's, and had secured this position through his influence. This magistrate, named Lechesneau, was an old practitioner in the criminal law; he, as well as Grévin, had been of much use to Malin in his judicial reforms in the Convention. So Malin had recommended him to Cambacérès, who had appointed him receiver-general of taxes in Italy. Unluckily for his prospects, Lechesneau became entangled in an intrigue with a great lady at Turin, and Napoleon was compelled to cashier the official as a prosecution was threatened by the husband on account of the abduction of a child born in adultery. Lechesneau, who owed his all to Malin, guessing the importance of the attempt, had ridden over with a captain and a picket of twelve gendarmes.

Before he started he had naturally requested an interview with the prefect; night was falling, so the semaphore was not available. He dispatched a messenger to Paris to report such an unheard-of crime to the minister of police and the Emperor. Lechesneau found Mesdames Marion and Grévin, Violette, the valet, the justice of the peace and his clerk assembled in the salon when he entered. The castle had already been searched. The justice of the peace, assisted by Grévin, was carefully collating the evidence. The magistrate was struck with the deep scheme that was revealed in the choosing of the day and hour for the attempt. The time was now too late to seek for circumstantial evidence. At this season, at half-past five o'clock, the time when Violette was first able to start in pursuit of the miscreants, it is almost dark; and, for delinquents, darkness often means impunity

13

for much. To choose a day of rejoicing when everybody
would be sure to go to Arcis to see the masquerade, and the
senator was equally sure to be found at home—did not this
insure that there would be no witnesses?

"Let us render justice to the perspicacity of the agents of
the prefecture of police," said Lechesneau. "They have con-
tinually cautioned us to be on the lookout against the nobles
of Cinq-Cygne; they told us that sooner or later they would
be up to some mischief."

Following the activity of the prefect of the Aube, who
sent messengers to all the prefectures in the neighborhood of
Troyes to search for traces of the five masked men and the
senator, Lechesneau began to lay the basis of his legal inquiry.

This work went rapidly along, with two such leading practi-
tioners as Grévin and the justice of the peace. The latter,
named Pigoult, had once been the head clerk in the attorney's
office where Malin and Grévin had first studied chicanery at
Paris; he was, three months afterward, named as president of
the tribunal at Arcis.

As regarded Michu, Lechesneau knew that he had previously
threatened Marion, and he also knew about the senator's escape
in the park that time. These two facts, one a consequence
of the other, were to be the premise of the first counts in the
indictment; they pointed to the ex-steward as the ringleader
of the malefactors, the more so as Grévin, his wife, Violette,
and Mme. Marion declared that one of the five masked
persons bore an unmistakable resemblance to Michu. The
color of his hair, his whiskers, and stout build made a disguise little less than useless. Whom other than Michu, in
addition, could have opened the gate of Cinq-Cygne with a
key?

The keeper and his wife, who were questioned on their return
from Arcis, deposed that they had locked both the gates
before leaving. The gates showed, when they were examined

by the justice of the peace, his clerk, and the country policeman, that there was no sign of a forcible entrance.

"When we dismissed him, he must have kept the duplicate
keys of the castle," said Grevin. "He must, also, have
been meditating some desperate deed, for he sold his land,
the purchase to be completed within twenty days; the money
was paid over in my office the day before yesterday."

"They have arranged so as to throw all the blame on him,"
exclaimed Lechesneau, struck by this circumstance. "He
takes their evil-doing upon himself."

Who could know their way about the castle better than the
de Simeuses and d'Hauteserres? Each of the assailants had
acted without making a mistake in their search; they had
gone about it in a manner which showed that they knew just
what they wanted, and where to look for it.

Every closet that had been left open showed that the locks
had not been forced; therefore the miscreants must have
possessed keys; and, stranger still, they had not created the
least disorder. It was no question of stealing. Finally,
Violette, after recognizing the horses as belonging to the
castle of Cinq-Cygne, had found the countess on the lookout
before the gate-keeper's pavilion. All taken in connection,
these facts with the depositions, afforded the strongest pre-
sumptions of guilt against the de Simeuses, the d'Hauteserres,
and Michu, before even unprejudiced justice; this degenerated
into certainty in the mind of the director of the jury. Now,
what did they want with the future Comte de Gondreville?
To force him to relinquish his estate; for the keeper-steward
had said, even prior to 1799, that he was ready with the
capital to acquire it? The whole aspect was at once changed.

The well-versed criminal detecter asked what the object of
that diligent search through the castle was. It could not have
been revenge, for the miscreants could easily have killed
Malin. Perhaps, though, the senator was already dead and
buried. Yet, if kidnapped, he was kept under restraint. Why

this sequestration after searching the castle through? Certainly, it was folly to think that the kidnapping of a dignitary of the Empire could long remain a secret. The news would spread so rapidly that any benefit to be gained by secrecy would soon be at an end.

To these objections Pigoult replied that justice could not always guess the motives of scoundrels. In all the private examinations of criminals there were depths that were never sounded between the examining judge and the criminal, obscurities into which no human power could throw a light except by the confession of the guilty one.

Grévin and Lechesneau gave assent to this by a nod, without ceasing, however, to try with all their eyes to penetrate the gloom surrounding the case.

"The Emperor had given them his pardon, too," said Pigoult to Grévin and Mme. Marion; "he struck their names off the proscribed list, though they were concerned in the last conspiracy against him."

Lechesneau, without further delay, hurried off his gendarmes to the forest and the valley of Cinq-Cygne, the justice of the peace going with Giguet, who became by the ruling of the Code his auxiliary officer of judicial police; the justice was instructed to gather evidence for the prosecution in the commune of Cinq-Cygne, and to proceed, if necessary, to make all preliminary inquiries; and, to save time, he rapidly dictated and signed the warrant for Michu's arrest in case the evidence bore out the suspicions against him.

After the departure of the gendarmes and the justice of the peace, Lechesneau went back to the important work of getting out warrants against the de Simeuses and d'Hauteserres, the Code requiring that every charge against a criminal shall be enumerated in each warrant.

Giguet and the justice of the peace came down upon Cinq-Cygne so quickly that they met the servants of the castle as they were returning from Troyes; they were arrested and taken to the mayor's office, where they were questioned. Each of them, being quite ignorant of the importance of their replies, answered in all simplicity that permission had been given them to spend the whole day at Troyes. In answer to the justice of the peace each made the same answer, that mademoiselle had offered them the holiday and that it had not been asked for.

These depositions seemed so serious to the justice of the peace that he sent the Egyptian soldier to Gondreville to beg Lechesneau come and be present himself when the gentlemen at Cinq-Cygne were arrested, while he would at the same time go to the farmhouse of Michu to apprehend the supposed ringleader. These new elements appeared so decisive that Lechesneau set out at once for Cinq-Cygne, giving instructions to Grévin to have a careful watch kept over the imprints of the hoofs of the horses in the park.

The director of the jury knew what satisfaction would be caused at Troyes by his proceedings against the old nobles, the enemies of the people, now become the enemies of the Emperor. In the like circumstances to these, a magistrate most readily takes presumptive evidence for full proof. But still, as he went from Gondreville to Cinq-Cygne in the senator's own carriage, Lechesneau, who for a fact was a good magistrate otherwise than for the passion which had led to his disgrace (owing to the Emperor having become prudish), could not reconcile the audacity of the young people and Michu, which was most foolish and little in harmony with what should be expected of Mlle. de Cinq-Cygne. For himself, he thought that there was something more in the abduction of the senator than the desire to extort a relinquishment of Gondreville.

In every profession, even in the magistracy, there exists what may be termed the professional conscience. Lechesneau's perplexities were the result of that state of mind with which a man sets about doing any work that is pleasant to him, that the savant finds in science, the artist in art, the judge in law. So, perhaps, for this particular reason the accused is safer with a judge than with a jury. The judge suspects everything but reasoning, while a jury is apt to be carried away by sentiment. The director of the jury posed himself with numerous questions; he proposed to come to a satisfactory solution of them by the arrest of these malefactors.

Although the news of Malin's abduction had already reached Troyes, Arcis remained in ignorance of the news until eight o'clock; for everybody was at supper when the gendarmes and the justice of the peace had been sent for; as for the people at Cinq-Cygne, not one, either in the valley or at the castle, had any idea that for a second time was the latter surrounded with gendarmes; but this time it was not for a political reason, but on criminal counts; a compromise possible in the one is impossible in the other.

Laurence had told Marthe, Catherine, and la Durieu to stay in the castle, neither to go out nor to look out of the windows, and this order had been strictly observed by them all. At each trip the horses had been stationed in the hidden way, opposite the breach in the moat, and from thence Robert and Michu, the strongest of the troop, had secretly carried the bags through the breach and into the cellar under the stairs in the tower called Mademoiselle's Tower.

Arriving at the castle at about half-past five, the four gentlemen and Michu had at once buried the gold. Laurence and the d'Hauteserres thought it would be advisable to wall up the cellar entrance. Michu was charged with this work, in which Gothard assisted him; the latter went to the farmhouse for some cement left after the building of the place, and Marthe went home to secretly pass the bags out to Gothard.

The farmhouse built by Michu was on the same knoll whence he had seen the gendarmes, and the way to it lay along the sunken path. Michu, nearly famished, did his work so speedily that toward half-past seven he had finished his labor. He hurried out to meet Gothard to prevent him bringing a last sack of cement, finding that he should not need any more. His house was already encircled by the justice of the peace, his clerk, and the gendarmes, who heard his footsteps and hid themselves until he had gone inside.

Michu met Gothard, a sack on his shoulder, and shouted to him:

"It is finished, my boy; return that and come and dine with us."

Michu, his brow bathed in perspiration, his clothes soiled with the cement and dirt from the stones taken from the debris of the breach, went in high spirits into the kitchen of his house, where Marthe and her mother had served the soup and were awaiting him.

At the moment that Michu turned the cock of the fountain to wash his hands, the justice of the peace made his appearance, accompanied by his clerk and the policeman.

"What do you want with us, Monsieur Pigoult?" asked Michu.

"In the name of the Emperor and the law I arrest you," said the justice of the peace.

The three gendarmes then came in, bringing Gothard with them.

Seeing the metal rims of the hats, Marthe and her mother exchanged looks of terror.

"Ah, bah! And why?" asked Michu, seating himself at the table and saying to his wife: "Serve me at once; I am starving."

"You know as well as we do," said the justice of the peace, signing to his clerk to begin on the report, and after exhibiting the warrant of arrest to the farmer.

"Well, you look astonished, Gothard. Don't you want your dinner—yes or no?" said Michu. "Let them scribble their rubbish."

"Do you know in what a state your clothes are?" asked

the justice of the peace. "You can no more deny that than you can deny the words you said to Gothard in the court-yard."

Michu was served by his wife, who was astonished at his coolness; he ate with voracity and answered no questions on any point; he had a full mouth and an innocent heart. A terrible dread had taken away Gothard's appetite.

"See," said the country policeman, whispering to Michu, " what have you done with the senator? They say that it is a matter of life or death for you, these justice people."

"Ah! my God!" cried Marthe; she had detected the last words, and fell as if thunder-struck.

"Violette has played us some villainous turn," cried Michu, remembering Laurence's words.

"Oh! you know then that Violette saw you?" said the justice of the peace.

Michu bit his lips and resolved on saying nothing again. Gothard imitated his reserve. Seeing the uselessness of en-deavoring to make him speak and knowing Michu's perversity, which the whole country was aware of, the justice of the peace ordered his and Gothard's hands to be tied by his men and to bring them to the castle of Cinq-Cygne; thence he went to join the director of the jury.

The gentlemen and Laurence had such keen appetites, and the dinner was an object of such intense interest, that none of them changed their dress. They went into the salon, she in her riding-habit, they in their white skin breeches and green jackets and riding-boots, and there found M. and Mme. d'Hauteserre, who were both very uneasy, for the goodman had seen their goings and comings, to say nothing of the distrust it implied in him, for Laurence could not give orders to him as she had to the servants. So, when one of his sons had avoided making a direct answer to his questions and sought refuge in flight, he said to his wife:

"I fear that Laurence has been doing it again."

"What kind of game have you been hunting to-day?" asked Mme. d'Hauteserre of Laurence.

"Ah! you shall some day know all the mischief that your children have participated in," answered Laurence, laughing.

Although spoken jestingly, these words made the old lady shiver. Catherine announced dinner. Laurence gave her arm to M. d'Hauteserre, smiling as she thought of the trick she had played her cousins, for one of the two was bound to offer his arm to the old lady, transformed into their oracle by their understanding.

The Marquis de Simeuse conducted Mme. d'Hauteserre to table. The situation grew so solemn that, the blessing said, Laurence and her two cousins could feel the violent palpitation of their hearts. Mme. d'Hauteserre, who helped them, was struck with the anxiety depicted on the faces of the two Simeuses, and the change presented in the sheep-like countenance of Laurence.

"Something extraordinary has taken place," she exclaimed, looking at them.

"To whom are you speaking?" said Laurence.

"To all of you," replied the old lady.

"As for me, mother," said Robert, "I am as hungry as a wolf."

Mme. d'Hauteserre, still troubled, offered to the Marquis de Simeuse a plate which was intended for the younger of the brothers.

"I am like your mother; I am always making mistakes, in spite of your cravats. I thought I was serving your brother," said she to him.

"You have helped him better than you think," said the younger, turning pale. "That is the Comte de Cinq-Cygne."

This poor boy, so gay, became sad forever; but he found strength enough to force a smile as he looked at Laurence, and repressed his mortal regrets. In an instant the lover was sunk in the brother.

"What! the countess has made her choice?" exclaimed the old lady.

"No," said Laurence; "we left it to chance, and you were its instrument."

She told of the stipulations agreed to that morning. The eldest Simeuse, who saw the pallid face of his brother, felt each moment like crying out: "Marry her; for myself, I will go out and die."

At the moment that dessert was served, the occupants of Cinq-Cygne heard a tapping on the window of the dining-room, on the side of the garden. The eldest d'Hauteserre opened it and gave admittance to the curé, whose breeches had been torn by the trellis as he scaled the park-wall.

"Fly—they are coming to arrest you."

"Why?"

"I do not know yet, but they are proceeding against you."

These words caused a universal burst of laughter.

"We are innocent," cried the gentlemen.

"Innocent or guilty," said the curé, "mount your horses and make for the frontier. There you may be able to prove your innocence. You may recover from a charge of contempt, but there is no getting over a charge arising from popular clamor; you are prejudged from the start. Do you remember the words of President de Harlay: 'If I were accused of carrying off the towers of Notre-Dame, I should run away at once.'"

"But to run away is an avowal of guilt, is it not?" said the Marquis de Simeuse.

"Do not run away," said Laurence.

"Always sublime in silliness," said the curé in despair. "If I had the power of God I would carry you away. But if they find me here, in this state, they will turn the singularity of

my visit against both you and myself; I must escape by the
way I came. You have yet time. The people of the law
have forgotten the wall of the parsonage grounds; on every
other side you are surrounded."

The trampling of feet and the ringing noise of the gendarmes'
sabres as they filed into the courtyard were heard almost before
the poor curé had departed. He had had no more success
with his advice than had the Marquis de Chargebœuf in his
case.

"Our communal existence," the younger Simeuse said to
Laurence, in a melancholy voice, "was a monstrosity, and
our love has also proven a monstrosity. This abnormal thing
has gained your affections. Perhaps it is because natural laws
are upset that all the stories of the lives of twins are so sorrowful. As for ourselves, you have seen the persistence with
which Fate has followed at our heels. Here is your decision
fatally retarded."

Laurence was stupefied. She heard as in a buzzing sound
these ominous words spoken by the director of the jury:

"In the name of the Emperor and the law! I arrest the
Sieurs Paul-Marie and Marie-Paul de Simeuse and Adrien
and Robert d'Hauteserre. These gentlemen," added he to
his companions, pointing to the splashes of mud on the
clothing of the accused, "cannot deny that they have spent
a portion of the day on horseback?"

"Of what do you accuse them?" asked Mlle. de Cinq-
Cygne, proudly.

"Don't you also arrest mademoiselle?" said Giguet.

"I will leave her at liberty under bail, until the evidence
has been more fully gone into."

Goulard offered himself as bail, simply asking the countess
for her word of honor that she would not escape. Laurence
crushed the Simeuses' old huntsman with a look of such hauteur that she made a mortal enemy of the man; tears started
to her eyes, tears of rage which bespeak a hell of anguish.

The four gentlemen exchanged terrible glances and stood immovable. M. and Mme. d'Hauteserre, fearing lest Laurence and the four young gentlemen had fallen into some error, fell into an indescribable state of stupor. Glued to their armchairs, these, who had passed through so many fears for their children and had now gotten them restored, stared before them with unseeing eyes; they listened, but heard not.

"It is unnecessary, I suppose, for me to ask you for bail, Monsieur d'Hauteserre?" exclaimed Laurence, to her former guardian; her cry ringing out shrill and clear as the trumpet of the last judgment.

The old man brushed away the tears from his eyes; he understood all that his young relative had said, and in a feeble voice:

"Pardon me, countess," he said, "you know that I am yours, body and soul."

Lechesneau had at first been struck by the tranquillity shown by the accused while dining, but his early suspicions revived as to their culpability when he noted the stupor of the old people and Laurence's thoughtful appearance; she was searching for the springe that had been set for them.

"Gentlemen," said he politely, "you are too well bred to make useless resistance; you will all four of you follow me to the stables, where it is required to detach in your presence the shoes off your horses; this may prove of the utmost importance at the trial, it may demonstrate your guilt or innocence. You will also come, mademoiselle."

The Cinq-Cygne blacksmith-farrier and his helper had been requisitioned by Lechesneau to attend in their quality as experts. While this operation was going on in the stables, the justice of the peace brought in Gothard and Michu. The work of removing the shoes from the feet of each horse, and the sorting and marking them, so as to be able to compare them with the impressions left in the park, took some time. Nevertheless, Lechesneau, when Pigoult arrived, leaving the accused with the gendarmes, went into the dining-room to dictate the *procès-verbal*, when the justice of the peace pointed out to him the state of Michu's clothing, and related the circumstances of his arrest.

"They must have killed the senator and plastered him up in a wall somewhere," said Pigoult in conclusion to Lechesneau.

"I am afraid so now," replied the magistrate. "Where did you get the cement?" he said to Gothard.

Gothard began to cry.

"The judge frightens him," said Michu, whose eyes flashed fire like a lion who had been caught in a net.

All the servants of the household, released by the mayor, had by this time returned; they crowded into the antechamber, where Catherine and the Durieus were crying in company; from them they learned of the importance of the admissions they had made. To all the questions put by the director and the justice of the peace Gothard replied with sobs, crying in fact so much that a sort of convulsive fit came on; this alarmed them and they left him alone. The little rogue, seeing that he was no more watched, looked at Michu and smiled, and Michu gave him an approving look. Lechesneau left the justice of the peace going out to hasten on his experts.

"Monsieur," at last said Mme. d'Hauteserre, addressing Pigoult, "can you explain the reason of these arrests?"

"These gentlemen are accused of having abducted the senator by main force, and of having sequestrated him, for we do not suppose, in spite of appearances, that they have killed him."

"And what penalty is incurred by the authors of such a crime?" asked the goodman.

"Well, as the laws that were not annulled by the Code still remain in force, the penalty is death," replied the justice of the peace.

"Penalty of death!" cried Mme. d'Hauteserre, and fainted away.

At this moment the curé and his sister presented themselves, and they called Catherine and Mme. Durieu.

"But we have not as much as seen your damned senator," exclaimed Michu.

"Madame Marion, Madame Grévin, Monsieur Grévin, the senator's valet, and Violette cannot say as much for you," replied Pigoult, with the sour smile of an unconvinced magistrate.

"I cannot understand this," said Michu; the reply had knocked him out; he began to think that the whole of them, masters and all, had been trapped in some plot against them.

At this time everybody returned from the stables. Laurence ran to Mme. d'Hauteserre, who recovered consciousness enough to say:

"The penalty is death."

"Penalty is death!" repeated Laurence, looking at the four gentlemen.

These words spread a dismay which was taken advantage of by Giguet, a man trained by Corentin.

"All can be yet arranged," said he, taking the Marquis de Simeuse into a corner of the dining-room; "perhaps you only did it for a joke, eh? What the devil! you are soldiers. Between soldiers all is understood. What have you done with the senator? If you have killed him, no more can be said; but if you have only sequestered him, why, then, give him up, you can see your game is at an end. I am certain that the director of the jury, in accord with the senator, will stifle the prosecution."

"We comprehend absolutely nothing of your questions," said the Marquis de Simeuse.

"If you take that tone, this will be carried to the end," said the lieutenant.

"Dear cousin," said the Marquis de Simeuse to Laurence,

"we are going to prison; but do not be uneasy; in a few hours' time we shall return. It is one of those unfortunate affairs that needs some explanation, that's all."

"I hope so for your sakes, gentlemen," said the magistrate, making a sign to Giguet to carry off the four gentlemen, Gothard, and Michu. "Do not take them to Troyes," said the lieutenant, "guard them at your station at Arcis; they must be present to-morrow, at daybreak, at the verification of the shoes of their horses with the impressions left in the park."

Lechesneau and Pigoult before going questioned Catherine, Monsieur and Mme. d'Hauteserre, and Laurence. The Durieus, Marthe, and Catherine declared they had not seen their masters since breakfast; M. d'Hauteserre stated that he had seen them at three o'clock.

When, at midnight, Laurence was seated between M. and Mme. d'Hauteserre, with the Abbé Goujet and his sister present, and without the four young men, who, for six months past, had been the life of the castle, its love and joy, she looked at them for a long time in silence, which no one ventured to break. Never was affliction deeper or more complete. At last they heard a sigh; they looked around.

Marthe, forgotten in a corner, rose to her feet, saying:

"To death, madame. They will kill them, in spite of their innocence."

"What have you done?" said the cure.

Laurence went out without replying. She wanted to be alone to recover her strength to meet this unforeseen disaster.

PART III.

A POLITICAL TRIAL UNDER THE EMPIRE.

At a distance of thirty-four years, during which three great revolutions have occurred, it is only elderly men that can remember to-day the prodigious uproar produced throughout Europe by the abduction of a senator of the French Empire. No trial, except, perhaps, that of Trumeau, the grocer of the Place Saint-Michel; that of the Widow Morin, under the Empire; those of Fualdès and Castaing, under the Restoration; or the trials of Mme. Lafarge and Fieschi, under the present government, had excited equal interest and curiosity to that of the young men accused of carrying off Malin. An unparalleled attack like this against a member of his Senate excited the Emperor's wrath; and when he was apprised of the arrest of the delinquents, the news of which came shortly after that of the misdemeanor, he learned of the negative results of the search. The forest had been probed to its depths, l'Aube and the departments about it had been thoroughly gone over, but not the slightest trace of their passage or the place of sequestration of the Comte de Gondreville could be found. The minister of justice, at the mandate of the Emperor, after obtaining information from the minister of police, came to his august master and explained the relations existing between Malin as against the Simeuse. The Emperor, then much occupied by weighty business, found the solution of the affair in the antecedent facts.

"These young men are crazy," said he. "A jurisconsult like Malin would be sure to revoke any deed extorted from him by violence. Keep an eye on these nobles and learn how they go about the release of the Comte de Gondreville."

He enjoined them to proceed quickly in this affair, which
(208)

he looked upon as an attack upon his institutions; a fatal example of resistance to the effects of the Revolution; an attempt at the great question of the National lands; and an obstacle to that fusion of parties which was to become the fixed idea of his interior policy. In fact, he believed that he had been tricked by the young men who had given him their promise to live peaceably.

"Fouché's prediction has been realized," he exclaimed, as he remembered the words which his present minister of police had let fall two years before; this he had spoken under the impression given him in Corentin's report on Laurence.

One cannot realize under a constitutional government where no person takes interest in public matters, blind and deaf, ungrateful and cold, the zeal which a word from the Emperor had given to the political machine of his administration. That powerful will of his seemed to impel other things beside men. Once his word was spoken, the Emperor, surprised by the coalition of 1806, forgot the affair. He was thinking of new battles to fight, he was occupied in massing his regiments to strike a deadly blow in the very heart of the Prussian monarchy; but his desire to see prompt justice done found a powerful factor in the uncertainty which affected the position of every magistrate in the Empire.

At this time Cambacérès, as archchancellor, and Régnier, minister of justice, were even then engaged in preparing the institution of courts of first instance, imperial courts, and courts of cassation; they were discussing the question of custom rights, to which Napoleon clung with much reason; they were seeking out some traces of the *parlements* which had been abolished and revising the list of officials. Naturally the magistrates in the department of the Aube thought that any proof of zeal in the matter of the carrying off of the Comte de Gondreville would be an excellent recommendation. The suppositions of Napoleon thus became certainty for his courtiers and the masses.

14

W

Peace still reigned on the continent, and admiration of
the Emperor was the unanimous feeling in France; he cajoled
men through their interests, their vanity, their appearance;
he flattered public bodies and all other things, even people's
memories. This enterprise seemed to everybody as an attempt on the public weal. So the poor innocent gentlemen
were covered with general opprobrium. A few of the nobility,
confined to their estates, deplored the affair among themselves,
but not one of them dared to open their mouths. How,
indeed, were they to oppose the outburst of public opinion?

All over the department they exhumed the corpses of the
eleven people killed in 1792, shot down from behind the
window shutters in the attack on the hotel de Cinq-Cygne,
and flung them at the heads of the accused. They feared
that the *émigrés* as a body would grow bold and intimidate
those who had acquired their lands, and make forcible protest against their unjust spoliation. These nobles were considered to have the traits of brigands, robbers, and murderers,
and Michu's complicity was especially fatal.

This man, or his father-in-law, had cut off every head that
fell in the department during the Terror; they were the sub-
jects of the most absurd stories. The exasperation was the
more lively because Malin had put nearly every functionary
in the Aube in his position. Not a single generous voice was
uplifted to contradict the public clamor. In fact, the unfortunate prisoners had no legal means of fighting this prejudice;
for, while submitting to the juries the indictment and the
judgment, the Code of Brumaire of the year IV. did not give
the accused that immense guarantee, the right of appeal to the
court of cassation, where a legitimate suspicion of unfairness
exists.

Two days after the arrests, the masters and servants of the
castle of Cinq-Cygne were summoned to give evidence before
the *jury d'accusation.** They left Cinq-Cygne in care of a

* A tribunal much resembling our grand jury.

MOST OF ALL, HE FELT THE ISOLATION.

tenant, under the supervision of the Abbé Goujet and his sister, who stayed there. Mlle. de Cinq-Cygne, M. and Mme. d'Hauteserre took up their abode in Durieu's little house in one of the long straggling suburbs that range around the city of Troyes. Laurence had a contraction of the heart when she perceived the rage of the populace, the malignity of the middle-classes, and the hostility of the administration; many little evidences which always befall the defendants and their relatives in a criminal trial held in a provincial town showed her this sentiment. Instead of encouraging words and compassionate exclamations, she heard conversations intended for her ear; clamorous, fearful desires for vengeance; demonstrations of hatred took the place of the strict politeness and reserve which ordinary decency demanded; but, most of all, she felt the isolation that is always experienced by people in such cases, felt the more keenly because misfortune begets mistrust.

Laurence had regained all her strength, the innocence of her cousins was evident, she despised the crowd too much to be alarmed at its silent disapprobation of the accused. She sustained the courage of M. and Mme. d'Hauteserre, all the time thinking of that judicial battle which, after seeing the swiftness of the proceedings, must soon be fought out in the criminal court. But she was to receive a blow which would undermine her courage.

In the midst of their disaster and the general ill-feeling, just as this afflicted family seemed as if alone in a desert, one man sprang into greatness in Laurence's eyes, and showed the nobility of his nature. The day following that on which the jury of accusation had returned the indictment approved by the formula *Oui, il y a lieu*—Yes, it is based on reason, which the foreman of the jury had written at the foot, and which had then been sent up to the public accuser, and when the warrant of arrest had been changed into an order for the safe custody of the body, the Marquis de Chargebœuf courageously came in his old *calèche* to the succor of his young relative.

Perceiving the promptitude with which the course of justice was moving, the head of the house had hurried to Paris, from whence he returned bringing with him one of the shrewdest and most honest *procureurs* of the olden time, one Bordin, for ten years, in Paris, the attorney of the nobility and whose successor was the celebrated Derville. This worthy lawyer immediately chose as counsel the grandson of an old president of the parlement of Normandy, who was destined for the magistracy and who had studied under his own tuition. This young barrister was looking for an appointment to a position revived by the Emperor ; as a fact, he was appointed as deputy public prosecutor at Paris, after this trial, and became one of the most celebrated magistrates. This M. de Granville took up the defense as affording an opportunity of distinguishing himself.

At that time barristers were replaced by officially appointed counsel or *défenseurs.* So that no case might be deprived of the right of defense, any citizen might plead the cause of innocence ; but the accused still took the old way of engaging a barrister in their behalf. The old marquis was alarmed by the havoc that grief had wrought on Laurence ; but he was admirable in his good taste and tact. He did not once allude to the counsel he had given which had been thrown away. He introduced Bordin as an oracle who must be obeyed to the letter, and the young de Granville as a defender in whom they could put implicit confidence.

Laurence held out her hand to the marquis and her warm grasp quite charmed him.

"You were right," said she.

"Will you now listen to my advice?" he asked.

The young countess and M. and Mme. d'Hauteserre made a gesture of assent.

"Well, then, come to my house ; it is in the centre of the

town, near the tribunal. You and your lawyers will be better
lodged there than in this place where you are huddled in a
heap, and too far away from the field of action. You would
have to cross Troyes every day."

Laurence accepted. The old man took her and Mme.
d'Hauteserre to his house, and there they and their lawyers
stayed during the trial. After dinner, after the doors were
closed, Bordin had Laurence give an exact account of all the
circumstances connected with the affair, begging her not to
omit one single particular; although both the lawyers had
already learned it in part from the marquis during their trip
from Paris to Troyes. Bordin listened, his feet to the fire,
without the least appearance of assumption. The young barrister was divided between his admiration for Mlle. de Cinq-
Cygne and the attention necessary to learn the elements of
the case.

"Is that really all?" asked Bordin, when Laurence had
recounted the events of the drama from its commencement to
the present time.

"Yes," she replied.

Profound silence reigned for some time in the salon of the
Chargebœuf mansion where this scene was passing; one of the
most solemn during a life, and one that rarely comes into our
experience. Every case is tried by counsel ere it comes before the judge, just as every invalid's death is foreseen by the
doctor prior to the final struggle with the laws of nature as
the other struggles against that of justice. Laurence, M., Mme.
d'Hauteserre, and the marquis sat with their eyes upon the
dark old face of the *procureur*, with its deep scars left by the
smallpox; what word would he pronounce—life or death!
M. d'Hauteserre felt the beads of perspiration on his forehead.
Laurence looked at the young barrister and noticed that his
face had a grieved look.

"Well, my dear Bordin?" said the marquis, holding out
his snuff-box, from which the lawyer abstractedly took a pinch.

Bordin rubbed the calves of his legs, draped in black floss silk stockings and black cloth breeches, and the long coat of the French fashion of a past age; he turned a cunning look upon his clients and gave an expression of misgiving which struck them icy cold.

"Must I dissect this case?" said he. "Shall I speak frankly?"

"Please go on, monsieur," said Laurence.

"All that you have done with the best of intentions can be turned into charges against you," the old practitioner went on to say. "You cannot save your relatives; you can but try to minimize the penalty. The sale which you ordered Michu to make of his land will be held as proof positive that you had criminal designs against the senator. You sent your people to Troyes purposely to be out of the way; it looks the more plausible because it is the truth. The eldest d'Hauteserre said a terrible thing to Beauvisage; you are all lost through that alone. You, yourself, said something in your courtyard which proves that for a long time you have borne ill-will against Gondreville. When you, you were acting as sentinel at the gate when the deed was done, if they don't prosecute you, it is only to eliminate any element of interest in the case."

"The cause is indefensible," said M. de Granville, "absolutely so."

"And less so," replied Bordin, "because the truth cannot be told. Michu, the Simeuses, and the d'Hauteserres can simply state that they were out with you in the forest for a portion of the day, and that they took breakfast at Cinq-Cygne. But if we can establish the fact that you were all there at three o'clock, the time of the deed, who then are the witnesses? Marthe, the wife of one of the accused; the Durieus, Catherine, all people in your service; monsieur and madame are the father and mother of two others of the accused. Such witnesses are worthless; the law will not admit their testimony against you—commonsense rejects their testimony in your favor. If, by bad luck, you say that you went out to find eleven hundred thousand francs in gold in the forest, you would send all the accused to the galleys as robbers.

"The public accuser, the juries, judges, audience, everybody in France would think that you had stolen that prize at the same time you sequestered the senator.

"Admitting the indictment as it stands, the case is not clear against you; but the whole thing, to speak the truth, becomes quite transparent; to the jury, the robbery would explain all that looks dark, for to-day royalist is but another name for brigand. As it stands, the case seems to point to an act of vengeance only, quite admissible in the present political conditions.

"The accused have incurred the penalty of death; that is not dishonorable in the eyes of the people; but if you bring in the abstraction of the specie, which always seems an illegitimate thing, you lose the advantage of the interest which naturally attaches the public to those condemned to death; that is, so long as the crime seems excusable. If, at the start, you had shown the hiding-place, the chart of the forest, the tin canisters, the gold, so as to have fully accounted for your day, it is not impossible that you would not have been held if brought before an impartial judge; but as things are, absolute silence must be maintained. God grant that not one of the six accused has compromised the case; but we shall see how the examination has resulted."

Laurence wrung her hands despairingly and raised her eyes to heaven with a look of desolation; she perceived now the whole depths of the precipice over which her cousins had fallen. The marquis and the young barrister both coincided with Bordin's terrible discourse. The goodman d'Hauteserre was crying.

"Why did you not give heed to the Abbé Goujet when he

wished them to flee?" said Mme. d'Hauteserre, in exasperation.

"Ah!" exclaimed the old barrister, "if you could have saved them and did not, you it is that has slain them. The contempt of court would have given time. Given time, innocent ones may clear their skirts. This is the blackest looking case that I have ever seen; I have seen a tolerably few crooked ones, too."

"It is inexplicable to every one, even to us," said M. de Granville. "If the accused are innocent, some one else must have done this deed. Five people do not come into a country by enchantment, nor are their horses shod in precisely the same way as those of the accused, nor do they change their appearances and put Malin in a pit, making themselves up to resemble the d'Hauteserres, the de Simeuses, and Michu purposely to ruin them. These unknown persons, the real miscreants, must have had some motive in slipping into the skins of these innocent folk; if we wish to find their traces, we, like the government, should need spies and eyes in every commune within a radius of twenty leagues."

"Which is, of course, impossible," said Bordin, shrugging his shoulders.

"It is useless thinking of it. Ever since society invented justice no community has discovered how to place at the disposal of the wrongfully accused a power equal to that exercised by the magistracy in the repression of crime. Justice is not bilateral. The defense, which has neither spies nor police, does not possess the powers of society in proving its innocence—this is only employed to prove guilt. Innocence has only argument upon which to rely; the reasoning that appeals to the judges is often wasted upon the prejudiced jury. The whole country is against you. The eight jurymen who approved the indictment are, each one, owners of nationalized land. The trial jury will be composed, like the first, of official folk or vendors and buyers of nationalized lands.

To conclude, we shall have a *Malin* * jury. A complete system of defense is therefore a necessity; we must stick to it and perish in our innocence. You will be condemned. We shall then appeal to the Court of Cassation, and endeavor to gain time there. If, in the interval, I can gather any evidence in your favor, you have an appeal to mercy still remaining. There you have the anatomy of the case and my opinion upon it. If we win (for everything is possible in law), it will be a miracle; but your barrister is, of all whom I know, the most likely to work a miracle; I shall give him all my assistance."

"The senator holds the key to the enigma," said M. de Granville, "for if anybody owes you a grudge you know whom it is and why. I see this man leaving Paris at the end of winter, coming to Gondreville alone without any of his suite, shut up with his notary, and giving himself up, as one might say, to these five men who kidnap him."

"Certainly," said Bordin, "his behavior is at the best as extraordinary as our own; but how, when the face of the whole country is against us, can we the accused become the accusers? It needs good-will, the help of the government, and a thousand times more proof than we can present to do this. I see premeditated malice of the subtlest in our unknown enemies; who know the position in which Michu stands in regard to the Simeuses and Malin? Not to speak, to take nothing—there is prudence. I can see plainly that they are anything but ordinary malefactors, those that wore the masks. But to speak of these things to the sort of jury they will give us—just think of it!"

This perspicacity in private matters, the impersonal clear-sightedness which makes some barristers and judges so great, astounded and confounded Laurence; her heart was seared by his remorseless logic.

"Of a hundred criminal cases," said Bordin, "there are

* *Malin*—malignant.

not ten which are thoroughly investigated by justice, and perhaps in a good third the secret remains unknown. Yours is one of those cases which remain inscrutable both to the prosecution and the defense, the court and the public. As for the sovereign, he has other peas to bind; even if the Simeuses had not attempted to overturn his government, he would not succor the MM. de Simeuse. But who the devil owes Malin a grudge? And why did they do this?"

Bordin and M. de Granville looked at each other, they seemed to doubt Laurence's veracity. This was the most agonizing moment to the young girl of all the sorrows she had passed through in this affair; she cast a glance at her two lawyers and their suspicion vanished.

The following day the report of the examination was remitted to her barrister, who was allowed to communicate with the accused. Bordin told the family that like good men the six accused "were keeping up well," to use the common term.

"Monsieur de Granville will defend Michu," said Bordin.

"Michu!" exclaimed M. de Chargebœuf, astonished at the change.

"He is the heart of the business, that is where the danger lies," returned the old lawyer.

"If he is exposed the most, that seems only just," exclaimed Laurence.

"We perceive a few chances," said M. de Granville, "and we intend to study them thoroughly. If we are able to save them, it will be because M. d'Hauteserre told Michu to repair one of the posts in the fence at the cross-roads, as there was a wolf in the forest; for in a criminal court all turns upon the pleading, and that in turn depends on little things which may become immense."

Laurence fell into a state of mental prostration, which in every energetic soul deadens it when it becomes apparent that action is useless and is so demonstrated. This was not throw-

ing down a man in power with the assistance of a body of
devoted adherents; there was no place for fanatical zeal enveloped in the clouds of mystery; she seemed to see all
society up in arms against herself and her cousins. She could
not go alone and single-handed break open a jail; nor can
one rescue the prisoners when the whole populace is hostile
to them, and the police are using their eyes everywhere owing
to the supposed audacity of the accused. So when this stupor
came over this noble and generous girl, a stupor which her
physiognomy exaggerated, the young barrister tried to raise
her courage; she only replied:

"I wait and suffer in silence."

The accent, the gesture, and the look were so sublime that,
spoken on a wider stage, the words would have become famous. Some time after, the goodman d'Hauteserre said to
the Marquis de Chargebœuf:

"The pains that I have taken with my two unfortunate children. I have saved until there is an income of nearly eight hundred thousand livres from the Funds. If only they had gone
into the service, they would have gained superior grades and
have married to advantage. Here they have gone completely
up."

"How," said his wife, "can you think of caring for their
interests when both their heads and honor are in jeopardy?"

"Monsieur d'Hauteserre thinks of everything," said the
marquis.

While the Cinq-Cygne folk awaited the opening of the trial
in the criminal court, and were making fruitless solicitations
for permission to see the prisoners, there was passing, at the
castle, in the profoundest secrecy, an event of the utmost importance. Marthe had returned to Cinq-Cygne soon after
her deposition before the *jury d'accusation;* her evidence
was so insignificant that the public prosecutor did not think
her presence would be needed at the trial. Like all people of

an excessive sensibility, the poor woman, who sat in the salon in the company of Mlle. Goujet, had sunk into a state of stupor most pitiable. To her, as to the curé, in fact, to everybody who did not know how the day had been spent, their innocence seemed doubtful. At times Marthe thought that Michu, with his masters and Laurence, had executed their vengeance on the senator. The unhappy wife knew well enough of Michu's devotion to understand that, of all the accused, he was in the greatest danger, one thing against him being his past and his leading part in the execution of this present affair.

The Abbé Goujet, his sister, and Marthe lost themselves in the probabilities to which this opinion gave rise; but the strength of this meditation grew upon them, and their minds gradually gave a certain significance to them. The absolute doubt which Descartes demands is as hard to find in the brain of man as a vacuum in nature, and the mental operation which makes this result is, in fact, something like an air-pump in its abnormal and exceptional action. Under every condition people have some kind of thoughts. Now Marthe was so afraid of the accused being guilty that her dread was equivalent to a belief; this state of feeling proved fatal. Five days after the arrest of the nobles, at the moment she was going to bed, being ten o'clock at night, she was called into the courtyard by her mother, who had walked over from the farm.

"A workman from Troyes wants to speak to you about Michu; he is waiting for you at the *rond-point*," said she to Marthe.

Both passed out of the courtyard through the breach in the moat. In the darkness of the night, in the lane, it was impossible for Marthe to distinguish more than the shadow of a man looming out of the gloom.

"Speak, madame, so that I can tell if you really are Madame Michu," said this person, in a somewhat unsteady voice.

"Certainly," said Marthe. "What do you wish?"

"Good," said the unknown. "Give me your hand, you need not fear me. I come," added he, bending over to whisper in Marthe's ear, "from Michu, with word from him. I am employed in the prison, and if my superiors knew of my absence we should all be lost. Trust me. At one time your brave father found me a position. So Michu could count on me."

He placed a letter in Marthe's hand and disappeared in the forest without awaiting any reply. Marthe had something like a shiver as she believed that at length she should learn the secret of the affair. She ran to the farmhouse with her mother and locked herself in while she read the letter, which follows:

MY DEAR MARTHE:—You may count on the discretion of the man who carries this letter; he can neither read nor write; he is one of the stanchest Republicans of the Babeuf conspiracy; he often served your father and he looks on the senator as a traitor. Now, my dear wife, the senator has been shut up by us in the cave in which we kept our masters hidden. The wretch has food for not more than five days, and as it is not to our interest to take his life, take him enough to last him for at least another five days, after you have read these few lines.

The forest is watched, so take as many precautions as we used to on behalf of our young masters. Do not speak to Malin, not a single word; put one of our masks on which you will find laying on the steps to the cave. If you would not compromise our heads you must keep absolute silence on this secret which I have been compelled to tell you. Above all, not one word to Mlle. de Cinq-Cygne, as she might get "scared." Fear nothing for me. We are certain to come out of this thing all right, and, if all comes to all, Malin will be our saviour. In conclusion, after you have read this letter, I need not tell you to burn it, for off goes my head if any one sees a single line of it. I embrace you many times.

MICHU.

The existence of the cave situated in the mound in the middle of the forest was only known by Marthe, her son, Michu, the four nobles, and Laurence, at least Marthe so sup-

posed, for her husband had never told her of his encounter
with Peyrade and Corentin. So the letter, which to all appearance had been written and signed by Michu, could only
have come from him. Certainly if Marthe had at once con-
sulted her mistress and her two lawyers, who knew of the innocence of the accused, the treacherous stratagem would have
revealed to the wily *procureur* and her barrister some light on
the means taken to embroil his clients; but Marthe, like most
women, acted on her first impulse, and was convinced of the
considerations placed in her sight; she threw the letter into
the fire. Yet, by a singular flash of prudence, she rescued
from the flames the side of the letter which had not been
written on and with it a few of the first lines; no sense could
be made of them that could compromise any one, so she
sewed it in the folds of her dress.

Knowing that the prisoner had been for twenty-four hours
without food, she became alarmed; this very night she would
carry him some wine, bread and meat. Her curiosity, no
less than her humanity, would not allow her to put this off
until to-morrow. She heated her oven, and made, with her
mother's assistance, a leveret and duck pie, a rice cake,
roasted two chickens, and baked two round loaves of bread.
About half-past two in the morning she placed these and three
bottles of wine in a basket, and, accompanied by Courant,
went on her way to the forest; the dog, who had always gone
with them on these expeditions, made an admirable scout.
He scented a stranger at a great distance, and would return to
his mistress, utter a low growl, and show, by the direction in
which he turned his muzzle, in which quarter the danger lay.

Marthe arrived at the pond at three o'clock; she there left
Courant on guard. After half an hour of hard work she
cleared the entrance and went through the doorway with a
dark-lantern; she had covered her face with the mask which,
as she had been told, was found on the steps.

The senator's sequestration had evidently been arranged for

a long time in advance. A hole about one foot square, which Marthe had not seen before, had been roughly made in the door of the cave, while the bolt was fastened with a padlock, lest Malin, with the time and patience at the disposal of prisoners, might succeed in reaching it and thus free himself. The senator had just risen from his bed of moss; he formed a suspicion, when he saw the approaching person was masked, that the time for his deliverance was not yet. He observed Marthe as well as the dim light of the lantern would allow, and at last recognized her; her dress, corpulence, and movements betrayed her. When she passed the pie through the hole, he let it fall to seize her hands, and with as much celerity as possible tried to draw two rings from her fingers—her wedding-ring and another little ring given her by Mlle. de Cinq-Cygne.

"You cannot deny whom you are, my dear Madame Michu?" said he.

Marthe no sooner felt her fingers grasped by the senator than she gave him a vigorous blow with her fist on his chest. Then, without speaking a word, she cut a stick sufficiently strong for her purpose and passed the senator the remainder of his provisions on the end of it.

"What do they wish of me?" he asked.

Marthe fled without replying. She had nearly reached home about five o'clock, and was on the outskirts of the forest, when she was warned by Courant of some one's unwelcome presence. She retraced her steps and went toward the pavilion that had been her abode for such a long time; but when she came out on to the avenue she was perceived in the distance by the gate-keeper of Gondreville; she at once made up her mind to go straight to him.

"You are very early, Madame Michu," said he, accosting her.

"We are so unfortunate," she replied, "that I have to do the work of a servant; I am going to Bellache for some seeds."

"What, you are without seeds at Cinq-Cygne?" said the gate-keeper.

Marthe made no reply. She went on her way, and, arrived at the Bellache farm, she asked Beauvisage to give her several kinds of seeds, as M. d'Hauteserre had been advised to change the strain he had for those of another kind. When Marthe had gone, the gate-keeper at Gondreville went to the farm to know why Marthe had gone there.

Six days after, Marthe, with becoming prudence, went at midnight with the provisions, so as not to be surprised by the game-keepers, who she knew were watching the forest. After having a third time taken provisions to the senator, she was seized with a kind of terror at hearing the curé read the account of the public trial of the accused, for it had now begun.

She took the Abbé Goujet aside, and, after having made him swear that he would keep her secret the same as if it had been revealed in the confessional, she showed him the fragments of the letter which she had received from Michu, and told him where the senator lay hidden. The curé at once asked Marthe to let him see some other handwriting of her husband's, so that the two might be compared. Marthe went home to the farmhouse, where she found a summons awaiting her to appear as a witness in the case at the court. When she returned to the castle, she learned that the Abbé Goujet and his sister had likewise been summoned on behalf of the defense. They were therefore all obliged to go to Troyes. So all the personages in this drama, and even those who may be called supers, were all assembled on the stage where the destinies of two families were then being played.

There are very few places in France where justice is surrounded with that impressiveness which contributes to its dignity and should never be lacking. After religion and royalty, is it not the noblest machine of society? Everywhere, even

in Paris, the bad arrangement of the premises, the shabby
setting, together with its lack of ornament, which in the eyes
of the vainest, most imaginative, and the fondest of theatrical
display of all modern nations, cannot but have a tendency to
lessen the effect of the enormous power of the law. All the
arrangements are much the same in every town.

At the bottom of a long rectangular hall there stands a
desk, covered with green baize, on the slightly raised platform,
where the judges sit in ordinary armchairs. At the left side
is the seat of the public prosecutor, and on his side is the
jury-box, along the wall, and containing chairs.

Facing the jury extends another raised space where a bench
is found upon which the accused and the gendarmes who form
his guard are seated. The clerk has his place below the platform at a table, upon which are disposed the documents connected with the case.

Before the institution of the Imperial Court, the commissary of the government and the director of the jury had each
a chair at other tables, one to the right and one to the left of
the judges' desk. Two ushers hover in the space left for witnesses. The lawyers for the defense are stationed beneath the
tribune occupied by the accused. A wooden balustrade con-
nects the two tribunes and forms an inclosure where benches
are placed for witnesses who have given their testimony and
a few privileged and curious auditors. Then, opposite the
court, over the entrance door, there is always found a little
shabby gallery, which is reserved for the authorities, ladies,
and others of the department admitted by the president, who
has the regulation of this privilege. The public are allowed
to stand in the space remaining between the door of the hall
and the balustrade. This normal physiognomy of the French
Courts and the courts of assizes of the present time was just
the same in the city of Troyes.

In April, 1806, neither the four judges nor the president,
who composed the court, nor the public prosecutor, nor the
15

director of the jury, nor any one else, except the gendarmes, wore any distinctive dress or badge of office to offset the general bareness of the place and the mostly insignificant countenances.

The crucifix was missing, and thus did not give its moral example either to the court or the accused. All was dismal and common. The pomp so necessary to the interests of society is perhaps also a consolation to the criminal. The interest of the public caused them to flock to the court-house, as such occasions always have done and will continue to do, so long as manners and customs remain unreformed; so long as France fails to recognize that while publicity is not by any means secured by the admission of the public, it becomes a painful ordeal, in such case, how distressing no legislator can have imagined, or never would it have been inflicted. Manners and customs are more cruel than the law. Manners are the people, but law is the intellect of the country. Custom, not seldom irrational, is stronger than the law.

A mob had congregated around the court-house. As in all sensational trials the president was obliged to place a guard of military at the doors. Inside, behind the balustrade, the space was so tightly packed with people that they were nearly stifled. M. de Granville defended Michu, Bordin appeared for the MM. de Simeuse, and a barrister of Troyes represented MM. d'Hauteserre and Gothard, the least compromised of the six accused; all these were at their posts before the opening of the case, and their faces inspired confidence. A doctor allows nothing of his misgivings to be seen by his patient, so in like manner the barrister always turns a hopeful countenance to his client. This is one of those rare cases when insincerity becomes a virtue.

When the accused entered there arose a murmur in favor of the four young men, who, after twenty days of detention, passed in painful suspense, looked somewhat pallid. The perfect resemblance of the twins excited the highest interest in them. Perhaps each person thought that Nature should have specially protected one of her most curious rarities. Everybody felt tempted to repair the irony of destiny which had befallen them. Their noble countenances, simple, and without the least trace of shame or bravado, touched all the women. The four gentlemen and Gothard were in the costume which they had worn when arrested; but Michu, whose clothing formed part of the evidence, was in his best clothes —a blue frock-coat, a brown velvet waistcoat of the Robespierre style, and a white cravat. The poor man paid the penalty of his sinister appearance. When he turned his tawny, keen, bright eyes upon the crowd by some chance movement, they responded with a murmur of horror. The audience saw the finger of God in his appearance in that dock, whither his father-in-law had sent so many victims. This man, truly magnificent, looked at his masters, repressing an ironical smile. He had the air of saying: "I am injuring you." The five other accused exchanged warm greetings with their counsel. Gothard still played the idiot.

After the counsel for the defense had with great sagacity used their right of challenge of the jury—information on this point being given by the Marquis de Chargebœuf, who most courageously sat between Bordin and de Granville—and when the panel was filled, the indictment was read, and the accused separated before being examined. Their answers were remarkably alike. After riding out in the morning, they returned at one o'clock to Cinq-Cygne for breakfast; after this repast, between three and half-past five, they were again in the forest. This formed the substance of the statement made by each of the accused, the details only being varied with the particular circumstances of their individual doings.

When the president asked the de Simeuses what reason they gave for going out at so early an hour in the morning, they one and the other declared that since their return they had formed the idea of trying to purchase Gondreville; and that they intended treating with Malin, who had arrived the day before; they had, therefore, with their cousin and Michu, gone to make an inspection of the forest as a means on which to base their offer. During this time MM. d'Hauteserre, with their cousin and Gothard, had chased a wolf which some peasants had seen. If the director of the jury had taken as much trouble in seeking for the foot-prints of their horses in the forest as they had expended care in examining those in the park of Gondreville, they could have seen that they were far away from the castle at that time.

The examination of the d'Hauteserres confirmed all that had been said by the de Simeuses, and was found to agree with their former statement, extracted by the examining judge. The necessity of accounting for their excursion had suggested to each the same idea of attributing it to a hunt. Some peasants had seen a wolf in the forest some days previous to this.

Nevertheless, the public prosecutor made the most of the contradictions between the present and the preliminary examination, when the d'Hauteserres had declared that they all went together after the chase; now it only left the d'Hauteserres and Laurence hunting, while the de Simeuses had been appraising the forest.

M. de Granville observed that the misdemeanor had been committed between the hours of two and half-past five; the accused must be allowed to know and explain how they spent the morning.

The public prosecutor responded that the accused were interested in concealing their preparations for the sequestration of the senator.

The ability of the defense then became apparent to all eyes. The judges, the jurymen, the spectators soon realized that the victory would be hotly contested for. Bordin and de Granville seemed provided for every contingency. Innocence gives a clear and plausible account of its acts. The duty of the defense is therefore to oppose a probable romance to the improbable romance of the prosecution. To the counsel for the defense who believes in his client's innocence, the indictment becomes a myth. The public examination of the four nobles gave a sufficient and favorable explanation of the affair. So far, all was well. But Michu's examination was a more serious matter, and closed the combat. Everybody now understood why M. de Granville had preferred to defend the servant rather than the masters.

Michu admitted having menaced Marion, but he denied absolutely that he had done the violence threatened. As to ambushing Malin, he said he had been simply promenading the park; the senator and M. Grévin might have been afraid when they saw the muzzle of his gun; they might have believed it to be a threat when really no threat was intended. He observed that when a man is unused to the handling of a gun he always thinks it is pointed at him, when it really is resting only on the shoulder. To account for the state of his clothing when he was arrested, he said that he had fallen as he was clambering through the breach on his way home.

"I was not able to see because of the darkness; in a fashion," said he, "I clutched at the stones to climb up the breach, when some of the loose stones came tumbling down with me."

As to the cement that Gothard was carrying, he replied now, as at every other time, that he needed it to fasten one of the posts on the hollow path.

The public prosecutor and the president asked him to explain how it was that he was at that time in the breach at the castle when he had been fastening a post on the high road, especially when the justice of the peace, the gendarmes, and policeman all stated that they heard him come up the hollow path. Michu replied that M. d'Hauteserre had blamed him for not having done that little job sooner, as it was likely to cause trouble with the commune as to the right of way; he

had therefore gone to the castle to tell them that he had repaired the fence.

M. d'Hauteserre had, in fact, placed a fence on the upper
part of the low path to prevent the commune from claiming a
right of way. He saw the importance of accounting for the
state of his clothing, and the use of the cement, so Michu had
invented this subterfuge. If truth often resembles fiction in
the eyes of justice, fiction more often resembles the truth.
Both the defense and prosecution attached much value to this
circumstance, which became the capital of the efforts of the
defense and aroused the suspicions of the prosecution.

At the hearing, Gothard, prompted without a doubt by M.
de Granville, declared that Michu had told him to carry some
sacks of cement; but up to now he had always begun to cry
when he was questioned.

"Why did not you or Gothard take the justice of the peace
and the policeman to this fence?" asked the public prosecutor.

"I never thought that it would be used against us in a
capital charge," said Michu.

With the exception of Gothard, all the accused were taken
out. When he alone was left, the president adjured him to
tell the truth, in his own interest, and he made the remark
that his pretense of idiocy was broken up. None of the jurymen thought him an imbecile. If he refused before the court,
he incurred heavy penalties; whereas, if he spoke the truth,
he would most probably be put out of the case. Gothard began to cry, then he finished by saying that Michu had told
him to carry some sacks of cement, but that each time he had
met him near the farm. He was then asked how many sacks
he had brought.

"Three," he answered.

On this an argument arose between Gothard and Michu as
to whether there were three sacks; counting the one he carried
when arrested, were there only two before that, or were there

three sacks without reckoning the last? This dispute ended
in favor of Michu. As for the jury, they held that only two
sacks had been used; it appeared they had made up their
minds to this; Bordin and de Granville deemed it advisable
to feed them to a surfeit on cement till they became so confused and weary that they understood less than nothing.
M. de Granville suggested, in conclusion, that experts be appointed to examine the state of the fence.

"The director of the jury," said the defense, "was content
to visit the place on their own behoof, less to obtain the
opinion of experts than to seek for proofs of subterfuge on the
part of Michu; but it failed, so it seems, and his error ought
not to be turned to our disadvantage."

The court ordered, in fact, that experts be sent to learn
whether one of the posts in the fence had recently been set.
On the other side, the public prosecutor wished to gain an
advantage from this circumstance before the experts reported.

"Why should you," said he to Michu, "choose an hour
when it was anything but light, between five and half-past six,
to fix a fence and do it all alone?"

"Monsieur d'Hauteserre had growled at me."

"But," said the public prosecutor, "if you used cement
on the fence, you must have used a bucket and trowel.
Now, if you so promptly went off to inform M. d'Hauteserre
that you had executed his orders, it is impossible to explain
how it comes that Gothard was bringing more cement to you?
You must have gone past your own farm, and then you could
have there disposed of your utensils and stopped Gothard."

This argument was a thunderbolt; it produced a horrid
silence in the court.

"Come, confess now," said the public prosecutor, "that
it was no post that you interred——"

"You perhaps think it was the senator, eh?" said Michu,
with an air and tone of intensest irony.

M. de Granville formally demanded that the public prose-

cutor be interdicted by his chief from pursuing this line.
Michu was accused of abduction and sequestration and not of
murder. This accusation was sufficiently serious. The Code
of Brumaire of the year IV. forbade the public prosecutor
introducing any new charge in the course of trial; he was
bound to adhere to the terms of the indictment, else the proceedings would be annulled.

The public prosecutor replied that Michu, the principal of
the affair, and who, in the interests of his masters, had taken
the whole responsibility on his own head, may most likely
have been compelled to block up the entrance to the unknown
place in which they had confined the senator.

Closely pressed, worried by Gothard being present, and
made to contradict himself, Michu struck on the ledge of the
dock with a mighty blow of his fist, and said:

"I have had nothing to do with kidnapping the senator;
I love to think that his enemies have just shut him up; but
if he makes his appearance, you will learn that cement had
nothing to do with it."

"Good," said his barrister, addressing the public prosecutor, "you have done more toward the defense of my client
than anything I can say."

The first day's hearing was over; the court rose after this
audacious assertion, which took the jury by surprise and gave
a fillip to the defense. The barristers of the town and Bordin felicitated the young counsel with much enthusiasm. The
public prosecutor was made uneasy by this remark; he feared
that he had stepped into some trap; and, in fact, he had fallen
into a snare very skillfully set for him by the defense, and
one in which Gothard had played his part to admiration.
The wits of the town said that the case had been cemented, that
the public prosecutor had made a botch of the job, and that
he had cemented and whitewashed the Simeuses. France is
the realm of jest, and it reigns supreme; the Frenchman cuts
his joke on the scaffold, in the Bérésina, at the barricades,

and some French pleasantry will probably be made at the last judgment.

The next day the witnesses for the prosecution were called; Mme. Marion, Mme. Grévin, Grévin, the senator's valet, and Violette, whose depositions were as might be expected after the events narrated. All of them with more or less hesitation recognized four of the accused, but were fully convinced as to Michu. Beauvisage repeated what had escaped the lips of Robert d'Hauteserre. The peasant, who came to buy the calf, deposed as to what Mlle. de Cinq-Cygne had said. The blacksmiths, when called, confirmed their report previously made that the tracks of the horses of the four gentlemen who were under indictment, and the imprints left in the park, were absolutely identical. This circumstance naturally caused a violent argument between M. de Granville and the public prosecutor. The defense put the Cinq-Cygne blacksmith on the stand, and it was shown by the examination that similar horse-shoes had been sold some few days previously to persons unknown in that country. The blacksmith declared that he had shod a number of horses in the same manner as those belonging to the castle of *Saint*-Cygne. Finally, the horse always ridden by Michu had, most extraordinarily, been shod at Troyes, and this imprint could not be found amongst the others in the park.

"The double of Michu was ignorant of that fact," said M. de Granville, looking at the jury; "and the prosecution has failed to prove that we used one of the horses from the castle."

He withered Violette's deposition concerning the resemblance of the horses, as seen at a long distance, and from behind. But despite of the incredible efforts of the defense, the mass of testimony was too strongly against Michu. The prosecution, the spectators, the court, and the jury all felt, as presented by the defense, that if the servant was guilty it followed that the masters were equally so. Bordin had well guessed where the stress of the trial would be when he had given de Granville the defense of Michu; but the defense by thus doing confessed their secret knowledge of the fact. So all that concerned the former steward-keeper of Gondreville possessed a palpitating interest. Michu's demeanor was superb, all through. He displayed in every discussion all the sagacity with which nature had endowed him; and he compelled the public to admit his superiority; but, strange to say, this man for that very reason appeared the more likely to be guilty.

The witnesses for the defense were taken less seriously than those for the prosecution; in the eyes of the jury and the law, the former appeared to do their duty, and were heard in such manner as acquitted the conscience of the jury. At the same time neither Marthe, nor M. nor Mme. d'Hauteserre could be sworn; then Catherine and the Durieus, being servants, were in the same box. M. d'Hauteserre said in effect that he had given the order spoken of to Michu to replace the broken post. The deposition of the experts, who at this moment submitted their report, confirmed the declaration made by the old gentleman, but at the same time it gave a point to the director of the jury, for they declared that it was impossible to say at what time this work had been done; it might have been some weeks since or it might only have been twenty days.

The appearance of Mlle. de Cinq-Cygne excited the most lively curiosity; but the sight of her cousins in the dock, after the separation of twenty-three days, so greatly affected her that she looked guilty. She felt an almost uncontrollable desire to be beside the twins, and was compelled, as she afterward said, to use her whole strength to repress her desire to kill the public prosecutor, that she might, before the eyes of all the world, stand a criminal with them. She artlessly related that as she was returning to Cinq-Cygne she had seen the smoke in the park; she thought that something must be on fire. For some time she thought that the smoke was caused by the burning of weeds.

"Nevertheless," said she, "I can remember one thing very particularly, that I think should be brought to the notice of the court. I found in the froggings of my riding-habit and in the pleats of my collarette some ashes which were, it seemed to me, of burnt paper carried by the wind."

"The smoke then was quite considerable?" asked Bordin.

"Yes," said Mlle. de Cinq-Cygne; "I thought something was on fire."

"This puts a new feature into the case," said Bordin. "I ask the court to at once make an order for the investigation of the place where the smoke was produced."

The president so ordered it.

Grévin, recalled by the defense, and questioned on this matter, declared that he knew nothing about it. But between Bordin and Grévin looks were exchanged which let in mutual light.

"There's where it lies," said the old *procureur* to himself.

"They are on to it," thought the notary.

But both of the cunning, sly couple knew that the investigation would be useless. Bordin knew that Grévin would be as discreet as a wall, and Grévin congratulated himself on having cleared off every trace of the fire. To clear up this point, which seemed but a puerile accessory, but which is of capital importance in the justification which history owes to these young men, the experts and Pigoult, who had been appointed to visit the park, declared that they could not find any trace of a fire anywhere. Bordin produced two laborers, who deposed that, by orders of the keeper, they had dug a patch of burnt turf under; but they had not noticed of what substance the cinders were. The keeper, recalled by the defense, said that after receiving the senator, at the moment when he was passing by the castle on his way to see the masqueraders at Arcis, the senator had told him to order a laborer to dig over that part, which the senator had noticed that morning when taking a stroll.

" Had papers or weeds been burned there ? "

" I saw nothing to make me think that papers had been burnt," replied the keeper.

" In short," said the defense, " if weeds had been burnt, means had been taken to remove all traces of the fire."

The deposition of the curé of Cinq-Cygne and that of Mlle. Goujet created a favorable impression. As they walked toward the forest after vespers, they had seen the gentlemen and Michu on horseback riding out from the castle in the same direction. The position and reputation of the Abbé Goujet gave weight to their words.

The address of the public prosecutor, who felt sure of securing a conviction, was in the usual style of such efforts. The accused were incorrigible enemies of France, its institutions, and its laws. They craved disorder. They had been implicated in plots against the Emperor's life, and formed a part of the army of the Condé; yet that magnanimous sovereign had stricken their names from the list of *émigrés*. Here was how they had repaid his clemency. In fact, all the oratorical declamations used afterward by the Bourbons against the Bonapartists, and which were again repeated at a later day against the Republicans and the Legitimists by the younger branch.

These commonplaces, which might have meant something under a stable government, must appear comic, to say the least, when history finds them in the mouth of the public prosecutor of every age. Perhaps the saying that sprang from former troubles might be applied: " The sign is changed, but the wine is always the same." The public prosecutor, who was indeed one of the most distinguished *procureurs* of the Empire, held that the misdemeanor showed the intention of the returned *émigrés* to protest against the occupation of their lands by others. He made his listeners shudder over the po-

sition in which the senator must be placed.   Then he massed
his proofs, semi-proofs, and probabilities with an ingenuity
which was stimulated by the certain reward of his zeal, and
he quietly sat down to await the fire of his adversaries.

M. de Granville made his first and last plea for the defense
in a criminal trial; but it made his name.   First, he opened
his argument with that irresistible eloquence which we to-day
so much admire in Berryer.   Then he was convinced of the
innocence of the accused; this forms a most powerful vehicle
for a speech.   Here are the principal points of the defense,
which were reported in full in the newspapers of the day.

He began by placing the truth of Michu's life before the
court.   This was a noble story to relate, a beautiful recitation
which sounded the highest sentiments and the finest sympathies.
Seeing himself rehabilitated by this eloquent voice, at one moment the tears started in Michu's tawny eyes and trickled down
his terrible face.   He appeared then as he was in reality—a
simple man with the cunning of a child, but a man whose life
had had but one thought.   He had suddenly been explained,
and his tears completed it and produced a great effect upon the
jury.   The clever counsel for the defense seized this feeling of
interest in which to bring in the discussion of the indictment.

"Where is the substance of the outrage?   Where is the
senator?" he asked.   "You accuse us of imprisoning him
and walling him up with stones and cement.   But, then, we
alone know where he is; and you as well as ourselves know
that, if you are kept in prison for twenty-three days, we
should be dead of starvation by now.   We become murderers,
and yet you have not accused us of murder.   But if he be
alive, we have accomplices; if we have accomplices and the
senator still lives, why do we not produce him?   When the
intentions you have attributed to us once failed, why should
we uselessly aggravate our position?   We might be condoned
by our repenting, as our revenge proved abortive; and yet we
persist in detaining a man from whom we can gain nothing!

Is not this absurd ?   You may carry off your cement, it is no good," said he, turning to the public prosecutor, " for we are either idiotic criminals, which you do not believe, or we are innocent ; the victims of inexplicable circumstances, both for us and you.   You had much better have looked for that mass of papers which were burned in the senator's grounds, which reveals that there is a stronger interest than that of yours, and some other way of accounting for his abduction."

He entered into these hypotheses with marvelous ability. He insisted upon the high character of the witnesses for the defense, whose religious faith showed a belief in a future and eternal punishment.   He was sublime in this and made a profound impression.

"And what ! " said he, " the criminals are peacefully dining after their cousin brings them news that the senator has been kidnapped.   When the officer of the gendarmes made the suggestion to them that if they would give up the senator the affair should go no further they refused ; they did not even know with what they were charged."

He then suggested that it was a mysterious affair, but that time would be when the solution would be known and the injustice of the accusation would be brought to light.   On this ground he had the audacity and ingenuity to so address the jury as being one of themselves; he represented his distress of mind when he afterward found a mistake had been made if he became the means of a cruel condemnation upon innocent men.   He depicted his remorse so vividly and recapitulated his doubts with such force that he left the jury in terrible anxiety.

Juries were not then so thick-skinned to such an appeal ; it possessed the charm of novelty and it left the jury visibly shaken.   After the fervid pleadings of M. de Granville, the jury were addressed by the wily and specious *procureur ;* he multiplied considerations, he set out all the obscure points of the trial and rendered them inexplicable.   In a manner he set himself to create an impression upon the mind and reason, like as M. de Granville had attacked the heart and imagination. Indeed, he perplexed the jury with such serious conviction that the argument of the public prosecutor was completely demolished. This was clear, that the d'Hauteserres' and Gothard's barrister left his case in the hands of the jury, finding that the charge as regarded them was abandoned. The prosecution asked that the morrow be given him in which to reply. Bordin vainly opposed this motion. He saw acquittal in the eyes of the jurymen, if they were permitted to deliberate on their verdict while the pleas were fresh ; he objected to throwing in another night of heart-crushing anxiety for his innocent clients.

The court held a consultation.

" The interest of society, it seems to me, is equal to that of the accused," said the president. " The court could not in justice refuse such a motion if made by the defense, so it must also be granted to the prosecution."

" Delays are dangerous," said Bordin looking at his clients. " Acquitted this evening, you may be found guilty to-morrow."

" In any case," said the eldest Simeuse, " we can but express our admiration for you."

Mlle. de Cinq-Cygne had tears in her eyes. After the doubts expressed by the barristers, she could hardly credit such a success. The people congratulated her, and each one assured her that her cousins would surely be acquitted. But this state of affairs was changed by a theatrical stroke, the most sinister and unexpected that ever changed the aspect of a criminal trial.

At five o'clock of the morning following that of the day on which M. de Granville had plead, the senator was found on the highway to Troyes ; released from incarceration while he slept by some unknown persons, he had started for Troyes, ignorant of the trial, and unaware that all Europe rang with his name, only happy to be again allowed to breathe the free air.

This man, who was the pivot on which the drama turned, was quite as astounded at the news he received as they in turn were amazed at seeing him. A farmer lent him a vehicle and he drove rapidly to Troyes, going direct to the prefect's office. The prefect at once sent for the director of the jury, the commissary of the government, and the public prosecutor, to whom he related his story. After the Comte de Gondreville had done this a warrant was made out for Marthe's arrest; she was found in bed at the Durieus.

Mlle. de Cinq-Cygne, who was at liberty on bail, was aroused from one of her brief periods of slumber had during the midst of incessant anxiety, and was taken to the prefecture for interrogation. Orders were given that the accused were to be denied communication with every one, even with their lawyers; this was impressed upon the warden of the prison. At ten o'clock the assembled crowd were informed that the hearing was postponed until one that afternoon.

This change, coinciding with the news of the senator's deliverance, the arrest of Marthe and Mlle. de Cinq-Cygne, and the counsel for the defense being denied admission to their clients, struck terror into the Chargebœuf mansion. All the town and those who had come thither out of curiosity to hear the trial, the reporters, and even the working people were moved by intense excitement. The Abbé Goujet came at ten o'clock to see M. and Mme. d'Hauteserre and the lawyers. They breakfasted together, if it seems like breakfasting under such circumstances. The curé took Bordin and M. de Granville apart, told them what Marthe had confided to him, and the fragment of letter he had received from her. The two lawyers exchanged glances.

"No more need be said; all seems lost for us," Bordin said after awhile; "but let us put a good face upon it."

Marthe was unable to resist the united force of the director of the jury and the public prosecutor. Moreover, proof against her was too plenty. Under the directions of the senator, Lechesneau had sent to search the cave, and found the bottom crust of the last loaf of bread taken thither by Marthe, together with a number of empty bottles and other things.

During the long hours of his captivity Malin had been con-, jecturing on his position, seeking for every sign of motive of his enemies; he naturally communicated his observations to the magistrate. Michu's farmhouse, recently built, had a new oven; the tiles and bricks on which the bread had lain while being baked had left the imprint of their joints in a sort of pattern on the crust. Then the bottles, sealed with green wax, were doubtless the same as those found in Michu's cellar. These subtle remarks, spoken by the justice of the peace in Marthe's presence, produced the results expected by the senator. The victim of the seeming good-nature of Lechesneau, the public prosecutor, and the commissary made her see that only her full confession could save her husband's life. Marthe acknowledged that the place where the senator had been hidden was known only to Michu, the de Simeuses, and the d'Hauteserres, and that on three several nights she had carried food to the senator. Laurence, questioned as to the hiding-place, was compelled to confess that it was discovered by Michu, that he had shown it to her, and had there concealed the nobles from the researches of the police.

As soon as these questions were ended, information was at once sent to the jury and the bar. At three o'clock the president opened the session, beginning by announcing that new elements had entered the case. The president had Michu confronted with three wine bottles, and asked if he recognized them as his; pointing out at the same time that the wax on two empty bottles was exactly similar to that on the full bottle, and which had that morning been brought from the farmhouse by the justice of the peace in the presence of his wife; Michu was unwilling to acknowledge them as his; **but** this new piece of circumstantial evidence had an appreciable effect on the jury, especially when the president explained that the empty bottles had been found in the place of the senator's detention.

Each of the accused was examined separately in reference to the cave situated in the ruins of the monastery. It was brought out in examination, after all the new testimony for and against the accused had been called, that this hiding-place had been found by Michu, and that only Laurence and the four gentlemen knew of it. One may judge of the effect produced on the spectators and jury when the prosecution announced that this cavern, known only to the accused by their own testimony, had served as the senator's prison.

Marthe was called. Her appearance caused the most lively anxiety to the audience and the accused. M. de Granville rose to oppose the admission of the wife's testimony against her husband. The public prosecutor made the point that she was an accessory after the fact; that therefore she was neither called nor sworn as a witness; she was to be examined only in the interest of truth.

" We have only indeed to read the interrogations and replies before the director of the jury," said the president, who at once instructed the clerk to read the *procès-verbal* drawn up that morning.

" Do you confirm these admissions?" said the president.

Michu looked at his wife, and she, who now saw her mistake, fell in a dead faint. It is no exaggeration to say that this news fell as a thunderbolt in the prisoner's dock and on the counsel for the defense.

"I never wrote my wife from prison, and I do not know one of the keepers," said Michu.

Bordin handed him the scrap off the letter, Michu had only to glance at it :

" My writing has been imitated," he exclaimed.

"A denial is your only resource," said the public prosecutor.

He then produced the senator with the due formalities.

His appearance was a theatrical stroke. Malin, called by the magistrate Comte de Gondreville, without pity to the old proprietors of that demesne, looked on the accused, being so bidden by the president, both long and earnestly. He recollected the clothing that his abductors wore and it was precisely the same as worn by the gentlemen; but he declared that he was so confused at the time of his captivity that he could not positively aver that they were the guilty ones.

"More than that," said he, "my opinion is that these four gentlemen had nothing to do with it. The hands that bandaged my eyes were rough and coarse. And so," said Malin, looking fixedly at Michu, "I can but think that my whilom keeper-steward undertook that charge; but I beg the gentlemen of the jury to carefully gauge my deposition. My suspicions are but meagre; I am not sure in the least. This is why:

"The two men who placed me on a horse and carried me off, put me behind the man who had blindfolded me, and whose hair was red the same as Michu's the accused. And now, although it was a curious thing to observe, yet I am forced to state it, though it is favorable to the accused—I beg him not to be offended. I was closely fastened to the back of this man, and, rapidly though we rode, I noticed the odor of my captor. Now I know that this was not my Michu's peculiar odor. As to the person who at three several times brought me provisions I am quite positive that that was Marthe, Michu's wife. The first time I recognized a ring which had been given her by Mademoiselle de Cinq-Cygne, and which she had not removed. The judge and the jury will note the contradictions which I state, but at present I am unable to explain them."

Favorable murmurs and unanimous approbation greeted

Malin's deposition. Bordin asked the court's permission to cross-examine so precious a witness.

"Monsieur le Senator, had you reason to think that your sequestration was attributable to any other cause than the supposed interests of the accused?"

"Certainly," said the senator; "but I am in ignorance as to what the motive might be; for I declare that, during the whole of my twenty days of imprisonment, I have not seen any one."

"Do you think then," said the public prosecutor, "that at your castle of Gondreville there could be any information, titles, deeds, or anything of value to the claims of the Messieurs de Simeuse?"

"I think not," said Malin. "I think the gentlemen incapable, in any case, of seizing them by violence. They had only to ask to have."

"Monsieur le Senator, did you not order papers to be burned in the park?" said M. de Granville, abruptly.

The senator glanced at Grévin. After a sudden, swift glance of the eye at the notary, and which had been noted by Bordin, he denied that he had ordered any papers to be burned. The public prosecutor then asked for information in reference to the previous narrow escape in the park, and whether he had not been in error as to the position of the gun; the senator said that Michu was on the lookout up a tree. This reply, according with Grévin's testimony, produced a lively sensation.

The gentlemen remained impassible and stolid during the deposition of their enemy, while he beslavered them with his generosity. Laurence suffered the most terrible agony; and the Marquis de Chargebœuf, from time to time, was compelled to catch her in his arms to hold her back. The Comte de Gondreville saluted the four gentlemen and left the stand; they did not return his bow. This little thing made the jury indignant.

" They are lost," said Bordin, in a whisper to the marquis.

" Alas! lost through pride, always the same," replied he.

" Our task has become too easy, gentlemen," said the public prosecutor, rising and looking at the jury.

He explained the use to which the two sacks of cement had been put, they were utilized in making the socket for the iron bolt that fastened the door and held in place the bar on the door of the cave outside, and which had been described that morning in the *procès-verbal* by Pigoult. He easily proved that only the accused knew of the existence of the cavern. He took up all the fictitious evidence of the defense; he pulverized their arguments by the new evidence so miraculously brought into the case. In 1806, it was too soon after 1793, and the epoch of the " Supreme Being," to talk of Divine Justice; he spared the jury giving thanks to heaven. In conclusion, he said that justice would keep on the lookout for those persons unknown who had liberated the senator, and took his seat to await the verdict with confidence.

The jury were certain that a mystery existed; but that mystery in their idea had been made by the accused; they would not speak because private interests of much importance were concerned.

M. de Granville knew that there were machinations of some kind; he rose, but seemed overwhelmed, and this, in fact, was so; nevertheless, it was not so much the new evidence that staggered him as the manifest conviction of the jury. He surpassed, perhaps, his pleading of yesterday. This second argument was certainly more logical and more terse than the first. But the sense of fervency was damped by the chilliness of the jury: he wasted words; more, he knew it. It was a situation horrible and glacial.

He remarked that the release of the senator, which was done as if by magic, and most certainly without the aid of the accused or Marthe, confirmed his first arguments. Surely yesterday the accused might have expected an acquittal, and if they had, as the prosecution seemed to suppose, they were the rulers as to the detention or release of the senator, they would not have released him until judgment had been given. He endeavored to make understood that enemies hidden in the shadows were the only ones possible to have committed this outrage.

A strange thing! M. de Granville troubled the conscience of the public prosecutor and the magistrates with his words; the while the jury just listened as a matter of duty. The spectators were the same, although always in favor of the accused, seemed convinced of their guilt. There is an atmosphere of ideas. In a court of justice the ideas of the crowd are felt by both jury and judges, and otherwise. Seeing these people's minds, both knowing and feeling its effect, the barrister rose in his peroration to a kind of fervered exaltation due to the conviction that his clients were guiltless.

"In the name of the accused I pardon you in advance the fatal error that nothing can dissipate," he exclaimed. "We are the toys of some unknown Machiavellian power. Marthe Michu is a victim of most odious perfidy, as society will see when the misfortune is irreparable."

Bordin, armed with the senator's deposition, asked the acquittal of the gentlemen.

The president summed up with the more impartiality, perhaps, because it was evident that the jury was convinced already, and leaned indeed toward the side of the accused, on the strength of the senator's deposition. A graciousness which could not compromise the success of the prosecution. At eleven o'clock at night, after the usual responses by the foreman of the jury, the court condemned Michu to death, the Simeuses to twenty-four years, and the two d'Hauteserres to ten years of hard labor; Gothard was acquitted. Every one in the hall wished to see the attitude of the five guilty ones in that supreme moment when they came in as free men to hear their condemnation. The four gentlemen looked at

Laurence; she threw them back a fiery glance from a martyr's tearless eyes.

"She would have wept if we had been acquitted," said the younger Simeuse to his brother.

Never did accused confront so quietly an unjust sentence, nor with a more dignified air, than these five victims of a terrible conspiracy.

"Our lawyers have pardoned you," said the eldest Simeuse, addressing the court.

Mme. d'Hauteserre fell ill, and kept her bed for three months, in the Chargebœuf mansion. The old d'Hauteserre returned peaceably to Cinq-Cygne; but, gnawed by his sorrows, the old man could not take up the distractions of the young; his frequent fits of absence of mind showed the curé that the poor father was always on the morrow of that fatal arrest. There was no need to try the beautiful Marthe; she died in prison twenty days after the condemnation of her husband, recommending her son to Laurence, in whose arms she expired. When once the judgment was known, this historical mystery, in the midst of matters of greater importance, passed from the memory. Society is like the ocean: it finds its level, it falls back into its old specious calmness after a disaster, and effaces every trace by the movement of its devouring interests.

Only for her firmness of soul and her conviction of the innocence of her cousins, Laurence would have succumbed; but she gave new proofs of the nobleness of her character; she astonished M. de Granville and Bordin by the apparent serenity by which the most extremely unfortunate show their noble souls. She nursed Mme. d'Hauteserre, sitting up with her every night, and spending two hours of every day at the jail. She said she would marry one of her cousins when they were removed to the hulks.

"To the hulks!" exclaimed Bordin. "But, mademoiselle,

there is only one thing to do now : that is, pray the Emperor to pardon them.''

'' Their pardon, and from a Bonaparte ? '' cried Laurence, with horror.

The spectacles took a leap from the nose of the dignified old lawyer ; he caught them as they fell and took a look at this young person who had at one leap become a woman ; he now understood her character to the full ; he took the arm of the Marquis de Chargebœuf and said :

'' Monsieur, let us hasten to Paris and save them without her.''

The appeals of the de Simeuses, d'Hauteserres, and Michu stood first on the trial sheet of the court of cassation. This was happily arrested by the ceremonies of the inauguration of the court.

Toward the end of the month of September, after three hearings of the appeals by their lawyers and Merlin, the attorney-general, who appeared in person, the petitions were dismissed. The Imperial Court in Paris had been instituted ; M. de Granville had been appointed deputy attorney-general, and the department of the Aube coming under that court's jurisdiction, he found it impossible in the court of which he was an official to take the steps necessary for the condemned. He wearied his patron, Cambacérès. Bordin and M. de Chargebœuf went, the morning after the day of the dismissal of the appeal, to his hôtel at the Marais, and found him in his honeymoon, for in the interval he had been married. In spite of all these events which had occurred in the life of his former lawyer, M. de Chargebœuf plainly saw, from the young deputy's distress, that he was yet true to his clients. There are barristers, the artists of their profession, who make their causes their mistresses. The case is rare ; you had better not count upon it. So soon as his former clients were alone with him in his study, M. de Granville said to the marquis :

'' I was not expecting your visit ; I have already used up

HE PRESENTED IT, SHOWING THE SIGNATURE OF MICHU

all my credit. It is of no use to try and save Michu; you can only obtain pardon for the MM. de Simeuse. There must be one victim."

"My God!" said Bordin, holding out to the young magistrate the three petitions for pardon. "Then how do you suppose that I am to suppress the demand of your old client? To throw this paper on the fire means to cut off his head."

He presented it, showing the signature of Michu. M. de Granville as he took it gazed at it.

"We cannot suppress it. But know this, that if you demand all you will get nothing."

"Have we time to consult Michu?" said Bordin.

"Yes. The warrant of execution is issued by the attorney-general; we can give you a few days. We kill men," added the barrister, in a bitter tone, "but we go through certain forms to do it, even in Paris."

M. de Chargebœuf had already been to the home of the chief justice, and the remembrance of what had been said gave great weight to M. de Granville's words.

"Michu is innocent, that I know, and I say so," said the deputy; "but what can one man do by himself when every one is against him? And bear in mind that now my part is a silent one. It is my task to raise the scaffold on which my old client will be decapitated."

M. de Chargebœuf knew Laurence sufficiently well to be aware that she would never consent to save her cousins at Michu's expense. The marquis took one last chance. He had asked for an audience with the minister of foreign affairs, to learn whether diplomacy in high quarters might not show a loophole of escape. He took Bordin with him to see the minister, to whom he had been of service at odd times. The two old men found Talleyrand absorbed in the contemplation of the fire, his feet stretched out in front, his head in one hand, his elbow on the table, a newspaper on the floor. The minister had just read the decision of the court of cassation.

" You will be seated, Monsieur le Marquis," said the minister. "And you, Bordin," added he, pointing to a place before him at the table ; " write:

SIRE :—Four innocent gentlemen, declared guilty by a jury, have just
been informed that their conviction has been confirmed by your court of
cassation.

Your Imperial Majesty alone can extend mercy to them. These gentlemen only beg this pardon of your august clemency that they may have
the opportunity of utilizing it to the death, in fighting under your eyes,
and they declare themselves your Imperial and Royal Majesty's most
respectful ——— etc.

" It is yours, my dear marquis, take it," said the prince.

"None but princes can know how to confer such obligations,"
said the Marquis de Chargebœuf, taking from Bordin's hand
the precious draft of the petition signed by the four gentlemen, and promising himself that he would obtain august
support for it.

" The lives of your relatives, Monsieur le Marquis," said
the minister, "now hang on the fortunes of war; try to arrive there the day after a victory, then you will save them."

He took up a pen and wrote a confidential letter to the
Emperor, and about ten lines to Marshal Duroc ; then he
rang the bell, asked his secretary for a diplomatic passport,
then quietly said to the old procureur :

" What is your real opinion of this trial ? "

" Then it is unknown to you, monseigneur, who has so
thoroughly entangled us ? "

" I have an idea that I do know, but I have my reasons for
making sure," replied the prince. "Return to Troyes and
bring here the Comtesse de Cinq-Cygne, at this hour to-
morrow; do this secretly ; take her to Madame de Talleyrand,
I will prepare her for your visit. If Mademoiselle Cinq-
Cygne, who shall be placed in such manner that she can see a
man in front of me, then recognizes the one who visited her

house at the time of the conspiracy of Polignac and de
Rivière, and to whom I shall talk, but she must not respond
—not a word ! not a gesture ! and no matter what I may say
or he reply. I do not think but what Messieurs de Simeuse
and d'Hauteserre can be saved ; but don't embarrass yourselves with your unfortunate scapegrace of a keeper."

"A sublime man, monseigneur," exclaimed Bordin.

" Enthusiasm ! and in you, Bordin ! This man must indeed
be something. Our sovereign is prodigiously proud, Monsieur
le Marquis," said he, changing the conversation ; " before
long he will dismiss me so that he may exploit his follies
without my intervention. He is a great soldier, who can
change the laws of time and space ; but he cannot change
men, though he would like to mould them to his use. Now,
do not forget that your relations' pardon can only be obtained
by one person—Mademoiselle de Cinq-Cygne."

The marquis left for Troyes alone, and informed Laurence
of the state of things. Laurence obtained permission to see
Michu, from the attorney-general ; the marquis went with her
as far as the prison door, where he awaited her return. When
she came out her eyes were bathed in tears.

" The poor man," said she, " he tried to fling himself on
his knees to beg me not to give him a single thought ; he forgot the irons on his feet. Ah ! marquis, I will plead his
cause. Yes, I would kiss the boot of their Emperor. And if
I fail, this man shall live for ever in my bosom, and be for
ever in our family. Present his petition for pardon to gain
time ; I must have his picture. Let us go."

The following day, when the minister learned by a precon-
certed signal that Laurence was at her post, he rang the bell,
and the attendant was instructed to bring in M. Corentin.

" My dear fellow, you are a very smart man," said Talleyrand, "and I wish to become your employer."

" Monseigneur——"

" Listen. By serving Fouché you make plenty of money,

but can never gain honor or position ; now by serving me as you did quite recently at Berlin, you will merit respect.''

" Monseigneur is very good——''

" You displayed much genius in that last affair of yours at Gondreville.''

" Of what does monseigneur speak ? '' said Corentin, neither too indifferent nor too surprised.

" Monsieur,'' the minister drily returned, " you will always remain nothing ; you are afraid——''

" Of what, my lord ? ''

" Of death ! '' said the minister in those rich, deep round tones of his. " Farewell, my dear fellow.''

" That is the man,'' said the Marquis de Chargebœuf as he came in; " but we have nearly killed the countess, she is stifled with rage.''

" He is the only one capable of playing such a game,'' answered the minister. " Monsieur, there is danger of your plans miscarrying,'' said the prince.

" Ostensibly take the road to Strasbourg, I will have your passports made in duplicate, the second set shall leave the route blank. Have doubles, change your road cleverly, and, more important still, change your traveling carriage; leave your doubles to be stopped at Strasbourg in lieu of yourselves, and gain Prussia by way of Switzerland and Bavaria. Not one word to a soul and be prudent. You have the police against you, and you don't know what the police is.''

Mlle. de Cinq-Cygne offered Robert Lefebvre a sum sufficiently large to induce him to come to Troyes to paint Michu's portrait; and M. de Granville promised the famous painter every facility possible. M. de Chargebœuf set off in his old *berlingot* with Laurence and one servant who spoke German. But near Nancy he rejoined Gothard and Mlle. Goujet, who had preceded them in an excellent *calèche ;* here those of the *berlingot* took the *calèche* and *vice versa.* The minister was right.

At Strasbourg the chief of police refused his *visa* to the travelers' passport, pleading absolute instructions. At this very moment the marquis and Laurence left France by way of Besançon with their diplomatic passports. Laurence crossed Switzerland in the early days of October, but she had no eyes for that magnificent country. She lay back in the depths of the *calèche*, in the torpor of the criminal when his last hour has come. All nature is covered about with a misty atmosphere at such times, and the commonest things take on a strange and unfamiliar aspect.

This thought: "If I am unsuccessful they will kill themselves," beat in upon her soul as the blow of the executioner's club falls upon the limbs of his victim who is broken upon the wheel. She felt more and more exhausted; she had lost all her energy in the cruel suspense as the swift, decisive moment drew nearer, when she would be face to face with the man on whom depended the fate of the four gentlemen. She had taken up a languid part that she might the better save her energy. Incapable of comprehending these calculations of strong minds which manifest themselves so diversely, for some superior souls abandon themselves to a surprising gayety, the marquis could not fathom Laurence's mood. Sometimes he feared that he would not be able to bring her alive to the audience, solemn only to suppliants, but certainly it assumed proportions beyond those of ordinary private life. For Laurence to humiliate herself before this man, the object of her hatred and scorn, meant the death of all generous sentiments.

"After all," said she, "the Laurence that survives will not bear much resemblance to the one about to die."

Nevertheless, it was very difficult for the two travelers not to perceive the general movement of men when they had once arrived in Prussia. The Jena campaign had begun. Laurence and the marquis saw the magnificent brigades of the French army being reviewed, and paraded the same as at the Tuileries. In this display of military splendor, which can only be given in the imagery and words of the Bible, the man who could animate these masses rose to gigantic proportions in Laurence's imagination. Very soon the words of victory rang in her ear. The Imperial arms had gained two signal advantages. The Prince of Prussia had been killed at Saalfeld, the day before that on which the two travelers arrived there, in their efforts to join Napoleon, who traveled with lightning speed.

Finally, on October 13th, that day of ill omen, Mlle. de Cinq-Cygne drove along by a river through the middle of the great army; she saw nothing but confusion; they were sent from one village to another and from division to division, until she began to be afraid for herself and the old man with her, who were drifting hither and thither in an ocean of a hundred and fifty thousand men, who faced one hundred and fifty thousand others. Quite tired of seeing the line of river by the hedge of box and the muddy road along the hill-side, she asked the name of it of a soldier.

"The Saale," he replied, pointing out the great army of Prussians grouped in large masses on the other side of the water-course.

Night fell; Laurence saw the watch-fires lighted and the glitter of steel. The old marquis, with chivalrous intrepidity, climbed to the seat beside the new servant, and himself drove the two strong horses bought the previous day. The old man well knew that he would be unable to find either horses or postillions on the battlefield. At the appearance of the audacious *calèche* everybody was surprised; it was an object of wonder to the soldiers; at length it was stopped by a gendarme of the army guard, who seized the bridle of the horses and shouted to the marquis:

"Who are you? Whence come you? What do you want?"

"The Emperor," said the Marquis de Chargebœuf. "I have important dispatches for him and Grand Marshal Duroc from the ministers."

"Well, you cannot remain here," said the gendarme.

Mlle. de Cinq-Cygne and the marquis were compelled to stop, and the day was nearly over.

"Where are we?" asked Mlle. de Cinq-Cygne, stopping two officers who came past, their uniform hidden by great-coats.

"You are in front of the van of the French army, madame," replied one of the officers. "You cannot stay here, for if the enemy makes a move the artillery will commence to play, and you will be between two fires."

"Ah!" said she, indifferently.

On this "Ah!" the other officer spoke.

"How comes this woman here?"

"We are awaiting a gendarme," said she; "he has gone to announce our arrival to Monsieur Duroc, who will extend his favor to procure us an audience with the Emperor."

"An audience with the Emperor," said the first officer. "Can you even think of such on the eve of a decisive engagement?"

"Ah! you are right," said she; "I should wait until the day after to-morrow, victory will sweeten him."

The two officers moved away some twenty paces, and mounted their horses, which stood immovably awaiting them. The *calèche* was at once surrounded by an extremely brilliant gathering of generals, marshals, and officers, who respected the carriage, precisely because it stood there.

"Good lord!" said the marquis to Mlle. de Cinq-Cygne, "I fear that we were talking to the Emperor."

"The Emperor?" said a colonel-general. "Why, that is he."

Then Laurence perceived, at some little distance, standing alone and in front of the others, that the one who had exclaimed: "How comes this woman here?" one of the two officers, was the Emperor himself, clothed in his famous greatcoat, which was over a green uniform, and he was mounted on a white horse, richly caparisoned. He examined the Prussian army, with a field-glass, where it lay on the other side of the Saale. Laurence now understood why the *calèche* was allowed to stay there, and why the Emperor's escort respected it. She was seized with a sudden revulsion, the hour had arrived. She then heard the dull sound of great masses of men moving in quick step, who placed their guns in position on the plateau. The batteries seemed to have a language all their own; the caissons vibrated and the metal shone.

"Marshal Lannes will take up position in front with his whole corps; Marshal Lefebvre and the guard to occupy the summit," said the other officer, who was Major-General Berthier. The Emperor dismounted. At his first sign, Roustan, his famous Mameluk, immediately came forward to hold his horse. Laurence was stupid with astonishment; she could not understand that this should be done so simply.

"I shall pass the night on this plateau," said the Emperor.

At this moment Grand Marshal Duroc, whom the gendarme had found, came up to the Marquis de Chargebœuf and asked the reason of his arrival; the marquis replied that he had a letter written by the minister for foreign affairs which would tell how urgently necessary it was that he and Mlle. de Cinq-Cygne should have audience with the Emperor.

"His majesty will doubtless dine at his bivouac," said Duroc, taking the letter; "and when I have learned what it is all about, I will let you know if it can be managed. Corporal," said he to the gendarme, "accompany this carriage and lead the way to the cabin in the rear."

M. de Chargebœuf followed the gendarme until the carriage came to a stand behind a wretched hut built of wood and earth, encircled by a few fruit-trees and guarded by pickets of infantry and cavalry.

One might say that the majesty of war shone out in all its splendor. From the summit of the hill the lines of both armies lay out in the moonlight. After waiting an hour, relieved by the continual movement of the aides-de-camp going and coming, Duroc, who came to look for Mlle. de Cinq-Cygne and the Marquis de Chargebœuf, took them into the hut, the floor of which was of trampled earth, like a barn floor. There at a table from which a meal had been removed, and in front of a smoky fire of green wood, Napoleon was seated in a rough chair. His boots, covered with mud, showed that he had been riding across country. He had doffed his famous greatcoat and wore the celebrated green uniform, crossed by a deep-red ribbon, relieved by white cashmere breeches and a vest of the same color; this attire most admirably set out his pale, stern Cæsarine face. He had his hand on a chart which lay unfolded on his knee. Berthier stood near him in the brilliant costume of a vice-constable of the Empire. Constant, his valet, was presenting the Emperor his cup of coffee.

"What want you?" said he with affected brusqueness, as he cast a glance like a ray of light at Laurence, which penetrated her soul. "You are not afraid now to speak to me before the battle? What is it about?"

"Sire," said she, looking fixedly at him, "I am Mademoiselle de Cinq-Cygne."

"Well?" he replied, in a sharp tone of voice, thinking that her glance dared him.

"Do you not understand? I am the Countess de Cinq-Cygne, and I ask your mercy," said she, falling on her knees and holding out the petition drawn up by Talleyrand, and with postscripts by the Empress, Cambacérès, and Malin.

The Emperor graciously raised the suppliant, and, throwing a shrewd glance at her, said:

"Are you wiser now? Do you understand what the French Empire should be?"

"Ah! I understand nothing but the Emperor at this moment," said she, overawed by the debonair way in which this man of destiny spoke the words which hinted pardon.

"Are they innocent?"

17

"All of them," said she, with warmth.

"All? No. The keeper is a dangerous man, who might kill my senator without so much as ' by your leave.' "

" Oh, Sire," said she, " if you had a friend that was devoted to you, would you desert him? Would you not——?"

" You are a woman," he interrupted, with a tinge of raillery.

"And you are a man of iron," she retorted, with an impassioned harshness that quite pleased him.

" This man has been condemned by the laws of his country," he replied.

" But he is innocent."

" Child ! " said he.

He took Mademoiselle de Cinq-Cygne by the hand and led her out upon the plateau.

" There," said he, with an eloquence all his own, that could turn cowards into brave men ; " there are three hundred thousand men—they are also innocent. Well, by to-morrow thirty thousand of these men will be dead, dying for their country. There may be among the Prussians some great mechanic, an idealist, some genius who may be mown down. On our side we shall certainly lose some great men who will die unknown. Indeed, it may be that my best friend will fall. Shall I adjure God? No. I shall be silent. Bear this in mind, mademoiselle, that one is bound to die by the laws of his country, the same as men will die here for glory," he added, leading the way back into the hut. " Go, return to France," said he, looking at the marquis, " my orders will follow you."

Laurence thought that this meant the commutation of Michu's penalty, and, in an effusion of gratitude, she bent her knees and kissed the hand of the Emperor.

" You are Monsieur de Chargebœuf, eh? " said the Emperor, confronting the marquis.

" Yes, Sire."

"Have you children?"

"A large family."

"Why not give me one of your grandsons? He should be one of my pages."

"Ah! there the sub-lieutenant peeps out," thought Laurence, "he wants payment for his pardon."

The marquis bowed, not making any other reply. Luckily General Rapp precipitately entered the cabin at this precise moment.

"Sire, the horse-guards and those of the Grand Duke de Berg cannot join us before to-morrow at noon."

"It's of no importance," said Napoleon, turning to Berthier; "we have yet some hours of grace, let us turn them to account."

On a signal of dismissal the marquis and Laurence withdrew to their carriage; the corporal set them on their way and conducted them to a near-by village where they passed the night. The next day they traveled further on from the field of battle to the sound of eight hundred pieces of artillery that thundered without intermission for ten hours, and, on the road, the tidings of the wonderful victory at Jena overtook them. Eight days afterward they entered the suburbs of Troyes.

An order from the chief justice, transmitted through the attorney-general of the Imperial Court of First Instance at Troyes, directed that the gentlemen should be liberated on bail, subject to the decision of the Emperor and King; but, at the same time, the order for Michu's execution was sent in to the court. These orders had arrived that morning. Laurence went to the prison immediately, it was two o'clock, and in her traveling dress. She obtained permission to stay with Michu to the last, sad ceremony of "the toilet," so-called. The good Abbé Goujet had asked leave to accompany Michu to the scaffold. When absolution had been given him he lamented that he had to die without being certain as to the fate of his masters; so when he saw Laurence he gave a cry of joy.

"I can die now," said he.

"They are pardoned; I do not know under what conditions," returned Laurence, "but they are pardoned; and I left no means untried to save you, my friend, in spite of their advice. I believed that I had saved you, but the Emperor led me astray by his royal graciousness."

"It stood written on high," said Michu, "that the watch-dog should die on the same spot as his old masters."

The last hour passed very quickly. Michu, when the moment of parting came, would not ask a greater favor than to kiss the hand of Mademoiselle de Cinq-Cygne; but she held up her cheek, and the sainted, noble victim there laid his last kiss. Michu refused to ride in the cart.

"The innocent can go on foot," said he.

He would not allow the Abbé Goujet to give him an arm, he marched with a resolute dignity to the scaffold. At the moment he lay on the plank he spoke to the executioner, asking him to turn down the collar of his greatcoat which covered his neck.

"My clothes belong to you, so do not stain them."

The four nobles had barely time to see Mlle. de Cinq-Cygne; an aide of the general commanding the division came bringing brevets as sub-lieutenants for them in the same cavalry regiment, with orders to at once repair to the headquarters of the corps at Bayonne. After heartrending farewells, for all had forebodings for the future, Mademoiselle de Cinq-Cygne went home to her desolate castle.

The twins died together, under the eyes of the Emperor, at Somosierra, one defending the other; both had become majors. Their last words were:

"Laurence—Cy MEURS!"

The eldest d'Hauteserre was killed, a colonel, in the attack on the redoubt at Moskova, when his brother took his place.

Adrien, appointed a brigadier-general after the battle of Dresden, was grievously wounded, going to Cinq-Cygne to be nursed. To save the last of the four nobles who at one time had been about her, the countess, now a woman of thirty-two, married him; but she could only offer him a blighted heart, which he accepted, like people do who doubt nothing, or who have not lost all faith.

The Restoration found Laurence without enthusiasm; the Bourbons for her returned too late; and yet she had no cause for complaint, her husband became a peer of France, with the title of Marquis de Cinq-Cygne; in 1816 he was appointed lieutenant-general, and was rewarded with the blue ribbon for eminent service rendered to the cause.

Michu's son, whom Laurence raised as her own child, was admitted to the bar in 1827. After having practiced his profession for two years, he was appointed assistant-justice of appeals of the Alençon tribunal, and became attorney for the crown at Arcis soon after; Laurence had invested Michu's capital; she handed over to him funds which brought in an income of twelve thousand livres when he attained his majority; she afterward espoused him to a rich heiress, Mademoiselle Girel, of Troyes.

The Marquis de Cinq-Cygne died in 1829 in Laurence's arms, adored by his father, his mother, and children, who were about him to the last. At the time of his death not a person had been able to penetrate the secret of the senator's abduction. Louis XVIII. did not refuse to make amends for this unfortunate affair; but on the subject of the causes of the disaster he was dumb; and from that time the Marquise of Cinq-Cygne believed that the King was an accomplice in the catastrophe.

CONCLUSION.

The late Marquis de Cinq-Cygne had invested his savings and those of his father and mother in the acquisition of a magnificent mansion situated in the Rue du Faubourg-du-Roule, and which comprised a portion of a great estate entailed for the maintenance of the title. The sordid economy of the marquis and his parents, which grieved Laurence, was thus explained. So since this purchase the marquise, who until now had lived on her estates and hoarded money for her children, spent the winters in Paris, the more willingly because her daughter Berthe and her son Paul were of an age when their education required the resources of Paris.

Madame de Cinq-Cygne went but little into society. Her husband could not be ignorant of the regrets which occupied her tender heart; but he ever showed her the most exquisite delicacy, and died having never loved any other woman. This noble heart, not fully understood for a length of time, but to which the generous daughter of the Cinq-Cygnes returned latterly as much love as that he gave her, was completely happy in his married life. Laurence lived for the joys of family life. No woman in Paris has been more loved by her friends, or more respected. To be received in her house is an honor. Gentle, indulgent, intellectual—more, simple and unaffected—she delights choice souls and attracts them toward her in spite of her aspect of sadness; each one seems to long to offer protection to this so really strong woman, with that sentiment of secret protection which counts for much in the charm of her affection. Her life, so sad and troubled during her youth, is beautiful and serene in its evening. All know of her past sufferings. No one asks whom the original of that portrait by Robert Lefebvre is, which, since the death of the steward-keeper, forms the principal though sad ornament of her salon. The countenance of Laurence has the appearance of fruit which has slowly matured. A kind of religious pride now dignifies that brow which has emerged from its trials.

At the time when the marquise went to her new house, her fortune, augmented by the law of indemnities, brought her in two hundred thousand francs of income, without counting her husband's stipend. Laurence had also inherited the eleven hundred thousand francs left by the Simeuses. From thence she spent one hundred thousand francs per annum, and laid the remainder aside for Berthe's *dot*.

Berthe is the living image of her mother, but does not possess her daring nerve; she has her mother's delicacy and wit and is "more womanly," as Laurence says with a sigh. The marquise was unwilling for her daughter to marry until she was twenty years of age. The savings of the family, wisely invested by old d'Hauteserre when the Funds made a sudden drop in 1830, made a *dot* of eighty thousand francs a year for Berthe, who in 1833 was twenty years old.

About this time the Princess de Cadignan, who wished to marry her son, the Duc de Maufrigneuse, had gained an intimate footing for him in Madame de Cinq-Cygne's family. Georges de Maufrigneuse dined with the marquise three times each week, he accompanied the mother and daughter to the Italiens, and curvetted about their carriage when they drove in the Bois. To the whole world of the faubourg Saint-Germain it was evident that Georges loved Berthe. As yet no one could decide whether Madame de Cinq-Cygne wished to see her daughter a duchess until she should afterward become a princess; or whether it was the princess who coveted the fine dowry for her son; or whether the fair Diane was making advances to the provincial nobility; or whether the nobles of the provinces were frightened by Mme. de Cadignan's celebrity, her tastes and ruinous life. In her desire to avoid in any way injuring her son's prospects, the princess grew

devout, immured herself in private life, and passed the summer season in a villa at Geneva.

One evening Madame la Princesse de Cadignan had at her
home the Marquise d'Espard and de Marsay, the president
of the council—she saw her old lover that evening for the
last time, for he died the following year—Rastignac, under-
secretary of State attached to de Marsay's ministry, two ambassadors, two celebrated orators from the Chamber of Peers,
the old Dukes de Lenoncourt and de Navarreins, the Comte
de Vandenesse and his young wife, and d'Arthez formed a
strangely assorted circle, the composition of which is easily
explained: It was a question of obtaining from the prime
minister a permit allowing the return of the Prince de Cadignan. De Marsay, who did not wish to take the responsibility
of granting this, came to inform the princess that the matter
was in good hands. An old political hack had promised to
bring a solution of the difficulty in the course of the evening.

The Marquise and Mademoiselle de Cinq-Cygne were announced. Laurence, whose principles were unwavering, was
not only surprised but shocked to see the most illustrious
representatives of Legitimacy in both Chambers chatting with
the prime minister of the man of whom she always spoke of
as "Monseigneur de Duc d'Orleans," and that they were
laughing and talking together.

De Marsay, like an expiring lamp, sparkled with a last
brilliancy. He forgot for a time the worry of politics. The
Marquise de Cinq-Cygne tolerated de Marsay much as the
Austrian Court had then accepted M. de Saint-Aulaire; the
man of the world outstepped the minister. But she arose as
though her chair had been of red-hot iron when she heard
announced:

"M. le Comte de Gondreville."

"Adieu, madame," said she to the princess curtly.

She left with Berthe, choosing her way across the room to
avoid encountering that fatal man.

" You have more than likely broken off Georges' marriage," said the princess to de Marsay in a low voice.

The old clerk from Arcis, former representative of the people, Thermidorien, tribune, councilor of State, count and senator of the Empire, peer of Louis XVIII., the new peer of July, made a servile bow to the Princess de Cadignan.

" Tremble no more, fair lady; we no longer war against princes," said he, seating himself beside her.

Malin had enjoyed the esteem of Louis XVIII., to whom his old experiences were anything but useless. He had aided not a little in the overthrow of Decazes, and had given seasonable advice to the Villèle ministry. Coldly received by Charles X., he took up Talleyrand's rancor. He was now in high favor with the twelfth government under which he had served and would one day, when to his advantage, also disserve; but, for the past fifteen months, he had broken the friendship which for thirty-six years had bound him to one of the most famous of our diplomatists. It was in the course of this evening that he spoke of the great diplomat in these words:

" Do you know the reason of his hostility to the Duke of Bordeaux?—— The pretender is too young."

" You are giving," remarked Rastignac, "singular counsel to young men."

De Marsay, who had become very thoughtful since the speech of the princess, did not rise to these pleasantries; he looked askance at Gondreville, and was evidently waiting for that old man to go to bed, which was usually at an early hour. Every one who had noticed the sudden departure of Madame de Cinq-Cygne, for reasons well known to them, imitated De Marsay's silence. Gondreville, who had not recognized the marquise, was unaware of the cause of the general reserve, but the habit of dealing with political matters had given him a certain tact; moreover, he was a man of quick wit; he knew that his presence was uncongenial and took his leave. De

Marsay, standing by the fireplace, in a manner which showed the gravity of his thoughts, watched the old man of seventy years as he slowly left the room.

"I did wrong, madame, in not giving you the name of my agent," said the prime minister, when the carriage had rumbled away. "But I will redeem my fault and give you the means of becoming reconciled with the Cinq-Cygnes. It is now thirty years since these things happened; it is as old to us as the death of Henri IV., which certainly, between ourselves and in spite of the proverb, is still a mystery like many another historical tragedy. I can, however, assure you, even if the affair did not concern the marquise, that it is none the less curious. As a matter of fact, it shows light on a famous passage of our modern annals—that of the Mont Saint-Bernard. Messieurs the Ambassadors will see," said he, with a profound bow to them, "that, in the matter of depth, our politicians of to-day are far behind the Machiavelli whom the waves of popularity lifted above the storm in 1793—some of whom, as the story says, 'have found a port.' To be anything in France in these days a man must have passed through those hurricanes."

"But it seems to me," said the princess, smiling, "that from your account, your state of affairs leaves nothing to be desired."

A well-bred little laugh was raised, even de Marsay could not help smiling. The ambassadors seemed eagerly awaiting the story; de Marsay coughed a preliminary and silence was obtained.

"One night in June, 1800," said the prime minister, "about three in the morning, just as the light of the candles grew pale in the dawn, two men tired of playing at *bouillotte*, perhaps they had only been playing to amuse others, left the salon of the minister for foreign affairs, at that time in the Rue du Bac, and withdrew to a boudoir. These two men, one of whom is dead, and the other of whom has *one* foot in

the grave, were, each in his own way, equally extraordinary.
Both had been priests; both had abjured their oaths; both
were married. One had been a simple Oratorian; the other
had worn the mitre. The first was named Fouché; of the
second I shall not tell the name; but both were then simple
French citizens—but anything rather than simple. When
they were seen to leave the salon and enter the boudoir, the
rest of the company manifested some little curiosity.

"A third person followed them. A man who thought himself far stronger than the first two, his name was Sieyès; as
you all know, he had also been in the church previous to the
Revolution. The one who walked lamely was the minister for
foreign affairs,* Fouché was the minister of police. Sieyès had
resigned the consulate. A stern, cold, little man left his seat
and joined the three men, saying, in a loud tone, as narrated
by the one who heard it, and who gave me the information:
'I mistrust priests' shuffled cards.' This man was Carnot,
minister of war.

"His remark did not trouble the two consuls who were playing cards in the salon. Cambacérès and Lebrun were then
at the mercy of their ministers, who were infinitely cleverer
than themselves.

"Nearly all these statesmen are dead; nothing need be
spared them: they pertain to history, and the history made
that night was terrible; I am telling you this, for only myself
knows about it; for Louis XVIII. never mentioned a word of
it to poor Madame de Cinq-Cygne, and the present government is indifferent as to whether the truth becomes known or
not.

"All four seated themselves in the boudoir. The lame
man carefully closed the door before a word had been spoken:
it has even been said that he drew the bolt. It is only people
of high rank who can readily think of such trifles. The

* Talleyrand, living when de Marsay gave this story, was lame.—
TRANSLATOR.

three priests had the haggard, impassive faces such as you all
remember. Carnot alone had any color in his face. The
soldier was the first to speak.

" ' What is on hand ? '

" ' France,' the prince must have said—I admire him as
one of the most extraordinary men of our day.

" ' The Republic,' was certainly said by Fouché.

" ' Power,' Sieyès most likely said. "

Each guest gazed at the other. De Marsay had given the
voice, look, and gesture of each with marvelous fidelity.

" 'The three priests quite understood each other," he went
on. " Carnot probably looked at his colleagues with dignity
enough ; but he must have felt quite bewildered in his own
mind.

" ' Do you believe in a success ? ' asked Sieyès.

" ' We may expect anything of Bonaparte,' replied the
minister of war ; ' he safely crossed the Alps.'

" ' At this very moment,' said the diplomatist, with calculating slowness, ' he is staking his all.'

" ' In short, say the word,' said Fouché ; ' what shall we
do if the First Consul is vanquished ? Is it possible to collect
another army ? Are we to remain his humble servants ? '

" 'There is now no Republic,' observed Sieyès ; ' he is
consul for ten years.'

" ' He has more power than even Cromwell had,' said the
former bishop, 'and he did not vote for the death of the
King.'

" ' We have a master,' said Fouché ; ' the thing is : shall
we continue him in power if he loses the battle, or shall we
return to a pure republic ? '

" ' France,' replied the sententious Carnot, 'cannot resist
unless she reverts to her old conventional energy.'

" ' I am of Carnot's opinion,' said Sieyès. ' If Bonaparte
returns defeated, we must put an end to him ; he has had too
much to say for the past seven months.'

" ' He has the army,' said Carnot, thoughtfully.

" ' We have the people,' exclaimed Fouché.

" ' You are too fast, monsieur,' replied the *grand seigneur*, in that sonorous bass voice of his, which he still retains, and which made the oratorian shrink within himself.

" ' Let us speak frankly,' said an old conventionalist, raising his head ; ' if Bonaparte is victorious, we shall worship him ; if defeated, we shall bury him.'

" ' You here, Malin ? ' said the master of the house, imperturbably ; ' then you are one with us.'

" He made him a sign to be seated. It is to this one circumstance that this person, an obscure member of the Convention, owes the position he afterward obtained, and finally became what we now see him. Malin was discreet, and the two ministers stood by him ; but they made him the pivot of the machine and the soul of their machinations.

" ' This man is not yet vanquished,' exclaimed Carnot, in a convincing tone ; ' he has surpassed Hannibal.'

" ' In case of the worst, here is the Directory,' replied Sieyès, signifying the five then present.

" ' And,' said the minister for foreign affairs, ' we are all interested in maintaining the French Republic ; three of us have cast our cassocks on the fire ; the general voted for the death of the King. While you,' said he to Malin, ' you own estates belonging to *émigrés*.'

" ' We have all the like interests,' said Sieyès, peremptorily, ' and our interests accord with those of the country.'

" ' A rare case,' said the diplomatist, smiling.

" ' Action is necessary,' added Fouché. ' The battle is now being fought, and Melas has the superior force. Genoa has surrendered, and Masséna has made the great mistake of embarking for Antibes; it is anything but certain if he will be able to rejoin Bonaparte, who will in such case be thrown on his own resources.'

" ' From whom had you this news ? ' asked Carnot.

" ' It is sure,' replied Fouché.   ' You will have the dis-patches by the Bourse opens.'

" They did not mince their words, these men," said de Marsay, smiling, and pausing for a moment.

" ' Now, it is not when the news of disaster has come that we can organize clubs,' Fouché continued ; ' appeal to pa-triotism, and make changes in the Constitution.   Our 18th of Brumaire ought to be ready.'

" ' Let us leave that to the minister of police,' said the diplomatist, ' and ware Lucien.'   (Lucien Bonaparte was then minister of the interior.)

" ' I'll arrest him,' said Fouché.

" ' Gentlemen,' cried Sieyès, ' our Directory ought not to be at the mercy of anarchy and change.   We must organize an oligarchic power, a life Senate and an elective Chamber, the control of which must be in our hands ; for we must profit by past mistakes.'

" ' With such a system I should have a quiet life,' said the bishop.

" ' Find me a sure man to intrust with our correspondence with Moreau ; for the army of Germany is our sole resource,' exclaimed Carnot, plunged in deep meditation.

" As a fact," said de Marsay, pausing awhile, " these men were right, gentlemen.   They were great in that crisis, and I should have done as they did.

" ' Gentlemen ! ' " cried Sieyès in a stern, solemn voice, said de Marsay resuming his story.

" That word ' gentlemen ! ' was thoroughly understood ; the same promise, the same loyalty could be read in all their faces—a promise of absolute silence ; unswerving solidarity in case Bonaparte returned in triumph.

" ' We all know what we have to do,' added Fouché.

" Sieyès had silently unbolted the door ; his priest's ear had well served him.   Lucien entered :

" ' Good news, gentlemen ; a courier has just brought

Madame Bonaparte a few lines from the First Consul—he has made a beginning with a victory at Montebello.'

"· The three ministers looked at each other.

" ' Was it a general engagement ? ' asked Carnot.

" ' No, a battle in which Lannes covered himself with glory. It was a bloody affair. Attacked, having ten thousand men by eighteen thousand men, he was only saved by a division sent to his support. Ott is in full flight. In fact, Melas' line of operations is broken.'

" ' When did this fight take place ? ' asked Carnot.

" ' On the 8th,' replied Lucien.

" ' And this is the 13th,' said the sagacious minister.

" ' Well, to all appearance, the destinies of France are being played for at this very moment when we are speaking.' (As a matter of fact, the battle of Marengo began at dawn of June 14th.)

" ' Four days of mortal suspense,' said Lucien.

" ' Mortal ? ' said the minister for foreign affairs, coldly and interrogatively.

" ' Four days ! ' said Fouché.

" An eye-witness assured me that the two consuls only heard the news after the return of the six personages to the salon. It was then four o'clock in the morning. Fouché was the first to go. That man of profound, infernal genius, working in the shadow, and but little understood, but who was of a certainty the equal of a Philip the Second, a Tiberius and a Borgia. His conduct in the Walcheren affair was that of a consummate soldier, a great statesman, and a far-sighted administrator. He was the only real minister that Napoleon ever had. You all know how he alarmed Napoleon at that time.

" Fouché, Masséna, and the prince are the three greatest men, the wisest heads alike in diplomacy, war, and government that I know. If Napoleon had frankly allied himself with them in their work there would no longer be any Europe, but instead a vast French Empire. Fouché did not entirely detach himself from Napoleon until he saw Sieyès and the Prince de Talleyrand pushed aside. In the space of three days, Fouché, all the time hiding the hand that stirred the ashes of the fire, organized that general agitation that arose all over France, and revived the Republican energy of 1793.

"As I shall throw some light on an obscure corner of our history, I must inform you that this agitation, starting from him, was all worked by a son of the old Mountain, and who produced Republican plots against the life of the First Consul, which was in peril from this cause after his victory of Marengo. It was the consciousness of the evil he had wrought which led him to warn Bonaparte, in spite of all opinions to the contrary, that Republicans were more concerned in the various conspiracies than were the Royalists.

"Fouché understood men to admiration. He counted on Sieyès because his ambition had been thwarted; on Monsieur de Talleyrand as he was a great lord; on Carnot as he knew his upright honesty; but the man he most dreaded was the one you saw here this evening. This was how he set about entangling him.

"In those days Malin was only Malin, and Malin was the correspondent of Louis XVIII. He compelled him, by the minister of police, to draft the proclamations of the Revolutionary government, its warrants and edicts against the factions of 18th Brumaire; and more, far more than all, this accomplice, in spite of his own will, was required to have these documents secretly printed and to store them in packages in his own house. The printer was arrested as a conspirator—for a Revolutionary printer had been chosen of set purpose—but he was released by the police about two months afterward. This man died in 1816, believing that he had been concerned in a conspiracy of the Mountain.

"One of the most curious pieces of comedy played by Fouché's police was, without question, the blunder caused by an agent who dispatched a courier to a famous banker of that time, and who announced the loss of the battle of Marengo. Fortune, if you recollect, was against Napoleon until seven o'clock in the evening. At noon the banker's agent sent word from the seat of war to the king of finance—for he considered the day was hopelessly lost—that the army was annihilated. The minister of police at once sent for bill-posters and public criers, and intended sending out a wagon-load of proclamations, when a second courier arrived with the news of a victory which sent France frantic with joy. Of course heavy sums were lost on the Bourse. But the gathering of criers and bill-posters were bidden to wait until the placards announcing the victory could be struck off; and these exalting Bonaparte were distributed instead of those of outlawry and depicting the political death of Bonaparte.

" Malin, on whom fell all the responsibility of the plot of which he was the working-agent, was afraid, so he carried off the whole of the papers in carts and took them down to Gondreville at a dark hour, where, no doubt, these sinister papers were entombed in the cellars of that castle, which he had bought in the name of another man—he nominated him as president of an Imperial Court—his name was—— ah ! Marion ! Then Malin returned to Paris in time to congratulate the First Consul.

" Napoleon, as you know, hurried from Italy to France with frightful celerity after the battle of Marengo; but it is certain, to those who know the bottom of the secret history of that epoch, that this promptitude was caused by a message to him from Julien. The minister of the interior had an inkling of the attitude of the Mountain, and, though he did not know from which quarter the wind blew, he feared a storm. Incapable of suspecting the three ministers, he attributed this movement to the hatred excited by his brother on the 18th Brumaire, and to the firm belief of the men of 1793 that the check in Italy was irreparable.

"The cry 'Death to the Tyrant,' shouted at Saint-Cloud, was always ringing in Lucien's ears.

"The battle of Marengo detained Napoleon on the plains of Lombardy until June 25th; he arrived in France, July 2d. Now, try to fancy the faces of the five conspirators, congratulating, at the Tuileries, the First Consul on his victory. Fouché at that same time told the tribune—for Malin had once played the part of a tribune—to have patience, for the end was not yet. As a fact, Bonaparte did not seem to Monsieur de Talleyrand and Fouché to be so wedded to the principles of the Republic as they were, and so, for their own safety, they buckled him down by the affair of the Duc d'Enghien. The execution of that prince is traceable, by visible ramifications, with the plot woven that night in the boudoir of the minister for foreign affairs, the night preceding the Marengo campaign.

"Certainly to-day, to those who have been well informed, it is clear that Bonaparte was played like a child by de Talleyrand and Fouché, who were determined to embroil him with the house of Bourbon, whose ambassadors were even then endeavoring to negotiate with the First Consul."

"Talleyrand was taking a hand at whist at Madame de Luynes," began one of those who had been listening to de Marsay. "At three o'clock in the morning he interrupted the game, pulled out his watch, and abruptly asked his three companions, without any preface, if the Prince de Condé had any other child than Monsieur le Duc d'Enghien. An inquiry so absurd from Talleyrand's lips caused marked surprise. 'Why do you ask this when you yourself know so well?' they said to him. 'This is to let you know that the house of Condé ends at this moment.'

"Now Monsieur de Talleyrand had been at the de Luynes' mansion since the evening commenced; he could not, therefore, have known that Bonaparte found it was impossible that he could grant the pardon."

"But," said Rastignac to de Marsay, "I don't see the point as to Madame de Cinq-Cygne."

"Ah! you were so young, my dear fellow, that I quite forgot the conclusion. You know the affair of the abduction of the Comte de Gondreville, the business that caused the deaths of the two Simeuses and the eldest brother of the d'Hauteserres, who by his marriage with Mlle. de Cinq-Cygne became Comte, and later Marquis of Cinq-Cygne."

De Marsay, begged by a number of persons to whom this adventure was unknown, gave the history of the trial, saying that the masked persons were five sharks sent down by the general police of the Empire, who were directed to obtain the proclamations printed by order of the Comte de Gondreville, and to destroy the very packages that the Comte de Gondreville had himself come down to burn, when he thought the Empire was firmly established.

"I suppose," said De Marsay, "that Fouché had search made at the same time for proofs of the correspondence between Gondreville and Louis XVIII.; there had been an understanding between them all along, even during the Terror. But in this cruel business there was a private animus on the part of the leading agent, who is still living. He is one of those great men, whom nothing can replace, who can properly fill a subordinate position; he has distinguished himself by most astonishing ability.

"It appears that Mademoiselle de Cinq-Cygne disdainfully treated him when he had gone down to arrest the Simeuses. So, madame, you have the secret of the affair. You can now explain to the Marquise de Cinq-Cygne, and make her comprehend why Louis XVIII. maintained silence."

PARIS, *January*, 1841.

MASSIMILLA DONI.

TRANSLATED BY JNO. RUDD, B. A.

To Jacques Strunz.

*My dear Strunz :—It would be ungrateful on my
part did I not set your name at the head of one of the
two stories that I could never have written but by your
complaisance and painstaking.   Receive this as a
friendly confession of the efforts you made (perhaps not
altogether successfully) to initiate me into the mystery of
musical science.   You have taught me, at the least, the
sum of the difficulties and laborious work genius must
bury in those poems which are for us the source of
pleasures divine.   You have also given me the opportunity of more than once laughing at the expense of a
pretending connoisseur.*

*I have been taxed with my ignorance, but those so
doing were little aware that I had taken counsel of
one of our foremost musical critics, and knew not that
I had the benefit of his best endeavor.   Perhaps I was
an inaccurate amanuensis.   Should this be so I were
indeed a traitor of a translator unknowingly, and still
I will ever sign myself one of your friends,*

DE BALZAC.

As every one versed in such matters must know, the nobility of Venice is the first in Europe. Its *Livre d' Or*
(Golden Book) dates prior to the Crusades, from an epoch
when Venice, a survivor of Imperial and Christian Rome,
which had thrown itself into the water to escape the barba-
rians, was even then all puissant and illustrious; the capital of
the world of commerce and politics. This brilliant nobility,

with a few exceptions, has gone to utter ruin. Among the gondoliers who serve the English—and who may in this read their own future fate as written of history—there are descendants of long-dead Doges bearing names that are older than those of their sovereigns. Upon some bridge as you sweep past it, if you ever visit Venice, you may admire some handsome girl in tattered garments, a poor child that maybe is a member of one of the most patrician of families. In a nation that has so fallen, it may well be supposed that certain strange characters may be encountered. It cannot astonish that sparks should flash out among ashes.

The nobility of Venice and those of Geneva, the same as those of Poland in earlier days, bore no titles. The name of Quirini, Doria, Brignole, Morosini, Sauli, Mocenigo, Fieschi, Cornaro, or Spinola was sufficient for the haughtiest pride. But all things become corrupt. At this time some of these families have titles. Even at a time when the nobility of the aristocratic republic were each the peer of the other, the title of prince was, in fact, given at Genoa to a member of the family of Doria, sovereigns of the principality of Amalfi. A similar title was used in Venice, having a precedent of ancient legitimacy in Facino Cane, Prince of Varese.

The last Cane of the elder branch left Venice thirty years preceding the fall of the Republic, condemned for various crimes. In the twentieth year of the present century it was represented by a young man by the name of Emilio, and an ancient palace long regarded as one of the chief ornaments of the Grand Canal. This scion of Fair Venice had for his sole fortune the useless palace and an income of fifteen hundred francs a year, the rental of a country-house on the Brenta. This small income spared the handsome Emilio the disgrace of accepting, as was done by many nobles, the indemnity of one franc per day, due to each poverty-stricken patrician by the stipulations of the cession to Austria.

At the beginning of winter this young noble was still stay-

ing in a country-house at the base of the Tyrolean Alps; it
had been bought by the Duchesse Cataneo the spring before.
The furniture was, like that of all Italian palaces, rich with
handsome silks, hung with exquisite taste, while valuable
paintings were favorably hung.   There were some by that
priest of Genoa kown as *il Capucino*, and several by Leonardo
da Vinci, Carlo Dolci, Tintoretto, and Titian.

The sloping gardens were filled with the marvels that money
has caused to be made.   Grottoes of rock and patterns of
shells—artistic lunacy—fairy terraces, arbors not too light,
where the cypress with his tall trunk, the three-cornered pines
and the melancholy olive were intermingled with orange trees,
laurels, myrtles, and pools of clear water in which swam blue
and golden fishes.   It matters not what may be said in favor
of the popular English garden, with its unartificial prettiness,
yet these trees pruned into the shapes of parasols and birds,
the yews being clipped into still more fantastic shapes; this
art of luxury, combined natural and artificial court graces;
those waterfalls down marble steps, the water so lightly spread
that it resembled a gauzy scarf blown aside by the wind and
quickly renewed; the bronze statues which silently inhabited
the glades; the noble mansion a landmark on every side,
uprearing its light outline to the foot of the Alps—the living
thoughts animating the marble, the bronze, the trees, this
lavish prodigality was in perfect keeping with the love of a
duchess and a gallant youth; for it is a poem removed far
from the coarse aims of brutish nature.

In this palace of the fairies, where one might expect to
see a negro slave, wearing a scarlet sash, holding an umbrella
over the duchess' head with one hand, while supporting her
long train with the other, this Duchess Cataneo accepted the
firmans of Victorine and wore the latest French modes.   She
had on a fine lawn dress, a wide straw hat, soft shoes, stockings of thread lace that the gentlest zephyr would have wafted
away, and over her shoulders a black lace shawl.   The one

thing that could not have been understood in Paris, where every woman is incased in her dress as a dragon-fly is sheathed in its ring-like armor, was the perfect freedom that this lovely daughter of Tuscany wore her French drapes; she had Italianized it. The utmost seriousness is accorded her skirt by the Frenchwoman; an Italian scarcely gives it a thought. She does not seek self-protection by a demure glance, for she knows her only armor is assured in a devoted love, a passion as sacred in her own estimation as it is in others.

At eleven o'clock in the morning, after a ramble, and near a table still strewn with the remnants of an elegant breakfast, the duchess, who was lolling in a low chair, gave him the freedom of these muslin draperies, not bestowing a frown upon him each time he stirred. Emilio, who was seated by her side, holding one of her hands between both of his, gazed at her in rapt adoration. Ask not if they loved; they loved only too well. They were not conning the same book, as did Paolo and Francesca; not so, for Emilio dared not say: "Let us read."

The glint of those eyes, the gray irises gleaming with streaks of gold starting from the centre like beams of light, making her gaze a sweet, star-like radiance, so thrilled him with a nervous rapture that it became almost a spasm. The mere sight of the luxuriant black hair crowning the adored head, kept in due bounds by a band of gold, would cause a singing in his ears, the mad rush of the blood through his veins seeming as if it would burst his heart.

Massimilla, heiress of the Doni, of Florence, was married to the Sicilian Duke Cataneo. Her mother, now dead, had hoped, by fostering this marriage, to leave her daughter rich and happy in the Florentine manner. She thought that her daughter, who emerged from a convent to embark in life, would attain, under love's guidance, the sacred union of heart with heart, which, in a woman of Italy, is the all and all. But Massimilla Doni, in her convent, had acquired a genuine liking for a religious life, and, after pledging her troth to the Duke Cataneo, she had the Catholic content to be his wife.

Here was an untenable position. Cataneo considered himself absurd as a husband, he only looked for a duchess; when Massimilla took umbrage at his indifference, he with much *sang-froid* bade her look up some *cavaliere servente,* going so far as to offer his services in introducing her to some pretty youths from which to choose. The duchess wept; he made his exit.

Massimilla gazed about her in the world that crowded her. She was taken by her mother to the various drawing-rooms of the ambassadors, to the Cascine—anywhere that it was likely young men might be met; she found none to her mind, and determined on travel. Then her mother died; she inherited her property, assumed mourning, and wended to Venice. There she saw Emilio, who, in passing her box at the opera, exchanged a glance of meaning with her. This was all. The Venetian was dumfounded, while the duchess heard a whisper in her ear: "This is he!"

Emilio was introduced to the duchess by the Signora Vulpato; he was the constant attendant in her box throughout the winter. Never was a love more ardent in two hearts, never so timid in its advances. The two children were each afraid of the other. Massimilla was not a coquette. She had not a second string to her bow—no *secondo,* no *terzo,* no *patito.*

This handsome pair had now been at the Rivalta for six months. Aged twenty, Massimilla had not abandoned her religious principles to her passion without a severe struggle. Still, although slowly, they had yielded; she was ready at any moment to consummate the love union her mother had made her understand, as she now sat, her hand caressed in that of Emilio's.

She was unconscious of the misfortune, a torture to Emilio,

which raised up a curious barrier between them. Massimilla, though very young, had the majestic mien ascribed by mythology to Juno, the only goddess which tradition has left without a lover; for Diana, the chaste Diana, loved! Only Jupiter himself could hold his own with his better-half goddess, the fashion upon which English ladies model themselves.

Emilio had placed his mistress far too high ever to touch her. Perhaps a year hence he might not be a victim to this grand mistake which only attacks very young or very old men. But like as the archer who shoots beyond the mark is as far from hitting it as the one whose arrow falls short, so the duchess found herself between a husband, who knew he was so far from being able to reach the target that he had stopped trying to get there, and a lover who was carried so far past it by the wing-feather of an angel that he could not get back at it. Massimilla could be happy with desire, not understanding its issue; but her lover, sorrowful in his joy, would occasionally obtain a promise from his so-beloved that was perilously near the verge of what many women call "the gulf," and found himself compelled to be satisfied by picking the flowers around the edge, not having more courage than to pluck off the petals, and smothering his love-pangs in his breast.

They had rambled out together that morning, singing such a hymn of love as was repeated by the birds among the branches. Upon their return, the youth, whose state can only be likened to the cherubs who are represented by the painters as having nothing between their heads and their wings, had become so inflamed by passion as to venture a doubt as to the entire devotion of the duchess, endeavoring to bring her to say:

"What proof can I give you?"

The question had been put with a regal air, and Memmi ardently kissed the handsome, guileless hand. Then he jumped up in a fury with himself and left Massimilla. The duchess still reclined in her voluptuous attitude on the couch; but now she shed tears, wondering why so young, so fair as she was, she could not give pleasure to Emilio. Memmi, on the other side, banged his head against the trunks of trees like a hooded falcon. But now came a servant in pursuit of the young Venetian to hand him a letter just come by express.

Marco Vendramini—pronounced also Vendramin in Venetian, which drops many final letters—his only friend, wrote informing him that Facino Cane had died in a Paris hospital. Full proofs of this were at hand, and so the Cane-Memmi were princes of Varese. A more important item to him, he thought, was the engagement at the Fenice of the great tenor Genovese and the no less famous Signora Tinti.

He ran to communicate this glorious tidings to the duchess, who knew nothing of the curious story which made La Tinti such an object of interest in Italy, so Emilio briefly related it.

This great and famous singer had been but a waiting-maid at a tavern, whose marvelous voice had captivated a wealthy Sicilian noble while traveling. This girl's loveliness—she was then but twelve years of age—being the peer of her voice, her patron had had her brought up in the like manner to which Louis XV. had Mlle. de Romans educated. He then waited most patiently until Clara's voice had been fully trained by an expert professor, by which time she was sixteen, before demanding aught of the treasure so successfully cultivated. La Tinti had made her debut last year, and had made captive the three most fastidious capitals in Italy.

"I am quite certain that her great lord is not my husband," said the duchess.

The equipage was soon ordered and Massimilla set out for Venice for the opening of the season. One evening in November, the new Prince of Varese watched the elegant gondola, navigated by men in livery, belonging to Massimilla; he could not help a retrospective glance at his life: he, whose only servant was an old gondolier of his father's.

"What a farce in fortune! A prince, with fifteen hundred francs a year! Owner of one of the finest palaces in the world, unable to dispose of the statues, wood-work, paintings, sculpture, which, by an Austrian decree, had been made inalienable. To live on a foundation made of driven piles of campeachy wood worth over a million francs, and yet possessing no furniture! Owning gorgeous galleries, and yet living in an attic over the highest arabesque cornice, built of marble brought hither from the Morea—that country through which a Memmius marched as a conqueror in the days of the Romans! To behold the effigies of his ancestors recumbent on their tombs of costly marble in one of the finest churches in Venice, in a chapel adorned with paintings by Titian, Tintoretto, Palma, Bellini, Paul Veronese—and yet debarred the selling a marble Memmi to the English for bread for the living Prince Varese! Genovese, the noted tenor, could earn more in one season by his warbling, the capital, the interest of which would be an income this son of the Memmi could live on. Genovese smokes an Eastern hookah, but the Prince of Varese cannot have even enough cigars!" He tossed the end he was smoking into the water.

The Prince di Varese obtained his cigars at the duchess' mansion; he would have been enraptured to lay at her feet the riches of the world. It was at her house that he made his only meal, for his whole income was expended on his clothes and his seat at the Fenice. His father's old gondolier was paid by him one hundred francs a year for his wage; to make this sum serve his necessities he could only obtain rice for food. Beside this Emilio retained enough to get himself a cup of black coffee every morning at Florian's to keep him in a state of nervous excitement until the evening; he hoped that this habit, carried to excess, would as surely be his death, in due time, as the use of opium would ultimately kill his friend Vendramin.

"And I am a prince!"

Speaking these words Memmi threw Vendramin's letter into the lagoon, not even stopping to read the conclusion of it; it floated off like a paper-boat launched by a child.

"See, now, Emilio," he muttered to himself, "is but three-and twenty.   He is a better man than Lord Wellington, who has the gout, than the Regent who has paralysis, than the epileptic royal house of Austria, than the King of France who——"

But as he thought of the King of France Emilio knit his brow, his skin of ivory became saffron-hued, his eyes filled with tears which hung a-down his long lashes. He raised a hand, handsome enough to be painted by Titian, and pushed back his clustering brown hair, and gazed once more at Massimilla's gondola.

"And this impertinent mockery of fate comes even into my affairs of the heart," said he.   "My soul and imagination are full of precious talents, yet Massimilla will none of them; she is a Florentine, she will cast me off. I sit by her side a figure of ice, yet her voice and glance fire me with celestial desire ! Ah, well, either my highness will end my days with a charge from a pistol, else will the heir of the Cane follow Father Carmagnola's example. We will turn sailors, pirates; it will be really amusing to see how long we can escape the hangman."

Emilio had a vision of the days when the Memmi palace had light streaming forth from every window, when the strains of music were carried afar over the Adriatic gulf, when gondolas by the hundred were made fast to its mooring-posts, the while graceful masked figures and the Republican magnates elbowed each other up the wave-kissed marble steps; of the time when its galleries and halls were crowded by intriguers and their victims; when the great banqueting-hall was filled with jolly revelers, the balconies with musicians, and when it seemed to embrace all the populace of Venice, laughing and gesticulating.

Some of the greatest sculptors of many ages had chiseled the brackets of bronze that supported the long-necked, pot-bellied China vases, and the chandeliers holding a thousand candles. Not a country but had given some contribution to the magnificence that ornamented walls and ceilings. But now the panels had been stripped of the splendid arras. Gone the Turkey carpets, the crystal vases brilliant with flowers, the statues, the paintings ; no more joy, no more money, the one means of happiness. The London of the Middle Ages, Venice, was crumbling stone by stone, man by man. The prophetic green weed, kissed by the sea and flung by the sea at the feet of every mansion, was, to the prince, the black border hung by nature, a token of death. But, alas ! as a finality, a famous English poet had descended upon fair Venice as a raven upon a corpse, and had croaked out in poetic song— the first, the last word of social humanity—the refrain of a *de profundis.* English poetry ! Flung in the face of the city that was the birthplace of the poetry of Italy ! Wretched Venice !

Think, then, of the astonishment evinced by Emilio when aroused from his reverie by old Carmagnola crying :

"Serenissimo, the palace is on fire, else have the old Doges arisen from their tombs ! See, there are lights showing in the windows of the highest balcony ! "

Prince Emilio believed that his dream had become fact by the wave of some magic wand. It was dusk, so, without being observed, the old gondolier was able to assist his master ashore, unnoticed by a hustling corps of servants who were buzzing around the landing like bees around a hive. Emilio stole into the great hall, giving upon the finest flight of stairs in the whole of Venice, up which he noiselessly ran to investigate this so strange occurrence.

Prince Emilio made his way to his own bedroom, which he was charmed to find had been made beautifully elegant. He seated himself in a cozy chair of gilded wood, and drew up to where an appetizing cold supper awaited him, and without more ado he began to eat.

"There can but be one Massimilla in all this world. Who but she could have thought out this surprise?" he reflected. "She has learned that I am now a prince. It may be that Duke Cataneo is dead, leaving her his fortune; if so, she is doubly as wealthy as before, and she will marry me!"

It gave him appetite. He ate in such manner as would have caused envy in an invalid Crœsus, could such have seen him, and he drank copiously of full-bodied port wine.

"Now can I understand the wise little look she wore as she said: 'Till this evening.' Will she come and break the spell, I wonder? What a fine bed! Such a pretty lamp, too! Really a Florentine idea!"

When Emilio had finished the bottle of port, eaten half a fish, and the greater portion of a French pâté, he felt drawn by longing to his bed. Perhaps he had a double attack of intoxication. He pulled aside the coverlet, opened the clothes, then, after doffing his attire in a pretty dressing-room, he lay down to meditate on destiny.

"Ah! I forgot poor Carmagnola, but doubtless my butler and chef will see to him," said he.

Just then in came a waiting-maid, lightly humming a scrap from "Il Barbiere;" she flung a lady's night-dress on a chair, the whole paraphernalia for the night, and said, when this was done:

"Here they are!"

And there entered a young lady dressed in the latest *mode de Paris*. She might have sat for some fancy English portrait to be engraved for a "Forget-me-not," an "Assembly of Beauties," or a "Book of Beauty."

The prince quivered with delight, alloyed with fear, for, you must remember, he was in love with Massimilla. But his blood was fired with desire. It agitated him, but did not infuse his soul with that celestially warm glow always felt on a word or look from the duchess. But the woman was not alone.

The prince beheld one of those forms believed in by no one when depicted from real life, where we wonder at them, to an imaginary life of mere literary description. The stranger's attire, like that of all Neapolitans, showed five colors, if the black of his hat may be accounted as one; his trousers were olive-brown, a red vest was covered with gilt buttons, his coat had a shade of green, his linen was more yellow than white. His eyes were like glass beads. His nose resembled the ace of clubs, and was awfully long and knobby; it did its very best, in fact, to hide a gash it were a horrible misnomer to dignify with the name of mouth; in this three or four tusks could be seen, endowed, apparently, each with a motion fitting to the rest of the features. His obese ears drooped of their own weight, and gave a whimsical look of a hound to the creature.

Some Hippocrates had doubtless prescribed metallic medicants to the extent of tainting his skin a blackish hue. His skull was Gothic and was barely supplied with a few, thin white hairs, which, like spun glass, crowned this grewsome face, covered with red blotches. Lastly, though the man was thin and but of medium height, his arms were long and shoulders broad. Despite this hideous aspect, and although he appeared to be about seventy, he did not lack a kind of Cyclopean nobility. His manners were aristocratic and his demeanor that of a man confident in his wealth.

His history could be read, engraved on the mud degraded by ignoble passions from the noble clay. Here was to be seen a man of gentle birth, who, wealthy from his youth up, had given his body over to debauchery for the sake of vulgar enjoyment. Debauchery had replaced the human being with a vile one made after its own likeness. Thousands of bottles of wine had made their way down the cavernous archway under that preposterous nose, but they had left their lees upon his lips. Slow and labored digestion had rotted away his teeth. The light of his eyes had become dimmed by the lamps of the gaming table. The blood, tainted with impurities, had impaired the nervous system. His intellect had deteriorated under the task of digestion upon his life-force. Finally, the passions of purchased love had thinned his hair. Every vice, like a greedy heir, had marked its possession on some portion of this living corpse. The student of nature will detect in her jests the most ironical. For instance, toads she puts in close vicinity with flowers; she had placed this thing by the rose of love.

"Will you play the violin to-night, my dear duke?" said the woman, as she loosed a cord to let fall a handsome portière over the door.

"Play the violin!" said Emilio to himself, "what has occurred in this my palace? Am I sleeping? I am here in that woman's bed, and yet she evidently thinks she is in her own house! She has taken off her mantle! Have I, as does Vendramin, inhaled fumes of opium? Am I, too, in one of those ravishing dreams of Venice, such as it was three centuries back?"

The unknown beauty, seated in front of a dressing-table, brilliant under wax-lights, was unfastening her lingerie with quiet calmness.

"Ring for Julia," said she, "I want to get my dress off."

At that moment the duke noticed that the supper had been tampered with; he glanced about the room, and soon discovered the trousers belonging to the prince, hanging over a chair-back at the foot of the bed.

"I will not ring, Clarina!" exclaimed the duke, in a voice shrill in its fury. "I will not play the violin to-night, nor to-morrow night, nor, in fact, ever again——"

"Ta, ta, ta, ta," sang Clarina, on the octaves of one note, flying from one to the other with the ease of a nightingale.

"In spite of that voice, which is the envy of your patron saint, Claire, you are absolutely too impudent, you hussy."

"You have not brought me up to give ear to such abuse!" said she with an assumption of pride.

"Did I bring you up to hide a man in your bed? You are not worthy of either my generosity or hate!"

"A man!—in my bed!" cried Clara, nervously looking around.

"And that, too, after eating our supper as if he were at home!" added the duke.

"Am I not at home?" exclaimed Emilio. "I am the Prince of Varese; this is my palace."

Saying this, Emilio sat up in bed, his handsome patrician head in a frame of flowered drapery.

First, Clarina laughed, a rushing fit of glee which seizes a young girl when she comes across a ludicrous adventure funny in the extreme. But her laughter soon ceased as she noted what a fine, handsome, and hale-looking young man he was, although but lightly attired; the madness of desire seized her in turn, as it had already done with Emilio; and, as she had no one whom to adore, no qualms of reason bridled her sudden fancy—that of a Sicilian woman in love.

"Though this is the palazzo Memmi," said the duke, "I must thank your highness to leave." As he spoke he took upon himself the distant irony of the polished noble and added, "I am at home here."

"Allow me to inform you, Monsieur the Duke, that you are in my bedroom, and not your own," Clarina said at length, as she recovered herself. "If you entertain any suspicions of my virtue, at least give me the benefit of my crime——"

"Suspicions? Say proof positive, my angel!"

"But I swear my innocence," Clarina made answer.

"Explain, then, what do I see in your bed?"

"Old ghost!" said Clarina. "Is it that you believe your eyes before my assertion, if so you have ceased to love me.

19

Go, do not weary my ears! You hear? Then begone, Monsieur the Duke. This young prince will readily recoup you the million francs you have expended on me."

"I won't repay anything," muttered Emilio in an undertone.

"But there is nothing due him! A million is too cheap for Clara Tinti when the adorer is so precious ugly. Now, get out," she added to the duke. "You it was that first dismissed me; now it is I that dismiss you. We are quits."

As the old duke made a gesture as though to dispute this command, given with a manner equal to Semiramis' best (the part in which la Tinti had earned her renown), the prima donna made a dash at the old monkey and ejected him out the door.

"If you do not leave me in quiet for to-night we never again meet. Understand, too, that *my* never counts for more than yours," said she.

"Quiet?" retorted the duke with a bitter laugh. "My dear idol, it appears the rather that I leave you *con agitata!*"

The duke went.

To Emilio this mean acquiescence was no surprise.

Clarina bounded like a fawn from the door to the bed.

"A prince, poor, young, beautiful!" she exclaimed. "Truly, it is a perfect fairy tale."

La Tinti perched herself on the bed with the innocent glee of an animal, the plant yearning for the sun, the airy undulations of a branch awaiting the zephyr. While unbuttoning the cuffs of her sleeves she commenced singing, not as she sung when winning applause at the Fenice, but a tender warbling, resonant with emotion. Her song was a soft breeze wafting the caresses of her love to his heart.

She stole a timid glance at Emilio, who was quite as much embarrassed as herself, for this lady of the stage had now lost all the boldness that had brightened her eyes and given decision to both voice and gestures as she had dismissed the duke. She was as humble as a courtesan who has fallen in love.

To depict la Tinti you must call to mind one of our leading French singers when she came out in "Il Fazzoletto," Garcia's* opera, then being sung by an Italian company at the theatre on the Rue Louvois. She was so extremely handsome that a poor guardsman of Naples had committed suicide in despair of winning her. La Tinti, whose name was something like that of the famous French singer, was just seventeen, and the unlucky prince three-and-twenty. What fateful hand of mockery had deemed it a jest to bring the match so near the powder? Here were a fragrant room hung with rose-colored silk bright with numberless wax-lights, a bed draped in lace, a dumb palace—Venice! Two young and handsome creatures! Every ravishing delight at once.

Emilio grasped hastily at his trousers, sprang out of bed, ran into the dressing-room, donned his clothes, came back and hurried toward the door. While dressing he thought :

"Massimilla, beloved daughter of the Doni, you in whom the beauty of Italy is a hereditary prerogative; you that are of equal worth to the portrait of Margherita, one of the so few pictures entirely painted by Raphael to his undying glory! My lovely and saintly mistress, shall I have earned you if I flee not from this abyss of flowery temptation? Should I be worthy you if I profaned a heart that is solely yours? No; I will not be caught in that vulgar snare spread for me by my rebellious senses! This girl has her duke, be mine the duchess!"

As he lifted the portière he heard a moan. The heroic lover turned around and saw Clarina on her knees, her face hidden in the bedclothes, choking with sobs. Will it be believed? The singer was infinitely lovelier as she knelt, her face unseen, than she was in her confusion and a glowing countenance. The hair drooping over her shoulders, the attitude of a Magdalen, the disorder of her partially unbut-

* Father of Mme. Malibran and composer of "The Caliph of Bagdad."

toned dress, the whole living picture had been arranged by the devil, who, as you are well aware, is a great colorist.

The prince clasped an arm around the weeping girl, who slipped from his grasp like a snake, clinging to one foot, which she pressed to her bosom.

"Will you please tell me," said he, jerking his foot from her embrace, "how you come to be here in my palace? How the impecunious Emilio——"

"Emilio Memmi!" exclaimed la Tinti, as she arose. "You said you were a prince!"

"A prince since yesterday."

"You are in love with the Duchess Cataneo!" said she, looking him over from head to foot.

Emilio stood dumb, seeing that the prima donna was smiling at him through her tears.

"Your highness perhaps does not know that the man who had me trained for the stage, the duke, is himself Cataneo. Nor that your friend Vendramin, desiring to serve you, rented your palace to him for three thousand francs during my season at the Fenice. My dear idol of my desire!" continued she, seizing his hand and drawing him nearer to her, "why fly from me, for whom most men would take the risk of broken bones? See, then, love is always love. It is the same in every place; the sun of our souls; we can warm ourselves wherever it may shine, and here—now—it is high noon. If I do not satisfy you, then to-morrow kill me! But I know I shall live, for I am a daisy!"

Emilio decided to remain. When with a gesture signifying his acquiescence, he noticed a thrill quiver through Clarina, seeming to him like a spark from hell. Never before had love come to him in so subtle a form. At that instant Carmagnola whistled loudly.

"What can he wish with me?" said the prince.

But bewildered by love, Emilio disregarded the old gondolier's oft-repeated signals.

If you have never traveled in Switzerland, you maybe will read this pen-picture with pleasure. If you have clambered among those mountains you will be glad to be again reminded of its scenery.

In that land of the sublime, in the heart of a boulder riven by a chasm, a valley as broad as the Avenue de Neuilly in Paris, but six hundred feet deep and cut into ravines, flows a torrent from some fearful height of the Saint-Gothard on the Simplon, which has formed a pool, how wide or how deep I cannot tell, bordered by split-up cliffs of gneiss upon the top of which meadows are found, with pine trees and great elms—where also grow the violet and strawberry. Here and there a châlet, at the window a rosy-cheeked Swiss girl with yellow hair. As is the mood of the sky so is the water of the lakelet, blue and green : blue, though, as is the sapphire—green as an emerald. There is naught in the world can give such an idea of depth, peace, immensity, heavenly love, eternal happiness, even to the least observant of travelers, the most hurried courier, the most common grocer, as this liquid diamond into which the snow trickles through its own channel, after accumulating on the highest Alps, bored through the live rock, whence it escapes below without a ripple of sound. The limpid sheet of water which overhangs the cascade descends so gently that not a ripple agitates the surface which reflects the chaise as you drive past. The postillion cracks his whip, you pass a crag, cross a bridge : suddenly arises a terrific uproar of waterfalls tumbling one upon another. The water has taken a gigantic leap and is desiccated into a hundred falls, is dashed to finest spray upon the rugged boulders ; a thousand sparkling jets fall from the heights that overtop the ravine and fall precisely in the centre of the path that has been cut by the most forceful of active forces.

If you have formed a succinct idea of this landscape, you may see in the waters that slept the passion that Emilio bore the duchess ; in the cascades, leaping like a flock of sheep, lies the idea of his amorous passion, shared with la **Tinti**. In the midst of his torrent of love a rock was upreared against which he broke. Like Sisyphus, the prince was always under the stone.

" What under heaven does the duke with his violin ? " he wondered.

" Is it to him I owe this sweet symphony ? " he asked Clarina.

" Dear child," for she could read that Emilio was but a child. " My dear child, that man who is at least a hundred and eighteen in the parish-register of vice, but only forty-seven in that of the church, has one sole joy remaining in life. A fact, all else is smashed, everything is in rags and tatters, his soul, mind, nerves, heart—all in man that can furnish an emotion or impluse, reminding him of heaven in desire or enjoyment, is fast bound in music, or really by one of the effects produced by music, a perfect unison of two voices or of a voice with the top open string of his violin. That old ape sits on my knee, takes his—instrument—he can play fairly well—makes the notes, and I, I imitate them. When at length the instant arrives that it is impossible to distinguish the tone from the violin and that produced by my throat, then does this old man become ecstatic, his dull eyes become light with their last remaining fire, he is happy, intoxicated, he rolls upon the floor in a drunkenness of rapture.

" There is the cause of his giving Genovese so large a price. His is the only tenor voice which, and that only occasionally, forms a perfect unison with mine. We really do exactly sing together perhaps once, perhaps twice (or the duke imagines that we do, the same thing), and for this imagined pleasure he has become the owner of Genovese ; for he is his. The tenor cannot be engaged by any theatrical manager unless I, also, am engaged, nor am I allowed to sing save with him. This is the whim that was the occasion of the duke's bringing me up, to gratify this caprice ; I am indebted to him for my talent, beauty, fortune, undoubtedly. He will die of an attack of perfect unison.

"Only the sense of hearing has survived his other faculties; this is the one thread binding him to life. Many a vigorous sprig shoots from a rotten stump. They say there are many men such as he. The Blessed Virgin keep them.

"But you, you are not like this! You can do all you desire—all *I* want you to do, I know!"

About daylight the prince crept away from her side; he found old Carmagnola lying, sleeping, across the doorway.

"Altezza," said he, "the duchess sends you this letter."

He handed Emilio a dainty three-corner folded note. The prince felt faint. He returned to the chamber, fell into a chair, his sight failed, and his hand was shaken as he read:

"My dear Emilio:—Your gondola stopped at your palace. Was it that you were unaware that Cataneo had taken it for Tinti? As you love me, go at once to Vendramini, who informs me that he has a chamber prepared for you at his house. What can I do? Is it possible that I should remain in Venice where Tinti and my husband may be seen together? Say, shall we not return to Friuli? Write but one word to say what letter it was that you cast into the lagoon.

"Massimilla."

The writing, the perfume pervading the paper, revived a myriad of memories in Emilio's mind. The sun of a fervent, single love cast his radiant beams upon the blue deeps, gathered in a fathomless pool, where they shone star-like. The youth could not keep back the tears that sprung to his eyes, for in the languid state caused by his night's satiety he was overwhelmed by the thoughts of that so pure divinity.

While she yet slept, his weeping was heard by Clarina. She sat up in bed, noticed the dejection of her prince, arose and flung herself at his knees.

"An attendant waits an answer," said Carmagnola, as he pushed the portière aside.

"Miserable that you are, you have undone me!" exclaimed Emilio, and he pushed la Tinti away with his foot.

Her entreating look, as she fondled the cruel foot, so begged an explanation that Emilio kicked her unmanly away, so wrathful was he at still finding himself in the toils of the passion that was the cause of his fall.

"You told me to slay you—then die, poisoned viper," said he.

He quit the palace and jumped into the waiting gondola.

"Now, pull!" he cried to Carmagnola.

"To where?"

"Where you like!"

The mind of the master was divined by that of the gondolier. By many a circuitous turning he brought the gondola to the steps of a marvelous palace, which you will surely admire when you visit Venice; no traveler but must stop to gaze upon those windows, each of a different design to the others, contesting as to which is the more fantastic. The lace-work balconies, the corners finished in high, willowy, twisted columns; the string-courses worked by so spirited a chisel that no forms are visible in the stone arabesques. How alluring the doorway! what an air of mystery in the arcade leading to the stairway! One must admire the steps carpeted in an everlasting pattern, one that shall last as long as Venice itself —as gorgeous as though wrought in a Turkish loom—but composed only of marbles inlaid in the same substance, but ivory-white. On entering, marble, wood, and silk could be seen, all showing exquisite marvels of the craftsman's art. Here the duchess had collected Venetian furniture of antique style; the ceilings had been restored by a master hand.

Emilio swung open a door of carved oak, went down the vaulted hallway, running from front to rear of a Venetian palace, and finally stopped before a door that made his heart increase its beats, it was so strangely familiar. He was perceived by a lady's maid, who gave him entrance into a library where the prince found the duchess prostrate before a madonna.

He had come to confess and beg forgiveness. Massimilla, praying, had converted him. He and God—naught else dwelt in that heart.

The duchess arose and, without affectation, held out her hand. Emilio did not take it.

" Did you not see Gianbattista yesterday ? " asked she.

" No," he responded.

"That ill-luck has caused me a night of wretchedness. I was afraid of your meeting the duke—I know his perversity so well. Why did Vendramin rent him your palace ? "

" Was it not a good thought, Milla? Your prince is a pauper ! "

The faith of Massimilla in him was so perfect, so beautiful and lovely was she, so glad in his near presence, that the prince became, as it were, suddenly awake. He went through the experience of a horrid dream, one that often torments people of a lively turn, in which, after finding himself in a ball-room crowded with women in full dress, he becomes all at once aware that he is stark naked, not having on even a shirt. Shame and fear in turn possess him, nothing but awaking can end his misery. So stood Emilio's soul in the presence of his mistress. None but himself knew this, for Massimilla clothed him so completely in virtues that her lover, the one she so adored, was incapable of being stained. Emilio had not taken her hand, so the duchess ran her fingers through the hair that had so recently been kissed by the prima donna. Thus she discovered that his hand was clammy, his forehead damp.

" What ails you ? " she asked, in a tender, flute-like voice.

" Never until this instant have I known the extent of my love for you," he answered.

"Well, my idol, what would you that I should do?" said she.

"Why should she ask me that? What have I done?" he pondered.

"Emilio, say, what letter was that you threw into the canal?"

"Vendramini's. I had not read it to the end, else should I not have gone to my palace and there met the duke; for it most likely would have informed me all about the matter."

Massimilla became pallid, but a caress reassured her.

"Stay all day with me; we will go to the opera together. We will not go to Friuli; your company will help me endure the presence of Cataneo," said Massimilla.

Though this could but be torment to her lover, he consented with seeming ecstasy.

If anything can give realism to a foretaste of the sufferings the damned must undergo on finding themselves so unworthy of God, is it not the state of a young man, not entirely polluted, in the presence of a mistress he adores, as he brings into that sanctuary of the divinity he worships the putrid air of the prostitute, and still perceives on his lips the vile taste of infidelity?

Baader had observed, like some Catholic writers, the intimate resemblance between heavenly and human love, and in his lectures illumined things divine by an imaging of erotic love. The piquant flavor of coquettish spice does not spur on affection so much as a gentle, tender sympathy. The chic of a trifler in love makes too clear the mark of apposition; it may be transient, it is still unpleasant; but an intimate comprehension depicts a true fusion of souls. The unhappy Emilio was impressed with this unspoken divination which had led the duchess to pity a fault to her unknown.

Massimilla could permit herself an expansiveness, for she knew that her love was strong in its absence of any sensual aspect. She bravely poured forth her angelic soul; she

"'EMILIO, SAY, WHAT LETTER WAS THAT YOU THREW INTO THE CANAL?''

stripped it bare, the same as, during that diabolical night, la
Tinti had unblushingly displayed the soft, voluptuous lines of
her body, and her firm, pretty, elastic flesh. To Emilio it
seemed as though a conflict was on between the heavenly love
of this so pure soul and that of the vehement, passionate, mus-
cular Sicilian.

The day was spent in deep meditations and longing looks.
The depths of tenderness was carefully gauged and found to
be bottomless. Modesty, who once forgot herself with love, is
the mother of coquetry, but she needed not to place her hand
before her eyes as she looked upon these lovers. For a crowning happiness, an orgy of joy, Massimilla pillowed her lover's
head in her white arms; now and again she would coyly press
her lips to his, as a bird dips its beak in the translucent crystal of a spring, anon gazing around lest it should be seen.
Their fancy wrought upon this kiss, which caused them tumul-
tuous and vibrating rushes of feeling as fevered their blood,
as a composer develops a musical fantasy on one idea.

In the evening the lovers went to the theatre. The manner
of Italian life is on this wise: in the morning, love; in the
evening, music; at night, repose. Is it not far preferable,
this existence, to that of a land where every one exhausts his
lungs and strength in politics without contributing to the
course of affairs as much real benefit as a grain of sand forms
in a cloud of dust. Liberty in those so curious countries consists in the right to squabble about public concerns, to look
after one's self, to squander time on some patriotic doing,
each one more foolish and futile than the last. Here, at
Venice, to the contrary, love and its thousand vagaries, the
luscious business of genuine happiness, engrosses each moment
of time.

There love is regarded as such a matter of course that the
duchess began to be looked upon as a monstrosity; for despite her violent attachment for Emilio, every one was confident of her immaculate purity. As for the young man, he

was looked upon as a victim to the rigid virtue of his lady
love, and the women expressed their pity for the ill-used one.
But yet none blamed Massimilla, for Italy is as religious as
she is amorous.

Massimilla's box on each recurring evening was the cyno-
sure of every opera-glass; each woman whispered to her lover
as she studied the duchess and her lover:

"How far have they gone?"

Then would the lover make study of Emilio, endeavoring
to trace some evidence of success; but finding only an expression of a pure, devoted, but dejected love. Then as the
visits between box and box were made would be muttered by
the men to the ladies:

"La Cataneo is not yet Emilio's."

"But she is foolish, she will tire him out," answered the
older women.

"Perhaps!"* would the young wives answer with that
so solemn accent which Italians can give to that great word
—the grand answer to so many questions.

It came that some women were indignant, the whole affair
was badly judged, it was very wrong that religion should be
allowed to smother love.

"My angel, give your love to that poor Emilio," said the
Signora Vulpato to the duchess, meeting her on the stairs, as
they were leaving.

"I do love him with my whole strength," answered
Massimilla.

"Why, then, does he not look happy?"

Massimilla replied by a slight shrug of her shoulders.

Now in France we—France as the increasing mania for
things English and English proprieties has made it—cannot
form an idea of the interest, serious interest, taken by Venetian
society in this affair. Only Vendramini knew Emilio's secret;
it was jealously kept between these two nobles, who displayed,

* The Italian *forse*—a universal exclamation.

for private enjoyment, their coats-of-arms in combination
with the motto: *Non amici, frates*—not friends, brothers.

As in every capital in Italy, so especially in Venice, the first
night of the operatic season is an event. The Fenice was
crowded. But in Italy a woman does not attend the theatre
to make a show of herself, as in other countries; the box is
absolutely as private as her own chamber—she is its mistress.
Elegantly draped with silk curtains, she reigns the queen of
that dimly-lighted closet; no children, no relatives, no Argus
eyes whatever are there to watch. Each box is freehold property, worth a considerable sum of money; some indeed are
valued at over thirty thousand lire; one family, the Litta,
possess three adjoining ones.

When the men are admitted each takes his seat on one of
the couches as he arrives; thus the first-comer, of course, is
next to the mistress of the apartment; when all the seats are
occupied, should another visitor enter, then the one who has
been the longest there arises, bids his adieux, and departs.
Each then moves up one, so that in turn each is next the
queen.

The box belonging to the duchess was on the parquet-tier,
or as the Venetians have it, *pepiano.* There she occupied a
place which allowed the brilliant light from the stage to
illumine her face, which stood out against the sombre background. The noble Florentine attracted every eye by her
wide, high brow, snow-white, and wearing a coronet of black
hair that gave her an imperial appearance; by the delicate
chiselings of her features, which resembled the gentle tenderness of *Andrea del Sarto's* heads; by the exquisite outline of
her face, the velvet eyes, nay, the setting themselves, which
proclaimed the bliss of a woman dreaming of happiness,
though loving, still pure; at once fascinating, dignified.

In place of "Moses in Egypt" being given, in which la
Tinti was to have sung with Genovese, "Il Barbiere" was
substituted; thus the famous tenor was to appear without the

celebrated soprano. It was announced by the manager that it was necessary to change the operas in consequence of la Tinti being seriously indisposed. The duke was not visible in the theatre.

Was Clarina's illness genuine, or was this a scheme of the management to secure two full houses by bringing Genovese and la Tinti out on separate occasions? Emilio could form an opinion of his own while others discussed the matter. The announcement gave him some little remorse, for he well remembered the singer's beauty and her vehement passion ; but the duke's absence was a cause for gratulation for both prince and duchess.

And Genovese, why he sang in such manner as effectually exorcised all remembrance of a blissful night passed in the illicit enjoyment of love, and prolonging the blessed happiness of this so joyous day. Only too glad to alone receive the applause of the house, the tenor made his best efforts; he used every phase of his great powers which have achieved the fame of all Europe. Genovese, who was now but three and twenty, was born at Bergamo; he was a pupil of Velutis, in love with his art, a fine man, handsome, quick to comprehend the spirit in a part, and was developing into that great artist whose destiny is to win fortune and renown. He had a raging success—a term only really true in Italy, where the applause of an audience becomes a frenzy when a singer conduces to its enjoyment.

A number of the friends of the prince came to chat over the news and to congratulate him on succeeding to his title. The sudden indisposition of la Tinti was much commented on, as it was only last evening that at the Vulpatos', whither she had been taken by the duke, she had sung in her usual fine style, with health as apparently sound. At the Café Florian, it was rumored that Genovese was violently smitten with Clarina ; that she did her utmost to avoid his attentions, and that the manager had vainly endeavored to obtain her consent to appear with him. On the other hand, the Austrian duke claimed that it was the duke who was ill and that the prima donna was acting as his nurse ; Genovese, he said, had been given orders to make amends to the public.

The visit of the Austrian general to the duchess was owing to the fact that a French physician had arrived in Venice, who was desirous of an introduction to her.

The prince, who could see Vendramin strolling around the *parterre*, took this occasion to join him and have a few moments of confidential talk, as he had not seen him for the past three months. As they walked round the aisle which forms the division between the seats in the parquet from the lower tier of boxes, he had an opportunity of noting the reception the duchess gave the foreigner.

" Who is the Frenchman ? " inquired the prince.

" A physician who has been summoned by Cataneo, who is anxious to know the length of his span of life," said Vendramin. " The Frenchman is awaiting Malfatti, whom he is to meet in consultation."

Like every Italian woman who is in love, the duchess kept her eyes on Emilio—for in that country a woman is so wholly engrossed in her lover that one scarce ever sees an expressive look cast at any other person.

"*Caro*," said the prince to his friend, "don't forget that I slept at your house last night."

" Have you then triumphed ? " asked Vendramin, putting his arm around Emilio's waist.

" No; but I hope at some time to be happy with Massimilla."

" Eh, well ! then you will excite more envy than any living man. The duchess is the most perfect woman in Italy. I see things through the radiancy meted out by opium ; it is perhaps owing to this that to me she seems the acme of expressed art ; nature, unknowingly, has made of her a picture by Raphael. Your passion seems to cause no concern to

Cataneo, since he has paid me the thousand crowns which I am to hand over to you."

"So," said Emilio. "Well, remember whatever you may hear, that I sleep at your house every night. Come, for every moment I am away from her, when I might be with her, is torture to me."

Emilio seated himself in the rear of the box and kept silence, listening, enchanted by her wit and grace, to the duchess. It was not for vanity's sake, but out of love for him, that Massimilla was prodigal of her charming speech, gemmed with Italian wit; her irony struck at things, not persons; her laughter was only caused by the laughable; the merest trifles were seasoned with Attic salt. In any other country she might have been tiresome.

But Italians are, eminently so, an intelligent people; they do not care to make show of their talents when such is not demanded. Their chatter is artless and without strain; it does not fence under the hand of the fencing-master, each one brandishing his own foil, as in France, and who, if he cannot find aught to say, must sit humiliated. Here conversation sparkles with a delicate satire, subtle and graceful, that touches lightly on familiar facts. Instead of an epigram an Italian can glance or smile in a meaning unutterable. They believe, and they are right in this, that to be expected to understand thoughts when they seek only enjoyment is a great bore. Indeed, la Vulpato once said to Massimilla:

"If you love him, you could not talk so well."

Emilio did not join in the small talk; he looked on and listened. Foreigners might have judged from this reserve that the prince was a person of little intelligence, a common impression of such of an Italian who is in love, whereas he was only a lover head over ears in rapture.

Vendramin took a seat by Emilio, facing the Frenchman, who, being a stranger, occupied the place of honor opposite the duchess.

"Is that gentleman intoxicated?" said the physician in a low voice to Massimilla, as he glanced at Vendramin.

"Yes," was the simple answer.

In that land of amours every passion contains its own excuse; gracious indulgence is granted all forms of error. The duchess breathed a profound sigh, while pain was expressed on her features.

"You will observe many strange things in our country, monsieur," she continued. "Vendramin exists only by opium, this one lives only in love, that other one is buried in science. Most young men have a passion for some ballet-dancer; their elders are misers. Thus each of us creates for himself some form of happiness or madness."

"The reason is simply because you are all trying to avoid having any fixed ideas; a revolution would be an effectual cure," the physician made answer. "The Genoese regrets his republic; the Milanese hungers for independence; your Piedmontese strongly desires a constitutional form of government; the Roman cries for liberty——"

"Of which it understands nothing," interrupted the duchess. "Alas! we have in Italy a number of men who are idiotic enough to desire your Code, by which woman's influence is sacrificed. A great number of my compatriots have to read your French books—all trashy rhodomontade."

"Trashy!" cried the Frenchman.

"See, now, monsieur, what can you discover in a book that is better than we have in our hearts?" said the duchess. "Italy is mad."

"I fail to see that because a country prefers to be its own ruler it is therefore mad!" exclaimed the physician.

"Gracious heaven!" cried the duchess, with enthusiasm, "does not that mean purchasing by much bloodshed the dreadful right of being able to quarrel over crazy notions, the same as you do?"

"Then you approve of despotism?" asked the physician.

20   Z

"Why then should I not give my approval to a plan of government which, in debarring us of books and absurd politics, leaves the men wholly to us?"

"I had an idea that Italians were more patriotic than that," said the Frenchman.

Massimilla said this in such a sly, mocking manner that her questioner was unable to detect any difference between mockery or serious meaning, neither could he distinguish her real opinion from sarcastic criticism.

"Then you are not a Liberal?" said he.

"May heaven preserve me!" she answered. "I cannot think of anything that shows worse taste in a woman than to hold such opinions. Could you now love a woman whose heart was occupied by all mankind?"

"All lovers are naturally aristocrats," the Austrian general said, with a smile.

"As I entered the theatre," went on the Frenchman, "the first person I saw was yourself. I remarked to his excellency that if any woman could personify a nation, that woman was yourself. I am thus pained to learn that although you possess the beauty, you do not possess the spirit of constitutionalism."

"You are bound, are you not," said the duchess, motioning to the ballet just being danced, "to find that all our dancers are detestable and our singers horrid? But London and Paris steal from us all our great stars. Paris judges them, London pays them. Genovese and la Tinti will not be ours again for six months."

At this moment the Austrian left the box. Vendramin, the prince, and the other Italians smilingly exchanged glances, and stole a look at the French physician. He felt that he had done or said some incongruous thing and felt some doubt of himself—a rare thing for a Frenchman. But the enigma was speedily solved.

"Can you believe that it would be prudent of us to speak our minds in the presence of our master?" asked Emilio.

"Here you are in a country of slaves," said the duchess, in such a tone and a so drooping head which immediately added to her countenance that look for which the physician had vainly looked.

"Vendramin," she continued, speaking so that none but the stranger could hear her, "took to opium-smoking, a horrible idea which an Englishman gave him, who, for totally different reasons to his, wanted an easy death; not death as men gaze on it in the form of a skeleton, but death tagged out in the frippery you Frenchmen call a flag, a virgin shape crowned with laurel and flowers. The figure of a maiden is seen in a cloud of gunpowder smoke borne along on a cannon-ball's flight—otherwise she is laid out on a bed between two courtesans; or, perhaps, she is seen rising in the vapor of a steaming bowl of punch, or maybe in the dazzling blaze of a diamond—a diamond in its native form as carbon.

"Whenever Vendramin wishes, he may, for three Austrian lire, be a Venetian captain, he can navigate the galleys of the Republic, he can conquer the gilded domes of Constantinople. There he can recline on the divans among the Sultan's wives in the Seraglio, the while the Grand Turk himself is the vassal of his Venetian victor. Then he returns to Venice; he restores his palace by the treasures of which he despoiled the Ottoman Empire. He can quit the Oriental women for the trebly masked intrigues of his much-beloved Venetians; he can fancy that he is fearful of the jealousy which has ceased to have being.

"For three zevanziger he is able to transport himself into the Council of Ten; he can wield their awful power, and departs from the palace of the Doges to sleep under the guardianship of a pair of flashing eyes; or to climb a balcony to which a fair hand has affixed a silken ladder. He has a woman to love, one to whom opium lends such bewitching grace and ravishing charms that we women of flesh and blood can never emulate.

"Anon he turns over, and finds himself confronted by the fearful frown of a senator, who grasps a dagger. He hears the poniard plunged into the heart of his mistress. She dies smiling on him, for she has saved his life.

"And she is a happy woman," added the duchess, glancing at Emilio.

"He makes his escape and hastens to command the Dalmatians to conquer the coast of Illyria for Venice the beloved. He wins forgiveness by his glory; he has a happy domestic life—home, a winter evening, a young wife, sweet children, whom he sees praying to St. Marco, an old nurse their guardian.

"Yes, for three francs' worth of opium he replenishes our empty arsenal, he takes note of the convoys of merchandise entering port, to be distributed to the four quarters of the globe. The force of modern industry and commerce reign no more in London, but here in his own Venice, where the hanging-gardens of Semiramis, the Temple of Jerusalem, Rome's marvels, live once more.

"He gives to the glories of the Middle Ages the added help of the power of steam; by new masterpieces of art under the wing of Venice, who protected it in time past. Monuments, nations crowd his little brain, yet is there room for all. Empires, cities, revolutions, come and disappear in an hour, while only Venice expands and grows; his Venice is the mistress of the seas. She has a population of two millions, holds the sceptre of Italy, is the master of the Mediterranean and the Indies!"

"What an opera is the brain of man! What an unplumbed gulf! yea, even to those who, as Gall did, have mapped it out," exclaimed the physician.

"My dear duchess," said Vendramin, "do not omit to mention the last service that my elixir does me. After listening to ravishing voices and imbibing music at every pore, after I have tasted the keenest delights of Mahomet's paradise,

I see then nothing but the most terrible images. I dream of my beloved Venice full of the distorted faces of children, like the dying; of women covered with fearful wounds—torn, shrinking; of men strangled and crushed by the coppered sides of great vessels; I see Venice as she is in reality—festooned in crêpe, naked, robbed, destitute. Pallid phantoms promenade her streets.

"Already the soldiers of Austria grin above me, already my visionary life is merging into my real existence; while six months ago my real life was the bad dream, and that of opium held passion and happiness, great affairs of moment and interests of state. Alas! In my grief I see the sun breaking over my tomb, truth and falsehood blend in a flickering light, neither darkness nor day, but which embraces both."

"Now you see that there is too much patriotism in this head," said the prince, placing his hand on the heavy, black curly hair that fell over Vendramin's forehead.

"Oh, if he really loves us he will quit the use of his dreadful opium!" said Massimilla.

"I will cure your friend," said the Frenchman.

"Do this and we will love you," said the duchess. "But we will love you still more, if, on your return to France, you do not calumniate us. We unhappy Italians are already too much crushed by foreign domination to be fairly judged—for we have known yours," she added, smiling.

"But it was more generous than is Austria's," exclaimed the physician eagerly.

"Austria squeezes and returns us nothing: you squeezed to extend and beautify our towns; you gave us stimulation by giving us an army. You had an idea that you could keep Italy, they are expecting they may lose it, therein lies the difference.

"The Austrians provide us what we may term a sort of torpor as stultifying and debasing as themselves; you swamped us by your over-violent energy. But what matters it whether death comes by narcotic or a tonic? Is it not death, just the same, Monsieur the Doctor?"

"Unhappy Italy. To me she is a lovely woman whom France should protect by taking her for his mistress," cried the Frenchman.

"But you could not love us as we would be loved," said the duchess, smiling. "We desire freedom. The liberty that I wish, though, is not that of your illiberal bourgeois kind which slays all art. I beg," said she in a ringing tone that echoed around the box, "I mean that I would beg for the resuscitation of every Italian republic: their nobles, citizens, the particular privileges for each caste. I would revive the old aristocratic republics with their internecine fights and rivalries that were the conception of our noblest art, that was the making of politics and upreared the great princely houses. When the acts of one government are spread over a vast extent of country they are frittered into nothingness. The republics of Italy were Europe's glory of the Middle Ages. Why, then, has Italy gone under while the Swiss, once her servants, triumph?"

"The republics of Switzerland were good housewives," said the doctor, "they busied themselves about their own matters and were without any reason for showing envy of each other. Your republics were proud queens, they would sooner sell themselves than show courtesy to a neighbor; now they are fallen too low ever to rise again. The Guelphs triumph."

"Do not waste all your pity on us," said the duchess, in a voice that startled the two friends. "We still remain supreme. Even now in her profound misfortune Italy rules through the better class that throngs her cities.

"Unhappily most of her talented ones came to a knowledge of life so early that they lay supine in poverty-stricken joys. And for those who are agreeable to play the sombre game for immortality, they well know how to clutch your gold and

force your applause. Grieved over as this land is for its fallen
state by idiotic travelers and hypocritical poets—its character
traduced by politicians—here, where all appears so languid,
feeble, ruinous, not old so much as worn, there yet remain
great minds in all departments of life ; genius, which shoots
forth vigorous suckers like as an old vine-stock shoots out
canes that afterward bear delicious fruit.

"This people of ancient rulers yet gives birth to kings :
Lagrange, Volta, Rasori, Canova, Rossini, Bartolini, Galvani,
Vigano, Beccaria, Cicognara, Corvetto. These Italians are
chiefs of the scientific heights whereon they stand, of the arts
to which they are devoted. It is unnecessary to speak of our
singers and musicians who ravish all Europe in their wonderful perfection ; Taglioni, Paganini, and so on. Italy remains the ruler of the world. The world will ever come to
her in worship.

"To-night do you go to Florian's ; in Capraja you will discover one of our brightest men who loves to remain unknown.
No one else, save my master, the duke, has such a knowledge
of music as he possesses ; he is known here by every one as *il
Fanatico.*"

For some time the Italians eagerly listened to the gage of
words between the duchess and the Frenchman ; her eloquence
confounded them, and they one by one took their leave to
carry the news to other coteries, that la Cataneo had easily
defeated the French physician and proved him in the wrong
on the question of Italy. This formed the talk of the evening.

Soon after the Frenchman found only himself with the
duchess and Prince Emilio ; he saw that they wanted to be
alone and he bade farewell. Massimilla bowed with such a
sweep of the neck as placed them so far apart, that it might
have brought upon her this man's hatred if he had been able
to withstand the charms of her eloquence and beauty.

By this toward the close of the opera, Emilio and Massimilla
found themselves alone, they clasped each other's hands and

listened to the strains of that delightful duet which ends " Il Barbiere."

" Music alone can give expression to love," said the duchess, moved by that strain as by two rapturous nightingales.

In Emilio's eye a tear glistened ; Massimilla, with the same sublimity of beauty that halos Raphael's Saint-Cecilia, pressed his hand, their knees touched, it seemed as though there was the bloom of a kiss upon her lips. The heart of the prince seemed surcharged to bursting as the tide of blood rushed there ; he beheld on her face a gleam of joy like as when a summer's day shines down upon the golden grain of harvest. He felt as if he heard a choir of angel voices. He would have given his life could he but have felt the fierce fire of passion with which at this time last night the odious Clarina had fired him ; now he was scarcely sensible of possessing a body.

Massimilla was much distressed at seeing this tear. She ascribed its origin, in her artlessness, to what she had said of Genovese's *cavatina.*

" But, *carino*," she whispered in Emilio's ear, " are you not superior to every expression of love, as the cause is better than the effect ? "

After having handed Massimilla into her gondola, Emilio awaited Vendramin to go with him to Florian's.

The Café Florian at Venice is an institution hard to designate. There merchants transact their business ; lawyers use it to talk over their difficult cases. It is an Exchange, greenroom, newspaper office, club, confessional, all in one. It is so suited to the wants of the Venetians that many wives never learn the business of their husbands, for when they wish to write a letter they use Florian's for that purpose.

Of course the genus spy is there, but this only serves to whet the wit of the Venetians, who here use the discretion once so celebrated. Numbers of persons put in their whole time at Florian's. Florian's is in fact so necessary to some men that they even go there between the acts at the opera, and leave the ladies under their charge in the boxes.

As the two friends threaded the narrow streets of the Merceria they did not talk, people were too many, but, turning into the Piazza di San Marco, the prince remarked :

" Let us not go direct to the café. I want to talk to you, let us stroll around."

He told all about his position and his adventure with Clarina. Vendramin promised that if Emilio, whom he thought had a despair almost akin to madness, would only give him a free hand to deal with Massimilla he would cure him. This gleam of hope came just in time to prevent Emilio from drowning himself on that very night, for, as he recollected the cantatrice, he felt an awful desire to visit her again.

Soon the two friends went to Florian's and entered an inner chamber ; there they listened to the town gossip of some of the leading men. The most interesting was, first, the eccentricities of Lord Byron, of whom the Venetians made much fun ; and afterward, Cataneo's attachment to la Tinti, for which they were unable to assign any reason, though twenty were suggested. Then came Genovese's debut, and, lastly, the tilt between the duchess and the French physician.

It was when the discussion had grown music-mad that Duke Cataneo entered. He bowed to Emilio most courteously, and this appeared so perfectly natural that none seemed to notice it, while Emilio as courteously returned it. Cataneo, looking around to see if any one was present whom he knew, at last recognized Vandramin and gave him greeting ; he bowed to a wealthy patrician, his banker ; and then to the one who chanced to be speaking, a famous fanatic in music, the friend of the Contessa Albrizzo ; not unlike a number of those who frequented Florian's, his habit of life was totally unknown. No one knew aught of him more than he himself chose to disclose.

This was Capraja, the nobleman named by the duchess to

the French doctor. This Venetian was of the race of dreamers with a powerful mind that could divine all things. He was a theorist, eccentric, and cared less for celebrity than he would have done for a broken pipe.

His existence was in accord with his ideas. At about ten o'clock, every morning, Capraja appeared beneath the *Procuratie*, but none knew whence he came. He sauntered about Venice smoking cigars. He regularly attended the Fenice, where he sat in the parquet stalls; between acts he strolled over to Florian's, took three or four cups of coffee there each day; his evening he ended at the café, and did not leave until about two in the morning. Twelve hundred francs a year was his full outlay; he only ate one meal a day, which he partook of at a restaurant in the Mercaria; at a stated hour each day the master-cook had his dinner ready for him, served at a little table in a rear room; the confectioner's daughter prepared his stuffed oysters, found his cigars, and took care of his money. It was owing to his counsel that this young girl never encouraged a lover, although she was decidedly pretty; she lived a steady life and wore the old costume of the Venetians. This pure-bred Venetian, when Capraja first interested himself in her, was twelve years old; when he died she was six and twenty. Although he never so much as kissed her hand or forehead, she was yet very fond of him; but she had no idea as to his intentions in regard to her. It came that this girl attained as much influence with him as has a mother with her child. She let him know when he needed clean linen; one day he would arrive minus his shirt, and she would hand him a clean one to don the next morning.

Never did he glance at a woman, either at the theatre or when promenading. He was descended from an old patrician family, but never thought his rank added to his dignity. When the night was come, though, after twelve o'clock, he awoke from his apathy and showed by his conversation that he had seen and heard everything that had taken place. This

gentle Diogenes, half-Turk, half-Venetian, who was incapable
of giving explanation of his theories, was stoutly built, short,
and fat; he had the sharp nose of a Doge, an eye inquisitive
and satirical, and a discreet, smiling mouth. When he died,
then it became known that he had lived in a small hut near
San Benedetto.

He possessed two millions of francs in the Funds of various
countries of Europe, and the interest, which had lain undrawn
on the securities since their purchase in 1814, had vastly increased his original capital. The whole of this was left to the
confectioner's daughter.

"Genovese," he was remarking, "will work wonders. I
don't know whether he really comprehends the grand aim of
music or only sings instinctively; but he is the only singer with
whom I have been absolutely satisfied. I shall not die without
having heard a *cadenza** executed like those I have sometimes
heard in my dreams, when I have awakened with a sensation
that the sounds were in the air surrounding me. The clear
cadenza is the acme of art; an arabesque adorning the chief
room of the house; too little, it becomes nothing; a shade too
much, it becomes confusion.

"The *cadenza* is set to arouse the soul to a thousand sleeping ideas—it ascends, takes its flight through space, scatters
seed upon the air to be received in our ears to bloom in the
heart. If you believe me, Raphael gave the preference to
music of poetry in his painting of Saint-Cecilia. In this he
was right; music appeals to the heart, writing is offered to
the intellect; its thoughts, like scent, is a direct communication. The voice of the singer does not thrust itself upon the
mind, nor yet upon the memory of delights; it stirs sensation,
thought's first principle.

"It is a shame that the people compel musicians to add
words to their expressions, factitious emotions—though if this
be not done it is all unintelligible to the vulgar. So it re-

* At that time the *cadenza* was an impromptu finale.—TRANSLATOR.

mains that the *cadenza* is the sole object remaining to the lovers of pure music; those devoted to art unfettered.

"A sorcerer crowned my brow and guided me through the ivory-door by which we gain access to the mysterious dream-land. To Genovese it is due that I was enabled to escape from my old husk for a few minutes; short minutes, perhaps, by actual count of time, but long when measured by sensation. A short spring-time, with its perfume of roses, was accorded me when I was again young—and beloved."

"But, see then, *caro* Capraja," said the duke, "there is in music a yet more magical effect than is found in the *cadenza*."

"What?" asked Capraja.

"The true unison of two voices or of a violin and a human voice—the tone of the former of which most nearly resembles the latter," replied Cataneo.

"On this perfect concord we are borne to life's very heart; we float on the surge of that element which resuscitates rapture, which carries man up into the midst of that luminous sphere whence his soul commands the whole universe. You still re-quire a *thema*, Capraja; but for my part the unalloyed element is sufficient. For you the current must flow through all the myriad channels of the machine, thence to fall in glistening cascades; the pellucid, tranquil pool contents me. My eye looks upon a lake without a ripple. I embrace the infinite."

"Say no more, Cataneo," said Capraja with hauteur. "What! Is it that you fail to see the fairy who swiftly drives through the sparkling air and gathers and binds in harmony's golden thread the gems of melody so smilingly poured upon us?

"Have you then never experienced the touch of her magic wand when she cries to Curiosity: 'Awake!' Up from the depths of our brain a divinity arises all radiant; she lightly touches Memory, fingering it as an organist does his keys; she brings us the roses of past days, divinely kept and still fresh. The mistress of our youth is revivified, she strokes the young man's hair; the heart overfull runs over; the flowery banks are seen laved by the torrent of love. Each burning bush we knew burst forth anew in flame; it repeats the heavenly strain we once heard and understood. The voice rolls on; it rapidly embraces those fleeting horizons; they melt away; these vanish and are superseded by newer, more profound joys—a future unrevealed, to which the fairy points as she reascends to the blue empyrean."

"And you," responded Cataneo, "you have never seen the direct ray of a star shining in the vista above; you have never climbed that ray that guides one to the skies, to the very centre of that first cause which moves worlds?"

The game which the duke and Capraja were playing was unknown to their hearers.

"The voice of Genovese thrills every fibre," said Capraja.

"La Tinti's fires the blood," the duke responded.

"That *cavatina* is a blessed paraphrase of love," Capraja continued. "Ah! Rossini was young when he wrote that interpretation of bubbling ecstasy. My heart was charged with renewed blood, a thousand desires tingled in my veins; never has the fairy waved such beautiful arms, smiled more alluringly; never did she more cunningly lift her tunic to display an ankle as she raised the curtain that conceals my other life!"

"To-morrow, old friend," said Cataneo, "you shall ride on the back of a glistening white swan, who will give you sight of the most lovely country; the spring-time shall be seen as children see it. You shall repose on silk of crimson, gazed upon by a madonna; you will feel like a happy lover kissed by a nymph, whose bare feet you will see, but who will presently disappear. Genovese's voice will be that swan, if he is able to combine it with its Leda—Clarina's voice. For to-morrow night 'Moses in Egypt' is to be performed—the greatest son of Italy's grandest opera."

The company present, not wishing to be the victims of

mysticism, did not take any part in the conversation. The French doctor and Vendramin were the only ones who listened to them for a few minutes. The opium smoked could enter into their imaginative flights; the keys of the mansion were in his possession—the palace through which they wandered. The doctor endeavored to and did understand, for his was a genius of the Pleiades of a Paris medical school, whence evolves, in the case of a true physician, the metaphysician, the expert analyst.

"Do you understand them?" said Emilio to Vendramin, as they emerged from the café at two o'clock in the morning.

"Yes, my dear fellow," said Vendramin, as they wended their way to his house. "Those two men belong to the legion of unearthly spirits to whom it is permitted here below to throw off their fleshly wraps; they can take flight on magic's shoulder to the blue empyrean in which celestial wonders are created by the intellectual life. Their art enables them to soar whither your great love bears you, the whither opium transports me. None can then understand them, but those who resemble them. The duke and Capraja were acquainted in Naples—there Cataneo was born; they are crazy on the subject of music."

"But what about that curious system that Capraja was anxious to explain to Cataneo?" said the prince. "Can you guess that?"

"Yes," Vendramin replied. "Capraja's great friend is from Cremona. He is a musician and is staying in the Capello palace; he has a theory that sound echoes to an element in man analogous to that producing the phenomenon of light and which creates ideas. In his idea, man has within him keys that are in accord and acted upon by sound; these correspond to his nerve-centres, and thence sensation and ideas take their rise. Capraja looks upon the arts as a collection of effects, which he can harmonize within himself; he takes all external nature, and a further mysterious nature, which he terms the inner life, and compounds them. He embraces all the ideas of this instrument-maker, who is now engaged in composing an opera.

"Try and conceive a sublime creation in which the wonders of the visible universe are reproduced with immeasurable grandeur, with vividness, rapidity, vastness; wherein is an infinity of sensation, whither certain privileged natures may penetrate, then you may form an inadequate idea of the ecstatic bliss which Cataneo and Capraja spoke of; each was a poet for himself alone. It is only in the intellect that so soon as a man rises above the circle of plastic art—a mere imitation—that he enters that sphere of transcendent abstraction where he understands all as an elementary principle; but that man then becomes unintelligible to ordinary intelligence."

"That is the explanation of my love for Massimilla," said Emilio. "My dear friend, there is in me a power which flames up under the fire of her glance or at her lightest touch, and wafts me into a universe of light where effects are produced that I cannot, dare not reveal. Often it has seemed to me that her delicate skin has impressed flowers upon mine as her hand lay in mine. Her words play on that inner key of which you have spoken. My brain is excited with desire; it stirs that invisible world in place of exciting my apathetic flesh; the atmosphere becomes rosy and sparkling; perfumes, unknown to my outer senses, but of great potency, relax my sinews; roses wreathe around my temples; my inanition becomes so great that I feel as though my life-blood was escaping through an opened artery."

"Smoking opium has the like effect on me," replied Vendramin.

"Do you desire to die, then?" exclaimed Emilio, alarmed.

"With Venice!" said Vendramin, motioning with his hand in the direction of St. Mark's. "Can you perceive a single pinnacle that is erect? Can you not understand that the sea awaits its prey?"

The prince inclined his head; he could not further speak of love to his friend.

To understand the meaning of a free country you must have traveled in a conquered nation.

When they arrived at the Vendramin palace they noticed a gondola moored at the water-gate. The prince put his arm around and affectionately embraced Vendramin, and said:

"A good night to you, my dear boy."

"What! a woman? for me; when I only sleep with Venice," cried Vendramin.

At this moment the gondolier, who leaned against a pillar, recognized the man he was looking for; he muttered in Emilio's ear:

"The duchess, monseigneur."

Emilio sprang into the gondola, when a pair of soft arms dragged him upon the cushions with a force of iron; there he felt the heaving bosom of an ardent woman. He was no longer Emilio; he was Clarina's lover. His thoughts and sensations were so confused that he yielded like one stupefied by her first kiss.

"Forgive the trickery, my love," said the Sicilian. "I shall die if you go not with me."

And the gondola sped over the discreet water.

At half-past seven of the following evening the audience was again assembled, each in their respective place, in the theatre, with the exception of those occupying the parquet, who sat where chance placed them. Old Capraja was in Cataneo's box.

The duke paid a call to the duchess previous to the overture; he made it a point to stand behind her and left the front seat next the duchess to Emilio. He made a few trifling remarks with the politeness of a stranger, and without a tinge of irony or sarcasm. But in spite of every effort he made to appear amiable and at home, the prince could not disguise his profoundly anxious expression. A bystander might have given jealousy as the cause for the change in his usually placid countenance.

The duchess without doubt reciprocated Emilio's feelings; she appeared gloomy and depressed. Between two sulky people the duke was fidgety, and he took the chance of the French doctor's entrance to slip away.

"Monsieur," said Cataneo to the physician, before letting fall the portière over the box entrance, "to-night you will hear a great musical poem, which is not easy to be understood at his first hearing. In leaving you with the duchess I am aware that you can have no more competent instructor, for she is a pupil of mine."

The same as the duke, the doctor was struck by the expression shown on the countenances of the lovers, a look of pining despair.

"Then does an Italian opera need a guide?" he asked of Massimilla, smiling.

Her position as the mistress of the box was recalled to her by this question, so the duchess attempted to disperse the clouds that shadowed her brow; she replied with eager haste, in order to open up a conversation in which she might give vent to her concealed irritation.

"This is more an oratorio than opera, monsieur," said she, "a work not without resemblance to a grand edifice; it will be with pleasure that I act as your guide. Trust me that you cannot give too much of your mind to our great Rossini, for you require to be equally a poet and musician to properly appreciate the whole theme of such a work.

"You pertain to a race whose language and spirit are too practical to receive such music without an effort; but, then, France is too intellectual to not learn how to love it, and cultivate it, and likewise to succeed in that as in everything else that she attempts. It further must be admitted that the music created by Lulli, Rameau, Haydn, Mozart, Beethoven,

21

Cimarosa, Paisiello, and Rossini, and as it will be written by
the future geniuses, is a new art, unknown to former genera-
tions ; they lacked our variety of instruments, they, too, were
unaware of the harmony upon which melody's flowers now
bloom as in some rich soil.

"A novel art demands the study of the public, that study
to be of a sort that develops the feeling to which music makes
appeal.   This sentiment as yet scarcely exists among you : a
notion given over to theories of philosophy, analysis, discussion, and always being torn by civil disturbances.   Modern
music needs peace, perfect peace, being the language of
loving, lofty souls, inclined to a sentiment of emotional
aspirations.

"This language, more full by a thousand times than that
of words, is to speech what thought becomes in its utterance ;
sensations are awakened and primitive ideas are born in that
portion of us in which such have their conception.   One of
the greatest truths of music is this power over our inmost
being.

" Every other art gives a definite creation to the soul ; those
of music are indefinite—infinite.   The poet's ideas we must
needs accept, so also those of the painter's picture, the statue
of the sculptor, but in music each interprets to himself the
will of the sorrow, his happiness, his hope, his despair.
Now other arts give bounds to our minds by attaching it to a
preconceived figure, while music frees it and allows it to roam
over all nature, it alone having this power of expansion.
You will hear how I interpret Rossini's ' Moses.' "

She bent over to the Frenchman so that she might be heard
only by him.

" Moses is the liberator of a race in slavery! " said she.
" Bear this in mind and you will understand the religious
hope that the Fenice will show in listening to the prayer of
the delivered Hebrews, and with what thunderous applause it
will respond."

Emilio sank into a rear seat when the leader lifted his bow. The physician by a nod was notified to take the vacancy. But the Frenchman was more interested in trying to learn what had gone amiss between the two lovers than to enter the domain of music created by the man whom all Italy applauded; for it was the day of the triumph of Rossini in his own land. He watched the duchess and observed how she was speaking in an enforced, feverish excitement. She recalled to him the dignity in sadness, the physical control that he had so admired in the Niobe at Florence; but yet her soul shone out through the warm blush of her cheek; her eyes seemed to dry away the tears by her scorching fires, though their anxiety was hidden under a cloak of pride. Her controlled grief was soothed, it seemed, when she gazed at Emilio, who never removed his eyes off her; it was readily seen that she was trying to disguise some mute despair. Her feelings, in the state they were, gave an enhanced height to the loftiness of her soul.

As most women who are under the trend of some absorbing agitation, she had somewhat of the Pythoness and acted beyond her usual restrictions—though she was still beautiful and calm. It was the figure of her ideas that was wrung by desperation, and not the features of her face. Perhaps it was that she wished to shine with all her intellect to give charm to life and keep her lover from death.

When the three chords in C-major had been given by the orchestra, there written by the composer to announce the opening of the overture; for the real overture is that great movement which begins with this severe attack and which ends only when the light appears at Moses' command. The duchess was unable to restrain a little convulsive start, which showed how entirely the music was in accord with her veiled distress.

"Those three chords cause the blood to freeze," said she. "They announce trouble. Hearken carefully to this introduction—the awful lamentations of a nation smitten by the hand of God. What a wail! The King, the Queen, their first-born son, every dignity of the country bewails; they are wounded in their pride, their conquests; they are checked in their avarice. *Dear* Rossini! You did well to fling this bone to the Tedeschi to gnaw, who declared that we possessed neither harmony nor science!

"Now you listen to the sinister melody that has been engrafted on this deep composition of harmony by the *maestro;* it is more than worthy of comparison with the most technical structures of the Germans, but without their fatigue and tiresomeness.

"You French will understand when this oratorio is given in your capital, you who carried through such a revolution of bloodshed, this noble dirge of the victims on whom God is avenging his own people. Only an Italian could have written this pregnant, inexhaustible theme—really Dantesque. Is it nothing, think you, to behold such a vision of vengeance even for one instant? Handel, Sebastian Bach, all the old German masters, your grand Beethoven even, down on your knees! Here is the queen of arts—Italy is triumphant."

The duchess had thus spoken while the curtain was being raised. Now the physician heard the sublime symphony introducing the great Biblical drama. It is written to express a nation's sufferings. In its expression suffering is universal, so especially physical suffering. Thus the man of genius, as he was, felt that there must be no variety of ideas, the musician had hit on the leading theme, he worked it out in various keys, he grouped the choruses and the *dramatis personæ* to bring out the theme through resolutions and cadences of wonderful structure. The power is found in its simplicity.

"There is something that is relentless in that slow phrase; it is cold and weird: it resembles an iron bar, wielded by some executioner of heaven, as it drops in regular rhythm on the limbs of its victims.

"As we hear it passing from C-minor into G-minor, return-ing to C and thence to the dominant, G, whence it starts anew, and *fortissimo* on the tonic, B-flat, resolving into F-major and returning to C-minor; in each key, more than ever terrible, chilly, sombre, we are forced as a finality to enter into the impression that the composer intends."

As a fact, the Frenchman was profoundly moved when this combined grief exploded in the cry:

> O Nume d'Israel,
> Se brami in liberta
> Il popol tuo fedel,
> Di lui di noi pietà !

> (O Lord of Israel,
> If Thou wouldst see in liberty
> Thy faithful people,
> Deign to have pity upon them and us.)

"There could never be a greater synthesis made up of natural effects; nature could not give a grander idealization.

"In a great national disaster for a long time each one laments for himself only, but soon, from out the crowd, there and here arises a more emphatic exclamation of anguish, until at length, when all have experienced the falling misery, it bursts out like a storm. When all can perceive the universal trouble, then the low murmurs of the people change to impa-tient cries. Thus Rossini has proceeded.

"After the outburst in C-major comes Pharaoh, who sings his grand *recitative*, '*Mano ultrice di un Dio*' (God's avenging hand); the orignal theme is here repeated with more signal expression; now all Egypt begs help from Moses."

Taking advantage of the pause necessary for the entrance of Moses and Aaron, the duchess gave this great introduction the interpretation:

"What, they weep!" she added passionately. "They have

done much evil. Egyptians, expiate your sins; expiate those of your insensate court! What wonderful skill the painter has displayed in making use of every sombre tone in music, of all that is gloomiest on the palette of music! What cling-ing darkness! What mists! Does not your very soul mourn? Is not the blackness of the land palpable to you? Can you not feel that all nature is wrapped in darkest shadow? Here are no palms, no palaces of Egypt, there is no landscape. And think what balm to your mind will be in the profound religious strain of the celestial physician who will stop this cruel plague! With what skill is everything done to bring the finish of that glorious invocation of Moses to God.

" By a scientific lucubration which Capraja could explain this prayer to heaven is only accompanied by the brass; this is what gives the solemnity of its religious features.

" Not only is this plan noble in its position, but notice the fertility of genius in its resources; Rossini acquires fresh beauty from the very obstacle he has erected. He keeps the strings in reserve to display the daylight when darkness is succeeded by it; in doing this he has achieved one of the grandest effects ever found in music. Such a result had never previously been known, until this inimitable genius led the way, to be obtained by a simple *recitative.* Thus far we have had neither an *aria* or duet. The poet relied only on the force of the idea, the vivid imagery, the realism of the declamation. This scene of despair, the darkness that can be felt, those cries of anguish; the musical picture in all is as fine as the ' Deluge ' by your great Poussin."

Moses waved his staff and it was light.

" Monsieur, does not the music here vie with the sun, whose radiance it has borrowed; with nature, whose phenomena it gives in every detail?" the duchess continued, in a low voice.

" Here art reaches its acme; beyond this can no musician go. Can you not hear Egypt awaking after its long somnolence? Joy comes with the day. In what work, ancient or modern, can you find so grand a phrase? The highest glad-ness contrasted with profoundest woe! What exclamations! What joyful tones! Now the oppressed minds breathe again. What delirium in that orchestral *tremolo !* What a fine *tutti !* that is a delivered people rejoicing. Are you not thrilled with joy?"

The physician, who was startled by the contrast, clapped his hands; he was truly carried away by his enthusiasm by one of the grandest compositions of modern music.

"*Bravo, la Doni !*" said Vendramin, who had heard the duchess.

"Now that the overture is ended, you have gone through a great sensation," cried the duchess, turning to the French-man. "Your heart beats; down in your imagination you behold a lovely sunrise; it floods a whole continent with light that before was cold and dark. Would you learn the method employed by the musician, that to-morrow you may admire him for the secrets of his handicraft after the enjoying of his works to-night? What, think you, causes that effect of day-light—so sudden, so mystical, yet so complete? It consists of the simple chord of C, many times reiterated, and only varied by its fourth and sixth. This reveals his magic touch.

"The morning of imagery is really and absolutely the same as the natural dawn; for light is one and the same in every-thing, ever alike in itself—its effects only vary with the thing on which it falls.

"Is it not so?

"Well, then, the musician has chosen as his fundamental bass, for its sole *motif*, a simple chord in C. The sun first sheds light upon the mountain heights, and afterward in the valleys. So the chord is first heard in the treble of the violins in Northern lightness; it spreads through the orchestra; one by one it awakens the instruments; it courses among them. Just as light glides from one object to the next, giving color as it goes, so does the music, and calls forth each rill of harmony till they join in the current of the *tutti*.

"Up to this the violins are silent, but now they give the signal with their light *tremolo*, slightly *agitato*, like the dawn's first rays. That bright, lively movement caresses the soul, and is skillfully supported by bass chords, as well as by a vague fanfare of the trumpets, confined to their lower notes; thus giving a vivid reality of the last cool shadows lingering in the valleys while the earlier warm rays tinge the peaks.

"Now the wind is gradually added to support the harmony. The voices join in with delightful sighs of surprise. At length flares out the brass, the trumpets sound; light, the source of all harmony, bathes all nature; every resource of music is brought out with turbulence—it is the splendor of the Eastern sun. Even the triangle, with its ever-recurring C, calls to our minds the shrill note, the joyous rhythm of early risen birds.

"The same key newly handled by the master thus expresses nature's every joy, the while it soothes the sorrow it had uttered before.

"There is the sterling-mark of real genius—Unity. It is the same: it is different. In the one same phrase we can trace a thousand varied woes, the despair of a whole people. In the one same chord we experience the various trifles of awakening nature—each expression of a nation's joy. These two tremendous themes are joined together as one by that prayer to an ever-living God, the maker of all things, the author alike of that joy and woe.

"Now, is not the introduction alone a grand poem?"

"It is, indeed," said the Frenchman.

"Next comes a quintet as Rossini only can give us. If ever he was justified in giving vent to that light, mellow, flowery grace for which the Italian music is often blamed, is it not in this graceful movement by which each one expresses gladness? The people who were enslaved are now delivered,

and yet a passion in danger must needs make moan. The
son of Pharaoh loves a Jewess, but this Jewess must leave
him.

"The thing that gives the ravishing grace to this quintet
is a return to love's homelier feelings, after the great pictures
of two immense national emotions—general misery, universal
joy, given forth with the magic force impressed upon them by
Divine vengeance, and with the miraculous inspiration of the
Bible. Now was I not right?" added Massimilla, as the
fine *stretto* finished :

> Voci di giubilo,
> D'in' orno eccheggino,
> Di pace l'Iride
> Per noi spunto.

> (Sound around us
> The cries of joy,
> While o'er us dawns
> The rainbow of peace.)

"With what deep skill has the composer constructed this
phrase!" she continued, after awaiting a reply. "He com-
mences with a horn solo, divinely sweet, accompanied by
arpeggios on the harps; for the first voices we shall hear in
this great piece of concerted music are those of Moses and
Aaron returning thanks to the true God. The strain reverts
to the sublimity of the invocation; it is soft and simple and
blends, notwithstanding, with the joys of the heathen.

"This transition combines the celestial and terrestrial in
such a manner as could only have been the device of genius;
it gives a tinge of color to the quintet *en ardante* that I can
only liken it to the glow shown by Titian on his Divine Persons. Did you notice the exquisite weft of the voices? the
skillful *debuts* by which the composer has gathered them about
the theme given sound by the orchestra? the scientific pro-

gressions which make us ready to grasp the festal *allegro?*
Did not you obtain a glance, as one might say, of dancing
ones, the dazzling whirl of a whole people rescued from bond-
age? When the clarionet gives the signal for the *stretto—*
' *Voci di giubilo* '—so bright, so gay, your soul was it not then
filled with the sacred fiery joy such as King David in the
Psalms speaks of, when he ascribes it to the hills ? ''

" Yes, it would make a right pretty dance-tune," said the
physician.

" French ! French ! always French ! '' exclaimed the duchess, stopped in her exultation by this keen thrust. " Yes;
undoubtedly you would be capable of taking that marvelous
outpouring of grand and dainty rejoicing and turning it into
a rigadoon. Sublime poetry cannot find mercy in your eyes.
The loftiest genius—saints, kings, disasters—everything the
most holy must bend beneath the chastisement of your carica-
tures. And the making vulgar of noble music by converting
it into a dance-tune is caricaturing it. With you, wit kills
soul as argument slays reason.''

During the *recitative* of Osiride and Membrea they all sat
in silence. These plot to annul the order issued by Pharaoh
to let the Hebrews go.

" Have I given you vexation ? '' asked the physician of the
duchess. " I shall be in despair. Your words are like a
magic wand ; they unlock the pigeon-holes of my brain ; they
kindle new ideas, let loose by this sublime music.''

" No," she answered, " you have applauded our great composer in your own way. With you, Rossini will be a success
by his wit and sensual gifts. It may be, let us hope it, that
he will find a few noble souls, in love with the ideal, to
properly appreciate the sublime, the height of his music. Ah,
now we have the famous duet between Elcia and Osiride ! ''
she cried, and she continued, during the respite caused by
three salvoes of applause which hailed la Tinti, who just now
made her first appearance on the stage :

" If it should be that la Tinti clearly understands the part of Elcia, you will hear the frenzied wail of a woman torn by her love for her race, and that of love for one of her people's oppressors, the while Osiride, filled with mad adoration for his lovely vassal, tries to detain her. The work is constructed as much on this idea as on that of Pharaoh's resistance to God and liberty; this must be thoroughly entered into or you cannot comprehend this stupendous opera. What can be more dramatic than the prince's love for this Jewess; it almost justifies treason to the power of the oppressor.

" Here, then, is what is expressed by this bold and marvelous poem in music; each nation has been stamped by Rossini with a fantastic individuality, for they are attributed with a historic grandeur subscribed to by every imagination. The songs of the Hebrews, their trust in God, are ever in contrast with the shrieks of rage of Pharaoh and his futile efforts, as represented by this powerful hand.

" At this moment Osiride thinks only of love; he hopes to detain his mistress by the reminiscences of their pleasures as lovers; he tries to conquer the feeling for her people. Here, then, we find delicious languor, a glowing sweetness, voluptuous suggestiveness; Oriental love displayed in the *aria 'Ah! se puoi cosi lasciarm'* (If you have courage to leave me, you will break my heart), sung by Osiride; and *'Ma perchè cosi straziarmi?'* Elcia's reply. No; two hearts in such a melodious unison could never part," she went on, turning to look at the prince.

" But now the lovers are suddenly interrupted by the exultant voices of the Hebrews as they journey in the distance; this recalls Elcia. Hear what a delightfully inspiriting *allegro* is in the theme of this march as they start for the desert. None, save Rossini, can cause reed and brass to express so much. And is not the art that can best express ' my native land ' truly nearer heaven than the others ? That clarion-call moves me each time so profoundly that I cannot find words to let you know how cruel it is to an enslaved people to see those freed ones march away!''

The eyes of the duchess were filled with tears; she listened thus to the grand *motif* which really is the masterpiece of the opera.

"*Dov'e mai quel core amante*" (What heart that loves but will partake my anguish), she murmured in Italian as la Tinti commenced the lovely *aria* of the *stretto* in which she implores pity for her sorrow. "But, say, what has happened? The parquet is in a turmoil——"

"Genovese is bellowing like a stag," replied the prince.

As a matter of fact, this duet, the first with la Tinti, was utterly spoiled by Genovese's complete breakdown. His so excellent method, rivaling that of Crescentini and Veluti, appeared to have completely deserted him. A *sostenuto* in the wrong place, an embellishment carried to excess, spoiled the effect; for a strident climax—forte—without a due *crescendo*, the sound of an outpouring of water tumbling through a suddenly opened sluice-gate, showed a willful neglect of all the canons of good taste.

The parquet was in the greatest excitement. The Venetian populace believed there was a deliberate plot between Genovese and his friends; la Tinti was recalled and received frenzied applause, while Genovese had a hint or so which warned him of the hostile feelings of the audience. During this scene, so highly amusing to a Frenchman, la Tinti was had to the front eleven times to receive alone the plaudits of the house, Genovese, all but hissed, not daring to offer her his hand—the doctor made a remark to the duchess about the *stretto* of the duet.

"Rossini, in this place," said he, "ought to have expressed the direst sorrow; on the contrary, I discover an airy movement, a sense of ill-timed cheerfulness."

"You are right," said she. "This error results from a tyrannical custom which all composers must obey. It was his prima donna he was thinking the most of, not of Elcia, when he wrote that *stretto*. But this evening I could throw myself into the situation so fully that, even if la Tinti had been more than usually brilliant, the passage, lively as it is, would have been to me full of melancholy."

The physician looked attentively from the prince to the duchess, but was unable to guess at the reason that held them apart ; that which made the duet seem so heart-rending.

" Here comes a splendid theme, Pharaoh scheming against the Hebrews. The grand *aria, 'A rispettar mi apprenda,'* is a triumph for Carthagenova, who will express in superb phrasing the offended pride and the king's duplicity. The Throne will speak : He withdraws the concessions he had made, he arms himself with anger.

" Pharaoh rises to his feet to grasp the prey that is escaping ! Rossini has never written anything grander in style ; or aught stamped with more irresistible, living energy. It is a finished work, grandly supported by an accompaniment of marvelous instrumentation ; but so indeed is every portion of this opera. Youth's vigor illumines the least detail."

The whole house rose to applaud this fine movement, which was thoroughly appreciated by the Venetians, as being so magnificently interpreted by the singer.

" In the *finale*," said the duchess, " you hear a repetition of the march, this is expressive of the joy of deliverance and of faith in God, who allows His people to rush off gladly to wander in the desert ! Whose lungs but would be refreshed by the aspirations of a whole race released from slavery.

" O ye loving, living melodies ! Glory to the grand genius who has known how to utter such noble thoughts ! That march is the essence of war, it proclaims that the God of armies is on the side of this nation.

" How filled are those strains of thanksgiving with deep feeling. The imagery of the Bible has arisen in our minds ; this most glorious musical *scena* enables us to realize one of the most stupendous dramas of that solemn, ancient world. The religious tone given in some of the voice parts, the manner of their entrance, one by one, to form a group with each other and the rest—give expression to all we have or ever can imagine of the sacred mysteries of that early age of manhood.

"And yet this finely concerted piece is only a development of the theme of the march into all its musical outcome. That theme is the inspiring element, alike of the orchestra and voices, the *aria*, the brilliant orchestration which supports it.

"Elcia now joins the crowd; here, to give shade to the joyful spirit of his number, Rossini causes her to utter her regrets. Hearken to her *duettino* with Amenofi; did ever blighted love express itself in sweeter song? The grace of a *notturno* fills it with the secret grief of a hopeless love. It is sad, sad! The desert will indeed be to her a desert!

"Afterward comes the fierce conflict between the Egyptians and Hebrews. All their joy is dashed, their march is stopped by the Egyptians. Pharaoh's edict is proclaimed in a phrase hollow and drear, the leading *motif* of the *finale;* in fancy we hear the tramp of that great Egyptian army as it surrounds the sacred phalanx of the true God, curling about it as a huge African serpent envelops its prey. But note the beauty of the lament of the duped and disappointed Hebrews! It is, though, less Hebrew than Italian. A superb phrase presages Pharaoh's arrival, his presence brings face to face the leaders and all the moving passions of the drama. The conflict of sentiments in that sublime *stretto* is admirable, that in which the wrath of Moses meets that of the two Pharaohs. What a medley of voices, what unchained fury!

"No subject with equal grandeur was ever conceived by a composer. That famous *finale* of 'Don Giovanni' at best only shows us the libertine at outs with his victims who implore heaven's vengeance; but here the world's dominions seek to defeat God. Here are two nations face to face; and Rossini has made marvelous use of the every means he has at command. He succeeds in giving the uproar of a tremendous storm which forms, as it were, the background to most horrible imprecations; yet he does not make it absurd. It is achieved by using chords in triple time and oft repeated; it moulds a rhythm of sombre musical emphasis grand in its monotony, so persistently repeated as to become absolutely overpowering. The Egyptians' terror at the pillar of fire and the cries for vengeance of the Hebrews require a delicate manipulation of harmony in the masses; see then how he makes the progression of the instrumentation follow the fugue of the chorus. In the midst of that deluge of fire the *allegro assai* in C-minor is terrific.

"You must needs confess," said Massimilla, at the time when Moses brings down the rain of fire by lifting his rod, where the musician brings out the full power of the orchestra and that of the stage, "that never did music more completely express so full an idea of distress and confusion."

"Which has spread to the parquet," said the Frenchman.

"What now? Most certainly the parquet is in a state of tremendous excitement," said the duchess.

In the *finale*, Genovese, who had fixed his eyes on la Tinti, gesticulated with such ridiculous flourishes that the parquet became suddenly enraged at having their enjoyment thus interrupted. To Italian ears nothing is so exasperating as a contrast between good and bad singing. The manager appeared on the stage to inform the house that Genovese, in answer to his remarks to him, had said that he was unaware in what manner he had given offense to the public, as at this same instant he had tried his utmost to reach the acme of perfection of his art.

"Let him be as bad to-day as he was yesterday—that would be good enough for us!" roared out Capraja in fury.

This exclamation restored good humor to the house.

The ballet, contrary to the usual Italian style, attracted but little attention. The subject of Genovese's strange acting and the manager's unhappy speech formed the text of conversation in every box. Those having the *entré* behind the scenes at once left the auditorium to learn the mystery of this curious performance. Soon it became rumored about that la Tinti had caused a terrible scene with Genovese, her colleague, and had accused the tenor of being insanely jealous of her success; that he had tried to prevent it by his preposterous behavior, and had actually endeavored to spoil the performance by pretending a passionate devotion to her. The prima donna was weeping bitterly over the catastrophe. She said she had been trying to fascinate her lover, who was somewhere in the house, though she had not been able to locate him.

Unless one understands the peaceful, humdrum round of daily life in the Venice of to-day, so lacking in incident that the altercation between two lovers, or, it may be, the huskiness of the voice of a singer, becomes the note of conversation, it becomes impossible to realize the excitement in the theatre and at the Café Florian, for it took on as much importance as the discussion of politics does in England. La Tinti was in love! la Tinti had been hampered in her performance! Genovese was either crazy or malignant of set purpose—he was actuated by the artist's jealousy so well known and familiar to Italians. Here was a mine to be worked by eager discussion.

The parquet was in a ferment of talk such as that on the Bourse; such a turmoil could not fail to astound a Frenchman accustomed to the quietude of the theatres in Paris. The boxes were in a ferment like the buzz of swarming bees.

One man alone remained pensive in the hubbub. Emilio Memmi, his eyes fixed on Massimilla, his back turned to the stage, seemed, in his melancholy expression, to live on her look; not once had he glanced at the prima donna.

"I need not ask, *caro carino*," said Vendramin to Emilio, "what result my negotiations had. Your pure, saintly Massimilla has been supremely kind; she has been, in fact, la Tinti."

The prince made reply by a negative shake of his head, full of profound sadness.

"Your love, then, has not yet descended from the spaces in ether in which you soar," said Vendramin, who was under the excitation of opium. "Not yet has it materialized. This morning, the same as for six months past, you could feel flowers opening their perfumed petals under the dome of your skull, which was an expanse grand in proportions. Your whole blood rushed to your throbbing heart, that seemed to rise to choke your throat. There—in there," said he, lightly touching Emilio's breast, "you experienced rapturous feelings. Massimilla's voice thrilled in your soul like waves of rippling light; her touch gave freedom to a thousand captive joys: they sprang from the convolutions of your brain and gathered around you in clouds, they bore your etherealized being through the blue air in a blaze of purple to far beyond the snowy peaks, to where the pure love of angels abides.

"Her smile, the kisses of her lips, tore off that venomous vestment and consumed the last remaining traces of your earthly nature. Her eyes, twin stars, changed you into a light without shadow. Together you kneeled down on heaven's palm-branches, there awaiting the opening of the gates of paradise; but they swung heavy on their hinges; you became impatient, you struck at them, but you could not reach them. Your hand could only touch clouds which were more elusive than your desires. Your companion, radiant and adorned with white roses, as a bride of heaven, wept at your anguish. It may have been that she was saying, in soft melodious tones, sweet litanies to the Virgin, the while the devilish cravings of the flesh were tormenting you with their indecent howlings: you have disdained the heavenly fruits of my ecstasy which is shortening my life, but in which I live."

"Your exaltations, my dear Vendramin," answered Emilio, calmly, "are much below reality. Who can in any way describe that absolute physical exhaustion in which we, who abuse the

22   2 A

dreams of pleasure, are left; which leaves in the soul an eternal longing, but the spirit in complete possession of its faculties? But this torment of Tantalus' I am weary of; to-night is my last on earth. After one other last attempt, our Mother shall again possess her child—my last sigh shall be received by the Adriatic——"

"Are you crazy?" exclaimed Vendramin. "No, you are mad; for the crisis we despise is madness; it is the remembrance of a former existence reacting on our being of the present. I have been taught that by the good fairies of my dreams, that and much beside!

"You would have one being made of the duchess and la Tinti; do not this, dear Emilio; take each separately, it is the wiser course. Only Raphael could unite form and idea. You would be the Raphael of love, but chance does not obey orders. Raphael was a *coup*, a lucky-stroke, of God's creation. It was preordained by Him that form and the ideal should be in antagonism; if it were otherwise naught could exist. If the first cause possesses more energy than the result, nothing can come of it. We must live either on the earth or in the heavens. Stay in heaven, it will always be too soon to descend to earth."

"I will accompany the duchess home," said the prince. "I shall make one final attempt—afterward."

"Afterward!" exclaimed Vendramin, anxiously. "Promise to call for me at Florian's."

"I will."

This dialogue had been held in modern Greek, a language unfamiliar to the duchess, although Emilio and Vendramin, like most Venetians, spoke it perfectly. And also to the Frenchman, who, quite without the little circle consisting of the duchess, Emilio, and Vendramin, yet had a glimmering of the truth, for he interpreted aright these Italian glances, by turns sly or keen, veiled or sidelong, which accompanied their speech. The duchess had urged Vendramin, by an earnest entreaty, to suggest this to Emilio, for she also suspected her lover's misery which he endured in that frigid empyrean in which he wandered—but she had no suspicions of la Tinti.

"These two young men are mad," said the physician.

"As regards the prince," said the duchess, "trust me to cure him. But for Vendramin, he must be wholly incurable if he cannot comprehend this divine music."

"If you would let me know the cause of their madness I could cure both," said the Frenchman.

"And since when have great physicians ceased to read the minds of men?" said she, ironically.

The ballet had now been ended for some time; the second act of "Moses" was about to begin. The parquet was quite at attention. It was rumored about that the Duke Cataneo had given Genovese a lecturing; that he had represented to him the injury he was working Clarina, the *diva* of the day. The second act would be superb.

"The Egyptian prince and his father are on the stage," said the duchess. "They have yielded again, and, though they are insulting the Hebrews, they tremble with rage. The son is congratulated by his father on his approaching marriage; his son is in despair at this fresh obstacle, but it only adds new fervor to his love which is opposed by everything. Genovese and Carthagenova are singing admirably. You note that the tenor is making peace with the house. How he brings out the beauty of the music! The theme of the son on the tonic, repeated by the father in the dominant, is truly in accord with that simple, serious plan which pervades the whole score; its soberness makes the endless variation of the music still more marvelous. All Egypt is there.

"In all modern music I do not think there exists a composition more truly noble. The majestic solemnity of a king is fully expressed in that wonderful theme; it is in harmony with that grand style which stamps the opera all through.

That idea of a son of Pharoah pouring out his griefs on the bosom of his father, surely could not be so admirably represented as in this noble imagery. For yourself, do you not feel a knowledge of that splendor we are accustomed to ascribe to that monarch of antiquity?"

"Indeed it is sublime music," said the Frenchman.

"The *airia* which the Queen will now sing, '*Pace mia smarrita*,' belongs to those *bravura* airs which must be introduced by every composer, though they detract from the general scheme of the opera; but unless the prima donna be duly flattered, an opera would more like than not never see the light. Still this musical *sop* is so fine itself that on every page it is given as it is written; it is so remarkably brilliant that the leading lady dare not substitute her favorite show-piece, such as is often done in operas.

"But now comes the really most striking movement of the score: the duet between Osiride and Elcia in the subterranean chamber, whither he has concealed her to withhold her from the departing Israelites and whence he intends to fly Egypt with her himself. But Aaron intrudes upon the lovers, he has been to warn Amatthea, and here we have the greatest of all quartettes—'*Mi manca la voce, mi sento morire.*' This *Mi manca la voce* is a masterpiece that will survive time itself—that destroyer of fashion in music—for it speaks the language of the soul which can never change. Mozart in his famous *finale* to 'Don Giovanni' holds his own; Marcello does the same by his psalm, '*Cæli en arrant gloriam Dei;*' Cimarosa by his aria, '*Pria che spunti;*' Beethoven by his symphony in C-minor; Pergolesi by his '*Stabat Mater;*' Rossini will live in his '*Mi manca la voce.*'

"The thing most to be admired in Rossini is his command of the variety in construction, he has here had recourse to the old construction of the canon in unison to produce the required effect; he brings in the voices and they become blended in the same melody. As the style of the lovely

melodies was new he set them in ancient framing; to give
still more relief he silences the orchestra, and the voices he
accompanies by the harps alone. It were impossible to display a greater ingenuity of detail or to produce a greater
general effect. Oh, dear! another disturbance!" said the
duchess.

Genovese, now that la Tinti was again on the stage, was
but a caricature of himself, although he had sung excellently
in his duet with Carthagenova. He had sunk from the great
singer to the most wretched chorus singer.

Now arose the most formidable uproar that had ever echoed
to the roof of the Fenice. It was only subdued in response
to the demand of Clarina; she, rendered furious at the diffi-
culties caused by the stubbornness of Genovese, sang "*Mi
manca la voce*" as it can never again be sung. The enthusiasm was tremendous; the house forgot its indignation and
rage in absolute, acute enjoyment.

"She drowns my soul in purple radiance!" said Capraja,
as he waved his handkerchief in a blessing to *la Diva*
Tinti.

"Heaven shower all its blessings on your head," cried out
a gondolier.

"Pharaoh," said the duchess, "will now revoke his commands." (The parquet had become calm again.) "He will be
overwhelmed by Moses even while upon his throne, who will
declare to him that every first-born son in Egypt shall taste
death; he sings out that strain of vengeance which proclaims thunders from heaven, while the clarion notes of the
Hebrews are heard above it. You must clearly understand
though that this *aria* is by Pacini; it is introduced by Carthagenova in the place of that written by Rossini. Doubtless
that *aria, Paventa,* will retain its place in the score; the
chance it gives the basso of displaying his voice is too good
to be lost, and here expression instead of science carries the
day. But, any way, the *aria* is filled with grand menace, and

it is possible that not for long we may be allowed the privilege of hearing it."

A thunderous clapping and cries of bravo hailed the song, followed by a deep, thinking silence; it was thoroughly Venetian and significant; nothing could have been more so, this turmoil and its sudden suppression.

"It is unnecessary to speak of the coronation march which announces the enthroning of Osiride, which is intended as a challenge to Moses, it only needs hearing to be comprehended. The celebrated Beethoven has never written anything finer. This march, filled as it is with earthly pomp, is in marked contrast to that of the Israelites. By comparing them you will see the purpose of the music.

"Elcia declares her love in the presence of the two leaders of the Hebrews; she then renounces it in the exquisite *aria* '*Porge la destra amata*' (Give to another the hand your adored one loves). Ah! what anguish! Just look at the house!"

The parquet was shouting *bravos*, as Genovese left the stage.

"Now freed from her deplored lover, we hear la Tinti sing: '*O desolata Elcia*'—that overpowering *cavatina* which is so expressive of love disapproved by God."

"Where art thou, Rossini?" cried Cataneo. "Would that he could hear the music invented by his genius so superbly rendered," he continued. "Is not Clarina worthy of him?" he asked Capraja. "To be able to give light to those notes by such flashes of flame which, starting from the lungs, feed on some unknown matter in the air, which are taken in by our ears and which bear us upward, onward in a heavenly rapture of love, she must be God!"

"She resembles that gorgeous Indian plant, which, deserting earth, absorbs invisible nutriment from the atmosphere, its spiral blossoms of white shed such fragrant vapors that fill the brain with ravishing dreams," replied Capraja.

When she was recalled, la Tinti appeared alone; a storm

of applause greeted her; thousands of kisses were blown from
as many finger-tips; she was pelted with roses; a wreath was
even made of the flowers ravished from the ladies' hats—
nearly all of which came from Paris.

The *cavatina* was encored.

"With what eagerness must Capraja have looked forward
for this *aria,* in his passion for embellishments, which derives
its whole success from the manner of its execution," said Massimilla. "Rossini has, one may say, given over the reins to the
fancy of the singer. Here *cadenza* and expression mean
everything; with a poor voice, or a feeble interpretation, it
would be worthless—the throat alone is responsible for this
aria's effects. The singer must display the intensest anguish,
the anguish of a woman who beholds her lover dying before
her eyes.

"La Tinti makes the roof resound with her *alt* notes; here
Rossini, leaving the singer free to do her utmost, writes it in
the simplest, clearest style. Then for a crowning effect he
composes those heart-rending cries: '*Tormenti! Affanni!
Smanie!*' What grief, what pain is in those runs. And,
you see, la Tinti has brought down the house."

Bewildered by this worshiping adoration of a vast theatre
for the source of its pleasures, the Frenchman had a glimpse
at the real Italian nature. But neither the duchess nor the
two young men paid the least attention to this ovation.

Clarina again began.

The duchess had a fear that this was the last time she would
ever behold Emilio. As for the prince, he was in the presence
of the divinity who uplifted him to the heavens; he had no
knowledge of where he was; he heard no longer the voice of
the woman who had initiated him into the mysterious sensu-
ality of earthly pleasures, for a profound dejection caused a
tingling in his ears; he heard a chorus of plaintive voices
which seemed partly drowned in a tempest of pouring rain.

As to Vendramin, he saw himself in a costume of ancient

Venice, gazing down upon the ceremony of the *Bucentaure.*
The Frenchman very plainly perceived that some painful
mystery had arisen between the duchess and Emilio, and he
was racking his brain in the conjecture as to what it might be.

The scene had changed.

In the centre of a fine picture, which depicted the Desert
and the Red Sea, the Egyptians and Hebrews made their
evolutions, but without producing any effect on the four persons occupying the box of the duchess. But when the first
chords of the harps gave the prelude to the hymn of the delivered Israelites, the prince and Vendramin rose and stood
leaning against the opposite sides of the box, while the duchess
supported her head on her hand, resting her elbow on the
velvet ledge.

Comprehending from this little stir the importance of this
justly famous chorus, the Frenchman listened, as did all the
house, with undivided attention.

With one accord the audience shouted for an encore.

"I feel as if I were celebrating Italy's liberation," thought
a Milanese.

"Music, such as this, lifts up heads that are bowed; it
revives the hope of the most indifferent," said one from
Romagna.

"In this scene," said Massimilla, whose emotion was dis-
cernible, "science is put aside. This masterpiece was dictated
by inspiration alone; it emanated from the soul of the composer like a cry of love! The accompaniment consists solely
of harps—only at the last refrain of this divine theme does
the orchestra appear. Never can Rossini rise higher than in
this prayer; he will do, undoubtedly, work quite as good, he
can never excel it; the sublime always equals itself; but this
hymn is one of those things that will remain sublime for ever.
The only companion for such a conception may be found in
Marcello's grand psalms, that noble Venetian, who was to music
what Giotto was to painting. The majesty of the theme is

only to be compared with the noblest inventions ever created by religious writers, as it unfolds itself in episodes of inexhaustible melody.

"How simple the structure! The attack is opened by Moses in G-minor, which ends in a *cadenza* in B-flat, thus allowing the entrance of the chorus, at first *pianissimo*, in the same key of B-flat, resolving itself into G-minor. Three times does this splendid treatment of the voices recur, and it ends its last strophe in a *stretto* in G-major of a most overpowering and majestic effect. It is a nation released from slavery; we feel it in this hymn, as it rises toward heaven, where it is met by the like strains falling from the higher spheres. With joy the stars make response to this ecstasy of a liberated earth. The rhythm in its rounded fullness, the deliberate dignity of the modulations which lead up to the outburst of praise and thinksgiving, its measured return, cause pictures of celestial joys in the soul. Can you not imagine that you see the heavens open; that you there behold angels swinging sistrums of gold, seraphims prostrated, waving their fragrant censers; the archangels resting upon their flaming swords with which they have vanquished the heathen?

"The secret of this music in its refreshing effect on the soul is that of but few works of human genius, I think; for the time it bears us into the infinite; it is within us; we see it in those melodies as boundless as those hymns sung round the throne of God. Rossini's genius carries us to prodigious heights, whence we gaze down upon our promised land; our eyes are fascinated by the divine light, and we gaze enraptured into limitless space. The last strain of Elcia brings a feeling, as it were, of earth-born passion, for she has nearly recovered from her sorrow, with this psalm of thanksgiving. This, see you, is another touch of genius.

"Aye, sing," cried the duchess, as she listened to the last stanza with a sombre enthusiasm like that given to it by the singers. "Sing! You are free!"

The words were spoken in such a tone of voice as made the physician start. With the intention of diverting Massimilla from her bitter reflections, he engaged her in argument in which the French excel, at the time that a furore of excitement recalling la Tinti was at its highest.

"Madame," said he, "to-morrow I shall come again with a more comprehensive understanding of this great work, thanks to you for your explanation, in its structural effects; you have often mentioned the color of the music; now, as an analyst and materialist, I must acknowledge that I have always rejected the affectation of a number of enthusiasts, who would have us believe that music is painting with tones. It would be, would it not? the same as Raphael's admirers speaking of him as singing in colors."

"In the language of musicians," answered the duchess, "painting awakens our souls to certain associations or definite images in our minds; now these memories and forms have each their respective colors—sad or lively. You do but fight for a word, that is all. Capraja's theory is that each instrument has its task, its mission; that it appeals to a particular feeling, the same as each color is allied to a certain idea in our souls. Take a pattern in gold on a ground of blue, does that arouse the same sensation in you as a red pattern on green or black? So in music there are no forms, no expressions of emotion—these are simply artistic; but no one gazes on them with indifference. Again, does not the oboe possess that peculiar tone always associated by us with the open country, the same it has in common with most wind instruments? The brass gives a suggestion of martial ideas, it arouses violent and, at times, even a furious feeling. The strings, which derive their material from the organic world, appeal to the finest fibres of our being—they reach the heart's depths.

"In speaking as I did of the sombre hue, the coldness of tone in the introduction to 'Moses,' I was, it seems to me, quite as justified as your critics are when they allude to

'color' in a writer's work. You confess to a nervous style,
a pallid style, a gay or bright-colored style, do you not?
Art can paint with words, sound, color, lines, shape. The
means are manifold, the result one.

"An Italian architect could give us the same feeling by
constructing an esplanade through, between and under,
gloomy, damp glades of tall, thick trees from whence we
emerge suddenly upon a valley filled with streams, flowers,
and mills, all radiant in the sunshine, as that created in us by
the overture to 'Moses in Egypt.'

"At their greatest the arts are but an exposition of Nature's
grand scenery.

"Go and talk with Capraja, you will be astonished at what
he will teach you; for myself, I am not learned enough to
propound the philosophy of music. He can inform you how
every instrument that depends on the touch of man for its
expression and temperament of tone is superior to color as a
means of expression, which must needs remain fixed, or speech
which has its limits. The language of music is infinite: it
includes all, it expresses everything. Can you now see in
what lies the preëminence of the work to which you have just
listened?

"I can explain it in a few words. Music is of two kinds:
one petty, poor, second-rate, never varying, its base the hundred or so phrasings which all musicians understand, a bab-
bling which is more or less pleasant, the life that most composers live. As we hear their would-be melodies, their themes,
which gave much or little satisfaction, and of which not a
trace is left in our minds, we know that by a century's end
they are entirely forgotten.

"But nations have preserved from time's birth until our own
day certain phrases which they have guarded as sacred treasures; these have contained an epitome of their manners and
instincts; they embrace, I might say, their history. Hark to
one of those primitive strains—take the Gregorian chant as an

example; it is, in sacred song, the heritage of the remotest races; in it you will lose yourself in deep dreams. Despite the severe simplicity of the rudimentary relics, strange, but portentous, conceptions will unfold before you. Once or twice in a century, never more frequent, a Homer of music arises; he is granted by God the guerdon of being ahead of his age. These men can concert melodies full to overflowing of facts accomplished, pregnant by massive poetry. Remember this, think of it. The thought, a germ, often turned over, will prove fruitful; melody, not harmony, it is that will weather the attack of time.

"The music in this oratorio is filled with a world of grand and holy things. An opera with that introduction and ending with that invocation is not mortal; it is as immortal as the Easter hymn *O filli et filiæ*, as the *Dies iræ* of the dead, as every song must be which in every country has outlived its splendor, its happiness, its dead prosperity."

As the duchess left her box she wiped away the tears which clearly showed that she was thinking of the Venice that is no more; Vendramin kissed her hand.

The performance closed in a chaos of turbulence. Hisses and abuse were showered upon Genovese, while a paroxysm of frenzy greeted la Tinti as applause. For a long time the Venetians had not experienced so enlivening an evening. The antagonism aroused had warmed and invigorated them, for such is never wanting in Italy, where the smallest towns have ever thrived on the diverse interests of two opposing factions. In every place the Guelfs and Ghibellines; at Verona, the Capulets and Montagues; at Bologna, the Geremei and Lomelli; at Genoa, the Fieschi and Doria; at every place the patricians and the populace, and the senate and tribunes of the Roman republic; at Florence, the Medici and the Passi; at Milan, the Sforza and the Visconti; at Rome, the Orsini and the Colonna; in fact, everywhere and upon all occasions the same impulse exists.

Already upon the streets there were "Genovists" and "Tintists."

The duchess was escorted by the prince; the former was still more depressed by the loves of Osiride; she dreaded a similar disaster to herself. She clung the closer to Emilio, as though trying to keep him next her heart.

"Remember your promise," said Vendramin; "I shall look for you in the square."

As Vendramin took the Frenchman's arm purposing a walk together on the Piazzo San Marco, as he awaited the prince:

"I shall but be too glad if he does not come," said he.

This formed the subject for a discourse between them, and Vendramin considered it a favorable opportunity in which to consult the physician. He told him of the peculiar situation in which Emilio was placed.

As every Frenchman does on every occasion, the Frenchman laughed. Vendramin was angry, for he viewed the matter very seriously, but he became mollified when that disciple of Majendie, of Cuvier, of Dupuytren, and of Brossais said that most surely he could cure the prince of his high-falutin rhapsodies, that he could dispel the celestial poetry he had wrapped about Massimilla as by a cloud.

"A pleasant form of misfortune!" said he. "The ancients were not quite the fools we believe them to be from their heaven of crystal and their ideas of physics, which in the fable of Ixion is symbolical of that power which annuls the body and creates the spirit lord of all."

Presently Vendramin and the physician met Genovese and, accompanying him, the fantastic Capraja. The august melomaniac was anxiously trying to learn the cause of the tenor's *fiasco.* Genovese, when questioned, spoke very rapidly, the same as all men do who become intoxicated in the bursting forth of ideas caused in them by a passion.

"Yes, signori, I love her; I adore her with such frenzy as I never thought I could experience, since I have become tired of women. Women play the devil with art. Work and pleasure can never get along together. Clarina fancies me jealous of her success; she believes I attempted to hamper her triumph at Venice; but in the wings I was clapping and shouting *diva* louder than any person in the house."

"Even so," said Cataneo, as he joined them, "but that does not account for your becoming, from a divine singer, one of the most execrable ones that ever pumped air through his larynx, without adding any of the charm which fascinates and ravishes us."

"I!" said the virtuoso. "I a poor singer! I who am the equal of the greatest masters?"

But now the doctor and Vendramin, Capraja, Cataneo, and Genovese had arrived at the piazetta. It was midnight. The glistening bay, in its outline of the Saint-Georges and Saint-Paul churches, at the end of the Giudecca, at the juncture of the beginning of the Grand Canal, that has its mysterious inchoation under the *Dogana* and the Santa Maria della Salute church, lay beautiful and placid. The moon shone on the barques alongside the Rive des Esclavons. There is no tide to the waters of Venice, and they seemed to be alive, dancing, as they were, in myriads of spangles. No singer had ever a more resplendent stage.

Genovese seemed to call upon the heavens and the earth as witnesses, as he made an emphatic gesture; then he commenced to sing, accompanied only by the lapping wavelets, "*Ombra adoratta,*" the *chef-d'œuvre* of Crescentini's.

This air, as it rose up amidst the statues of Saint-Theodore and Saint-Georges, right in the breast of sleeping Venice, which were radiant in the moonlight, the words, so peculiarly harmonizing with the scene, the melancholy passion of the singer, bound the Italians and the Frenchman as by a spell.

Vendramin's face became wet with tears at the first notes.

Capraja stood as motionless as one of the statues in the ducal palazzo. Cataneo showed some emotion. The Frenchman was pensive, he was taken quite by surprise; he seemed like a scientific man face to face with a phenomenon which has upset the axioms upon which he is founded. These four so different minds, with so little faith; these that believed in nothing but themselves for themselves, with nothing to follow, who looked upon their existence as at best a chanceling and fortuitous being, like the petty life of a plant or a bug, gained a glimpse of heaven. No music could so surely deserve the epitaph—divine. Those so soothing notes were poured forth and bathed their souls in soft and languorous airs. These vapors, which seemed to the listeners to be almost visible, resembling the marble forms around them in the silvery rays of the moon, had angels seated upon them, waving their wings in love and adoration. The simple, artless melody penetrated the soul like a ray of light. It was a sacred passion!

But the vanity of the tenor awakened them like a sudden blow.

"Say, now, am I a poor singer?" he cried as he finished the air.

His audience regretted that the instrument was not a heavenly thing. It was no more, this angelic song, than the outcome of a man's wounded pride! The singer experienced nothing, thought nothing of the pious feelings and divine imagery that he had created in the others; not more, in reality, than Paganini's violin can understand what he makes it declare. They, in imagination, had seen Venice lifting its shroud and giving utterance to song—and here it was but the result of a tenor's *fiasco!*

"Can you guess what such a phenomenon means?" the Frenchman asked Capraja; he wished to make him talk, as the duchess had alluded to him as being a deep thinker.

"What phenomenon?" said Capraja.

"Genovese, who, in the absence of la Tinti, is most admirable, and when singing with her makes the braying of a donkey.''

" He obeys a supernatural law of which one of your chemists might be prepared to give the mathematical formula, and which the succeeding generation may probably express in a report filled with x, a, and b, stirred up among a number of algebraic signs, nodes, and quips that give one the colic; for, as a fact, the greatest mathematics ever conceived add nothing to our sum-total of happiness.

" If an artist becomes so unfortunately full of the passion that he would fain express, he cannot fulfill his desire because then he is the real thing and no longer its image. Art is the work of the brain, not the heart. When a subject possesses you, then you are no longer its master, but its slave; you are a king besieged by his people. When you have too keen a feeling, at the instant you wish to represent that feeling, you cause an insurrection of sense against the faculty of government.''

" May we not be able to convince ourselves of this truth by some further experiment?'' said the doctor.

"Cataneo,'' said Capraja to his friend, "contrive to bring your tenor and the prima donna together again.''

"Very well, gentlemen,'' replied the duke, "sup with me. We ought to effect a reconciliation between Genovese and la Clarina; if not, the season is ruined for Venice.''

The invitation was accepted.

"Gondoliers!'' called Cataneo.

"One moment,'' said Vendramin, "Memmi is awaiting me at Florian's; I cannot leave him to himself; if we do not make him tipsy to-night, he will kill himself to-morrow.''

"*Corpo santo!*'' cried the duke. " I must keep that young man alive, if only for the future prospects of my line. I will also invite him.''

They all returned to Florian's, where an eager and stormy discussion was going on in the crowd, to which an end was put by the tenor's arrival. By a window in a corner, gloomy, in a fixed gaze and dejected attitude, stood the prince, looking at the balcony, the very image of dismal despair.

"'That crazy fellow," said the physician in French to Vendramin, "knows not what he wants. That man can create in Massimilla Doni, a being apart from the rest of creation; he possesses her in the skies in the midst of an ideal splendor that no earthly power can make real. He sees his mistress always sublime, ever pure; he always hears within him what we heard by the sea; he lives forever in the light of a pair of eyes which create for him the warmth and golden radiance that halos the Virgin in the Assumption by Titian, after Raphael had invented it for him and revealed it to him in the Transfiguration, and this man wishes to smear the poem. My advice is that he makes a combination in one woman of his sensual delights and his divine worship. In short, like all and every one of us, he must be given a mistress.

"He had a divinity, and the miserable creature insists that it shall be a female! I can assure monsieur that he will resign heaven. I won't answer, though, for it that he may not at the last die of despair.

"O, ye faces of women, so daintily outlined in a pure and lovely oval, which reminds us of art's creations where it has very successfully rivaled nature! Celestial feet that cannot walk; a form so slender that an earthly breeze would break; a frail shape which cannot conceive; virgins that visited our dreams when we grew out of childhood, those we adored in secret, and worshiped without hope, clothed in the ray of some unwearying, voluptuous desire; maidens whom we shall never again behold, but the smiles from whom remain ever supreme throughout our lives, what hog of Epicurus will insist on dragging you down to the filth of this world!

"The sun, monsieur, gives heat and light to the world only because it is placed at a distance of thirty-three millions of leagues away. Come nearer to it and science warns you

23

that it is not really hot nor luminous—for science is of some use," he added, turning to Capraja.

"For a Frenchman and a doctor, that is not so bad," said Capraja, as he patted the foreigner on his shoulder. "In those few words you have solved the question which Europeans have least understood in the whole of Dante—his Beatrice. Yes, Beatrice, that ideal form, the queen of the poet's phantasies, chosen in preference to all the elect, consecrated by tears, deified in his memory, always young in the fact of his perpetual desire!"

"Prince," said the duke to Emilio, "come and sup with me. It is impossible you should refuse the poor Neapolitan from whom you have stolen both his wife and his mistress."

This broad Neapolitan jest, spoken as it was with aristocratic grace, made Emilio smile; he permitted the duke to take his arm and lead him thither.

Already Cataneo had sent a messenger to his house from the café.

As the Palazzo Memmi was on the Grand Canal, but a short distance away from Santa Maria della Salute, the way thither was either by gondola or on foot by passing around the Rialto. The four guests would not hear of separation, so all walked; the infirmities of the duke compelled his making use of a gondola.

Toward two o'clock in the morning the passers-by would have seen the light pouring out of every window of the Palazzo Memmi and across the Grand Canal; they would have heard also the delightful overture to "Semiramide," performed at the base of the stairway by the orchestra from the Fenice, in seranading la Tinti.

The company was at supper on the third-floor gallery. From the balcony la Tinti in return sang "Buona sera," Almavida's *aria* in "Il Barbiere," the while the steward of the duke distributed largess from his master to the impecunious artists, and bade them to dinner on the coming day. These civilities are expected of great lords who protect singers, and of fine ladies who have their tenors and bassos. In such cases there is naught for it but to marry the whole *corps de théâtre.*

Cataneo did things in great style; he was the banker for the manager; this season alone had cost him two thousand crowns.

The palace had been furnished by him; he had wines from every country and had imported a French chef. The supper, therefore, was a royal banquet.

All through the meal the prince, who was seated next to la Tinti, was vividly alive to what is termed by the poets "the darts of love."

As the thought of God is sometimes obscured in clouds of doubt in the consciences of solitary thinkers, so was the transcendental vision of Massimilla eclipsed to the sight of Emilio.

Clarina believed herself the happiest woman in the world; knew it when she saw that Emilio was in love with her. She felt assured of keeping him, and her delight was plain to be seen in her countenance; her beauty was so radiant, so dazzling, that none of the men could refrain from expressing their admiration as they lifted their glasses; it was impossible to resist a courtly bow to her.

"The duchess cannot be placed in comparison with la Tinti," said the Frenchman, who had already forgotten his theories under the burning glance of the eyes of the Sicilian.

The tenor ate and drank perfunctorily; he appeared to only wish to identify his life with that of the prima donna; he seemed to have lost that keen sense of enjoyment so characteristic of Italian male vocalists.

"Come, signorina," said the duke, looking imploringly at Clarina, "and you, *caro primo uomo,*" he continued to Genovese, "let your voices unite in one true sound. Give us the C of *Qual portento,* when the light comes in the oratorio we have just listened to, and thus convince my old friend

Capraja that the unison is far superior to any embellishment of harmony.''

"I will bear her away from that prince whom she loves; she worships him, it is apparent in her eyes," muttered Genovese to himself.

The astonishment of the guests can only be imagined when, after hearing him in the open air, he began to bray, coo, mew, squeak, guggle, bellow, bark, thunder, squeal, shriek, and produced sounds even which can only be described as a hoarse rattle; he went, in fact, through a non-understandable farce; what time his face was transfigured with an expression of rapture, like a martyr, as painted by Zurbaran or Murillo, a Titian or Raphael. The universal yell of laughter became changed to nearly tragic gravity when they comprehended that Genovese was terribly in earnest.

La Tinti saw that her associate was enamored of her; that he had spoken the truth when on the stage with her in that land of falsehood.

"*Poverino!*" she whispered, as she stroked the hand of the prince beneath the table.

"By the holies!" exclaimed Capraja, "please let me know what score you are reading at this time—murderer of Rossini? Pray instruct us of what you are thinking—what demon is it that struggles in your throat?"

"Demon!" cried Genovese, "nay, the rather say: God of music. My eyes, like St. Cecilia's, see angels pointing with their fingers to show me the staff of the score writ in fiery notes; I am trying to keep pace with them. *Per Dio!* do you not comprehend? My being is filled with inspiration; it crowds my heart, my lungs; my soul and my throat possess the one life.

"Have you never heard in a dream the most entrancing strains, the thoughts of unborn musicians who have utilized pure sound, which has been hidden by nature in everything—sounds which we, more or less truthfully, bring forth, employing the instruments we use to create groups of various colors? These in dream-concerts are heard free of every imperfection of those performers whom it is impossible shall be all emotion, all soul. And I, I give you that perfection and you upbraid me!

"You are as crazy as the parquet at the Fenice when they hissed me! I have contempt for the vulgar crowd who are unable to mount with me to those alps where I reign over art —I make my appeal to remarkable men, to a Frenchman— why, he is gone!"

"Half an hour since," said Vendramin.

"It is a pity. Perhaps he might have understood me, as worthy Italians, lovers of art, do not——"

"There you go!" said Capraja, smiling and giving a light tap on the tenor's head. "Ride away on the celestial Ariosto's hippogrif; chase, then, your dazzling chimera, musical *teriaki* as you are!"

For a truth, every one else believed that Genovese was simply drunk, and they let him talk without paying any attention to him. It was only Capraja that understood the case put by the French physician.

The wine of Cyprus had loosened every tongue, and each one pranced around on his own particular hobby; meanwhile the Frenchman was in a gondola awaiting the duchess, to whom he had forwarded a note written by Vendramin.

Massimilla made her appearance in her night-wrapper; she had been so alarmed at the prince's adieu and further startled by the hope suggested in the letter.

"Madame," said the Frenchman, as he handed her to a seat, desiring the gondolier to start, "at this instant the life of Prince Emilio is in jeopardy and only yourself can save him."

"What must be done?" she asked.

"Ah! Will you resign yourself to perform a degrading act—despite the noblest face in Italy? Is it that you can

descend from your heaven of azure into the bed of a courtesan? In short, can an angel of refinement as you are, of
such true and unspotted beauty, beseem yourself to imagine
what the love of a Tinti can be—put yourself in her place so
much as to deceive Emilio's ardor, and who is too much
intoxicated to be altogether clear of sight?"

"And is that all?" said she, with a smile that betrayed to
the Frenchman one view of the delicious nature of an Italian
woman in love which he had not before perceived. "I will
out-Tinti la Tinti if necessary to save the life of my friend."

"Then you will blend two species of love into one; he
now sees them as separated from each other, divided by mountains of poetic imaginings; these will melt away like snow
upon a glacier under the fierce rays of a midsummer sun."

"I shall be your debtor throughout eternity," said the
duchess soberly.

When the Frenchman returned to the hall, he showed a
look of satisfaction which Emilio, who was absorbed by la
Tinti, did not observe; the banquet had now become an orgy
and was stamped with Venetian frenzy. The prince was promising himself a further indulgence in the ravishing delights he
had already tasted, while la Tinti, a genuine Sicilian, was idly
floating on the sweet current of a maddening passion now on
the verge of being again gratified.

When the Frenchman whispered a few words to Vendramin,
la Tinti was evidently troubled.

"What are you plotting?" she asked the friend of the
prince.

"Are you a good girl?" inquired the doctor in her ear,
assuming the operator's sternness.

These words thrust themselves into her understanding as
though struck by a dagger in her heart.

"It is to save Emilio's life," added Vendramin.

"Come here," said the doctor to Clarina.

The poor singer arose and walked to the end of the table,

seating herself between the doctor and Vendramin, and looking like a criminal in the presence of the confessor and executioner.

She held out for a long time, but at length she yielded, out
of love for Emilio.

The last words of the doctor were:

"And you must cure Genovese."

As she returned around the table she spoke a few words to
the tenor. Then she went to the prince, she placed her arms
around his neck, she kissed his hair, a despairing expression
on her face, noticed by the only two who seemed to have any
sense remaining, Vendramin and the doctor, and then vanished into her chamber.

Emilio, who noticed that Genovese had left the table, while
Cataneo and Capraja were engrossed in a long-winded argument on music, then crept to the door of the bedroom,
raised the portière, and slipped in like an eel into the mud.

"But see you, Cataneo," said Capraja, "you have extracted
the last particle of physical enjoyment, now here you are,
strung on wires like a harlequin of cardboard, all patterned
with scars, and never making a move except the string of
perfect unison is pulled."

"And you, my Capraja, you who have squeezed dry every
idea—are you not also in the same boat? You only exist by
riding the hobby-horse of a *roulade;* is it not so?"

"I? I possess the whole world!" exclaimed Capraja, with
the gesture of a sovereign and an extended hand.

"And I have devoured it!" answered the duke.

The prince's sleep was disturbed by a dream, next morning,
after a night of unalloyed happiness. On his heart he felt the
trickling of pearls let fall by an angel: he awoke, and found
himself laved in the tears of Massimilla Doni. He lay in her
arms and she had watched him as he slept.

The same evening, though la Tinti would not let him arise
until two o'clock in the afternoon—a thing which is con-

sidered very bad for a tenor voice—Genovese, at the Fenice, sang most divinely his part in " Semiramide."

Together with la Tinti he was many times recalled, new diadems were presented, the parquet was delirious with joy; the tenor had done with trying to charm the prima donna by the angelic method.

Vendramini was the only one whom the physician could not cure. Love for a country that no longer exists is a passion beyond remedy. This young Venetian, who by living in his republic of the thirteenth century and in the embrace of that pernicious harlot known as opium, when he found himself in this work-a-day world, brought thither by reaction, at last succumbed, pitied and regretted by his friends.

How shall the conclusion of this adventure be given, for it is so disastrously humdrum. One word is enough for those who adore the ideal:

The duchess was big with child.

The Peri, the naiads, the fays, the sylphs of ancient lore, the Muses of Greece, the Marble Virgins of the Certosa at Pavia, Michael Angelo's Day and Night, the little angels which Bellini was the first to place at the feet of his church paintings, and which Raphael painted so exquisitely in his Virgin with the Donor, and the shivering Madonna of Dresden, Orcagna's exquisite Maidens in the church of San-Michele, Florence; the celestial choir round the tomb of Saint-Sebaldus, Nuremberg, the Virgins of the Duomo at Milan, the whole population of a hundred Gothic cathedrals, all the race of beings who burst through their mouldiness to visit you, all grand imaginative artists—each and all of these angelic and disembodied maidens gathered about Massimilla's bed and wept.

PARIS, *May 25,* 1839.

INDEX TO THE COMÉDIE HUMAINE.

TITLES OF VOLUMES.

A   The Wild Ass' Skin.
B   The Chouans.
C   The Country Doctor.
D   The Quest of the Absolute.
E   Eugénie Grandet.
F   The Country Parson.
G   Father Goriot.
H   Ursule Mirouët.
I   The Celibates.
J   A Bachelor's Establishment.
K   Modeste Mignon.
L   The Lily of the Valley.
M   A Distinguished Provincial at Paris.
N   Lost Illusions.
O   César Birotteau.
P   Béatrix.
Q   About Catherine de' Medici.
R   The Peasantry.
S   A Woman of Thirty.
T   The Seamy Side of History.
U   Seraphita.
V   A Daughter of Eve.
W   The Poor Parents.   Part I.
X   The Poor Parents.   Part II.
Y   The Harlot's Progress.   Vol. I.
Z   The Harlot's Progress.   Vol. II.

AA   Jealousies of a Country Town.
BB   The Thirteen.
CC   Muse of the Department.
DD   The Deputy for Arcis.   Part I.
DS   Droll Stories.
EE   The Deputy for Arcis.   Part II.
FF   A Prince of Bohemia.

GENERAL INDEX.

The letters in Capitals denote the *title* volume; the italic letter giving the one in which each story is found.

For example:

"The Atheist's Mass," *c,* will be found in C—"The Country Doctor."

The Comédie Humaine.

A full list of titles classified in the manner obtaining for a generation after Balzac's death, being arranged by himself, except that the "Député d'Arcis" was not then completed.

SCENES FROM PRIVATE LIFE
(Scènes de la Vie Privée).

SIGN OF THE CAT AND RACKET,	*La Maison du Chat-qui-Pelote.*
The Sceaux Ball,	*Le Bal de Sçeaux.*
The Purse,	*La Bourse.*
The Vendetta,	*La Vendetta.*
Madame Firmiani,	*Mme. Firmiani.*
A Second Home,	*Une Double Famille.*
THE PEACE OF THE HOUSE,	*La Paix du Ménage.*
The Imaginary Mistress,	*La Fausse Maîtresse.*
A Study of Woman,	*Étude de femme.*
Another Study of Woman,	*Autre étude de femme.*
The Great Bretêche,	*La Grande Bretêche.*
Albert Savaron,	*Albert Savarus.*
LETTERS OF TWO BRIDES,	*Mémoires de deux Jeunes Mariées.*
A Daughter of Eve,	*Une Fille d'Ève.*
A WOMAN OF THIRTY,	*La Femme de Trente Ans.*
A Forsaken Woman,	*La Femme abandonnée.*
The Pomegranate Trees,*	*La Grenadière.*

* As here we have "The Oaks," "The Beeches," etc., as house names.

The Old Maid,	*La Vieille Fille,*
The Collection of Antiquities,	*Le Cabinet des antiques.*
THE LILY OF THE VALLEY,	*Le Lys dans la Vallée.*
LOST ILLUSIONS:—I.,	*Illusions Perdues, I.:*
The Two Poets,	*Les Deux Poëtes,*
A Distinguished Provincial at Paris. Part 1,	*Un Grand homme de province à Paris, 1ʳᵉ partie.*
LOST ILLUSIONS:—II.,	*Illusions Perdues, II.:*
A Distinguished Provincial at Paris. Part 2,	*Un Grand homme de province, 2ᵉ p.,*
Eve and David,	*Ève et David.*

SCENES FROM PARISIAN LIFE
(*Scènes de la Vie Parisienne*).

THE HARLOT'S PROGRESS:	*Splendeurs et Misères des Courtisanes :*
Esther Happy,	*Esther heureuse,*
What Love Costs an Old Man,	*A combien l'amour revient aux vieillards,*
The End of Evil Ways,	*Ou mènent les mauvais chemins.*
VAUTRIN'S LAST AVATAR,*	*La dernière Incarnation de Vautrin.*
A Prince of Bohemia,	*Un Prince de la Bohème.*
A Man of Business,	*Un Homme d'affaires.*
Gaudissart II.,	*Gaudissart II.*
The Unconscious Mummers,	*Les Comédiens sans le savoir.*

* An integral portion of the previous volume.

24

THE THIRTEEN :
    Ferragus,
    The Duchess of Langeais,
    The Girl with Golden Eyes,
	Histoire des Treize :
	    Ferragus,
	    La Duchesse de Langeais.
	    La Fille aux yeux d'or.

FATHER GORIOT,*	Le Père Goriot.
CÉSAR BIROTTEAU,	César Birotteau.

THE FIRM OF NUCINGEN,
The Secrets of the Princess of
    Cadignan,
The Workpeople,
Sarrasine,
Facino Cane,
	La Maison Nucingen.
	Les Secrets de la princesse de
	    Cadignan.
	Les Employés.
	Sarrasine.
	Facino Cane.

THE MIDDLE CLASSES,†	Les Petits Bourgeois.

THE POOR PARENTS :‡
    1. COUSIN BETTY,
 	
    2. COUSIN PONS,
	Les Parents Pauvres :
	    1. La Cousine Bette,
	
	    2. Le Cousin Pons.

SCENES FROM POLITICAL LIFE
(Scènes de la Vie Politique).

A HISTORICAL MYSTERY, An Episode of the Reign of Terror,	Une Ténébreuse Affaire. Un Episode sous la Terreur.
THE SEAMY SIDE OF HISTORY:	L'Envers de l'Histoire Con- temporaine :

* "Old Goriot" would be preferable as a title.

† "The Lower Middle Classes," correctly, but this has no significance in this country.

‡ A literal translation, although "The Poor Relations" is a better one.

Madame de la Chanterie,	*Mme. de la Chanterie,*
Initiated,	*L'Initié.*
Z. Marcas,	*Z. Marcas.*

THE DEPUTY FOR ARCIS,	*Le Député d'Arcis.*

SCENES FROM MILITARY LIFE
(*Scènes de la Vie Militaire*).

THE CHOUANS,	*Les Chouans.*
A Passion in the Desert,	*Une Passion dans le désert.*

SCENES FROM COUNTRY LIFE
(*Scènes de la Vie de Campagne*).

THE COUNTRY DOCTOR,	*Le Médecin de Campagne.*
THE COUNTRY PARSON,	*Le Curé de Village.*
THE PEASANTRY,	*Les Paysans.*

PHILOSOPHICAL STUDIES
(*Études Philosophiques*).

THE WILD ASS' SKIN,	*La Peau de Chagrin.*
THE QUEST OF THE ABSOLUTE,	*La Recherche de l'Absolu.*
Christ in Flanders,	*Jésus-Christ en Flandre.*
Melmoth Reconciled,	*Melmoth réconcilié.*
The Unknown Masterpiece,	*Le Chef-d'œuvre inconnu.*
THE HATED SON,	*L'Enfant Maudit.*
Gambara,	*Gambara.*
Massimilla Doni,	*Massimilla Doni.*

THE MARANAS,	*Les Marana.*
Farewell,	*Adieu.*
The Conscript,	*Le Réquisitionnaire.*
The Executioner,	*El Verdugo.*
A Seaside Tragedy,	*Un Drame au bord de la mer.*
The Red House,	*L'Auberge rouge.*
The Elixir of Life,	*L'Elixir de longue vie*
Maître Cornelius,	*Maître Cornélius.*

ABOUT CATHERINE DE' MEDICI :	*Sur Catherine de Médicis :*
The Calvinist Martyr,	*Le Martyr calviniste,*
The Ruggieris' Secret,	*La Confidence des Ruggieri,*
The Two Dreams,	*Les Deux Rêves.*

LOUIS LAMBERT,	*Louis Lambert.*
The Exiles,	*Les Proscrits.*
Seraphita,	*Seraphita.*

DROLL STORIES,	*Contes Drolatiques.*